IN TOO DEEP

**Center Point
Large Print**

ॐ श्री गणेशाय नमः

IN TOO DEEP

JANELLE TAYLOR

CENTER POINT PUBLISHING
THORNDIKE, MAINE • USA

BOLINDA PUBLISHING
MELBOURNE • AUSTRALIA

This Center Point Large Print edition is published in the year 2002
by arrangement with Kensington Publishing Corp.

This Bolinda Large Print edition is published in the year 2002
by arrangement with Dorie Simmonds, Literary Agent.

The text of this Large Print edition is unabridged.
In other aspects, this book may vary from the original
edition. Printed in Thailand. Set in 16-point Times
New Roman type by Bill Coskrey.

US ISBN 1-58547-169-0
BC ISBN 1-74030-684-8

Library of Congress Cataloging-in-Publication Data

Taylor, Janelle.
    In too deep / Janelle Taylor.--Center Point Large Print ed.
        p. cm.
    ISBN 1-58547-169-0 (lib. bdg. : alk. paper)
        1. Large type books. I. Title.

PS3570.A934 I5 2002
813'.54--dc21

                                                           2001047654

Australian Cataloging-in-Publication

Taylor, Janelle.
In too deep / Janelle Taylor.
1740306848
1. Large print books.
2. Single mothers – Fiction.
3. Romantic suspense novels.
I. Title
813.54

British Cataloging-in-Publication is available from the British Library.

❖IN TOO DEEP❖

Santa Fe, New Mexico

Obie Loggerfield was truly disgusting, especially up close. Detective Hunter Calgary tried not to breathe too deeply. It was a certainty Obie hadn't bathed for decades. Grime mixed with sweat and body oils had become a black sheen that covered every visible inch of flesh and filled the lines on his face.

The only time the drunken lout got near water was when it rained, Hunter knew, and even then the man did his best to avoid it. Which was why, during this morning's cloudburst, he'd taken up residence on the steps of the police station and why Hunter had allowed him inside.

As an advertisement for the colorful Southwest, Land of Enchantment, Obie was a poor bet. Luckily for tourists and residents alike, rainfall was next to nil most of the time; and Obie lived well north of town where he could offend no one, in a makeshift canvas tent pitched in the shadow of a jagged red rock formation.

Now, he gave Hunter a crafty look as he settled his filthy bulk into an old oak desk chair. "You gonna keep me, copper?"

The odor the old man threw off was indescribable. A mixture of so many things that Hunter's generally excellent vocabulary provided only one adjective: bad. "I'm going to give you a lift out of town, Obie. Either that or someone around here might think about putting you in jail."

"Jail cells are dry," Obie said hopefully.

Through the opened door of Sergeant Ortega's office

came a snort. "Don't even think it," Ortega's stern voice warned Obie, who started scratching in places that were not often scratched in public. "Those cells are meant for criminals, not transients."

"I ain't no transient."

Hunter hid a smile. This was actually true, since Obie had never lived anywhere else but his tent in the six years Hunter had been with the Santa Fe force.

Obie's answer ignited Ortega's volatile temper. "I'll tell you what you are, Loggerfield. A pain in the b-u-t-t! And one I want out of that room. No one can breathe with you stinking up the place. Calgary, get him out of there!"

Hunter reached for the keys to his Jeep. "Come on, Obie. Let's go home."

Three steps toward the door, however, and their way was blocked by a thin man with silvery hair and nervous hands. He clutched a briefcase as if his life depended on it, but his voice was smooth and controlled, "Detective Hunter Calgary?" he asked.

The hair on the back of Hunter's neck lifted, and for a moment he regarded the man in silence. A lawyer, he'd guess. Somebody's agent. Someone with money, by the cut of the man's suit and the high polish on his shoes. "That would be me," he drawled.

Obie regarded this newcomer curiously. The man's nostrils twitched involuntarily as he took in Obie, and Hunter suppressed a smile. Obie certainly could have that effect.

"I'm Joseph Wessver of Wessver, Moore, Tate, and McNeill. I'm here at the request of Allen Holloway. Mr. Holloway would like to hire you."

Once more Hunter viewed the man in silence. There was

no need to ask who Allen Holloway was. Holloway—or Holloway's huge company—owned a chunk of Santa Fe and several other towns and cities across New Mexico, Arizona, and Texas. He'd started with one Tex-Mex restaurant in Dallas, the Rancho del Sol, which had then mushroomed into a very successful chain. There were Rancho del Sols across the Southwest. By all accounts, Holloway had invested his profits in land and the stock market, and made millions. His name appeared regularly in the regional papers for an endless parade of good deeds. Holloway also owned office buildings and retirement homes; and had financed several independent films which had been shot around Santa Fe. It added up to major money, and a social circle Hunter was no part of, and wanted nothing to do with.

The big question: What would a man like Allen Holloway want with him? Though there was a connection between them, Hunter doubted Allen knew of it. And if he did, why was he contacting him now, after all these years?

Wessver frowned, as if contemplating the same question. "I was given to understand that you had left your job. Are you currently working with the police?"

"No." Hunter considered explaining himself, then decided it wasn't really anyone's business but his own.

"I see," Wessver said, when he clearly didn't. He glanced again at Obie and coughed lightly. The man's body odor was overwhelming. Sliding his fingers under the lapels of his raincoat, Wessver wished he could bury his face under the layers of material to keep from smelling it. "Well, could I have a word with you in private?" he asked Hunter on a gasp.

The detective sighed. He always—but always—knew

when something bad was about to happen to him. "I'm taking Obie home," he said wearily. "I'll be back in about an hour. You can wait, leave a number, or ride along . . . ?"

"I'll wait," the thin man said quickly.

Hunter shot him the glimmer of a smile and slapped Obie on the back, which produced a choking cloud of dust. Then they headed out the door.

It was nightfall by the time Hunter returned. Pulling up in front of the station, he cut the ignition, then sat in the Jeep listening to the tick of the cooling engine. The rain had ceased and pinpoint stars pierced the dark sky. Easing his shoulders back, Hunter relaxed against the torn seat.

He liked New Mexico. Its clear, thin air and wide open spaces suited him just fine. He'd lived in Los Angeles most of his life but his tolerance for the city had slowly vanished after Michelle's death. He hadn't regretted his decision to get out for good years ago.

His fury with the L.A.P.D. and the district attorney and everyone else involved in that fiasco had faded over those six mercifully uneventful years, but Hunter's belief in justice was nearly gone. He'd tried to rekindle his passion for law enforcement in Santa Fe but the damage had been too deep.

He was burned out, and that was that.

With a sigh, he climbed from the Jeep and headed up the steps to the station. He'd quit the Santa Fe force a month earlier to spend time on his isolated ranch and get his head together, but he still stopped in from time to time, more to see Ortega than anything else. Ortega hadn't forgiven him for leaving. First he'd begged, then ordered, then stomped around in a frustrated tantrum, then finally, grudgingly accepted Hunter's decision. "You'll be back," was his faintly ominous prediction as he handed Hunter his last paycheck. "Sooner than you know."

Now, Ortega was nowhere in sight as Hunter pushed through the main doors and headed toward the back offices. His own door was closed and probably locked. The place was empty except for Mr. Wessver, who sat primly on the carved wooden hall bench, his briefcase balanced on his lap. He stood up as Hunter strolled toward him.

"My car is outside. Could we continue this meeting at Rancho del Sol, Mr. Holloway's restaurant?" he asked. "Mr. Holloway would like to buy you dinner, no matter what your decision is."

Hunter inclined his head in a silent yes and followed the shorter man to his dark green Lexus.

Rancho del Sol, Santa Fe, was a low, rambling building with *vigas*—dark rounded beams that protruded through the stucco to the outside—and distressed, red-brick arches. It was known for its authentic southwestern cuisine and also was a steak house, one of the best around. Hunter usually ordered their rib-eye and had never been disappointed. Tonight, as always, the first bite melted in his mouth. He would never understand vegetarians.

Joseph Wessver chose the wine. Not a wine connoisseur, Hunter tasted the merlot: like the beef, it was good. Midway through his second glass he realized Wessver was only pretending to drink his own, and Hunter decided it was time to get to the point.

"What does Mr. Holloway want?" he asked, sinking into his chair a bit. His long legs were cramped and he wanted more than anything to get up and walk around. He wore black jeans and a gray shirt, open at the throat. If he was underdressed by Wessver's standards, he didn't give a damn. No one cared about things like that in Santa Fe.

"He wants you to protect his daughter."

"His daughter?" Hunter frowned, stretching one leg as far as he could without kicking the nervous Mr. Wessver. "From what?"

"Her ex-husband." He paused, eyeing Hunter warily.

The detective froze. He knew where this was going.

Wessver continued, "His daughter Geneva—known as Jenny to her friends—was married briefly to a man whose only interest in her was her fortune, or more accurately, the fortune she would eventually inherit. Jenny's father helped ease her through her divorce, and he's made certain the man has stayed away from her all these years."

"How many years?" he asked slowly.

"Fifteen."

Hunter swallowed more merlot, his gaze fastened on the other man's serious face. "And he's reappeared?"

"Yes." Wessver took a deep breath and indulged himself in a dramatic pause.

"Why do you want me?" Hunter asked at last.

"You're acquainted with the man in question."

The hairs on the back of his neck rose to full attention. Gooseflesh broke out on his forearms. Hunter again waited in silence until Wessver said quietly, "Troy Russell."

Not a muscle moved in Hunter's face. Wessver almost smirked. It was exactly what he'd expected. "Shall I go on?"

Hunter nodded curtly. His heart began to beat in a slow,

deep rhythm. Troy Russell was the man responsible for his sister Michelle's death.

⬧ CHAPTER ONE ⬧

Thhat man at table fourteen is watching you."
Jenny Holloway glanced up from the produce bill in her hands, trying to keep up with her friend Carolyn Roberts, who was carrying an armload of steaming pasta dishes and weaving through the tables with the artistry of a ballet dancer. "What?"

"That man. Table fourteen." Carolyn nodded toward the back of Riccardo's L-shaped dining room. There, an arched, stone doorway led to a smaller room filled with square tables draped in white damask cloths. But the table in question was around the corner. All Jenny saw were the soft, glimmering shadows thrown against the stone walls by the crystal votive candles on the tables.

"I'll take your word for it. I can't see table fourteen," Jenny said, heading for Riccardo's kitchen and back offices. A frisson of unwelcome fear slid along her spine. *Someone watching her?* She'd had that strange sensation for the past few weeks but she'd chalked it up to nerves. She was anxious—excited, really—about the decisions she'd made concerning the money she was about to inherit.

Remembering her mother's promise still brought tears to her eyes. "I've saved something for you, Geneva," Iris Holloway had whispered to her as she lay in the hospital bed. "But it won't be yours until you turn thirty-five. Just know it's there and it comes from love." But teenaged Jenny, plagued with self-doubt and sick with fear over her mother's imminent death from pancreatic cancer, had been unable to think about anything but her own misery. She'd cried furious tears, angry at her mother for dying too soon, and her father, whose affair with a woman closer to Jenny's age—and subsequent marriage—had estranged father and daughter forever.

But now, so many years later, Jenny could see how wise her mother had been, and how farsighted. If Jenny had come into all of her inheritance when she was young, she might have frittered it all away. Now, with a teenager of her own and some hard-won experience to guide her, she was ready to invest the money in the business her family knew best: restaurants.

She had more than one reason to be edgy. So what? She wasn't being paranoid or anything. Just cautious.

"I *know* table fourteen's around the corner," Carolyn said, catching up to her outside her office door. "Just go look! He's a hottie with a capital H!"

Jenny snorted and laughed. This sounded a lot less sinister than she'd thought. Carolyn described any guy with a decent face and powerful physique as a "hottie." During her last five years with Riccardo, Jenny had learned to discount anything the petite blond waitress had to say about men. Carolyn was actively looking for Mr. Right, a search Jenny had given up years earlier.

"I think I'll pass," she said.

"You'll be sorry. He'll be gone in a few minutes and you'll miss a date with destiny."

"I'll take my chances."

Carolyn shook her head dolefully at Jenny's unwillingness. But she knew that Jenny had suffered at the hands of

" Alberto's eyes had strayed to the *ribolita*, ... that resembled Thanksgiving Day turkey ... than anything else but tasted like heaven, in ...ion. It was being prepared by the newest junior ...king his tongue, Alberto practically shoved him ... way, ignoring the other chef's resentment as he ...ed on about everything the inexperienced man had ...rong.

...y winked at the others in the kitchen. Their expres-... varied from sympathetic to satisfied—but all of them ...ected Alberto's manic attention to detail. Either one ...rned, or one was let go. There was no compromise at ...iccardo's.

Settling into her office chair once again, Jenny listened to the familiar squeak and groan of the beat-up old thing, her own addition to the cramped quarters. If she had to straighten out these financial messes, she was darn well going to be comfortable. Alberto couldn't care less. Jenny was thorough and quick, and she knew what she was doing.

It didn't hurt that her background was in food service. She'd grown up in the restaurant business and the Rancho del Sol chain was one of the best. Allen Holloway might have been the brains and financial brawn behind its success, but young Jenny had been an apt pupil. He'd always planned to put her in charge or so he'd said. But then circumstances had changed everything and Jenny had stopped adoring her father.

Carolyn blew into the kitchen again, on her way stopping at Jenny's office door. "Well?"

"Well, what?"

a self-absorbed, abusive husband, and it had put her off men in general.

Spying her boss, Jenny waved to Alberto Molini, owner of Riccardo's. Carolyn groaned. "Don't make Alberto the only man in your life."

"Too late." Jenny grinned, and she called out, "Hey, there," to the rotund restaurateur as Carolyn threw her hands in the air, then returned to fetch another order.

"*Bella!*" Alberto cried, stretching out his arms to Jenny, greeting her as effusively as ever.

Dodging his flour-dusted arms and apron, thinking of her black sweater and skirt, Jenny waved him off. "Don't you dare," she chided. "I can't afford the cleaning bill."

"Then I will kiss you from here," he declared, smacking the tips of his fingers.

Jenny chuckled. Alberto was the grandson of the original Riccardo, first proprietor of the popular Houston restaurant. Five years earlier, when Jenny had come in looking for work, Alberto turned his gaze to the heavens and declared that his prayers had been answered. "You are my daughter," he'd cried joyously, embracing her as if she were indeed some long-lost child who'd finally come home. Bewildered by his unexpected enthusiasm, she had simply stared, wondering what on earth possessed the man.

"*Bella!*" he had declared. "You are a gift! A godsend! I was praying just for you!"

Jenny remembered wondering if that were some strange come-on line. "You were?"

"Ah, yes. And here you are! God has looked down at his poor Alberto and said, 'You work hard, and you deserve something beautiful.' And here you are."

She had quickly learned that Alberto was effusive in every way. He was loving and generous—and exacting and tyrannical, at least when it came to Riccardo's cuisine.

Now, as Jenny disappeared into her tiny office, she smiled to herself. She *felt* like his daughter. He'd certainly been more of a loving father to her than her own had ever been. But when she'd broken the news that she planned to move to Santa Fe and start her own restaurant, Geneva's, Alberto had tried to stop her. Wringing his hands, he'd begged, "Stay with me. Be my partner! We could expand. Don't leave!"

"I'm sorry, Alberto," she'd said gently. "But it's time for me to leave Houston. Find a new life."

"What kind of food? What will you do?"

"I plan to go southwestern," she'd replied. *Compete with my father . . .*

Jenny still wasn't sure her decision had been all that wise. Her combative relationship with Allen Holloway hadn't improved much over the years. She'd been happy to become Alberto's protégée, and though she'd been around her father's Rancho del Sol restaurants all her life, it was Alberto who'd really taught her the business. Accepting him as a mentor was the one good choice she'd made after a series of really bad ones. Her ex-husband, Troy Russell, at the top of that particular list.

But she wasn't going to think about him now. She'd married Troy mostly to escape living with her father and his silly, anorexia-thin wife, Natalie. But at least that brief and unhappy union had given her one beautiful gift, her son Rawley. Rawley was all that mattered to her now, and she hoped her move to Santa Fe would benefit him as much as

her. Alberto might bemoan her dec was the right choice.

Her overbearing father mig from Houston, but she di anyway. As warm and g father was cold and self-invo nately, depending on how one Jenny had as little to do with him mother's death, and Allen's remarr longer daddy's little girl. And she was obedient wife, either. She was a thirty divorcée and mother who was on the verge of

Glancing at the produce bill she'd nearly forgott Jenny stuck her head outside her office. Spying he again, Alberto cried, "*Bella!*" She laughed aloud. It w routine that had developed into near farce; the surrounding chefs and waiters alike simply smiled at them.

"I've about got this figured out," Jenny told him, fingering the bill which she'd marked with questions and underlined in several places. The produce bill was invariably wrong. Not that the members of Gaines Produce had any intention of cheating Alberto; it was just that their company, also privately owned, was in a constant state of flux. Had Jenny been the one to make all the decisions she would have switched suppliers long ago, but Alberto was stubbornly attached to the Gaineses. Their friendship went way back. He put up with the inconveniences of their haphazard delivery and lack of inventory with a dismissive wave of his hand while Jenny was left to sort everything out. It was just one of the things Jenny planned to do better in her own restaurant.

"Did you check him out?"

"Who?" Jenny was preoccupied with the week's payroll.

"The *hottie!* Good grief, my dear. You didn't even *look!* Are you completely unaware of the male sex? What does it take to get your attention! If you don't want him, turn him my way. Now, go. Right now!"

"I . . ."

But Carolyn was yanking on her arm, dragging Jenny from her chair and herding her through the kitchen to the main dining room beyond. "Go," she urged. "And I can't be doing this all the time, you know. I have work to do."

"What does he look like?" Jenny said. "Maybe I know him."

"Tall, dark, and handsome. It doesn't get any better than this, honey."

Tall, dark and handsome. That was how she'd described Troy to her friends when she'd first met him. She'd been giddy with delight that this "older man" had fallen for her. Only later did she learn he'd fallen for her money. Later still that he possessed a sadistic side that bordered on criminal . . .

She drew a deep breath. But Troy was out of her life now. Paid off by her father, a plan she'd disapproved of but had secretly been grateful for, especially when she learned that she was pregnant with Rawley. By the terms of her father's agreement with him, Troy could never enter her life again. And one thing she knew for certain about her ex-husband was that he would never give up cold, hard cash for anything.

"Jenny," Carolyn said, looking peeved. "Go now and look. Go, go, *go!* I swear, if you miss him I'll have a hysterical fit right here!"

"Okay."

"Okay?" Carolyn gave her a hard look.

Jenny lifted her hands, in an I-give-up gesture and nodded vigorously. "Okay! Okay!"

"All right, then." Carolyn scurried back to her tables. For a moment Jenny simply stood where she was, enjoying the rich aromas of garlic and tomato and basil and onion, and the low hum of conversation, punctuated occasionally by a ripple of laughter. The votives flickered. To her right, one of the waiters poured a deep red chianti into a glass for a white-haired gentleman to savor. Sensing Jenny's gaze, the man lifted his glass appreciatively in a silent toast to her.

Walking toward the archway to the smaller dining room, she slowed, apprehensive again. She didn't want to confront some man who may or may not have been watching her. The whole idea made her uncomfortable. She'd been the object of male interest since she was a teenager. Her blue eyes, the unruly auburn locks now firmly held at her nape in a tortoiseshell clip, and her slim, athletic body had attracted many an admiring glance. But since her divorce, she rarely wore makeup, and her clothes were somber and businesslike. It didn't take a psychotherapist to figure out the reason why: she didn't want any man to be interested in her. Not any more.

Still hesitating, she glanced inside. The stone walls were topped by cream painted plaster and a ceiling that arched high above the narrow room. Heavy, almost gaudy, chandeliers hung above, their crystal drops refracting light over the gleaming tableware and white damask tablecloths. The room was welcoming, even cozy, but Jenny shivered involuntarily. A male voice spoke from somewhere near her right and she jumped, startled.

In a bad Italian accent, she heard, "Madam, this *insalata Caprese* lacks spirit even though the balsamic vinegar is speaking with joy. I suggest a different olive oil, possibly something with deeper flavor and emotion."

Lips parting, Jenny blinked, then gave the speaker a hard look. Hidden behind Riccardo's burgundy leather menu was a dark-haired male with a very familiar tenor voice. Reaching over with one finger, she pulled the menu away from the handsome face of her son Rawley.

So, this was her male "watcher"! Relief and delight flooded her. "And just what are you doing here?" she asked, surprised that he would deign to come see her at all. At fifteen Rawley had become a handful.

His blue eyes, so like her own, flashed with humor. But he also resembled his father, something that occasionally squeezed her heart with fear. Troy had been—and undoubtedly still was—an unrepentant bully. In the few short months they'd actually lived together as man and wife, Jenny had learned to fear him and it had taken all the courage she possessed to leave him.

Her father's unspoken "I told you so" had been the final blow to her pride. Knowing that he had essentially bought her freedom was so humiliating that she had trouble even allowing herself to remember the details.

But it was all over now. Troy was history, and though it sometimes weighed on her conscience that Rawley had never met his father, she knew it was better that way. Her son didn't need to know Troy.

"I was just remarking on the salad," said Rawley, as if he

were a connoisseur of Italian cuisine.

"Sounded like Alberto's complaining to me," she teased gently. She had to be careful with Rawley these days. His moods were mercurial, loving one moment and surly the next.

Now, he flashed her his devastating smile, so full of dash and vigor and fun that the girls were already ringing the phone off the hook. Unfortunately, that smile, too, reminded her of Troy. She'd fallen for Troy's good looks and ignored his immaturity and half-hidden viciousness.

And, of course, her father had been against her relationship with Troy from the get-go. A fact that had turned her toward him like a vane spinning in the wind.

"First of all, that is not *insalata Caprese*. There's not a teaspoonful of balsamic vinegar or olive oil to be seen. You've got your basic American garden salad there, buddy. The only greens you'll eat, as far as I know. For your information, *insalata Caprese* consists of tomato slices, fresh mozzarella cheese, and fresh basil leaves. The last time I served it you made gagging sounds and thoroughly disgusted me and our guest, Benjamin."

Rawley grinned wider. "Benjamin couldn't care less."

Jenny smothered an answering smile. Benny was the neighbor's big, scruffy mutt with a tail that cleared the top of a coffee table in mere seconds. Jenny shooed him out every time, while Rawley sneaked the happy hound in whenever her back was turned.

"I thought you were going to be at Janice and Rick's tonight."

"I had soccer practice at 3:00 P.M. Rick came to watch, but afterwards I just wanted to leave." He shrugged.

Rawley seemed to think of their neighbor, Rick Ferguson, as a substitute father these days. He'd wanted to be someone's son—anyone's son—for a long time. She understood completely, but Jenny was still loathe to talk to her son about his real father. A few months earlier, she'd found a picture of Troy in Rawley's old baseball cards and personal junk. Though he never asked about his father, he was obviously thinking about him, and Jenny suspected it was just a matter of time before she'd have to explain more.

Jenny often wondered what Rawley was thinking. He knew Troy had never contacted him. A tough situation for a boy whose friends' fathers almost always attended their soccer games and other sports and school events. She had the feeling that Rawley's hidden emotions on this issue were about to explode. And there was nothing she could do about it.

"I told Janice that you wanted me down at the restaurant," he said. "And Alberto said I could order anything I wanted."

"Alberto would," Jenny murmured. "Was Janice picking you up, or do you need a ride?"

"I can walk."

Jenny nearly choked. Their apartment was miles and miles away and the multilane highway that led to their neighborhood wasn't exactly the best place for a kid to be walking, especially after dark. But Rawley didn't want to be babied. He was teetering on the verge of manhood, and it was a knife's edge. The wrong word from Jenny would end up cutting them both.

And so far he hadn't put up too much of a fuss about

moving to Santa Fe. If she could keep him happy on that score, everything else would fall into place.

"I wish you'd ride. It's safer," she said, holding up a hand to forestall his protests.

"But I'd be fine."

"I know—"

"I'd be fine! You don't trust me at all."

"It's not you," she declared in exasperation. "It's every-body else! Good grief, you know the way they drive in Texas! I just wouldn't be able to stand it if I thought you were walking home alone. It has more to do with me than you."

Rawley rolled his eyes. "I'm not five years old."

"I know." She glanced around, not wanting this battle. "I've got to get back to work. If Janice can't come, I'll take you home."

Rawley retreated behind the menu, stiff with anger. Jenny sighed inwardly. Until last year she and Rawley had been fast friends. Other mothers had warned her about ado-lescent obnoxiousness, but she'd blithely believed that Rawley, whose good manners were remarked on and envied by others, would not succumb to teen-itis. She'd been astonished by the change in him.

Returning to her office, Jenny placed a call to Janice, her neighbor and friend. Janice and Rick lived around the corner from Jenny's ground floor apartment in a comfort-able, two-story house. Since they were Benny's rightful owners, Jenny was more tolerant of the dog than she might normally have been and consequently Benny crossed the Holloway welcome mat as often as his own.

"Hello?" Janice sounded harried. A distant cacophony

reached Jenny's ears.

"Bad timing?" she suggested.

"Oh, hi, Jenny. It's the twins. They can't play a board game together. Becky cheats, and Tommy throws the game pieces and dice at her."

"Ahhh . . ." Janice's seven-year-olds were going through a tough phase, according to their parents. They were exhibiting just the kind of behavior that Jenny had congratulated herself on never seeing in Rawley. My, my, how things could change.

"Is something wrong?" Janice asked suddenly. "Aren't you at work?"

"Yes, yes. Rawley's here. I was just kind of checking up."

"He said you wouldn't mind having him there." In the background, Becky commenced a keening wail. "Jenny? Can you call back? I've just got to take care of this and I'll be able to talk."

"Never mind. Everything's cool. I'll talk to you later. Thanks for keeping tabs on Rawley."

She exhaled a deep breath as she hung up. It was becoming increasingly difficult for Jenny to ask much of the Fergusons. Their twins were a handful, and their older son, Brandon, was Rawley's age and not exactly a choirboy. The arrangement that had once worked so well was falling apart fast. But what could she do? Rawley was too old to have a babysitter and a little too headstrong to be left by himself.

And what will you do in Santa Fe?

"Start over," she said aloud, as if someone had actually asked her a question.

Well, maybe their upcoming holiday together would help ease the transition. Friends had asked her and her son to join them at their rented villa in Puerto Vallarta. It was an incredible hillside manor, only accessible via a winding stony road, with a full staff including a cook, maids and gardeners. The villa had eight bedrooms with as many baths, a kidney-shaped pool, a view to die for, and a rented Jeep for the week.

A time for family bonding. A time for fun. A time to set things straight again.

Retracing her footsteps, she found her son tucking in to a plate of ravioli and Italian sausages. He gave her a sidelong look.

"I called Janice and she was playing referee with the twins." Rawley grunted acknowledgment which encouraged Jenny. "I'll take you home. I'm about ready to leave." Since this was a blatant lie, Jenny mentally crossed her fingers.

"I can walk. I've got two legs."

"Let's not argue."

"When are you going to let me be me?"

She wanted to laugh out loud. "When haven't I let you be you?"

"Now!"

"Shhhh," she said gently, but firmly. "Alberto gave you a free meal because he likes you. Behave yourself in his restaurant."

"I'm behaving myself. Besides, Romeo said he didn't want me to starve. He insisted I order two sausages."

Romeo was Rawley's nickname for Alberto. He'd seen Alberto work his Italian magic on the single women who frequented the restaurant. His shameless flirting amused Rawley to no end even though Jenny, and the targeted customers, knew it was all in fun.

"He likes you," Jenny said.

Rawley grinned. "I know."

"You've got to stop taking advantage of his sweet nature. I mean it."

This time Rawley didn't argue with her. Jenny had some hope that all was not lost when it came to her son's worrisome behavior. He did know when he was being a brat—even if it had to be pointed out to him now and again.

She glanced over her shoulder. There was still so much left to do. Could she really afford to leave? Maybe. As long as she could find a few hours tomorrow, on Sunday, to come in and make up some work. Her birthday . . .

"I'll be ready whenever you are," she said on a note of finality.

He nodded. She marveled as he stuffed half an Italian sausage into his mouth with little effort. Retracing her steps to the kitchen once again, she felt another frisson of uneasiness run down her spine and wondered what in the world was wrong with her. She'd never been so susceptible to atmosphere and mood.

Catching up with Alberto, she told him regretfully, "I've got to head out. My son needs a ride home, and I think we should spend some time together." She wagged a finger in front of his nose. "And you shouldn't let him twist you around his little finger."

"He is like my grandson. What I have, is his." The twinkle in Alberto's dark eyes gave him away; he was totally unrepentant.

"Hmm." Jenny gave him a mock glower.

"He needs to be fed, that boy. To be strong." Alberto lifted his chin and flexed his biceps. "To be a man, to take care of his mama."

"Oh, right," Jenny muttered.

Alberto laughed aloud, and Jenny shook her head. It was useless to talk to him. He and Rawley had an unspoken agreement—a male pact—and there wasn't anything she could do about it.

Five minutes later, her paperwork in hand, Jenny headed out of her office for the last time, standing for a moment in the kitchen, the heart of the restaurant. Plates of steaming calamari and scallopini in garlic butter and savory osso bucco flew by. She loved all the mouth-watering aromas and lush-sounding names of the dishes. It was a kind of olfactory and auditory ecstasy.

Soon, soon, she would be involved in Geneva's. And she had her own amazing chef who was waiting in the wings, ready to step in as soon as the final renovations on the restaurant were completed. Gloria was one of the main reasons Jenny had chosen Santa Fe. Part Hopi, part Mexican, and a kitchen wizard with a true cook's temperament, Gloria had been born and raised around Santa Fe. She was, like Alberto, a demanding personality, but her perfectionism translated into dishes that were indescribably luscious. She'd once worked for Jenny's father, who had tried to force her into the Rancho del Sol mold and that had been a recipe for disaster. Sparks flew from the onset. Sparks? No. More like an exploding volcano. And Gloria had flat-out refused to work for another Holloway at first. When Jenny then explained her relationship with her father, the woman signed on with a flourish, ready to thumb her nose at the man she considered "stupid about food." Jenny was thrilled to have someone so strong willed and talented on her side.

She smiled to herself again. She and Gloria would be up to their elbows in work within a few weeks, but for now there was Puerto Vallarta. And Jenny planned to use the trip for culinary exploration, as well. If there was something out there with just the right flavors and presentation, she would coax Gloria into giving it a try.

At least that was the theory.

Alberto was currently standing over the chef he'd upbraided earlier. The younger man looked ready to explode. But for once Alberto held his tongue. Whatever issue he wanted to address remained hidden for the moment as kettles and deep-dish frying pans bubbled and hissed on top of the burners.

Jenny said, "Anytime you want our extra customer out there to wash some dishes for his meal, feel free to put him in front of the sink."

"Ah, *bella*, you are so cruel!" Alberto spread his hands expansively, stepping away from the other chef so that peace reigned—at least for the time being. "He is so thin. He needs my pasta to build strong muscles."

"Why are you patting your stomach as you say that?" Jenny observed.

"Oh, funny, funny lady."

Chucking her under the chin, he then waved her away. Jenny shut the door to her office and locked it. On her way out at last . . .

Carolyn caught her in the main dining room. "Did you

see him?"

"Yes, I saw him." She smiled at her friend. "And he's very handsome. A little young, perhaps, but hey, what's twenty-some years."

Carolyn looked nonplussed. "What are you talking about?"

"Rawley. I found him. And he's in trouble whether he thinks so or not. He can't just show up and expect a meal just because I'm here. He sure as heck knows how to work the system."

"Rawley?"

"Yes, Rawley . . ." Jenny trailed off. With a jolt she suddenly realized her son had not been seated at table fourteen. He'd been at table eleven.

"Not him! This was an honest-to-goodness hunk," Carolyn declared. "Go look again! Maybe he's still there. I want you to see him. I mean, the way he watched you when he first came in . . . wow. And then when you walked by while I was taking his order . . . He didn't think I saw, but his eyes were all over you, like he was studying you or something."

"Oh?"

She nodded. "He was mentally taking notes. I'm surprised you couldn't *feel* it."

"You're creeping me out, Carolyn."

"Oh, no, no. It was in a good way. I wouldn't have minded him looking at me that way."

"Well, you're not me."

"Look, he's sexy. That's all I'm saying. Go look. Table fourteen . . ."

Filled with trepidation, Jenny slowly approached the

stone archway one last time. Her gaze jumped from Rawley's table to the now vacated table fourteen. Her heart beat quick and fast. Her breath jumped in and out of her throat. Nothing. No reason to be so jittery.

"Come on," she said to her son, shooting a glance around all the darkened corners just to make sure. "Let's go home."

Outside Riccardo's a slender yellow moon rose over the forest of commercial buildings, wires, and parking lots—ugly reminders of urban humanity. Hunter waited in his Jeep. He was tired. He'd driven from Santa Fe to Houston nonstop and had been unable to sleep much since, especially when he was lying on some hard motel bed and staring at the ceiling.

But his weariness went further than that. It was bone deep, a product of long hours and lost hopes. These last six years in Santa Fe he'd managed to fight it back, but from the moment Joseph Wessver brought up Troy Russell it had come back with a vengeance. Oh, sure, part of him still wanted to get Russell, a hope that refused to die no matter how many times he reminded himself of the hard realities of "no evidence."

Troy Russell had killed Michelle Calgary as surely as if he'd put a gun to her head and pulled the trigger. That Michelle had leapt from the roof of her five-story apartment building near La Cienega Boulevard in Los Angeles didn't cut any ice with Hunter. He *knew* Russell was responsible, and Hunter had lost his job with the L.A.P.D. because of it.

He'd been unable to convince anyone that Michelle, who

had a healthy fear of heights, would never choose to end her life that way. Troy Russell had pushed her off that building after mentally and physically abusing her for several years. That was Hunter's theory. But that she'd been about to leave him, that she'd broken down and told Hunter she would testify against him, anything, *anything* to put him behind bars, was not enough to prove the man had been with her on the roof that day.

But Hunter knew . . .

Now, he closed his eyes and felt a familiar ennui settle over him. He'd outrun it for a few years, but it was apparently still there. Burnout. Bad case. A lack of passion for anything. He'd recharged some in Santa Fe, but when it came right down to it, the battery was essentially dead.

But he'd promised to watch out for Allen Holloway's daughter. Be a bodyguard. Save her from Troy Russell. Her ex-husband.

That, at least, still penetrated.

Sighing, Hunter thought over his meeting with Wessver, and then the subsequent one with Holloway himself. He'd learned a great deal about the man, and about his daughter, and about their relationships with the man Hunter wanted to bring to justice more than anything else. So, he'd agreed to be Jenny's protector, only to learn that she had no knowledge of Allen Holloway's plan and the danger that lurked in the shadows.

"She won't appreciate my interference," Allen Holloway had told him. "Mention my name, and you won't get near her. But I need you to be near her. Now, more than ever, because Russell's putting on the heat. The man's a bloodthirsty lunatic and he wants my daughter more than money these days."

"That's what he said?" Hunter had asked.

"No. He said he wanted to up the ante. More money. And if it were just that, I'd be glad to do it. I don't care. But it's not. He might know about the boy. I'm not sure. Jenny's kept a pretty low profile for a long, long time. But Troy's been out of Texas ever since the divorce, and now he's back. Contacted me from the Warwick, which isn't cheap. He lives high. Needs to, to pick up women."

Holloway's words pricked Hunter like needles. Michelle had fallen for Troy Russell's good looks, perfect charm and apparently endless supply of money. Holloway's money.

"I want her safe. She's flying to Puerto Vallarta in about a week. Here . . ." He flipped an airline ticket Hunter's way. "Get close to her. I'd rather be paying you than Russell," he added emphatically.

So, here he was. Following her. Had been ever since that meeting with her father. But it wasn't for the money. It was for Michelle, and for himself, and yes, for her safety. And in the process he'd become immersed in Jenny's life, waiting outside her apartment long after the last light had been turned off. What had started out as a job was fast becoming an obsession. And about all he felt was a kind of exhausted relief.

Which was crazy, when he thought about it, but he was just glad to have a focus. A purpose. Quitting the Santa Fe police department to hang out on his dusty little ranch had seemed self-defeating at the time, yet he'd been unable to do anything else.

Hearing voices brought him out of his reverie. Sure enough, there she was, coming out the back door of Riccardo's and walking toward her car alongside a rangy teenaged boy. He knew her by sight now. Geneva Holloway Russell, though she'd dropped her married name even before the divorce was final. The boy was her son. Rawley Holloway. No last name of Russell for him, either, apparently. A good sign, as far as Hunter was concerned.

He watched her walk with the boy to a blue Volvo sedan. Twisting the key in the ignition, he waited until she'd driven nearly out of sight before he eased into traffic behind her. When she turned into the parking lot of her ten-unit apartment building, he passed by, circled the block, then returned in time to see the master bedroom light turn on. He parked across the street and switched off his engine.

Her building had only two stories. A person might be able to survive a fall from the roof here, he mused, his thoughts dark.

A car drove past, slowed, crept for a block and a half, then sped up. Hunter memorized the license plate, but it looked like a rental. It didn't return again, but he wrote the number down anyway. He might not be the only watcher out tonight.

Eventually her bedroom light was switched off. Settling down further into his seat, Hunter dozed fitfully. Hours passed and nothing happened. In the gray hours of dawn he fired up the Jeep's engine and drove to his cold motel room on the edge of the loop, the circle of freeways that girded Houston's center. Standing in the dark in the center of the room he breathed in the musty scents of mildew and disuse. For a moment he had a flash of desire to be back at his own place, alone as always.

I wish I had a dog.

Hunter felt mild surprise at such an alien, *normal* thought invading his mind.

Switching on his desk light, he glanced down at the travel documents in his name. A bright red brochure from Hotel Rosa lay beside the airline ticket.

"It's practically right on the bay," Holloway had told him. "Great open air restaurant and bar. Thatched roof. Authentic, reputedly incredible Mexican cuisine. If so, Jenny'll be there to taste the food. She fancies herself a restaurateur and I understand that she's renovating a place in Santa Fe. Hang around the hotel and you'll catch up with her eventually. Everyone goes there."

Hunter responded to the one thing that bothered him ever so slightly. "Santa Fe?"

"You're almost going to be neighbors," Allen said with a sniff of disapproval. "She's opening a restaurant on one of those arty little streets with all the galleries. Geneva's. For the grandmother she's named after. Yes, I know more about her than she thinks I do, but I want you to learn even more."

Now, Hunter gazed down at the brochure and airline ticket. There was an underhanded element to this whole scheme that normally would have bothered him. But Allen wanted to stop Troy Russell.

And there was nothing Hunter wanted more.

CHAPTER TWO

*S*o *many things to do . . .*
Jenny scratched off one item on the list and sighed as she studied the remaining twenty-plus errands. She was leaving for Puerto Vallarta in a week and she felt overwhelmed.

A throbbing beat from Rawley's bedroom speakers shook the apartment hard enough to measure on the Richter scale. Marching down the hall, she rapped loudly on his door. "Rawley! Rawley!"

She didn't doubt that he couldn't hear her. He'd need the alertness of a hunted animal to discern anything beyond that awful noise. She slammed her palm against the door panels until her hand smarted, then twisted the knob and opened the door a crack.

"Hey!" Rawley yelled, affronted. "Don't I deserve some privacy?"

"Not when your music is blowing away half of Houston." His mutinous glare followed her as she walked to the speakers and deftly lowered the volume. "There are rules. I don't make them. I just have to abide by them because I signed a lease to that effect. And I don't feel like getting kicked out two weeks before we leave at the end of the month."

Benny barked as if to answer from the other side of Rawley's bed. He bounded across the room, jumping up against her, muddy paws dirtying her denim shirt.

Frustration filled her and it took effort to hold back her anger. Grabbing Benny by the collar she half walked, half dragged the dirty pooch to the door and pushed him onto the outside deck that led to the stairs to the street. Instantly, he tried to turn around and wriggle back inside but Jenny clamped her legs against the doorjamb, blocking his entry. "For the love of Pete, go home!" she declared in exasperation.

Moments later she slammed the door and turned back to Rawley's room. The volume was somewhat higher than when she'd left, but at least it wouldn't make her ears bleed. "There are muddy footprints across the carpet. Please clean them up," she said in a tone that warned of future injunctions should her reasonable request be ignored.

Closing his door softly behind her, Jenny inhaled a deep breath and blew it out slowly. Some birthday, she thought. She thought of her inheritance, due to be transferred to her account tomorrow, and wondered why it didn't cheer her up. Right now all she wanted to do was sit down and cry.

Rawley didn't remember today was her birthday.

But why should he? She hadn't mentioned it. And teenagers weren't known for looking outside themselves. Had she been like that when she was young? So self-absorbed that she couldn't even recall her parents' birthdays? No. She'd always known her mother's. She'd wanted to. It was important.

As she wiped off Benny's pawprints from her shirt and slacks Jenny's mind opened on her past. She remembered how ill her mother had been for so long. It had seemed like an eternity. She'd been alternately angry at her mother and consumed with despair. Iris Holloway had quietly passed away when Jenny was on the verge of adolescence and she had pretended to stoically accept her mother's death during the daylight hours although she cried silent, bitter tears at night in the sanctuary of her lonely room.

Her once close relationship with her father had ended at nearly the same time. Four months after Iris's death he married Natalie, who'd barely passed her twenty-first birthday at the time of the wedding. The rest of Jenny's high school years were a blur and only when she met Troy Russell did they focus on some kind of reality.

What a mistake! She'd eloped with him at eighteen and spent six miserable months in a marriage her father had tried to break with every legal means available. And she had ended up leaving Troy the last time he shoved her against the wall hard enough to break through the sheet rock.

She blocked the memories right there, fighting back an involuntary shudder. She'd made a life for herself and Rawley over the last fifteen years, and she rarely thought about those dark days. She'd walked through the fire and come out on the other side only slightly singed. She was one of the lucky ones.

With new resolve she went in search of the carpet spot remover. It was all well and good to demand that Rawley clean up, but he always needed nagging if she wanted results. And sometimes she just did the darn job herself rather than wage the battle.

After scrubbing up the worst of the pawprints from the hall carpet, she set the blue can of spot remover on the edge of the kitchen counter and set about making herself a cup of tea. She'd certainly made huge mistakes during her teen years, but she'd never been as outwardly rebellious as her son. Was it a matter of gender, or the times, or just fate?

Whatever the case, Rawley was making a very noisy statement today.

More memories came back to her. Her first Troy sighting, that summer after high school, when Jenny was supposed to be preparing for college. But all she thought about was Natalie holding hands with her father, Natalie girlishly squealing when Allen bought her a diamond necklace, Natalie learning tennis from a personal trainer who winked at Jenny a little too suggestively every time he walked by. It was revolting and Jenny spent endless hours driving her blue Mercedes convertible in aimless circles, wishing for something to happen.

Lost, angry and searching for escape, she had literally run into Troy's beat-up Dodge truck with her car. He'd just parked in one of the private spaces reserved for the Holloway elite at Houston's original Rancho del Sol. Jenny hadn't meant to hit him. She'd just been so distracted that she slammed her foot on the accelerator instead of the brake and bumped hard into the back of his car. His look of horror was almost comical, and Jenny leaped out of her car and apologized over and over eventually running out of steam since he never responded with so much as a syllable.

"I'm sorry," she said for the umpteenth time. "I'll pay for it."

"Never mind," he finally replied. "I shouldn't have been in your parking spot."

"Oh, no!" Jenny was eager to take the blame. "It's my fault. Come inside. I've got my insurance information . . ."

And that was how Troy was introduced to Allen. Jenny, reverting to childish ways, let her father handle all the particulars. It turned out Troy was looking for a job. He had a business degree from UC Berkeley, or so he maintained, and wanted to work in restaurant management. It was all a lie, but he had enough phony credentials to back up his claim; and Allen, happy to have his daughter's accident so easily dispensed with, hired Troy then and there.

And Troy played the part of everyone's favorite guy. Cool even in the worst Houston heat. A trait Jenny had admired and learned later to distrust completely. Someone somewhere had said that there were two types of physical abusers: those that flew into a white rage and were dangerous because they were out of control; and those whose heartbeat actually *decelerated* in the anticipation of a physical battle. Calm and cool but imbued with the swiftness and intensity of a cobra. That was Troy.

Hero-worship had consumed her, despite Allen's disapproval. And when her shocked father stumbled upon the two of them in an embrace, his gaze flicking from Troy to Jenny and back again, she found her weapon against him without even trying.

Allen hustled her into his back office and gave her an ultimatum: she was not to see Troy Russell as anything but an employee.

She eloped with Troy the following spring. Her first inkling of trouble was at the end of the ceremony, when Troy Russell kissed his new bride and then looked down at her with a smile on his face. Not the loving smile of a new husband. The smile of a conqueror . . . the smile of a scam artist who'd just pulled off an enormous coup.

"Mom?"

Rawley's voice brought her back to reality. He stood at the edge of the counter, eyeing her worriedly before his gaze dropped to the blue can of spot remover. "Oh," she murmured, turning around and reaching for the paper towels. "Here. Maybe you could clean up the pawprints in your room."

He took the paper towels and the can and asked, "What were you thinking about?"

"Nothing much."

"Yeah?"

"Just the work I need to finish before we go on vacation."

He nodded. "I'm going over to Brandon's for a few minutes. After I do this," he added, indicating the spot remover.

"Wait. Don't go."

"Why not?"

"I just kind of want you here, today. This afternoon . . ."

"What for?"

What for, indeed? *To make your mother's birthday something to remember?* "I don't know. Oh, never mind." She smiled wanly. "Have a good time."

The tears she'd been battling suddenly welled in her eyes. Rawley gazed at her in consternation.

"Mom . . . ?"

"I'm okay . . . really . . . I'm just tired." With that, she collapsed onto one of the two bar stools, struggling to get her emotions under control.

The doorbell rang and Benny, still on the porch, started barking at whoever was standing outside with him. Instantly Rawley ran to the rescue, cracking open the door, collaring Benny as he streaked inside. "Oh, hi," he said to the newcomer.

"Hello, there. You've grown a few inches since the last time I saw you. Pretty soon you'll be looking for a job at

Rancho del Sol!"

Jenny brushed her tears away and got up, stopping short at the archway in stunned amazement. Her father . . . Allen Holloway . . . stood in the doorway.

Rawley hung onto Benny for dear life and managed an uncomfortable smile. "I guess . . ."

"Well, hello," Jenny greeted him, forcing a lightness she didn't feel. Her father had never come to her apartment. He'd never been invited and she hadn't even known he knew where it was.

"Are you going to invite me in or make me wait out here all day?" Allen asked with an attempt at humor as flat as Jenny's smile.

"Of course. Come in." She walked across the room as Rawley stepped aside, one hand still on Benny's collar. "What in the world are you doing out this way?"

He wore a pair of gray slacks, a navy suit coat and a polo shirt, his normal dress for a Sunday afternoon at his club. If Jenny had been thinking, she would have realized the reason for his visit immediately, but she was just so surprised to see him—and wary—that her brain seemed to stall.

"It's your birthday, isn't it?" he asked.

Rawley threw his mother a stricken look.

"Well, yes, it is," she said, aching for her son and wishing Allen could have been the one to let the event slip by rather than Rawley.

"Happy birthday, honey." Awkwardly he pulled her into an embrace and Jenny did her darnedest to hug him back with feeling. But too many memories intruded, memories of other birthdays and events where the hours they spent together were filled with him badgering her about her future and her sinking into resolute silence. Even after Troy was out of their lives, he'd called and cajoled and tried to force her to come work with him. Her resistance, and refusal of all monetary help, frustrated the hell out of him.

Now, however, Jenny swallowed as her gaze flew over the magazines and leftover mail scattered on the coffee table. She mentally congratulated herself for recycling the bottle of chianti she'd begun with a frazzled Janice Ferguson a few days earlier and finally finished the evening before. She would have liked her father to see her place in its most immaculate state, but a muddy pawprint caught her attention and she realized that was hopeless. Why it mattered, she wouldn't consider. It just did. She didn't want him to start in again about how much she needed his financial support.

"So, how does it feel to be the ripe old age of thirty-five?" Allen asked her.

She half smiled. Her father always knew the worst thing to say to her. "Not a day over thirty-four."

His laughter sounded choked. In the mirror above the entry table she caught sight of her wildly curling auburn hair which remained forever untamed even in this era of chic, straight cuts. Birthday blues had kept her from even bothering to even clip it back. Wouldn't you know her father would show up? Some things were destined.

As Rawley dragged Benny back to the cement landing, Jenny held the door. Allen stepped quickly aside, avoiding Benny's light-colored fur although some of it ended up on his pants. Allen's snort of disgust made Jenny's lips twitch. "Whose animal is that?" he demanded. "Not yours, I hope."

"The neighbors'."

"Mom . . . ?" Rawley said, shifting his weight from one foot to the other.

"Go." She waved him away with a smile. "And take Benny with you." He was out the door like a shot. Benny's disappearing barks and Rawley's noisy footsteps said they were fast on their way.

"That's all he says to his grandfather?" Allen demanded.

"You're lucky he wasn't in one of his silent moods," Jenny said, instantly defending her son. Rawley might drive her to distraction, but she did not need her father telling her how to raise him.

Allen let that one go by. "I brought you a gift," he said, pulling an envelope from his inside pocket and handing it to her with a flourish. Reluctantly Jenny accepted it. She didn't want to open it. She knew what it was. Money. Another bribe to get her to come back into the family business. "Aren't you going to open it?" he demanded, settling himself gingerly on her couch, alert for more dog hair.

She sat down opposite him in a painted rocking chair that tended to squeak. She wasn't poor, but she'd been saving her money for years and years and some things just weren't as important as others. "I'm getting my inheritance from Mom," she said, the envelope heavy in her hand.

"I know. I just wanted you to have enough."

"Enough?"

"I know you're opening a restaurant in Santa Fe," he admitted.

Jenny felt the noose slip over her neck. This was how it started with her father. Carefully she opened the envelope.

Glancing at all the zeroes at the end of that check, she folded it up and held it out to him. He, however, refused to reach for it.

"I appreciate it, but I can't accept it."

"Geneva . . ."

"No." She cut him off. "Obviously you've been keeping tabs on me."

"Well, of course I have! You're my daughter."

"I'll do fine with what Mom left me and what I've saved. Better than fine."

"You need the money," he argued. "Take it. And if you don't put it in your business, save it for your son. It's a birthday gift."

It's a bribe . . . She didn't say it. She wanted to, but she didn't.

"I understand you're naming the restaurant Geneva's," he said, ignoring her outstretched hand until Jenny had to drop it in her lap.

"After my grandmother, not myself."

"I figured." A small glimmer of a smile. "It's not easy to make it in this business."

"I've spent a lot of years being an apprentice," she pointed out.

"Hmmm." He didn't argue. Why should he? He probably knew as much about Jenny's expertise as she did herself. That was just the way Allen worked.

"Do you also know it's southwestern cuisine?"

"Yes." He got to his feet and walked stiffly around the room. "And I think you're foolhardy. You won't work at Rancho del Sol to save your soul, but you'll jump into your own restaurant with no knowledge of what it really takes to run this kind of business. And don't tell me about all the years you've worked for that Italian. It's not the same."

" 'That Italian' owns Riccardo's and it's one of the best restaurants in this city," she answered in a steely voice. " 'That Italian' has a name: Alberto Molini."

He waved her fury away. "You won't listen to me no matter what."

"Not when I know you're wrong."

"Tsk, tsk." He shook his head at her, his facade cracking. He hated being thwarted. Hated it.

"I'm not going to take this check. Thank you." She set the folded-up piece of paper on the coffee table.

"Fine. I'll deposit the amount in Rawley's stock portfolio."

"Rawley doesn't have a stock portfolio."

Another tight smile. "Yes, he does."

Jenny was thoroughly annoyed. This high-handedness was typical of him. "How much is in that account?" she demanded.

"Enough to cover his mistakes."

"What's that supposed to mean?" Now she was furious.

He spread his hands. "It cost a lot to get you out of that Troy Russell fiasco."

Jenny felt like she'd been slapped. Her father hadn't ever thrown that in her face. He'd been as relieved as she was when it was over.

As if realizing he'd crossed the line, Allen inclined his head. "I'm just trying to prevent him from making similar mistakes. I should have set up your own account and let you have some financial freedom. Maybe then you wouldn't have jumped into marriage so soon."

"Money wasn't the reason I married Troy!" Jenny looked at him as if he'd lost his mind. "My family had the money. *You* had the money. That's why he married me!"

"Still . . . I want Rawley to be safe."

"What are you talking about?" Something about his tone made gooseflesh rise on her arms.

Allen seemed momentarily at a loss. He took a deep breath. "Your birthday isn't the only reason I stopped by today."

"No?" Jenny braced herself. Now they were getting to it. And she could already tell she wasn't going to like it.

"Sometimes things happen and there is nothing to do but act," he said cryptically, running a palm down the back of his silvered hair. "I know you're planning a trip to Puerto Vallarta with friends before you leave for Santa Fe. Is Rawley going with you?"

"Yes." She tensed. Waiting.

But he seemed to relax a little. "Good. Good." He rubbed his hands together and nodded.

"What's wrong?"

"I just wanted to get that clear."

"No. It's something else. If you're not here to badger me about coming to work for you, then you've got some other purpose. Frankly, you're scaring me."

Allen stared at her, or more accurately, *through* her. It was as if his vision were transfixed on some otherworldly object and whatever he saw was decidedly unpleasant.

Uneasiness feathered across Jenny's skin. Her heart beat in a deep, painful cadence. *Troy*, she thought as her father said grimly, "Your ex-husband contacted me."

Jenny felt the blood rush from her face.

"He came to the house to tell me he was sorry. He said he wanted to make up for all the trouble he caused."

"I don't believe you," she said dully.

"It's the truth."

She shook her head. "I mean, I don't believe this is happening. Troy doesn't know how to feel remorse. He's— he's been living in California, right? What's he doing here? What's he *really* doing?"

"I don't know." His sober tone reflected how they both felt at the moment. "I don't trust him at all. And I don't want him trying to insinuate himself into your life again."

"Neither do I."

"You're sure? You fell for his lies once before."

"I'm a lot older and wiser."

"But he's clever. He fooled all of us once."

"He won't fool me again."

"Okay." He nodded. "I was going to suggest Rawley stay with me and Natalie."

Oh, he'd love that, Jenny thought but wisely kept that to herself.

"I was worried Troy might try to contact him."

Jenny's heart leapt in fear. "He never has before!"

"He's never turned up before, either. I bought that man off, Geneva. And now he has the gall to come laugh in our faces. If I could've, I would have had him arrested on the spot!"

Jenny darted a glance to the hall and her son's closed door. "Rawley's got a different view of Troy than we do."

"That's because he doesn't know the man." Allen harrumphed. "It's just as well, since Russell's a criminal."

"He's never been convicted of a crime, so he's not a

criminal," Jenny reminded him.

"He's a criminal," Allen responded, his voice softening ever so slightly. For a moment he didn't meet Jenny's eyes, then he surprised her by coming to where she stood and reaching for her hand. "I'll never forgive him."

Jenny swallowed hard, refusing to give in to emotion one more time. It made her skin crawl to even consider seeing Troy again. She had never told the whole story of his physical and mental abuse, but her father had read between the lines. "I would really hate to face Troy again.

"The bastard had the nerve to smile at me and stick out his hand, like we were old friends or something." Allen's jaw tightened. "I refused."

Jenny had a momentary flashback. Troy had backhanded her twice, sending her reeling across the room. Both times it had been over nothing, and she'd been shocked by the power of what had seemed like an effortless hit on his part. She'd stayed away from people for several weeks, waiting for the bruises to fade. Why she hadn't been able to tell she couldn't really say. But it was true that she no more wanted to talk about those days now than she had during the worst of them.

She'd been so naive. But Troy had crushed all her girlish dreams of white knights and men of honor in the space of a few months. Her illusions had vanished as swiftly as the bonds of her marriage.

"What do you think he really wants?" she asked now, her voice sounding odd even to her own ears.

Allen's jaw worked several times before he finally admitted tightly, "I don't know."

The second time Troy hit her she'd just learned about

Rawley. She never told him about the pregnancy. And when her father came to her with another plea to leave Troy, she'd accepted gratefully. She'd never told Allen all the whys and wherefores, but her father was a man who knew things before they were even uttered.

"I'm not going to dwell on this while I'm in Puerto Vallarta," Jenny said, thinking aloud. "And then I'm only here for a few more days before we leave for Santa Fe."

"I never thought I'd be glad to have you moving out of Houston, but this time I am." Her father looked at her. "Doesn't mean I think you'll make it in the restaurant business."

"Heaven forbid." Jenny lifted an ironic brow, earning her another one of her father's rare smiles.

"Keep the money," he said as he made to leave and Jenny reached for the folded-up check. "Please."

Since she'd never heard him say "please" in all her life, Jenny froze in the act of picking it up.

"I've made arrangements to keep you safe," he added.

"What do you mean?" Jenny asked warily.

He hesitated, then said, "I've got someone checking the bastard out. Seeing what he's been into these last years. I want to know what's in that man's head."

Jenny inhaled and exhaled heavily. "So do I."

"Happy birthday, honey," he said again, a trifle gruffly.

"Thanks." She almost added "Dad" but couldn't quite get the endearment past her lips.

"If you need anything, call."

"I will."

"I'm there for you, you know."

"Yes."

She closed the door behind him and collapsed against it. He would be there for her, but her father's love came with a price—she could never forget that. She glanced down at the check again. Making a face, she decided to take his advice and put the money in an account for Rawley. That way, she could make herself believe she hadn't just somehow fallen under her father's control again.

The sound of the front door creaking open brought her screeching from an afternoon doze to painful awareness. She leapt to her feet in time to see her son sheepishly tiptoeing into the room.

"What are you doing?" she demanded, blinking, her heart racing. "You scared me half to death."

"Sorry. I was trying to . . ." He stopped short, unable to come up with any kind of explanation that made sense. "Is Grandpa gone?"

Grandpa . . . She shivered again, thinking things were fast slipping out of her control. "He left a while ago."

"I didn't really want to talk to him much." He shifted his weight from one foot to the other, hesitated, then mumbled under his breath, "Here," and thrust a small package wrapped in red paper in front of her nose. The wrap job was pure fifteen-year-old boy—sloppy and haphazard. "Sorry I forgot."

"It's okay."

"You never forget my birthday."

"Well, that's different. I'm your mom."

She was touched beyond reason by her son's thoughtfulness and yes, his guilt. It didn't matter. She opened the box to discover a necklace with several pinkish imitation pearls clustered together. "Rawley, it's beautiful!" she said.

"It's not much." His toe scuffed the floor.

"Yes, it is." She clasped the chain around her neck and the pink pearls nestled in the hollow of her throat. "It's the nicest gift I've ever had," she said, truly touched and Rawley shot her a suspicious look from under his lashes.

"Oh, sure."

"No," she said with all sincerity. "It really is the nicest gift I've ever had. I wouldn't say it if I didn't mean it."

His embarrassment took over as she saw his face turn a shade of red. Mumbling something unintelligible, he headed for his room and soon the decibel level was reaching glass-shattering levels once again. This time Jenny didn't object.

She touched the necklace and smiled. Checking the clock, she made a sound of annoyance, grabbed her purse and flew from the house. There were still things to do at the restaurant, and she didn't want to delay any further.

Alberto was in the kitchen, scowling at one of the junior chefs when Jenny entered. "*Bella!*" he cried, hugging her enthusiastically. Jenny hugged him back, a little tighter than she normally would. Seeing her father only made her want to connect with Alberto even more . . . even though she was leaving.

In her office, she quickly ran through the list of book-keeping problems she'd left for today, then sat back, feeling nostalgic at the squeak of the wooden chair. The mere thought of all she was leaving behind made her misty-eyed. Yet she knew she'd been here too long. But it had been a safe place to learn to think for herself—and understand those choices she'd made when she was young that had led her into her disastrous marriage. Two hours later, she closed up her office, then stared down at the key in her hand. The new bookkeeper, a man, was scheduled to start in the morning.

"I think you're going to need this," she said to Alberto, extending the key with one hand as she slung her purse over her shoulder with the other.

"Oh, no. No." He dolefully shook his head.

"I'm going to be away for a week, and when I get back, I'll just be in to troubleshoot a little, in case you need it."

He clasped his hands over his stomach and stared at the key. He was so forlorn that Jenny had to look away before emotion overcame her as well. Gently, she pressed the key in his palm and kissed him on the cheek. Then she hurried out before one of them burst into tears.

Outside the restaurant she took several deep breaths. Pressing the remote to her car, she heard the locks click open. She took three steps toward the driver's door, and glanced around swiftly. It was as if she could actually feel someone's stare. It was creepy. Totally creepy, as Rawley would say.

Inside the Volvo, she pushed the automatic locks, but even the click of all of them locking at once was not comforting. Her heart beat faster. Placing her hands on the steering wheel, she sat perfectly still, waiting for . . . something.

Several people walked out of Riccardo's back door. One man stopped to light a cigarette. Jenny's eyes glued to his silhouette, but as he walked down the back steps she realized he was a stranger. A car drove by on her right and turned into a parking spot. A young couple with a preschooler climbed out and headed into the restaurant, holding the child between them and swinging her up the steps.

Nothing. No lurking stranger.

Jenny started the engine and backed out of the lot. Her eyes kept darting to the rearview mirror on the drive back to her apartment; and because she was paranoid, she drove an extra mile and circled around through the neighborhoods before finally parking in her usual spot at the apartment. She ran up the steps and quickly let herself inside.

"Mom?"

She nearly jumped out of her skin. "Rawley!" she said in relief, half-laughing as she collapsed against the door.

"What's wrong?" He was standing in the doorway to the kitchen, looking worried and oddly ill-at-ease.

"I just keep thinking someone's following me. It's ridiculous."

Rawley nodded, but the frown didn't leave his face. "I'm making popcorn," he said by way of invitation.

"Great." She moved to the couch, thoroughly annoyed with herself. Just the mention of Troy's name had sent her nerves screaming into overdrive. There was no reason to panic. Even if he approached her, she could handle it. He was a man, not a demon. A really sick, worthless twisted man with no heart, she reminded herself with an ironic smile. But then, no one's perfect.

"What are you smiling about?" Rawley asked as he flopped down beside her and handed her the bowl of popcorn.

"Oh, I don't know. Being silly and afraid for no reason. Having a birthday and a wonderful son."

Rawley gave her a sidelong look that said he didn't have a clue what she was talking about.

Jenny leaned over and gave him a quick kiss on the cheek. Clearing his throat, he said, "I have a question for you, but maybe this isn't really the right time."

"Okay . . ." New warning bells sounded in her head.

"Do I have to go to Puerto Vallarta? There's a soccer camp during spring break that I can go to with Brandon, and the Fergusons said I can stay with them. I really don't want to go on the trip. We're leaving Houston in a couple weeks and this is my last chance to see Brandon. Do you mind? I mean, really a lot? Could you go to Puerto Vallarta with your friends and leave me here? At the Fergusons, I mean?"

It came out in such a rush that Jenny couldn't break in. Dropping her handful of popcorn back in the bowl, she fought back the rush of feelings that threatened to spill into words. Of course she minded. Of course it was a terrible idea! How could he give up this trip? Everyone was expecting him.

And Troy was out there, somewhere . . .

"Is this what you really want to do?"

He nodded anxiously, evidently afraid that she would say no. She wanted to. Oh, how she wanted to.

"And it's all right with Janice and Rick?"

"No problem. You can call 'em. I think they're expecting you to."

Sighing, Jenny reached for another handful of buttery popcorn. Damn the calories. She could eat a tubful of the stuff. "Looks like I'm going solo."

He hugged her so hard and fast that she was still reeling

when he jumped over the back of the couch and whooped with joy. Then he ran for the phone. "Brandon!" he yelled. "I can stay!"

And Jenny blinked rapidly and reached for another handful of popcorn.

❋ CHAPTER THREE ❋

The steep, curving stone lane to the villa provided a thrill ride straight out of Disneyland. The Jeep that Magda Montgomery drove was little more than a canvas top on a wagon body. Jenny clung to the sides and desperately tried to keep herself from slamming her right foot through the floorboards in a futile attempt to brake. Dizzyingly, the road twisted and switchbacked, only a foot or so away from a sheer drop to the orange-tiled roofs of other villas and the sparkling waters of the Pacific ocean, far below.

"Isn't this great?" Magda yelled above the engine and thunkety-thunk of the tires over the rough stone road.

"Gr-rr-eat," Jenny chattered.

She held on to her hat with one hand, the low door with the other. She wasn't normally afraid of heights, but she was no daredevil either, and she couldn't wait to arrive at the villa. She tried not to think of all the reasons she shouldn't have come. *Numero uno:* Rawley's decision to stay with the Fergusons. Jenny had considered canceling the trip altogether.

Even after she'd capitulated she'd still tried to change his mind. "We've got airline tickets and reservations at the villa. They've held a room for us."

He looked at her with those huge blue eyes. "But I never really wanted to go. I was just doing it to make you happy."

In the end she'd knuckled under; she should have known her last-minute objections were useless. And it was understandable that Rawley would want to spend his last few days in Houston with the people he considered a second family. She should be grateful, she supposed, that he wasn't pitching a fit about the move. For reasons she didn't fully understand, Rawley wasn't complaining about the relocation to Santa Fe. She was grateful for that.

"There!" Magda exclaimed. She yanked on the brake before the Jeep came to a complete stop, nearly sending Jenny through the windshield.

Jenny released the grip on her hat and the door and glanced at the stucco building. Wrought iron decorated the arched windows and flower boxes filled with bougainvillea spilled bright blossoms down the walls. A plank door with iron bars opened upon their arrival and Magda's husband, Phil, wearing a blue beret jauntily over one eye, greeted them with a tray of margaritas.

"Welcome to Puerto Vallarta," Phil sang, kissing Jenny on both cheeks.

"Euro-Phil," Magda sniffed, loving every display of her husband's character. Phil was a born actor who just happened to make a living in real estate in Santa Fe. Jenny had met them at the restaurant. The Montgomerys always ate at Riccardo's when they cruised through Houston. They, like Alberto, had unofficially adopted Jenny and made her their friend, and it was Magda who had talked Jenny into making the move to Santa Fe. Magda was a skilled artisan who made unique jewelry; and she shared space in a shop in Santa Fe along Canyon Road, a street famed for its galleries and shops. She'd found a great location for Geneva's, and she'd been instrumental in urging Jenny to take the chance.

The Montgomerys had been wonderful to her from the start.

Euro-Phil helped them both from the Jeep, then served the frosty glasses. Lifting her margarita, Jenny toasted Euro-Phil; it was time to put everything out of her mind and enjoy the moment.

"How's that boss of yours doing?" Phil asked as he hefted her bag from the back of the Jeep.

"I think it finally hit Alberto that I was leaving when I told him he'd have to keep an eye on our produce company. He started to wail and beg, and for once I don't think it was an act."

"He'll be destroyed without you," Magda predicted.

"Oh, no. He'll survive." Jenny smiled. "He just wants it his way. Like every other male I know."

"Ouch!" Phil declared.

"Except you, Euro-Phil. "

"*Très bien.*"

"*De nada.*"

They laughed as they crossed the threshold of the huge stucco building and Magda led the way up a spiral staircase to a suite on the upper floor which looked over the bay far below. Stepping onto the balcony, Jenny closed her eyes and breathed deeply. How wonderful to put her cares aside! Maybe it was better if Rawley wasn't here. She could see herself floating in the pool, drinking margaritas and doing nothing at all.

After Magda left and Phil dropped her bag on a chair, Jenny changed into a two-piece swimsuit and bright blue sarong which she tied across her hips. She sipped her drink and watched the sun lower until it touched the horizon. Then she hurried downstairs, appearing on the lowest floor as a servant placed a tray of appetizers on a counter of painted blue and yellow Mexican tiles. A long, cloth-covered table stood set with silver and glass; something savory bubbling out of sight made her mouth water.

Phil and Magda were lying on lounge chairs, soaking up the sun. "Isn't this heaven?" Magda called.

"It sure is."

"The others will be back from their sightseeing tour later. Dinner's at eight."

The others were friends of Magda and Phil whom Jenny had never met. She'd been given the invitation when one couple backed out, and she'd debated on whether to accept because she'd been trying to scrimp and save. But Magda and Phil had offered her a major discount based on their friends' need to get out of their share of the villa rental. It had been too good a deal to pass up. Consequently, all she knew about the others was that they consisted of two couples, two single women, and one single male.

Arranging herself on a lounge chair, Jenny slathered on sun block, sank back into the cushions and immediately fell asleep. Exhaustion was like a drug and before she could remember where she was, excited voices pulled her groggily back to the present. The others had arrived.

Tom and Alicia Simmons were from Santa Fe, and the Brickmans, Sam and Carrie, hailed from Dallas. Lisa and Jackie, the two single women, were Carrie Brickman's college friends; and all of them knew either Magda or Phil from work, or mutual friends, or some roundabout way that, once mentioned, passed through Jenny's mind and was instantly forgotten. The one single male was Matt Somebody-or-other, but he'd apparently been prowling Puerto Vallarta's cafes and bars, getting a jump on the night life, and therefore wasn't currently with the group. Clearly, they were all eager to hit the club scene directly after dinner, something Jenny did not want to do.

"It's mostly young people," Magda admitted as they dug into enchiladas, quesadillas, refried beans, tortillas, and rice. "But it's a ton of fun."

"I am so tired. I don't think I can make it tonight," Jenny said, which evoked a chorus of disagreement from everyone.

"You can rest tomorrow!" Magda declared, grabbing Jenny's arm as if expecting her to bolt from the table and disappear. "Tonight's for dancing!"

"You must come with us," either Lisa or Jackie maintained. "It'll be fun."

Carrie Brickman added her two cents. "It's like a hedonistic tradition. Lay around all day and soak up the rays and sleep. Party till dawn."

Jenny laughed. "I turn into a frog at midnight."

"That's okay. We don't mind frogs," Tom Simmons said with a smile. He'd shaved his head, according to Magda, as a statement against going bald. But he'd kept a huge, red mustache which sprouted a good two inches on each side of his face.

After that, Jenny gave up. With zero enthusiasm, a faint headache, and tiny burn splotches here and there where she'd missed with the sunblock, Jenny found herself squeezed in a cab during the first run to town, then squeezed into one of the clubs along Puerto Vallarta's waterfront, her blue denim sundress sticking to her skin. She was barely able to turn around without rubbing against another body. And she felt at least a decade too old for the bumping, grinding, screaming crowd.

Wow . . . Talk about a one-hundred-eighty-degree turn from the responsibilities of real life! It was a party and a half. One of the initiation rites appeared to be straight shots of tequila followed by biting into a lime and licking salt off one's own hand. She had a sudden vision of the quiet wine dinners at Riccardo's and realized she was just a little too old for this kind of nonsense. It was a young person's paradise, and had Rawley been about six years older, he would have been in heaven.

"It's a good thing Rawley's not here!" Jenny yelled in Magda's ear.

"Huh? Why?"

"Because he's only fifteen and he'd be tempted to find out about margaritas and Mexican beer in a hurry!"

"They probably wouldn't serve him."

Who was she kidding? This wasn't the good old U.S. of A. and Jenny didn't think age regulations of that sort were seriously enforced here. Whatever the case, she was feeling better that Rawley had chosen to stay with the Fergusons, even if she still suffered twinges of fear over what Troy might have in mind.

By eleven o'clock Jenny was done with a capital D. However, Magda and Phil and the others didn't seem to be slowing down. Since they'd come by cab, Jenny considered hailing one alone, but in the end she just walked along the sidewalk at the edge of the beach, enjoying the hot breeze and scattered crowds of people. Puerto Vallarta bars closed late, some when the sun was rising. Jenny thought about her bed at the villa, then considered how it would feel to arrive there completely alone. She wanted—something. Company. People around, even if she wasn't part of the conversation.

She just didn't want to feel so alone.

There was a hotel not far away with an arched blue tile entry set into thick plaster walls that looked cool and inviting. She stepped through into a walled patio, where, overhead, stars shone against a darkening royal blue sky. All eyes turned her way, but she ignored them. Finding a place at the bar, she slid onto a stool and lifted her gaze to the open sky above. It was just too beautiful and serene to worry.

The bar was fairly crowded, but the thundering music and thrashing limbs of the other nightclubs was thankfully missing. People sat beneath umbrellas which were slowly being removed from the tables because there was no threat of rain. Jenny ordered a sparkling water, glad to observe the clientele here at—she squinted at the name on a matchbook from the wicker basket on the bar—the Hotel Rosa was closer to her age.

Hotel Rosa. She'd accidentally wandered into the very place she'd planned to check out for their wonderful Mexican cuisine. Smiling to herself, she wondered if she ought to live a little and order something more exotic to drink. With that, she picked up a laminated drink menu and wondered who in their right mind would order a Flaming Volcano. Something about tabasco and rum and a jalapeño pepper. She shuddered.

Three men asked to buy her a drink. She shook her head each time and finally ordered a Corona. Once the beer, with its wedge of lime, was placed in front of her, she glanced around. Her three would-be suitors were standing by. This was a circumstance she hadn't imagined, though she should have. Sighing to herself, she debated whether to give it up for the evening and catch a taxi to the villa after all.

One of the suitors wedged himself between Jenny and the customer seated on the stool next to her. Jenny inwardly groaned. He was young and buff. He had that "I know what women want" attitude that always annoyed her.

"Come here often?" he asked, stupidly grinning like a jack-o-lantern. The older man on the stool got up and left in a huff, shooting Jenny's newfound friend a look of disgust as he left.

"Not really." Jenny fought the urge to be unpleasant.

"You come in on the cruise ship?"

"No."

"Just visiting?"

She nodded. "Staying with friends."

"Yeah?" He glanced around. He might be in good shape, but he was losing his hair, and he kept running a palm over the thinning strands, self-conscious, yet unable to keep from drawing attention to himself. Jenny felt a pang of something like empathy in spite of her disdain. Tom's shaven head seemed like a much healthier approach. "So, where are they?" he asked.

"My friends are still down the way," she said, inclining

her head to the door.

"Meeting you here?"

"Hope so."

"Mind if I keep you company till they show?"

Her smile froze. She wanted to scream at him to get lost, but she just couldn't speak. "Not at all," she heard herself say, then glanced at her reflection in the mirrored wall behind the bar and sighed.

What am I doing here?

What the hell is she doing? Hunter asked himself, feeling weary all over at the naiveté of women. They picked up men the way they picked up stray animals. Like this half-bald bozo with his tongue practically hanging out.

And you'd think Jenny Holloway would know better by now.

Tossing down the rest of his beer, Hunter wiped the back of his hand over his lips. He hadn't expected her to just turn up like this. Sure, it was the Hotel Rosa, but it was her first night and he'd expected her to crash at the villa with her friends. He'd been here a day already and had driven up past Villa Buena Vista, scouted out the surrounding area and returned to the hotel. He'd thrown open the doors to his balcony, lain down on his double bed, listened to the cease-less dull roar of the ocean, and fallen into a comalike sleep until he wakened, shocked, dazed, and confused.

As he understood it, depressed people sometimes slept for days or weeks, never wanting to rise and face their problems. On the other hand, it had been so long that he'd actually slept more than a few minutes at a time that it could be a sign of healing. Grimacing, Hunter had decided he really didn't give a rat's ass what it meant, and it was lucky he didn't have to tell some shrink that.

The upshot was he'd stumbled awake and headed downstairs for some food. Allen Holloway had been right about the cuisine. The chili relleno was delicious. He scooped up some of the cheese-stuffed pepper and turned it around on the end of his fork, staring at it. Wow. If Jenny had come down here to learn the Hotel Rosa's secrets, he was all for it. The idea of her opening a restaurant in Santa Fe suddenly held new interest for him.

But for the moment . . .

The guy bothering her had moved closer, his beefy arm lying across the bar, his sunburned head thrust toward her. The loser really deserved to be grabbed by the back of his thick neck and thrown into the street. Was she humoring him? The way she smiled and courteously responded to his inane questions needled him. Losers like this guy were all over this trashed-out planet and Hunter had seen way too many of them. When did women learn? He would have thought a woman as wealthy as Miz. Holloway would have ignored a barfly, but she was being so downright friendly it boggled his mind.

The guy leaned in even closer, struggling for a look down her blue denim sundress for a quick peek at a pair of beautifully rounded breasts. Hunter automatically reached for his beer. Finding the bottle empty, he squeezed his fingers into his palms until his hands were balled fists.

Wait, he cautioned himself, as he fought an urge to lunge forward and forcefully remove the bozo from the scene. He shifted his weight, counting silently to himself. It wouldn't do to attract attention to himself that way. *Wait* . . .

Jenny didn't seem alarmed. Observing her closely, he recognized the faint signs of female boredom. Instantly he relaxed. She was just being polite. As long as her overeager friend kept to a certain level, she could handle things herself.

Snorting at the realization, Hunter lifted a desultory hand at the waiter standing by the bar, then pointed to his empty bottle. The beer was replaced and he picked the bottle up by the neck. He was sprawled on a caned chair in the corner of the patio, partially hidden by the trunk of a thick tree whose gnarled roots had already lifted some of the red floor tiles. It was a massive miscalculation by the owners. A few more years and the tree would topple over, possibly taking a patron or two with it. But it served its purpose tonight.

Hunter hadn't expected Jenny to appear so soon. It was actually his second night on alert, because he'd arrived a day ahead of her. Last night he'd walked around the hotel grounds and wandered down the streets, stopping in at the nightclubs to witness some world-class tequila drinking and gyrating bodies in the skimpiest clothing outside of the beach.

He'd rented a Jeep today. A Wrangler. The tourist vehicle of choice, it appeared, and his own personal favorite. He'd gone to the airport to wait for Jenny's flight to land; then watched her as she drove off with a woman whose wild red hair, bracelets, skimpy dress, and loud exuberant manner earned her sidelong looks from the tourists and locals alike. He'd winced at the way the woman had ground the gears. Tough to hear a vehicle treated that way.

Following Jenny Holloway was getting interesting again.

She was responding to the man without encouraging him. She didn't have to. She was encouragement enough just sitting there. Her hair lay in lush, thick waves against a smooth neck and back. She was slender in the right places and curvy in the others, unlike other rich women who made thinness an obsession.

But she was rich. She was Allen Holloway's only daughter. Hunter had done some research on the man himself before committing to this assignment, only to learn the expected, though unpalatable truth: Holloway owned half of Texas and most of New Mexico.

Okay. Maybe that was an exaggeration. But the guy was loaded. Supremely loaded. Hunter had suffered through the pains of being involved with the very rich: his ex-wife had possessed way too much money and that dependence on the almighty dollar had been the main reason that marriage had failed.

That, and his own bad attitude about the whole thing, Hunter knew. It was a fact. Pure and simple. And boy, could Kathryn be an out-and-out bitch. But then he'd married her for all the wrong reasons, too. The three "S"s. Sex, stupidity, and sentimentality.

Once a fool, always a fool . . .

Except the mistakes of romance were behind him now. His disillusionment over Kathryn meant little compared to the death of his sister Michelle. In fact, he hadn't really thought about Kathryn much the past few years. She called now and again, and though he tried not to listen to her, she managed to convey enough information to remind him how lucky he was that it was over. She'd married again, divorced again, and had gotten into fitness in a way that had turned her thin as a whippet. Unlike Jenny . . .

His breath caught. Was the slimeball putting his hand on her *thigh?* She swung her legs to one side, as if she'd anticipated the move and with a quick turn she was off the stool, saying good night and dipping her head to hide her expression. Hunter wanted to squeeze the lounge lizard's neck for ruining this perfect observation. Now, he was going to have to think fast and with a couple of beers under his belt, it was the last thing he wanted to do.

But providence saved the day. Geneva's friends, in a whirl of drunken gaiety and noise, swarmed into the bar. One of the women caught her heel on a broken tile heaved up by the tree roots, then whirled like a pinwheel as Hunter half stood. She cried out, slammed an elbow into the tree trunk, then landed with a plop in his lap, cropping them both to the chair, hard.

"Ohmigod!" she declared, slipping around unsteadily so that Hunter clung to her with all his might. She wasn't heavy, but she was drunk as a skunk.

Jenny appeared instantly and grabbed her friend's arms. "Magda? You okay?"

The redheaded pal squinted at her. "*Olé!*" she cried, laughing like a hyena. Hunter couldn't help but smile, and when Magda swung around to look at him, she declared, "Whoa, whoa! What have we here? Good heavens! A good-looking man. Hey, Jenny. Look what I found!" She collapsed into a second fit of hysteria.

Jenny Holloway's blue eyes regarded Hunter with gratitude and a hint of suspicion. "Good catch," she said softly.

Hunter righted Magda onto her feet. She moaned in dismay at the broken strap of her sandal. "Never pay more than a hundred dollars for a pair of shoes," she declared, stumbling toward the bar. "It's just not worth it."

A hundred dollars for those hemp strings and strips of leather? Hunter thought in shock. A hundred dollars *plus*? Instantly he kicked himself for being surprised at anything the rich did. He knew better. He knew so much better.

"Do I know you?" Jenny asked curiously and Hunter's pulse leapt in spite of himself.

He glanced at her, keeping his expression neutral. What the hell was going on here? He wasn't certain what to think of his sudden sensitivity. He hadn't reacted to anything in so long that for a moment he sat in silence, marveling. He decided to ignore his feelings and answered flatly, "No."

"Oh." She stiffened. "I guess not. You seemed . . . familiar. Sorry." She shot him a fleeting smile. "I don't know what I was thinking."

The bozo took the opportunity to step up. "You all need a ride somewhere? I could drive you."

"No, thanks."

"Hope your friends aren't driving," the guy pointed out, as Magda and friends headed for the bar.

"We cabbed it," Jenny assured him in a voice that had grown colder by the syllable.

Hunter was amused by the exchange. The guy just wouldn't get the message. Jenny had been patient and polite, but she was becoming out-and-out annoyed. About time, too, he felt.

"Well, if you want a driver, I'm offering," the guy responded. With that he pulled a card out of his wallet and Hunter noticed he wasn't as fast on the draw as he purported to be. Bozo had downed a few too many Mexican beers himself.

"Probably not a good idea for you to be behind the wheel, either," Hunter observed.

The man threw him a belligerent glance. "Yeah?" he challenged.

"You're trying to hand her your insurance card."

He glanced down, muttered a curse and searched on.

Jenny said firmly, "Thanks, but we're fine. I really have to get back to my friends."

He cursed again, swept his hand over the back of his head, threw Hunter a furious look, then staggered outside.

"Hey, good-looking!" Magda waved Hunter to the bar. "Join us."

Hunter hesitated. The open seat was right next to Jenny Holloway. Gathering up his half-downed beer, he ambled over. His days of following her without her knowing it had just come to an end.

Jenny wasn't sure whether to wring Magda's neck or kiss her. The only man in the bar worth noticing was the dark-haired stranger who'd caught her, but Jenny was worn out. At this point she just wanted to go back to the villa.

Still, as he unfolded himself in a slow moving, sensual way, she couldn't help the thrill of feminine awareness that swept through her. When his jeans-clad legs moved into her line of vision, she had to ignore the way his belt lay low on his hips and the taut muscles of his bare forearms. Nope, she reminded herself. Physical attractiveness was only skin deep. She'd been there and back.

"What's your name, Tex?" Magda asked, checking him out, but much more boldly than Jenny.

"Hunter."

"That a first or a last?"

Jenny swallowed a smile. You had to hand it to Magda. Always uninhibited.

"First." He signaled the bartender who promptly snapped the cap on another beer and slid it across the bar.

"Well, Hunter, what are you doing here?" Magda asked.

"Reliving *Night of the Iguana*."

Jenny gave him a long, long look. "That was shot here in Puerto Vallarta."

"Yep." He took a pull at his beer and swung around on the stool, regarding her in a way that sent off strange vibes inside her.

"Are you a fan?"

"A fan?"

"Of the film." Jenny felt a little tongue-tied. As she spoke she could feel her pulse thunder ahead as if it had joined some race in progress.

"Never seen it. Is it good?"

"I have no idea." She laughed, but it was a flirtatious noise that made her cringe inside. She had to get out of here. "I've never seen it either. Supposed to be good, though. The hotel where it was set is supposed to be south of town, I think. I'm not sure."

She was babbling. With determination she signaled the waiter and pointed to Hunter's beer. "I'll take one of those, please." Something to drink would give her mouth something to do besides make a fool out of her.

"What's it about?" Hunter asked her.

"What?"

"*Night of the Iguana?*"

"Oh." She swallowed from the bottle, pleasantly surprised at the foamy light bitterness. Beer wasn't a thing she normally drank. "Lost souls and revelations, I think."

He arched a brow. "Maybe I should see it."

She wanted to stare at him, examine the lines of his face and the hard curve of his jaw. He was handsome, she decided, but it was a masculine kind of attractiveness that had a lot to do with intensity and power. She suspected his nose had been broken, maybe more than once, and there was a scar on his chin that reminded her of Harrison Ford. "Do you have a lost soul?" she asked lightly.

"I think so." A brief smile and flash of white teeth dazzled her. It was quickly over, extinguished, like dousing a flame with water.

"What's your last name?" she asked.

A long moment passed. She wondered if he were seriously considering withholding that information, then he extended his hand.

"Hunter Calgary, and you are?"

"Jenny Holloway," she answered a bit breathlessly, shaking his hand. His palm was strong, warm and dry and held all the masculine strength she'd noted. Her mind spun. What the hell was wrong with her? She was acting like a giddy teenager.

"Jenny short for something?" he asked.

"Uh, yes. But not Jennifer . . . it's Geneva. After my grandmother."

"Geneva," he said, rolling the syllables on his tongue as if he were tasting the effect.

Jenny watched his lips, fascinated. She shook herself to attention and turned to Magda who was once again moaning about her ruined sandals. "I have to go home," Jenny said, shaken. "Really. It's late and I'm exhausted."

"Really?" Magda screwed up her face, silently pleading for her to relent.

"Really."

"Well, we won't let you leave!" Phil declared. "We've got to dance!"

"No." Jenny grabbed her purse and slid from the stool, desperate to be away. "Sorry."

"One dance." Phil swept her into his arms and they swayed to a soft Latin beat while Jenny kept one eye on the broken tiles to avoid a snapped sandal or a twisted ankle.

She humored him for the length of the song, but finally shook her head and pulled away. "Party on," she told him, turning toward Magda and the others. Hunter Calgary was nowhere to be seen.

With a feeling of disappointment way out of proportion to the event, Jenny hugged Magda and Phil and extricated herself from their arms, kisses, and pleas. She would get a cab and find her way back to the villa.

But the bozo barfly was waiting for her outside and she inwardly groaned as she stepped onto the street. "I got a car right over there," he said, pointing down the street.

"No, thank, you." Jenny was polite but firm.

"Now, come on. I'm not gonna bite."

Jenny turned to walk away, her senses on alert, listening to see if he followed her. Sure enough, his footsteps fell in line behind hers.

"Hey!" he yelled, irritated. "Hey!"

Jenny walked faster. "Please, please, please . . ." she murmured aloud.

And then Hunter Calgary stepped out of a parked Jeep Wrangler and simply grabbed the man by the arm, jerking him around.

The man grunted and ducked his head, as if he were going to charge. Hunter waited on the balls of his feet, legs apart, arms away from his sides. He'd been attacked by the best of them, and he wasn't going to be taken by surprise by a guy who might or might not be the kind who liked to fight.

But bozo stumbled a bit. He was a hell of a lot drunker than he believed. "Back off!" he growled at Hunter.

"Careful." Hunter kept his eyes trained on the guy's face, watching his eyes. "Leave her alone or she'll call the police. You don't want to get in trouble in Mexico, pal."

"I just want to give her a ride!" he wailed.

"Go back to your hotel. Catch a cab."

"I'm staying at this hotel!" he declared.

Wouldn't you know, Hunter thought, as the bozo swiveled around and headed back inside the hotel bar, muttering obscenities under his breath. What a piece of work. Turning, he saw that Jenny had continued walking rapidly down the street. He debated on following after her, but then decided against it. The last thing she needed was to be approached again, even by him. She was done with would-be Romeos for the night. Sighing, he headed back to his Jeep, careful to keep one eye on her disappearing form. He could still see her as he slipped inside the Wrangler. She was attempting to hail a cab, but she was competing with a lot of tourists as the night wore on, and no one stopped. Rethinking his plan, he jerked the vehicle in gear and cruised up beside her. Initially she tried to ignore him, finally shooting him a grim look. Then she recognized him.

"At the risk of being rejected, would you like a lift?" Hunter asked her.

"Oh!" She hesitated a moment, then yanked open the passenger door before Hunter could even offer help. "I really would, as a matter of fact. Thanks."

"He wasn't taking no for an answer." This time he eased the Jeep into gear and moved smoothly into the stream of traffic.

"No kidding." She sighed and half smiled, dropping her head against the headrest. "Why is that? Is it alcohol? Or was he just a thick-headed guy?"

"Combination, I'd say."

"I couldn't get a cab to save my soul."

"One would have come along."

"I'm glad you were there, all the same."

Hunter wished, suddenly, that he had a cigarette. Not that he'd ever been much of a smoker. He'd given it up altogether upon becoming a cop. It was just too much trouble to bother with, he'd felt, though his friends on the force felt differently. But now, for reasons that troubled him at a level he didn't feel like exploring, he could damn well use a smoke.

They bumped across the uneven stone road, then onto the highway, then up the broken rock roads that would flood so badly during the rainy season it was like trying to drive up a waterfall. Her villa was perched precariously on the edge of the hillside, as most of them were, and Hunter pulled over onto the curb to get off the road.

"Thanks," she said, reaching for the door once again before he could offer help.

He nodded, glimpsing the curve of her calf and trim bones of her ankle before she managed to drop to the ground. The tightening he felt inside was part sexual response, part recognition of potential danger.

He cursed himself. That sense of impending doom was stronger than ever.

Jenny leaned inside, hands on the edge of the door frame. "Are you staying long in Puerto Vallarta?"

"I'll be here awhile."

"Maybe we'll run into each other again?" She sounded hopeful.

"I'm at the Hotel Rosa."

"You are?" She was surprised. "You didn't have to leave to bring me home."

"No problem. I wasn't eager to run into our mutual friend, now that I know he's one of the guests."

"Maybe he'll find another female at the bar. Of course, then you'll be called into service again, saving damsels in distress."

"Not my best role." He smiled with an effort. Why was she getting to him? He couldn't understand it, and he knew it was going to screw up his plans if he didn't set the ground rules fast.

"Really? Seems like a natural to me."

She glanced toward the front door of the villa, filled with indecision. He suspected suddenly that she might throw caution to the winds and invite him inside. Quickly, he suggested, "Come by the hotel bar tomorrow evening. I'll buy you a margarita and some free tortilla chips."

She laughed then, relieved the decision had been made for her. "All right, I'll be there, Hunter Calgary. Thanks again." With that she turned and walked to the moonlit door and the image burned on Hunter's brain was of long, silky legs walking away from him. He waited until she was safely inside, turned the Jeep around and drove away. A simmering, unwelcome heat had taken him over. Sex. Ordinarily he would have thrilled at the return of feeling but Jenny Holloway was off limits for many, many reasons. He'd be better off to pour a cold beer in his crotch than entertain any thoughts about what and where and how they could do things together.

The idea had merit. But as he walked through the bar on his way to his room, he saw the bozo again, hunkered at the bar and hoping for a second chance. The man glowered at Hunter who hooked a beer and threw his head back, pouring the liquid down his throat, dousing the flames of sexual desire from the inside out. It worked, too, until he went upstairs and flung himself on his bed. He stared up at the ceiling fan overhead, watching its blades turn in a desultory circle which barely moved the thick air.

Kathryn had gotten to him the same way. Long limbs, perfect breasts, unconscious sex appeal—or so he'd thought until he'd gotten to know her and learned too late how calculating she could be. He'd listened to his cock instead of his brain; and when he learned that lovemaking with Kathryn was as wonderful as he'd envisioned, he'd married her.

What a mistake.

Just thinking about it constricted his chest to this day. Life with Kathryn had been pure, unadulterated hell. He'd learned right away that those wonderful nights of sex had been a conscious trap on her part. She had no serious interest in him, but she sure as hell could act! She was also exacting, spoiled, used to being treated like a princess, and determined to change him from an L.A. police detective to a real estate investor and decorative piece of arm candy. He'd left her after six months, divorced her a year and a half later. She'd never forgiven him and still called whenever her latest relationship fell apart and she was lonely. He'd never gone back, however, not even for a taste. And he'd congratulated himself on climbing out of the trap and recognizing the pitfalls ever since.

But Jenny was different . . .

Closing his eyes he groaned softly. Was it all in his imagination, this sexual chemistry? Maybe she didn't feel the same way. Maybe she'd just been grateful for the ride and that was as far as it went.

He was floating in this state of pain and pleasure when the phone rang. Instantly alert, he picked up the receiver, listening a moment before answering. "Yes?" he asked cautiously.

"How's my girl?" Allen Holloway asked. "Have you found her yet?"

The man's voice was like an avalanche of ice on his sexual thoughts. *This* was why he couldn't even dream about Jenny. She was a job. A paycheck. And a means to an end.

"Yep." It bugged him that Holloway had called him.

"She's with those fools the Montgomerys?"

No wonder she objected to her father's interference. Allen Holloway was opinionated as hell and felt no compunction to keep his thoughts to himself. "She's at Villa Buena Vista."

"No sign of Russell?"

"None that I've seen." Not that he'd been looking. Not that he'd been able to do much but envision Jenny without that sundress on.

"Good. Keep an eye out."

"Don't call here again," Hunter answered. "I don't want any link between us. Let me call you."

"You think that's necessary?"

"Yes," Hunter answered truthfully. "If you want to get your money's worth."

That stopped him. Holloway would have liked to argue, but he also wanted results. "I want a full report as soon as you're back in the states."

"Have you heard anything more from him?" Hunter asked.

"From Russell? No."

"Even if you do, don't call me. Wait."

The Allen Holloways of the world did not like being told what to do. Hunter could hear the man's deep breathing—almost a growl—before he muttered something about wanting Hunter to give him full and timely reports. With a grunt that meant "maybe," Hunter hung up the phone. Lust had faded from his thoughts with Allen's call.

Now, staring at the ceiling, all he could envision was Troy Russell's cold eyes and characterless face.

CHAPTER FOUR

C harm. That's all it took. Good looks helped, but he'd seen even the ugliest men in the world get what they wanted with a little charm. And women were suckers for it. They'd open their legs and their pocketbooks for it. He should know. Charm was his stock in trade.

Troy drummed his fingers on the steering wheel of his rented Ford sedan. It was that color usually called "champagne," which really meant the metal was a nondescript light goldish-brown no one looked at twice. He'd picked it for its blandness. Bland was the order of the day when one had to be invisible. Bland was what kept Jenny from looking over her shoulder once too often.

He'd had a bad moment the other night at the restaurant. She'd been skittish as a colt, and he'd had to actually slide down on the sedan's seat and stay there until he heard her engine slip into gear and her wheels move away. Her head had been turning from the moment she stepped out the back door of the restaurant and he'd dropped down instantly. She'd sat in her car quite a while and he'd wondered if she'd seen him, but then she'd pulled out. He'd waited, then followed slowly. She'd actually driven past her apartment building an extra mile, then circled around and cruised back. He'd had to stay a long way behind, but since he knew where she was going it had been a cinch. Still, her little safety precautions amused him. Little did she know they weren't going to do a damn thing for her. Not if she was protecting herself from him.

He laughed silently to himself. Stupid bitch. They were all stupid bitches. Sluts at heart, even the seemingly good, ones like dear old Jenny. All of them secretly panting for a guy to rip off their clothes and give it to them hard. He hadn't known that quite as clearly when he'd been with Jenny. He'd learned a thing or two over the years, and he was red-hot and ready to give her the benefit of his education.

He hadn't actually been inside her place . . . yet. But he'd calculated which room was hers and which was the boy's. The kid looked to be about thirteen, gangly and awkward and on the verge of rebellion. Troy remembered those days, although he'd been in a very different situation. Whose kid was he? he wondered, feeling really pissed that Jenny had gone out and got herself pregnant almost the moment Troy left. Allen Holloway had been anxious to throw him some cash in those days. Anything to keep his wicked son-in-law away from his precious little girl.

So, who'd knocked her up? Allen hadn't mentioned the boy at their meeting. Come to that, Allen hadn't mentioned anything much. He'd demanded, that's what he'd done. Demanded and demanded, while his lips twitched in an effort to fight back an emotion Troy understood implicitly: fear. Holloway was afraid of him.

"Good," he said now, meaning it. He glanced at the wrought iron gates that led to the Holloway grounds. A mansion. The old guy lived there with his beautiful wife— a woman who was as vacant as an empty lot. Troy had learned her habits, too. He'd managed to run into her at one of those pricey stores that sold all natural stuff. She had been examining some kind of nitrate-free bacon, and he brushed his shoulder against hers, apologizing profusely. Natalie. That was her name. He wondered if she would recognize him. They hadn't had a lot of contact in those faraway days. She'd been at the wedding reception Allen had insisted upon when he and Jenny got back from their elopement, but she'd been so involved with her own appearance that he'd be surprised if she even remembered what Jenny looked like. And then she'd got drunk on champagne and Allen had paid someone to take her home. Troy hadn't really seen her after that. Holloway wasn't in the habit of inviting his daughter and her new husband to the house. Still . . .

But no. Natalie hadn't made the connection at all. She accepted his apology and smiled in that vacant way of hers, as if her mind were elsewhere. Another time Troy might have considered it a challenge. Turn on the old charm and see if he could rustle up some sexual interest. But he had other things in mind, and Natalie Holloway wasn't one of them.

Jenny was.

She was where the money was.

He'd told Allen he wanted to make amends for the past. What a joke. Who the hell ever wanted to make amends unless they wanted money or found God, and Troy Russell sure as hell hadn't got religion all of a sudden. But he could act like a man who'd seen the light. Acting was easy. It was just a facet of charm.

"What do you want?" Holloway had demanded. "Why are you really here?"

"I've had a lot of time to think things over. I just want to make things right."

"I paid you to stay away from Jenny. I paid you a lot of money."

"And that was a lot of years ago," Troy conceded. "I'm

here to make amends."

"You come near her, and I'll make you wish you hadn't."

Ultimatums were a coward's stock in trade. Lots of talk, talk, talk. Words thrown out like spears, but nothing to back it up. Troy had learned not to let them bother him and he kept his own anger easily under control. Holloway was a skinflint who kept all his money in stocks and real estate. He hadn't apparently lavished tons of the green stuff on his daughter since she was slaving away in a restaurant and living in a dumpy apartment. Maybe Holloway detested the boy's father even more than he detested Troy.

But it didn't matter. Jenny would get the entire estate upon the death of the father. Natalie was nothing. An ornament. A hefty chunk of change and she was on her way. Jenny was the true heir.

Troy grimaced. He'd really blown the sweet deal he had with Jenny, because he'd been too young to realize how to play the game. He'd let his anger get in the way. He knew that now. And now, if he was furious, he found other outlets to let the steam escape. It was so fuckin' easy to fool people.

Smiling, he pulled out a pack of gum, folding a stick in his mouth. He'd given up smoking. Smoking didn't win you the skinny, rich women with hot pussies. They could sure as hell smoke, but they wanted their studs Lysol clean. He liked doing them, but one eye was always on their pocketbooks. Sometimes he got them drunk and stole their cash on his way out. But not often. Mostly he used them to learn the names of their friends, and their friends, and so on. Twice he'd seriously caught a wealthy one who wanted to shower him with all her riches, but both times there had been a wedge. The same wedge. Michelle Calgary. Just thinking about her sent Troy into a cold fury. Gotten herself pregnant and crying all the time. He couldn't take it. Just couldn't take it.

And now he'd been in a long, dry spell. Oh, there was Patricia, but her money wasn't enough. He wanted his fair share, but that took millions upon millions. He showed up now and again and gave her what she wanted, but he'd peeked at her finances and they weren't at the level of Allen Holloway. Tough luck for Pat. He just didn't come that cheap.

Putting the Ford into gear, he slid into traffic and drove toward Jenny's apartment. It was dark. Again. Had been for the last couple of days. She was on a trip, he realized suddenly, furiously.

Allen must have warned her about him.

His anger swept over him in such a cold wave that he white-knuckled the steering wheel. He yanked the car back toward Holloway's mansion, then changed his mind a few moments later, turning instead in the direction of her restaurant. He practically jumped out of the car before it came to a halt.

"Fucking bastard," he said through his teeth. He was going to kill Holloway. As surely as there would be a tomorrow, he was going to kill him.

"Welcome to Riccardo's. Table for one?" the pert receptionist asked him.

Fuck you, he thought, but the smile that crept across his face was a purposely sexy one. "Unless you'd care to join me . . . ?"

She grinned slyly and led him to a table by a rock wall, the votive candle sending up flickering shadows against the rugged, gray stones. She sashayed away, showing him some sweet cheeks.

Charm, he reminded himself as he watched for the waitress who'd talked to Jenny as if they were the best of friends. He'd watched them from a corner table and then left before Jenny actually spotted him. He'd thought Jenny wasn't working that night, then had been surprised when she'd walked by within ten yards of his table. He'd slipped out after leaving enough money on the table to cover his drink plus a nice tip. Didn't want people remembering the man who dined and dashed. Gotta keep it bland.

There she was. Friendly as hell. When he realized he hadn't been seated in her section, he simply moved. Let them work it out. "Hi, there," she said with a jaunty smile. "Weren't you here a few days ago?"

"Can't seem to stay away."

"Uh-huh." She leaned back on one hip, surveying him with twinkling eyes. "Have you had a chance to look at the menu?"

"What would you recommend?"

"It's all wonderful. And if you like pasta, you've come to the right place."

He finally settled on ziti in a marinara sauce with calamari and clams. She brought it to him with a glass of chianti and then she gave him his second jolt of the evening, "She's not here tonight," she said in a stage whisper. "Vacation."

So, she knew he'd been watching Jenny. He was infuriated with his sloppiness. "She take her son with her?"

"Rawley? I think so. No, maybe not. Do you know her?" She sounded confused, like she hadn't expected it.

Following her lead, Troy chose his words carefully. "Just by seeing her around here."

"Well, you'd better make your move when she gets back, because it's only going to be for a few days. She's moving, you know. I'm not even sure she's coming back to the restaurant before she goes."

Troy's fingers curled into fists beneath the table. "Oh, that's right. Last time I talked to her she was talking about getting out of Houston. Where's she going again?"

She eyed him from head to toe, as if debating on how much she could trust him. Troy shrugged at her, making like a harmless puppy. "You don't have to tell me. I'll call her at her apartment."

"New Mexico," she answered. "What's your name? I'll tell her you stopped by."

"Mike Conrad." He grimaced. "I'm afraid I'm gonna miss her. I'm heading back to Cincinnati tomorrow."

"Bummer! Well, okay, Mike Conrad, I'll let her know that she missed a serious opportunity."

"You do that."

As he watched her walk away, he felt a certain amount of contentment. New Mexico was a big state, but all he had to do was tag after her and the information would come his way. And she had that son . . . Rawley. All in all, it had been a pretty good night.

Perspiration dripped down Jenny's temples as she lay on the white chaise longue. Her eyes were closed and she was baking. Steaming, actually, under a merciless Mexican sun.

When she opened her eyes, heat devils danced and wriggled in the distance. Sighing, she let her lids drop once more, wishing she could enjoy this vacation as much as Magda, Phil, and the others did.

They were already warming up with afternoon margaritas during a time when any self-respecting Mexican would be having a siesta. Jenny was all for quitting during the heat of the day and picking up the pace when the shadows lengthened. Why she was even out in the sun was a mystery to her, although snoozing in her room had lost its appeal when the air conditioning unit dropped a puddle of condensation on the foot of her bed. Joaquin, the houseboy, was apparently taking care of the problem.

Her thoughts seesawed from anticipation—thoughts that had Hunter Calgary in their center—to anxiety. The anxiety had to do with Troy. She'd so effectively shut him out of her life that he'd become a distant memory over the past fifteen years, nothing she wanted to ever think about. But now, with Allen's revelation just days old, a flood of recollections had left her feeling nervous and jumpy. Sometimes she wanted to leap out of her skin and scream.

Back in her room, she showered, towelled off, then blow-dried her hair, clipping the unruly mane at the back of her nape with a tortoiseshell barrette. Drawing a breath, she pursed her lips, then blew her fluffy bangs upward. In the mirror serious blue eyes stared back at her ironically. The dimple that appeared when she smiled was hidden beneath the sternness of her expression.

"You can't hurt me, Troy," she said in a voice that matched her expression.

In the salon, Magda, Phil, and the others had moved from

desultory sipping to out-and-out drinking. Discussion revolved around the cost of taxis. No one wanted to drive, given their current state of inebriation. Jenny fought an urge to scurry back to her room. She wasn't generally judgmental about drinking, but they were all so far ahead of her that it made her feel even more like an outsider.

"Jenny, my love!" Magda waved fingers at her with one hand and sloshed frozen margarita mix out of her drink and onto the Mexican tiles with the other.

"Let me fix you a drink." Phil was once again in his Euro-Phil beret. Jenny half smiled and nodded. She didn't want to be the wet blanket. In fact, she was tired of being Miss Responsible, Miss Go-to-Bed-First, Miss Boring. She'd made mistakes in her youth, but she'd atoned for each and every one of them. It was time she had a little fun. Besides, Rawley was safe with the Fergusons and there was nothing to worry about. Nothing.

It took an almost physical effort to push her worries about Troy aside. Still, she glanced toward the phone. It required a credit card and a better knowledge of Spanish than she possessed if she wanted to check in with the Fergusons, just in case. Rawley might be happy at soccer camp, but she couldn't stop herself from fretting completely. Maybe another margarita will help, she told herself with new resolve.

Time to become the life of the party.

"Here ya be," Phil declared, bestowing her drink in her hand with a flourish.

"Thanks."

One of the others detached himself from the group and came her way. It was the single man. Matt Something-or-other. Jenny searched her brain for something to say, berated herself for being a flirting failure, and just settled on a welcoming smile. He'd been bantering with Lisa and Jackie throughout the afternoon, but she suspected it was now her time to share his wonderful personality. Cynical? Yes, she was. But it had served her well for the past fifteen years . . .

"Hey, there," he said, plunking himself down on the end of her chaise.

"Hello." She mentally groaned. He reminded her a bit of an overgrown Rawley. The teenage vernacular was certainly the same.

"Come here often?" He grinned like a satyr.

"Every day for the next week."

"My name's Matt. And you're Jenny."

She lifted her drink in a silent salute. She wanted to say something clever and sassy, but for the life of her she couldn't. What a drag! Life was too short to waste it trying to be perfect.

"My mother's name's Jennifer."

"Oh?"

"And my father's name's Ted." He grinned. "I'm boring the hell out of you, aren't I?"

She shook her head even though it was close to the truth. How many hours were there before she could gracefully get away? Hunter had promised her a margarita. She wondered if she could skip dinner and hightail it out of here right now. But then, what would she do? Wait for him at the bar? Try to call his room?

The answer was so obvious she was surprised she hadn't considered it before. As Matt opened his mouth to throw out another get-to-know-you line, Jenny glanced at her watch. "Oh! I didn't realize how late it was. I've got to get to the Hotel Rosa. I'm having dinner there tonight."

"You are?" Magda waved an arm adorned with one of her silver and turquoise bracelets. Her own creation, a design from what she'd dubbed her "Tourist Trap" line. Still, it really worked for her.

"For the restaurant," Jenny said. "I've heard their food's wonderful, and I'd like to get some ideas." She smiled. "I only steal from the best."

"I'll come with you," Matt promptly invited himself.

"No, Matt!" Magda gave him a scolding look. "We can't abandon all this food! What would the staff think? They'd get their feelings hurt!"

"You all stay here and Jenny and I will check out the Hotel Rosa." He winked at Jenny. "You tell me what to order, and I'll buy."

Jenny gaped at him, mad at herself that she couldn't respond with equal rudeness. With a shrug, she headed upstairs to change, noticing Lisa and Jackie's crestfallen glances at Matt. He phoned for a cab while she was gone, and by the time she was downstairs he was there beside her, wearing tight jeans and a black shirt, open to the navel.

Oh, God, she thought, preceding him out the door.

Matt was a problem she didn't need. From the moment he helped her into the cab,. his attentions became proprietorial. Jenny longed for the company of Lisa and Jackie but they had scorned her last-ditch invitation, throwing dagger glances at Matt.

Matt was completely unaffected. As they bumped down

the rocky hillside to the town itself, he wound an arm over her shoulders. "I didn't think you'd go out with me," he revealed with a toothy grin. "You're one icy lady, if you know what I mean."

"Go out with you?" she questioned, lifting one brow.

"I know the Hotel Rosa is supposed to have great food, but some of the other spots around are better for music and dancing."

"I'm only interested in the food, Matt. That's why I'm going to the Hotel Rosa."

He made a face. "All right," he said with a lugubrious sigh.

Jenny ran some rude comments around in her head but couldn't quite get up the gumption to toss them out. Too many years of training. It really irked her. But she had to do something. She had a pseudo-date with Hunter Calgary, didn't she? What would he make of Matt?

As Matt helped her from the cab in front of Hotel Rosa, she said, "I haven't been exactly honest with you. I'm meeting someone here. I just thought you should know." She rooted around in her purse for some money, but Matt stayed her with a hand on her wrist.

"I've got it." He paid the cabbie and gave him a tip. "You could have let me know."

"You didn't ask!" She headed for the door to the restaurant.

"Hey, wait up." He hurried ahead to open the door for her which only irritated Jenny all the more.

"Look—"

"No. I'm sorry, I—"

"No, listen," she cut him off. "We're going to be staying

together at the villa for the entire week. Let's get things straight right now. I'm just here on vacation. That's all I'm doing. You know what I mean?"

"Sure. Some R & R."

She nodded. "So, let's not misunderstand each other. I don't want this to feel awkward."

He grinned again. He had a Tom Cruise-like mouthful of big white teeth that probably dazzled most women instantly. But then he spoke, spoiling the illusion. "Hey, I haven't asked you to marry me yet. Relax, okay?"

With that he led the way inside.

Hunter nearly groaned aloud as he saw Jenny Holloway enter with a companion. The guy had blond hair, cut short and sort of spiky, a killer tan that looked as if it had been obtained by careful hours in the sun, jeans tight enough to split, and a black shirt open to the navel. A quick first impression would have put him in his early twenties, but the kind of intense visual inspection Hunter had learned to quickly give perps told him that the man was over thirty. Who the hell was he? And why was she with him?

The answer clicked in almost as quickly as the thought: he was a guest of the villa. And he was being incredibly familiar with Jenny . . . and she wasn't liking it one bit. Hunter eased back and watched. He stayed to one side of the bamboo-framed doorway between the room they'd entered and the one where he'd taken a table.

She wasn't certain what to do. She looked everywhere but at her companion, absentmindedly rubbing her throat with one hand, as if she were incredibly hot, or incredibly uncomfortable. Maybe both, considering the rather steamy heat of the place, a heat that was as yet unrelieved by the deepening sky. For once, no breeze seemed to be coming from the ocean. The whole restaurant felt still and close.

He was torn between walking forward and appropriating Jenny on the spot, and melting back into the shadows, content to keep up his silent surveillance. He would have liked to observe her longer, but they had made a date and that wasn't going to work. So, after a long moment he emerged from the darkened doorway and walked into the room behind the maitre d' who stood ready to seat them.

She looked up, saw him, and the smile she sent his way both flattered his ego and pricked Hunter's conscience. She was starting to rely on him, and he wasn't a man who could be relied on. Not in that way. Not in any way that mattered beyond pure safety.

"Hello, there," she said, then glanced at the blond man uncertainly. Hunter flicked him a look that conveyed his disinterest, but the man did a classic double take at him. He blinked several times, took a step away from Jenny, then crossed his arms over his chest and frowned at Hunter.

"I—um—brought reinforcements," Jenny said. "Matt is staying at the villa with us. Matt, Hunter Calgary."

Matt reluctantly thrust out one sweaty paw. "Matt Kilgore."

Hunter shook his hand. The guy was about two inches shorter than he was, and had the pampered, pouty look of a mama's boy. He had to be after her money, Hunter decided coldly. He'd probably wangled an invitation. Knowing his assessment was undeniably harsh and possibly completely wrong, he asked, "Longtime friends?"

"Oh, no!" Jenny was quick to correct him. "I've known

Magda and Phil awhile and they arranged this whole trip. Matt and I just met a few days ago." She looked askance at Matt, who hadn't said one word.

Hunter gazed at him and he finally said, "Yeah, I know Magda and Phil, too."

Jenny's brows lifted. "Oh, I thought you came with Lisa and Jackie."

"I did. We came together," he said blasé, glancing around. "There was a spot that opened up, so they had me come along. But I know the Montgomerys pretty well."

Like hell, Hunter thought Sounded like he'd mooched aboard this magical mystery tour. And since his job was to keep Jenny out of harm's way, he put Matt Kilgore into his "keep an eye on" file, something to be examined later more carefully.

The maitre d' seated them at a table near the ocean. Here the floor actually gave way to the beach and a little sand had drifted into the room through an open doorway. The walls surrounding them were merely removable slats of bamboo to be taken down when the weather changed. A candle in a red holder offered uncertain illumination, and a string of tiny white Christmas lights crisscrossed over the open space of what would have been the roof. From this angle a breeze filtered off the ocean, relieving the stuffiness. The surf was loud, and their voices grew louder just to be heard.

Matt beat Hunter to helping Jenny with her chair. Fine. Let him rush around and make an ass of himself. Besides, it was also better to keep her at arm's length. Getting too close was dangerous. She was a rich man's daughter and too pretty to trust.

Pulling his chair back from the table, Hunter sank down and stretched out his legs. His shoe accidentally brushed Jenny's sandal and she swept her foot back as if contact had electrified her. Matt lit a cigarette and Jenny wrinkled her nose. The princess didn't like smoke, it appeared, though Matt seemed oblivious to the effect.

Letting out a sigh of contentment, he said, "God, it's good to be able to smoke. Know how many restaurants don't allow it anymore? It's an epidemic. And in California, forget it. You can't even smoke in the bars. Hell, I don't know how to *drink* without a cigarette!"

In a gesture of casual friendship, he tossed the pack in Hunter's direction. Hunter flicked a look at it. Funny how he'd thought he wanted one a few nights ago; now he had zero urge to indulge.

Jenny had turned away, either from the smoke or from the men themselves. She seemed a bit melancholy all of a sudden, and Hunter, understanding his own malaise, hated seeing her like that. It was all he could do to keep from reaching out and grabbing her hand and saying—what? Some incredibly trite line about everything being all right? Nothing to worry about, now that he was on the job?

He stayed where he was.

Jenny closed her ears to the conversation between Matt and Hunter, concentrating instead on the dull thunder of the ocean, the sound a soft, incessant growl that whipped to a lion's roar when the winds and waves were beating against the shore. Her expectations for the evening had risen too high, she realized, and Matt's appearance had brought her back to reality with a bang.

Which was just as well. Having Hunter lounge in that chair, his long denim-clad legs mere inches from her own, his own shirt unbuttoned at the throat, not with the *Saturday Night Fever* outrageousness of Matt's but in a rugged, uninhibited, roguish way. . . . It was enough to do her in. She could scarcely believe it. All this time, all these years of being damn near immune to the opposite sex and now she was overwhelmed by his mere presence. Damn him. He just seemed so utterly . . . collected.

And she didn't know what the hell to do about it.

Have a fling. Find romance. Make love all night long. . . . She nearly covered her face with her hands, embarrassed by her own thoughts.

"Hey, Jenny!" Matt said, slapping his palm down on the table. She jumped about a foot from her chair. "Whoa!" He gave her the once over. "Take it easy!"

She smiled faintly. He was reminding her more and more of a teenager. She was liking it less and less.

"What would you like to drink?" he asked, signaling for the waiter who quickly approached their table.

"Sparkling water?" She glanced at the waiter almost apologetically.

Matt made a disgusted sound and ordered a couple of shots of tequila. Hunter asked for a beer.

"Wait . . . no . . . make it a margarita."

She needed something stronger than water. Besides, liquid courage sounded like a good idea in the face of rampant sexual thoughts. Actually, it sounded like a bad idea, but she didn't care. Miss Responsible was taking a night off and that was that.

Matt chattered on while they waited for their order, since

neither Jenny nor Hunter could find much to say. When the drinks came, Matt knocked his first shot back, then cocked his head and asked, "So, how do you two know each other?"

"We just met last night." Jenny glanced at Hunter, who scraped at the edge of his beer label with his thumbnail. He met her gaze, however, and she had to look away quickly.

"Yeah?" Matt glanced at her, then at Hunter. "In Puerto Vallarta?"

"At the Hotel Rosa," Hunter offered, when Jenny couldn't seem to think of a response.

"No kidding. And you made a date for tonight." He pushed his chair back. "Jenny, Jenny, Jenny, you should have let me know what the real deal was between you two."

"There is no real deal," she stated evenly, furious with herself for blushing. Thank God for the dim lighting. "We just had an—an encounter here last night with Magda and Phil and the Others. Magda broke her sandal."

"She fell into my lap," Hunter supplied with a glint in his eye.

"Jenny?"

"No, Magda," Jenny explained. "She tripped and spun around and—" She gestured to Hunter's lap, her gaze resting briefly on his belt and the taut denim before moving away.

"I was thinking about introducing myself," Hunter drawled, "and the opportunity just dropped into my lap."

Matt knocked back his second shot. "So, should I stay or not?" he asked, the nicest thing he'd said all night. Nice enough that Jenny stopped feeling so resentful toward him.

"Stay," she told him, and Hunter wanted to groan yet again. He could see the way she'd softened, and he nearly shook his head in wonder at the susceptibility of females. Didn't she know? Couldn't she see? The man was after her for all the wrong reasons.

"Thanks," Matt said, giving Jenny one of his toothy grins. He seemed genuinely happy that she'd deigned to include him. "Let's get another round! And this time, Jenny, you're having a shot with me!"

Hunter thought darkly that Matt should be drawn and quartered.

Two hours later, after a meal that had lived up to its reputation, Jenny felt as if her bones were melting as she sank into the chair, nearly sprawling in that relaxed way that Hunter Calgary seemed to have perfected. Matt had turned out to be okay. It was as if he'd made a conscious decision to hand her over to Hunter and, that done, he could just enjoy his surroundings. Men were so much better when they weren't on the make, she thought, smiling with a slightly drunken grin. Matt was even farther along down the tequila highway than she was, but Hunter's quiet impassivity and detachment hadn't altered one iota. Clearly his beers weren't doing the trick, and he steadfastly refused any tequila.

Her heart contracted. Was she making an idiot out of herself?

"Think I'll circulate," Matt said with a lecherous wink. He stumbled a bit, climbing from his chair, then glanced around and said loudly, "It's okay. I'm oh-kay . . ."

Hunter watched him swing toward the bar where a

couple of blond women in halter tops were slurping margaritas of their own. He glanced back at Jenny who'd sunk a bit in her chair. He guessed she'd consumed a little bit more alcohol than normal, and her touch-me-not aura had pretty much disappeared. She looked—adorable. And he sure as hell wished she didn't.

She gave him a long look and leaned her elbows on the table. "Okay, we're alone," she said boldly. "Now come the hard questions."

"Shoot."

"You're vacationing in Puerto Vallarta. What do you do back in the states?" She hooked a thumb northward to emphasize her point.

"I'm currently unemployed. Had a job. Just quit it."

"What kind of job?"

"Government."

"That narrows it down." She squinted at him. "You're an IRS agent."

He grinned.

"No . . ." She laughed herself silly, wondering why everything seemed so blasted funny. "You're a postal worker. No, no, no . . . You're a senator from a western state. Idaho. Or maybe Wyoming. You look like a cowboy."

He lifted one brow. "A cowboy?"

"Well, not really." She struggled. "You just walk like one."

"Bow-legged?"

"You're trying to make this hard," she accused. "No, you move like one. Kind of slow and easy and relaxed." *And sexy,* she didn't add. "Of course, I've never known any cowboys, so I'm probably all wrong."

"Houston's full of cowboys. Or men who think they are."

A slow smile crept across his lips. A sexy, sexy smile she was not going to fall for. Uh-uh. No way. She knew about those things. She was thirty-five years old, for crying out loud. None of that stuff worked any more.

Squinting through a fuzziness she knew was a bad sign, she asked, "Did I tell you I was from Houston? I don't remember telling you that."

"You said your father lived there."

"Oh . . . yeah . . ." She had mentioned her father, in an oblique reference to parenting when Matt had made some disparaging remark about his own family. Hunter seemed disquietingly sober, and she was past her usual stopping point.

"And you're in the restaurant business," he added.

"I'm starting my own. Is that a mistake, do you think? Everybody tells me you can't make it in the restaurant business. It's too volatile. Restaurants open and close up within a month." She snapped her fingers, proud of herself for being so on top of her game. "My father's done okay, though, and I've been working in the business for years."

"I think you can do it."

His words penetrated deeply even though she knew it had to be just a throwaway comment for him. But she could count on one hand the times anyone had ever believed in her, and suddenly, ridiculously, she was near tears. To cover up, she swallowed most of her latest margarita, blinking rapidly.

"I don't normally drink like this," she blurted out. "I know every lush on the planet says the same thing, but in my case it's true. Sorry." Carefully, she set down her stemmed glass.

Hunter wanted to reach over and kiss her. She didn't have to tell him she scarcely ever drank, it was written all over her. "Nothing to be sorry for. You're fine."

Her blue eyes gazed at him. "You're just saying that."

He shook his head.

"Maybe I need some coffee."

"Want to go for a walk on the beach?"

She thought about it and nodded gravely. "Yes. That would be a good thing."

He threw some money on the table and guided her past the bamboo partitions to the beach. The ground turned from sand to pebbles at this point, quickly giving way to rocks and lapping waves. They stayed closer to the restaurant, avoiding the sharp little stones, then Hunter grabbed her hand and they squinched through the sand in silence for a few yards.

"Know why I'm here?" she asked, as if on the verge of confession. "I'm escaping. That's what I'm doing."

"That's what vacations are for," he said, thinking he should take his own advice.

"But I'm escaping real life while I'm here. I suppose that's why everybody's here at some level, but I really am. I'm switching gears. I'm changing my life, and Magda wanted me to come, so I did."

"Sounds like a pretty good idea."

She nodded. "I think it's been good. Although when Matt said he was coming tonight . . ." She lifted her face toward the distant moon and chuckled. "I didn't know what to do! I was supposed to meet you, and then I couldn't shake him.

I wanted to tell him to take a hike. *Pronto*." She gave him a sideways look. "Notice my use of Spanish, there."

Hunter laughed. He was shocked to hear it and momentarily bemused to think how long it had been since he had laughed. "You sound like a native."

"Don't I, though?" She swung their clasped hands as they walked. "Anyway, I couldn't make myself be rude. Miss Responsible stepped in and wouldn't let go. You know, she really needs to relinquish control a bit."

"Miss Responsible, huh?"

Jenny's grin was impish. She stretched on her tiptoes and whispered in his ear. "I'll tell you a secret. I don't even like her."

"Do I get to meet her?"

"Oh, you have, you have." She waved that away. "She's boring as hell. Always does the right thing, says the right thing, blah, blah, blah. She has given up wearing the right thing, though, so that's an improvement."

"I like what she's wearing now."

"She isn't here now," Jenny scolded him.

"Who is?"

She stopped and turned to him, the fringe of her wraparound sarong flickering slightly in the faint breeze. Tendrils of hair swept across her eyes and lips and she brushed them away. "This is a dumb conversation," she said, suddenly sounding remarkably sober and shaken. "I don't know what I'm saying."

He wanted to kiss her. He gazed down at her lips and seriously debated about going for it. He told himself not to be an idiot.

"I'm not normally so—silly."

"You're not silly. I think it's okay to give Miss Responsible the night off once in awhile."

She closed her eyes and sighed. "We were talking about you. I don't know how I started talking about me."

"I like talking about you."

Jenny shook her head. "No. I'm not all that interesting."

"Everybody's interesting. Just depends on how much they're willing to tell about themselves."

Opening her eyes, she smiled up at him, a return of her earlier humor. "You're a spy. With the CIA. You're getting into my mind. That's your government job."

"You found me out;" he answered, mock serious.

She laughed again, then clapped a hand over her mouth. "I am going to die of embarrassment tomorrow. I can already tell."

"Nothing to be embarrassed about."

"I'm way too giddy. It's that evil drink."

Hunter smiled, enjoying the moment as much as he'd enjoyed any in years. "You should do it more often. You're too serious most of the time."

"How do you know that?" She was instantly wary, almost scared.

"You said you were."

"Oh."

"And I've seen you with your friends," he added. "You stand out a mile. You're the one who's thinking ahead, seeing the pitfalls, weighing the future. It's a curse, most of the time, because life keeps on going, and you feel like you've missed the train."

She stared at him, long and hard. "You're speaking from experience."

"For a woman who's been complaining about being too silly, you're remarkably sharp."

"What are you going to do about it?"

"What?"

"How are you going to make the train?"

Hunter frowned, albeit reluctantly. "That was just a metaphor."

"I know," she said softly. "But how are you going to make the train?"

What the hell was he doing, waxing philosophic? What the hell purpose was there in getting to know each other? "That train came and left, and I don't plan on catching another anytime soon."

"Pity," she said, releasing his hand, and he felt like a heel for somehow disappointing her. "Well, thank you for the walk, Hunter Calgary. Looks like it's time to go back."

Had she dreamed it?

Jenny awoke in her room to streaming sunlight and a faint headache around her temples. She squinted through eyes that felt as sandy as the beach they'd walked on the night before. What in God's name had she been thinking?

Have a fling. Find romance. Make love all night long . . .

She groaned with real pain and pulled her pillow over her head. But that only made her headache worse. With an effort she climbed out of bed, rooted around in her makeup bag and found some aspirin. But there was no water to drink, so she suffered through a shower and the effort of dressing before she could walk downstairs and grab some orange juice.

Magda, Phil and the others were all seated at the table for

breakfast. Matt was nowhere to be seen.

"So, how was your evening?" Magda asked, smiling knowingly.

"What?" Jenny popped the tablets and swallowed them down with a gulp of orange juice.

"You're looking pretty worn out this morning," she sing-songed.

"And there's no sign of Matt," Lisa said under her breath. Jackie's lips tightened as she nodded agreement.

"I wasn't with Matt."

"You left with him," Lisa pointed out.

"Well, I didn't come home with him."

"What happened to him, then?" Jackie challenged.

Jenny shrugged and shook her head. Part of her was irritated at their probing, and part of her was glad she didn't have to talk about Hunter. Let them think what they would about Matt.

A bloodcurdling scream sounded from the top floor. "My stars!" Alicia cried, a hand crushed to her heart.

"What the hell is that?" Phil said, jumping from his chair and heading for the stairs.

Jenny scraped back her chair and followed at a slower rate, wincing a bit. The maid stood at the gallery where the stained-glass doors to the small, upstairs balcony were flung open to the outside. She could smell jasmine and hear birds wittering loudly. The maid's face was full of confusion.

"What's wrong?" Phil demanded, just as Jenny spied a pair of male, jeans-clad legs sprawled on the tiny landing. Peeking around the balcony doors, she saw Matt lying face down on the tiles.

"He was locked out by mistake," Jenny realized, amused.

Phil assured the shattered maid that everything was all right. She gave them a last backward glance. "Crazy Americans," he murmured.

"No kidding. Matt," she said, shaking him awake.

He lifted his head and glanced around, bleary-eyed. "Where'm I?" he mumbled. Then he moaned and pressed his forehead to the tiles. "Oh, yeah. I didn't have a key and none of you guys heard my knock."

"What time was that?" Phil asked.

"Four? Five?" He squinted an eye toward the sun and shuddered. "I climbed up to the balcony but those damn doors were locked too, so I just crashed here."

"Well, you can come in now," Phil said with humor, helping Matt to his feet. Matt gave Jenny a crestfallen look.

"Why do you look so friggin' perky?" he demanded. "What happened last night?"

"Nothing."

"Oh, come on. You and Hunter looked ready to eat each other up."

Phil chortled as Matt dragged himself to his room and stumbled inside.

They headed back downstairs and Phil described Matt's predicament. Lisa and Jackie tore upstairs to make certain he was all right. Magda looked vaguely amused. "You're lucky you didn't stick around with him," she observed to Jenny.

Phil flicked Jenny a glance. Silently she begged him not to say anything, but he just couldn't help himself. "Jenny had another date. With our friend from last evening."

"It wasn't actually a date," Jenny demurred.

"Oh, stop being so modest. That man couldn't take his eyes off you." Magda poured herself another cup of coffee and sighed in contentment. "Ahhhh . . . the medicinal effects of java. Do you think it's too early for a Spanish coffee?"

The rest of the morning was a delightful waste of time. Jenny wandered around the villa, declined a trip with the group to the beach, tried to read a book, then finally settled onto a chaise longue at the pool and determined she'd subject herself to the blazing sun. That lasted about fifteen minutes before the heat did her in and she slid beneath the cool water of the pool.

Closing her eyes, she struggled to forget the way Hunter's all too evident sexuality had attracted her so powerfully. What was it about him that intrigued her? She didn't know whether to be worried or elated. It had been far too long since she'd yearned for a man.

Grimacing, she couldn't help an unwanted trip down memory lane, back to that time when she'd fallen so hard for Troy. She'd spent so many years making up for those few months of foolishness. She'd been so lonely for so long.

But now . . .

It's purely physical, you know, a judgmental little voice said somewhere in her mind. *You don't know him. You certainly can't trust him. And apart from a few cryptic comments, he's a mystery man who's told you nothing about himself.*

Well, darn it, that was what was so appealing about him! She needed someone who would sweep her off her feet, spending sun-drenched days and soft, warm nights with her. Wasn't that the essence of true romance? No ties. No worries. No . . . nothing . . . when it was over?

No husband who married you for your money and then slapped you or slammed you against a wall when things weren't going his way.

No Troy Russell.

Shivering, Jenny climbed from the pool and hurried up the tile steps to her bedroom.

Houston's brilliant sunshine had changed to longer and longer shadows by the time Troy slipped into a parking spot near Jenny's apartment complex. Her building could be entered through an inner courtyard which connected to a line of garages, each one numbered with the corresponding unit. The courtyard gate was a low, wrought iron affair with an easy-to-lift latch. The only problem: the units all faced inward to this courtyard, and anyone coming and going would be noticed and quite possibly remembered by the nosy inhabitants. At least that was the risk he would face.

But he'd driven around and around, staring up at the backside of the buildings and it had gotten him nowhere. She wasn't here anyway.

Troy idled the car and considered. Eventually, he cut the engine and got out, leaning against the door, placing a cigarette between his lips and striking a match to light it. He smoked in silence. Not one car went by. Dusk fell and light from the house across the street spilled from the front windows. Another house, farther along the street, opened its front door and released a dog, a golden retriever. It trotted up the street, snuffled around Troy's car, then headed toward the courtyard. Grinding out his half-smoked cigarette beneath the heel of his leather shoe, Troy followed.

The dog slid right under the wrought iron fence. Lifting the latch, Troy casually stepped into the courtyard. His footsteps caught the dog's attention. It stopped and turned back, panting softly, its pink tongue lolling out the side of its mouth.

Troy coldly gazed back. He had no love for animals, wild or tame. And they knew it. Even this dumb hound knew it. It emitted a soft "woof" that sounded like a question, then checked out the yard, nose to the ground, marking its territory on a post, the soft tuft of grass in the center and a straggly shrub that looked to Troy's untrained eye like some kind of sagebrush but was probably something far more exotic.

He zeroed in on her apartment. Second floor. Casually, he strolled to the steps, climbing them easily, acting as if he hadn't care in the world. He debated on whistling but decided that would bring unwanted attention.

The dog suddenly lifted its head, stared at Troy, then padded swiftly to the stairs, shooting past Troy, a tawny-brown streak. It stopped at Jenny's door and whined and scratched, then gazed at Troy, waiting for him.

His eyes narrowed on the dog whose tail wagged like a furry flag. A bit warily. It wasn't sure yet of Troy's allegiance. Clearing his throat, he whispered, "Here, boy. . ." A low growl sounded in the beast's throat and it bared some wicked looking teeth.

So he wasn't welcome after all.

Didn't matter.

Turning around, Troy headed downstairs again with new conviction. He glanced back once but the stupid dog had curled itself on the threshold.

At the car he hesitated, gazing across to the house with the lights and the small street beyond. Strolling, he entered that street and examined the house behind it. A cottage from the forties, redone, except the paint was chipping a bit. From inside he could hear squabbling voices, a girl's and a boy's. They were playing some kind of game and apparently cheating.

The mother's frazzled voice tried to make peace. Troy thanked whoever that he'd never had children. They were clinging, miserable, whining creatures who ruined everything they touched. One, the boy, was crying for somebody named Brandon. This appeared to be the older brother, but the mother reminded him tiredly that Brandon was at soccer camp. Fresh wails split the air at this news and the girl declared that she hated that soccer camp and she hated Rawley, too, 'cause he'd made Brandon go. If Brandon were here, he would make sure Tommy played fair! Tommy then insisted that *she* was the one who cheated. She always cheated. She was just a dumb girl!

Troy was beginning to like Tommy—as long as he stayed out of sight. *She* began wailing again. When was Brandon coming home? "When?" she demanded tearfully.

"At the end of the week," the mother answered, still weary.

"Will Rawley go away too?" the girl questioned, certain there was a trick in there somewhere.

"Yes, yes, yes," the mother responded. Rawley would go home when his mom got back from Puerto Vallarta. And that was next Sunday, she added, forestalling the next question. Soccer camp ended the same day.

"Three Winds Soccer Camp!" Tommy declared with a ring of triumph.

"Oh, shut up," the girl demanded with another siren-like wail.

Three Winds Soccer Camp . . .

Troy smiled into the night. He'd stood outside their window several nights running, but this was the first useful information he'd acquired. Rawley, Jenny's son, apparently hadn't gone to Puerto Vallarta with his mother.

Idly he wondered where this Three Winds Soccer Camp might be. The information was surely in Jenny's apartment. Folding another stick of gum in his mouth, he retraced his steps to Jenny's apartment. He examined the door casing carefully and recognized how easily he could break the lock. One or two swift kicks and it would splinter inward.

But the dog . . . the neighbors . . .

The tawny beast lying in front of the door growled again. Troy smiled coldly at it. Something would come to him. It always did.

❋ CHAPTER FIVE ❋

Hunter wrenched the wheel of the Jeep, yanking the vehicle to the edge of the road, stopping for a moment on his drive down the coastline. The Pacific lay on his right, shadowed by low clouds, unusually threatening for this time of year in Puerto Vallarta. Spattering rain hit the hood, becoming huge drops that left splashes in their wake. More and more of them, until a torrent washed over the windshield and plopped through the open sides of the vehicle onto his legs.

He was glad for the rain. The storm matched his emotions, and its tumultuous energy was a kind of relief. With only a moment's hesitation he stuck his head outside the window and let rain soak his hair and head. Flopping back against the seat, he shook rain from his hair, feeling as elemental as the sudden cloudburst.

He'd never been good at surveillance.

Untrue, his rational mind reminded him. He had been ruthlessly excellent at surveillance most of the time. He'd been terrible when it had involved his sister. Hunter scowled and switched on the ignition once more, turning the Jeep back toward the city. Instead of merely following and watching, he'd purposely harassed Troy Russell after Michelle's death. At first, Russell had ignored him, and the man had even seemed to enjoy the cat-and-mouse game. Several times he'd grinned at the sight of Hunter's barely suppressed rage until Hunter had gotten his hand around the man's throat and squeezed.

He wouldn't have killed him. Even Russell, as lowly a worm as ever crawled on this earth, couldn't make Hunter actually murder someone. But he'd wanted to scare the bejeezus out of the bastard and that he had managed to do. It had cost him his job and the respect of his friends on the force, but it had served its purpose. Troy Russell was on notice. Every subsequent move he'd made had been analyzed and examined and tested to the point that the man would never be able to hurt, injure or kill again.

Or so Hunter had thought. It hadn't quite turned out that

way. No one in Los Angeles wanted to spend their time chasing after a man who'd made evading punishment a full-time occupation. It had been Hunter who'd been put on notice, and he'd left Los Angeles in disgust, spending the last six years in Santa Fe, drifting through his days. With the memory of his sister's untimely death forgotten by everyone but himself, Hunter had to curb his obsessive interest in Russell and try to stop feeling as if his life had no purpose.

He'd left the Santa Fe force in the belief that he needed to figure out what the rest of his life was all about. He'd had no clear plan, but he'd at least walked away from a job that demanded half his skills and none of his attention. Okay, that was a little harsh, but he'd never felt the alertness and intensity he'd experienced in L.A. Santa Fe was just slower-paced, and therefore the city's crime rate was lower than the City of Angels'.

Wind blew against his face and hair and Hunter glanced out the open side of the Jeep, watching the breakers froth against stones and spread rapidly onto stretches of tan beach. Negotiating a turn, he inhaled and smiled grimly. Allen Holloway's job offer had arrived at just the right moment. Hunter had been looking for something—and a chance to take care of unfinished business was like finding the path out of darkness.

Jenny Holloway. His mind's eye critically reviewed her looks, from the swing of loose auburn curls that framed her face, to the wary blue eyes, to the lithe figure and tense stature. He'd only seen her fully relaxed while under the effects of a few drinks, a guilty pleasure long denied. She had too much on her mind, including the responsibility of raising her son. Russell's son. A son Russell did not realize was his, if Allen Holloway could be believed. Was that why he was back in the picture now?

Fifteen minutes later Hunter yanked on the emergency brake, climbed out of the Jeep and slopped through the puddles in the broken cement walk to the hotel. The torrent had stopped as if some slowly wakened god had finally noticed and turned off the taps. The air was slightly refreshed but the oppressive tropical humidity promised more rain, and soon.

The desk employees smiled at him as he headed for the stairs. Screw the elevator. Hunter needed exercise to release tension. He took the steps two at a time and strode impatiently to his door. In his room he stripped off his shirt and walked onto the balcony. Three floors below lay the beach. If he fell, he suspected he would survive.

But no one survived a fall from ten stories onto pavement.

His phone rang, surprising him. *Jenny!* he thought, then berated himself for both feeling so much hope and letting himself think of her in such intimate terms.

"Hello," he said flatly, giving nothing away.

"Calgary?"

Frustration licked through his veins at the sound of Allen Holloway's voice again. For a moment he didn't respond, but that didn't stop Holloway.

"I know what you said." His voice was clipped. "But something's happened here. My wife thinks she ran into Russell the other day."

Hunter froze. "Where?"

He snorted. "The grocery store. Russell made a point of

addressing her, although he acted like he didn't recognize her."

"What did he say?"

"Nothing much. Just apologized for bumping into her. Small talk. But it was the way he looked at her. She didn't make the connection immediately, but she thought about the meeting because it seemed odd to her. She told me about it today."

Picking up the Hotel Rosa desk pen, Hunter rolled it over with his fingers. "Don't call me again."

"I just thought you should know. He's up to something, and I want to know what it is!" Holloway sounded frightened beneath his autocratic tone. "Keep my daughter safe!"

"Then don't give her whereabouts away," Hunter said through clenched teeth.

"I'm worried about Rawley. What if he's not safe?"

Hunter thought of Rawley. Rawley Holloway who was really Rawley Russell, Troy Russell's child. That bad feeling returned. "I'm going to cut this trip short and come back."

"No!" Holloway was beside himself. "No! Troy doesn't know about Rawley. Stay with Jenny."

"What if you're wrong?"

"I know where Rawley is. I know those friends of hers who are taking care of him. He's all right. It's Jenny who's at risk. That's what I'm paying you for."

Twisting the pen through his fingers until they hurt, Hunter said, "I'll stay through the end of the week."

"Fine, fine."

"Next time, I call you. Understand?"

Holloway swallowed back whatever else he wanted to say and grudgingly agreed. Hunter dropped the phone in its cradle and stared at the thing with loathing. It wasn't that he truly believed Troy Russell capable of tracking Holloway's calls; the man was a coldhearted bastard with a penchant for violence, not a clever criminal with information resources and steel nerves. There was a vast difference between the two types, as Hunter well knew from years of dealing with both. But it didn't hurt to be careful.

Easing his shoulders back several times, Hunter sought to release tension. In Santa Fe he worked around his ranch, mending fences, checking on the neighbor's cattle who wandered aimlessly from that man's vast spread to Hunter's smaller, livestockless several acres. He'd never had the time that a real running ranch required, so he'd never done more than help out his neighbor. He'd never put down roots. Still, it had kept him reasonably satisfied and sane and that's all he'd wanted after Michelle's death. And it had helped keep him in shape without the need of a local gym.

The phone rang again. Hunter narrowed his gaze on the machine. "Yes?"

"Hunter?" Jenny's voice came across the line like a wave of cool water.

"Oh, hello there." Frustration receded, replaced by a kind of hopeful despair he didn't want to feel. He wanted to smack himself hard.

"I didn't want to bother you, but I wondered if you'd like to come to dinner here tonight? At the villa? We've got more than enough. I'd—like you to come," she added, though he could tell it took an effort for her to be so direct.

Silky legs. Soft, musical voice. Butterfly-quick smile. If he forgot who she was for an evening . . .

His heartbeat throbbed at his temple. She was off-limits. He could only indulge himself in a sweet, somewhat painful fantasy which would never, ever come true.

"Hunter?"

"What time?" he asked hoarsely.

Jenny gazed at the table, counting the plates, asking herself if she'd gone a little crazy in this hot, relentless sun. Bringing Hunter here was as good as announcing to Magda, Phil, and the others that she and Hunter had a real relationship of some kind. And bringing him here felt scary, as if she were bringing him home to meet the family.

"Don't be ridiculous!"

"Who're you talking to?" Matt asked, coming up behind her.

"Me, myself and I."

"Are you all listening?"

She turned and laughed shortly. "I'm afraid none of us are paying a whole lot of attention."

Matt, from being the bane of her existence the night before, was fast becoming Number One Friend. "This got something to do with your boyfriend?"

"I've invited Hunter to dinner with us. Magda told the staff to set an extra plate."

Matt smirked. "Tell me again how you met this guy?"

"At the Hotel Rosa bar. After Magda fell in his lap."

He chortled and walked over to the counter where Rita, the prettiest member of the villa's staff, was preparing another jug of margaritas. Winking at her, he picked up one of the empty glasses. Faintly smiling, Rita whirred the blender, then poured him an icy drink, letting her gaze linger on his muscular chest. None of the men at Villa Buena Vista bothered with shirts, even at dinner, since the table was outside, protected only by a dark green cloth awning and a twisting branch of hot pink bougainvillea.

Over her protests, Matt graciously handed Jenny the first glass. He picked up another and clinked the edge of his against hers. "Bottoms up," he said and knocked back three-quarters of the frosty tequila and lime in one gulp.

"We're all going to be raving alcoholics after this trip," she said, sipping at her own. She didn't even want it, especially today, but ice felt good no matter what flavor it was.

"But this is the time to do it," Matt argued. He drank the rest of his, licked his lips and held the glass to Rita for a refill. "Life back home is hard, so when you're away from it, the rules don't apply."

"What's so hard about your life?" Jenny asked, lifting a brow. Matt didn't appear to be struggling too much.

He shrugged. "Nothing more than anyone else. It's just a grind. Payments. Work. More payments. When I'm on vacation, man, I'm like a sailor on leave! What about you?"

"I don't go on vacations, normally."

"What do you do, then?" He frowned, as if she were some indefinable new species.

"Bookkeeping. Work. Restaurant management. Raise my son."

"Ugh. Sounds like you need to cut loose even more than I do." He lifted one eyebrow. "That's where Hunter comes in, right?"

She gazed at him helplessly, uncertain whether to laugh or groan. "Give it a rest, Matt."

He grinned again as Magda and the others appeared, sans Phil. "Montezuma's revenge," Magda declared in a stage whisper. "We'll have to go out partying without him!"

"I'm not going anywhere tonight," Jenny stated firmly. "No amount of pleading will change my mind."

Magda waved a languid hand at her. "You won't have to. You've got a date coming here!"

"Lucky you," Lisa murmured.

"Who is this man?" Tom Simmons wanted to know. He placed a beefy arm around Alicia, who cuddled up to him as if they were newlyweds. Another time Jenny might have found it too cute for words, but tonight she felt a tug at her heartstrings. Tom and Alicia had been married a long time and it worked for them. The Brickmans looked over and wrapped their arms around each other as well.

"Stick around and you can all meet him," Jenny invited.

"I think we'll do that!" Alicia said brightly. "Won't we, honey?" They gazed at each other and wrinkled their noses. Tom's moustache twitched.

Jenny quickly got over her sentimentality. *Yech!*

Everyone went over to Rita and the blender; and Jenny moved to the far side of the patio, gazing out toward the Pacific where white-ruffled waves moved inward to a beach she could just see toward the north. For reasons she couldn't explain she had a sudden urge to call Rawley. Glancing toward the kitchen phone, she wondered if she dared try to phone with everyone hovering around, staff and guests alike. She'd figured out the system. With a credit card and an eye on the time since the rates were unbelievably high, she could place a call to the Fergusons. Though Rawley was with Brandon at soccer camp, she could talk to Janice or Rick and catch up on his activities. Rick, soccer fan that he was, was bound to have visited the camp to check on the boys.

But was it foolish to be so overprotective? Maybe she should wait another day.

Why? she questioned herself immediately. *He's your son. You have a right. And Troy's out there somewhere, nosing around.*

"Excuse me, I need to use the phone," she told Rita as she squeezed past her behind the counter.

Rita couldn't have cared less. Like Lisa and Jackie before her, her eyes were fully on Matt Kilgore.

By the time Hunter arrived at the villa, the party was in full swing. He stood on the stoop beneath the wrought iron balcony and listened to the drone of the doorbell. Moments later, one of the housemaids opened the door and from below he heard Mexican music, loud talk, and laughter.

With a smile the maid gestured him inside, then pointed to the curving blue tile stairs that led downward. He descended into an open-sided room that led to the patio and pool. Beneath an awning sat a table already set with plates, glasses, napkins, and silverware. The food was in the kitchen ready to serve, as the guests pirouetted around the pool and balanced brightly colored glasses full of tequila, judging by the labels on the empty bottles next to the blender.

"Welcome! Welcome!" the one who had fallen into his lap greeted him. Magda. That was her name. "Come on in and have a drink!"

That drink materialized at his elbow, in the hands of the girl who had admitted him. He accepted it as his gaze fell on Jenny's back. She was standing in a corner of the kitchen, facing the counter, and he realized after a moment that she was on the phone.

Magda grabbed him by the arm, nearly dumping his drink over both of them. "Come and dance. My husband's out of commission for a while, so I need a partner."

The last thing Hunter felt like doing was dancing. He sought for a way out, but Magda was nothing if not persistent. Drink in hand, he settled for swaying on his feet and keeping one eye on Jenny. She was speaking animatedly to someone, brushing hair from her eyes, her fine brows drawn into a frown. She wore a yellow sarong around her hips and her tank top was a dusty blue. She looked so touchable that he had to force himself back to the moment, worried at his reaction. How many times did he have to remind himself that she was a job? A rich woman who just happened to have a few problems he was hoping to solve.

Magda slipped into his arms and it was all he could do to keep his drink from spilling down her tanned back. "Just drink it," she encouraged, waiting while he swallowed the frosted lime margarita.

"I'm not much of a dancer," he pointed out, setting the empty drink down.

"Oh, who cares." She hugged him close and grinned. "I like dancing with handsome blue-eyed men. Phil just doesn't get sick often enough." She spun away from him and spun back. "Do you hear that, Phil?" she yelled, stepping back from the awning and gazing at the upper floors.

"I'm falling in love with another man down here. Thin
you should rescue me?"

Hunter glanced above the awning to the double door
that led into one of the bedrooms. Phil wandered onto th
balcony and waved a hand at them. "Take her," he saic
"I'll win her back after I'm well."

Magda looked concerned. "You okay, honey?"

"No, I'm dying. Have a good time." He went back insid
and closed the door.

She sighed. "There's always someone who gets the bug
Ice cubes," she said, peering suspiciously at her own drink
"From those out-of-the-way places where the water isn'
pure. We hit a little roadside café yesterday and Phil had ;
couple of tacos and a couple soft drinks with ice. You'v
got to stick to the established businesses to trust the food.'

"And even then you take a chance," another man said
"Tom Simmons," he introduced, grabbing one of Hunter'
hands and pumping it heartily.

Hunter accepted this information silently, amused tha
they felt they had to warn him about the hazards o
drinking the water.

"I'm in insurance," Tom said. "What about yourself?"

"Oh, shut up," Magda butted in, blowing the totally balc
Simmons a kiss. "Nobody wants to hear about that."

"I was just talking," he responded, wounded, his rec
moustache looking a little wilted. He went back to his wife
who looked about as wide as she was tall. She smoothec
her palm down his arm and he kissed her on the lips.

"Your drink looks empty," another lady told him, fluttering around. "Let me refill it."

"No, thanks."

"Oh, I insist!" she said, plucking the glass from his fingers.

At that moment Jenny returned from the phone. "I was talking to friends of mine who are taking care of my son," she explained, her eyes following the woman as she asked for a refill on Hunter's drink.

"How is the little darling?" Magda asked, finally releasing Hunter in the need to refill her own cocktail glass.

"He's fine. He's at a soccer camp with his friend Brandon. Brandon's parents, the Fergusons, are taking care of him, and Rick Ferguson is a soccer fanatic so he's been up at the camp once already." She picked up a tortilla chip and scooped it into the fresh guacamole in an earthenware bowl on the counter. "Janice said Rick made a nuisance of himself, offering advice and butting in—her words, not mine—and they asked him not to come back."

"Sounds like Rawley's having fun though." Magda settled herself in a lounge chair at the far side of the pool so that she could look upward and check out what was going on at her bedroom balcony. A tiny furrow of worry had appeared between her eyes. Worry for her husband. Hunter, who'd been reserving judgment, warmed to her.

"He is." Jenny picked up a bowl of taco chips. "Want some?" she asked, holding it toward him. It was an invitation he couldn't resist. He came to stand beside her, conscious of the opening in the sarong that showed one slim leg up to the top of her thigh and the edge of her blue bikini bottoms. With more concentration than necessary, he dipped a tortilla chip into the guacamole, way too conscious of the rest of her body.

She threw him a smile and said, "The Fergusons—

they're the ones taking care of my son—anyway, their dog Benny has been practically living at my apartment, apparently. He's camped outside the door and when Janice takes my mail in, it's all she can do to keep him from sneaking inside."

"Benny's your dog?" Tom asked, completely missing the whole point. He and his wife had seated themselves at the table, ready for their meal.

"*Their* dog," Jenny corrected, sharing an amused glance with Hunter. "Except he's adopted Rawley and me. I told Janice to relax. Benny's practically part of the family. He can make a mess even faster than my son can."

Hunter listened. He had seen the dog. Oblivious to leash laws, it wandered Jenny's apartment complex, wagging its tail and patrolling. Jenny wasn't the only person in the complex who let Benny visit, but her apartment was the only one Benny seemed to consider home.

"How's Benny going to take the move?" Matt asked. He, like Magda, had chosen a chaise longue. The other couple, whom Magda had introduced as the Brickmans, sat in chairs and smoked, listening and holding out their empty glasses to the pitcher of margaritas currently being served by the houseboy.

"Badly, I suspect," Jenny said quietly. To the rest of the crowd, she explained, "I'm moving from Houston to Santa Fe."

"Jenny's opening a restaurant," Magda put in. "I'm sure I told all of you earlier. Geneva's. Southwestern cuisine."

Two women joined the group who'd been missing earlier. Magda introduced them to Hunter as Lisa and Jackie. Their eyes darted over his body, and they shared a look.

He'd been catalogued and rated, and by the looks on their faces, he'd passed the test with flying colors.

Jenny lifted an amused brow. "You've made a hit."

"I was trying to."

"I don't think you have to work too hard."

"Tell us about yourself," Tom's wife, Alicia, said encouragingly as they all sat down at the table.

"He works for the CIA," Jenny said, a smile tilting the corners of her mouth.

"Do tell," Magda murmured, interested.

"No, seriously, what do you do?" This was from the one called Jackie.

Hunter had formulated what he was going to say when he'd received the invitation. "I worked for a security firm in Los Angeles up until a few years ago."

"Retired?" Tom lifted his brows and gave Hunter the once over, as if implying he was far too young to be out of the nine-to-five grind.

"More like on sabbatical," Hunter said.

"What kind of security firm?" Jenny asked.

"Electronics. Home and business installation." He shrugged and accepted the bowl of refried beans. The meal was family style and tonight's menu was decidedly Mexican. Carne asada and tamales were served with beans and white rice. A salad heavy with avocados and tomatoes sat next to a covered dish of floured tortillas.

"Every night it's a little something different. Usually Mexican. We can make some choices, but it's always fabulous," Alicia told him as she scooped up a healthy portion of refried beans.

"I wish Phil were here." Magda sighed.

"How long are you staying in Puerto Vallarta?" Lisa asked. "Is this business, or pleasure?"

"Pleasure?"

They all glanced over at Jenny who froze; fork raised in midair. "What?"

"What do you think?" Magda teased.

"Oh, no. Don't look at me." She set down her fork and lifted her hands in mock surrender.

Magda drawled, "Oh, but we are, honey. And we're looking at him, too."

That started a volley of remarks about the weather, the state of the country and the plans for the evening, anything to cover up the moment. The conversation went on in a similar vein until most everyone had finished their meal. When individual cups of flan were passed around, Hunter begged off. Jenny took a bite, savored it on her tongue, and made an "mmm" sound which made the cook clasp her hands over her broad stomach and beam at Jenny.

For Hunter, it was an odd feeling to be part of this eclectic crowd. A loner by nature, he usually avoided parties; and the only reason he'd accepted Jenny's invitation this evening was because she was his job. A flash of inner honesty reminded him that wasn't the only reason, but he set his jaw at the thought. He needed to get over that fast.

Still, he'd enjoyed the dinner and what normally would have been a teeth-gritting experience had been mildly pleasant, even fun. He was mulling that over while the group gathered and ordered taxis for the trip to town. Though he hadn't minded sharing the evening with them, he was glad to see them go.

The staff gathered up their belongings and began

preparing to leave for the night. In the interim, neither Jenny nor Hunter seemed to know what to say to each other. They waited in silence on the back deck, and by the time they heard the front door close, the sun had dipped near the sea, spreading its last golden rays across the huge expanse of blue-gray water. Leaning their elbows on the rail, they watched it disappear by degrees, finally fading to a fuschia glow on the far horizon.

"You really work for a security firm?" she asked, breaking the silence.

"You really plan to open a restaurant in Santa Fe?"

"I asked first."

"I asked second."

She shook her head, hiding a smile. "You're a difficult man to get answers from. I'm still leaning toward the CIA gig."

"I just quit my job," he said. "That's the plain truth. And I don't know what I'm going to do next."

"Is that what this trip is about? Self-discovery?"

"Does a trip always have to be about something?"

She considered. "Maybe not. It kind of is for me, though. I'm just—marking time. Trying to shift from one phase to another."

"What was phase one? And what's phase two?"

"Oh . . ." She groaned and pushed her hair away from her cheek. He followed the movement of her hand. She gave him a straight look. "Do you really want to know?"

"Yes." *More than anything.*

"I've been . . . treading water for fifteen years," she said, getting right to the point. "I was a spoiled kid who never got over her mother's death and detested her father's second wife. I still detest her, I suppose, although it's more that I just don't have to like her." It sounded almost like a question so he nodded in response. "She wasn't the cause, but I blamed her, and I blamed my father. It's so trite, I hate talking about it.

"I was fifteen when my mother died, and I was married by twenty. My father was against my marriage, and of course, that made it all the more attractive. But to be fair, I was smitten."

Hunter's skin grew cold. He glanced away from her, afraid to react. Oblivious, Jenny went on, "He was everything that was wrong for me, and that's what made it so right. I just *wanted* him."

Michelle's words floated in his head. *You don't understand, Hunter. I just want to be with him. I feel like I can't live without him. He's all I've got, besides you, and he's all I've ever wanted . . .*

"So I married him," Jenny added flatly, her mouth turning down at the corners, her eyes growing colder. "And it lasted all of two weeks before I knew I'd made a dreadful mistake. Within six months I was divorced. My father helped with that. I had to turn to him. It was—awful. Troy married me for the money he thought I would inherit." She laughed shortly. "Must have killed him when he realized it would be a long, long time before I ever got one dime." She swallowed, then added fiercely, "I will never, ever want that money."

She sighed. "Well, as long as I'm being trite, let me offer you another cliché: money can't buy happiness. It can't even buy peace of mind. It can only buy things, and maybe those things add to your comfort, maybe they don't. Sometimes it can buy people. My father bought off my ex-husband, and I was glad. But I want that to be the last thing he buys me."

"How did he do that?"

"Gave him a chunk of change to disappear from my life forever." She leaned her chin on her hands, suddenly looking like a desolate little girl.

"Did it work?" Hunter's mouth was dry.

"For fifteen years."

"That sounds open-ended."

"If you mean it sounds like it's not over yet, you'd be right. Troy contacted my father and put the bite on him."

"He asked for more money?"

"Oh, no." She shot him an ironic look that masked a world of anguish and pain. "He said he wanted to put things right. 'Make amends,' my father said. The money demands will come later."

"You think he's going to harass you." It was a statement, not a question.

"I know he is. He's in Houston now, or was, but he'll find me in Santa Fe. It's inevitable."

Hunter knew she was right. He wished he could offer words of reassurance, but Troy's smirking mug swam across his vision and he knew he could never lie like that. "What about your son?" he asked, knowing he was punching the hot button.

"Rawley's the reason that my father will give in to the blackmail." She turned, regarding him straight on. "Troy is Rawley's father, but he doesn't know it. Yet."

They stared at each other as a breeze started up, playing with her hair, forcing her eyes to squint, the lashes long and lustrous. He swept a strand away from her cheek and held it back for her. "You're giving me a lot of information," Hunter said, his gaze lighting on her mouth. He forced his eyes downward, away from the curve of those luscious lips.

"Am I scaring you?"

"No."

"I didn't think I would," she said with just a touch of relief. He was still as stone. "What?" she asked, suddenly afraid she'd spoken more than she should.

"Nothing."

"Something," she disagreed, watching him.

"I'm not good with divulging secrets," he said finally, scowling.

She kept her beautiful blue eyes trained on him and he worried that she was looking into his soul.

"I think that could be an asset in your line of work. believe you're in security. And I don't know if you're looking for a job"—she laughed faintly—"or maybe a lost cause, but I need someone to help. I guess I'm offering you a job," she said in a smaller voice. "I didn't intend that when I asked you to come here tonight, but maybe at some deeper level I was hoping . . ."

Hunter dragged his gaze away from her, staring out to the Pacific to where the sinking sun was just a memory. There was only the faintest violet afterglow. "What did you have in mind?" he asked.

"I don't know. But whatever it is, it will require you to be in Houston until I move, and then in Santa Fe."

Hunter stood in silence, wondering how to respond.

"Listen to me," she said, sounding annoyed with herself

"I'm pussyfooting all around because I'm scared. I'm scared of what Troy will do when he finds out about Rawley. I'm scared for my son, who doesn't know the truth about his father."

"Which is?"

"Well, Rawley knows Troy's his father. I told him Troy left before he was born, which is the truth. And he knows what Troy looks like—he has a picture I found . . ." She let the sentence trail off.

"Then what truth is he missing?"

"What?"

"You said you're scared for your son because he doesn't know the truth about his father. What truth is that?"

Jenny started. "Oh. Just that—Troy is an ugly human being. You can't tell a son that about his father."

"You said the marriage lasted six months but that you knew after two weeks that it was a mistake. What happened?"

"I just knew it was a mistake, that's all!" She pushed away from the rail, restless and anxious under his steady gaze. "Troy was a fortune hunter. He wanted the money."

"Why is he an ugly human being?"

She froze and her nostrils flared a bit. Unconsciously, she wrapped her arms around her torso, hugging herself. "He just is."

"He hurt you," Hunter said softly.

She swallowed. "Yes, he did."

"He married you for your money, but he wanted you, too. And it wasn't in a healthy way." She shuddered involuntarily and Hunter hated himself a little. But he knew exactly what Troy Russell had done to his sister, and he also knew that Michelle had refused to face it until it was too late. Jenny was braver, but she didn't want to admit the extent of her mistake, even fifteen years later.

"I'm afraid of him," she admitted, the words torn from somewhere deep in her soul.

"He physically abused you."

Tears stood in her eyes. Her mouth worked and she tightened her lips to keep them from trembling. A moment later, she whispered, "I can't look at all those things. I still can't. I've got them inside a box, under lock and key, and I've put that box on a shelf and shoved it way, way to the back. But when he contacted my father, that box fell down and cracked open and now—now I'm out of control."

"Shh . . ." Hunter pulled her into his arms. His heart beat hard. He wanted to kiss her. Make it all go away for her.

"It makes me feel so helpless," she said in a suffocated voice. "If he ever laid a hand on Rawley, I'd kill him. I would kill him."

Not if I got there first, Hunter thought grimly.

❁ CHAPTER SIX ❁

Jenny lay on her bed and stared out the window at the indigo sky. She wished she had the energy to either get up and do something or fall asleep. An odd languor had taken hold of her, unusual for someone as self-directed as she generally was. She felt suspended in time.

Someone knocked on her door. Turning her head on the pillow with an effort, she called, "Come in," and Magda entered, bringing with her a whiff of alcohol and some kind of coconut fragrance that was undoubtedly body lotion.

"I thought you and your fabulous new friend would come and join us downtown." She perched on the edge of Jenny's bed.

"I sent my fabulous new friend home. Well, actually, I think I scared him away."

"What? No. He kept his eyes on you the whole time. It was devastatingly sexy."

"He thinks I'm an overwrought nutcase."

Magda waved her away. "Yeah, right."

"I told him about Troy and Rawley. I just blabbed and blabbed. And then I was embarrassed."

"Oh, everybody's got a skeleton or two in the closet. He doesn't strike me as the kind of guy who'd be afraid of your evil ex."

Jenny struggled upward, propping herself against the pillows and shaking her head. "I sound like a teenager talking about her crush. The last thing I need is to worry about whether some guy likes me or not."

"It's the first thing you need!" Magda argued. "Jenny, my dear, you've been living without love for so long that you think you don't deserve it. Believe me, you do. Trust me on this one. And why not with Hunter, hmmm? He's gorgeous and he's got that strong, silent thing going that makes my knees go weak."

"*Your* knees," Jenny reminded her.

"And your knees," she argued right back. "I think you're ready for a fling."

Jenny gave an unladylike snort.

"I think flings are fabulous. And cost-effective. A fling could help ease the worries fluttering around in your head. You could think back on it for the next decade. Why not have a guiltless one-night stand?"

"That's impossible," Jenny pointed out.

"Okay, two-night stand. Or the rest of the week. Wait a minute, it could even last longer. Why not? You could see each other when you get back!"

"I don't even know where he lives."

"Yet," she said. "Yet."

Jenny sighed and shook her head. "I practically asked him to be my bodyguard. I don't know what I was thinking."

Magda nodded appreciatively. "Nice tactic."

"Oh, stop!" Jenny threw a pillow at her. "It wasn't like that at all. It was—worse." She covered her face with her hands and groaned. "I feel like I've been living someone else's life these past fifteen years. Going through the motions. But I didn't know it until now."

"If you want to have an affair, honey, just have one! There's no need to explain." She smiled at Jenny without artifice. "You've been waiting a long time for this without even knowing it. That's what a trip south of the border is for."

"I just don't want to do anything stupid," Jenny murmured, drawing up her knees and hugging them with her arms.

"*Do* something stupid. Break out."

Jenny glanced out the window again. "Maybe I will. . . ."

The lobby of the Hotel Rosa was crowded with jade plants and philodendrons and willow bark furniture upholstered in bright colors. Arched doorways opened to the reception area, the pool, and a hallway that led to elevators and access to the beach. Jenny strolled up to the counter, tugging her straw bag over her shoulder. "I'd like to ring Hunter Calgary's room, please." The desk clerk punched numbers on his dial, then waved her to a guest phone hung on the wall next to one of the arched doorways. The line rang and rang with no answer. She hung up, disappointed. The hotel obviously didn't offer automatic message service.

What to do?

Walking down the hallway toward the beach, Jenny stepped into a blinding day. Twenty feet away from the hotel, vendors plied her with Mexican hats, blankets, trinkets, and pottery. No amount of shaking her head and saying no kept them away, and she had to go back to the hotel. Here, the lounge chairs were all occupied and since she wasn't a guest, she wasn't entitled to use one anyway.

The half-bald man who'd approached her that first night she'd met Hunter lay sprawled in one. Spying him, Jenny tiptoed out of range. She could tell by his pink skin that he'd been out too long already, and she thought the way he held his frosted drink to his forehead said more about the night before than the current day's heat. It made her feel slightly sorry for him, and that brought her back to her own situation.

What was she doing here anyway? Hunter hadn't invited her. She'd just come to the hotel to . . . start a whirlwind affair. She almost laughed to herself. Who was she kidding? She couldn't do this. Not with Troy in the background and her worries over Rawley and her own innate sense of what was proper. She couldn't.

Could she?

Swiftly she turned back, considered leaving a note, then headed for the door to the street. Then, to her relief and consternation, Hunter strode into the lobby and up to the desk. Smoothing her skirt, Jenny took a deep breath, tried on a smile, and walked toward him. After her soul-baring of the night before—a memory that made her shudder now—she'd been terrible company, edgy and uncomfortable and embarrassed, and it hadn't taken Hunter long to get the message and take his leave. But since her talk with Magda, she'd stiffened her resolve, at least to keep seeing him, and so she'd decided to take this flirtation a few steps further.

The desk agent was handing him an overnight package. Jenny flicked a glance at it, then waited for Hunter to turn around and see her. When he did, he stopped short, and his hard expression brought all her doubts to the forefront.

"Hi," she said, feeling like an idiot. "I hoped I'd run into you. I thought I was a little over the top last night, and I wanted to prove I have some sanity."

"You weren't over the top." The package swung downward from his other hand, seemingly forgotten for the moment. "I was planning to call you today."

"You were?" she asked lightly.

"I was thinking we could go for a drive down the coastline."

"Sure." She nodded eagerly.

"Stay here. I'll be right back."

He touched her arm reassuringly and then headed for the elevators. The car rumbled downward, collected him, then rumbled back upward again. Jenny sank into a chair and settled in to wait, wishing she didn't feel like she'd interrupted something.

She'd seen the package. Hunter wanted to kick the wall in frustration. It wasn't anything he'd had to have, but he'd made the mistake of asking for some information from Ortega. The Santa Fe sergeant had squawked and complained and demanded Hunter come back to work, but he'd grudgingly sent the information along anyway, asking a lot of questions that Hunter refused to answer.

Quickly he ripped the FedEx package open and scanned the contents. A small newspaper notice about Geneva Holloway's elopement with Troy Russell and a picture. Several more articles concerning the civic-minded Allen Holloway and his good deeds. A couple on Holloway's real estate acquisitions. Information he'd already seen once during his investigation over Michelle's death, but it now held new meaning for him.

He examined the picture of Russell and Jenny. It was a quickie snapshot, something Jenny had probably had done in a hurry since Hunter believed Allen Holloway would not have wanted the world to know about Jenny's marriage, no way, no how. Her smile was wide and a little forced; Russell's was a knowing smirk.

Hunter felt a familiar resentment burn in his chest and he took several deep breaths to clear away the feeling. The clearest emotion he could name was a blood-thirsty desire for revenge. That hadn't waned. That hadn't been tempered by his depression.

With Jenny waiting downstairs, he shoved the articles into a side pocket of his bag, threw the bag on a chair, grabbed his keys, and hurried back to the elevator.

Ten minutes later they were outside a grocery store in the center of town. Jenny gazed at him with smiling blue eyes, and Hunter couldn't help but feel a twinge of guilt that he was deceiving her, even if it was in the name of a greater good.

"So, what's in store?" she asked.

"Come on." He held the door for her and they headed down the crowded aisles. The first thing he searched for was a bag, something about the size of Jenny's beach bag, and then he started throwing items inside the grocery cart: cheese, bread, wine and Mexican beer. "A picnic," he told her. "See something you like, throw it in."

"Mmm . . ." She tilted her head. "How about some greasy tortilla chips?"

"Whatever vice you're into."

"Watch it," she scolded. "You nearly ran over that little boy's foot!"

The boy gazed at them with huge, liquid brown eyes. He glanced in their cart and made a face, clearly disgusted with their choices. Jenny took a look inside his mother's cart and saw more traditional Mexican cuisine supplies: corn husks and refried beans and tortilla shells. Jenny smiled at him and he smiled back, his front two teeth missing. Glancing at Hunter, he scowled fiercely, then ran away after this show of strength.

"I should have taken off a toe," Hunter said mildly.

"You don't seem to have a way with children," she teased. Then hearing herself, "Ever had any of your own?"

"No."

"Are you married?" she suddenly asked, the words jumping to her lips. Despite her dithering about approaching him, she'd never once considered this. Her own naiveté shocked her. She felt almost ill.

"Divorced," he admitted after a long moment.

"Oh." Her heart rate slowly returned to normal and she offered him a wan smile. "We're the same."

"From the sounds of it, mine wasn't quite as ugly as yours. Ugly enough, though."

"How long ago?"

He didn't want this conversation. He hated getting personal, and he really didn't want to go over it with Jenny. "Years."

"Why?"

He gave her a sharp look.

"Why did you get a divorce?"

"Irreconcilable differences. We couldn't stand each other," he added helpfully.

She ducked her head, trying to think of something to say and settled for a helpless little shrug. Hunter found the tortilla chips and tossed them in along with a plastic tub of fresh salsa. They wove through the other carts and families and stacked displays of goods and finally stopped in the long line snaking toward the register.

"I never went grocery shopping with Troy," Jenny said. "Not once."

Hunter thought that over. "I never went grocery shopping with Kathryn."

"Maybe that's where we made our mistakes," she said lightly.

"I don't think Kathryn ever went grocery shopping. We had a cook who took care of all those mundane chores."

Jenny blinked. "Really."

His grin was twisted. "I married into wealth. Not a mis take I intend to ever make again."

Why was he telling her this? What purpose did it serve? Even as the questions crossed his mind, he knew, he *knew* He didn't want to want her. He didn't want her to want him He was throwing up roadblocks right and left even while he reached out to her from some inner desire that couldn' be controlled.

She made no response to that as they gathered their gro ceries and headed to the Jeep. On the road, she held her hair back with one hand as the wind tore through the open win dows of the vehicle and Hunter accelerated out of town.

"Tell me about yourself," she half shouted to be heard.

"What do you want to know?"

"Where you grew up, where you went to school, how you met Kathryn, when you knew the marriage was over . . . anything."

Hunter groaned and shook his head. He opened his mouth to deny her, but she wagged a finger at him. "Fair's fair. You tell me something about yourself, I'll tell you something about myself."

He was going to have to lie, and though he shouldn't care, he did.

"I'll start," she said, when he remained stubbornly silent. "Fact one: I'm an only child. Definitely a brat. I thought I owned the sun, the moon, and all of Texas. My mother tried to exert some influence but she hadn't a prayer, really. Too headstrong. Too arrogant . . ." She darted him a side ways look and her voice fell. "Not a nice little girl."

Hunter shot her a quick smile. "You just painted a picture of my ex-wife."

"Ouch."

"She had her good points." He turned the wheel and they sped around a corner. "I just wish I could remember what they were."

"Double ouch." Jenny pointed a finger at him. "Okay, it's your turn now."

"What do you want to know?"

"No, no. You have to offer it up. Don't make me work for it." Folding her hands primly in her lap, she was forced to close her eyes as she let the wind take charge of her wildly whipping hair. It was all he could do to keep from reaching over and smoothing it back. He wanted to see that smooth cheek, that roses-and-cream complexion, that gently curving jaw line.

"I was born in Phoenix and my family moved to Las Vegas. My father gambled his paychecks away and my mother cleaned hotel rooms. My sister Michelle sketched caricatures of hotel guests and became quasi-famous around town. I dragged myself through college." Hunter stopped. To this point, he'd stuck to the truth, but he was going to have to veer off track quickly. He didn't want her to know he'd been a cop.

"What did you study?"

He slid her a look as they turned down a particularly breathtaking stretch of coastline. "It's your turn."

Jenny smiled. "All right, I went to college, too. Studied literature and philosophy and boys for one full semester before Troy . . ." She gazed out toward the sea. A boat was dragging a white, billowing cloud of sail behind it and a parasailor. She could see the tiny black form of the person beneath the parachute.

Hunter pulled into a lookout with a rocky climb down to the beach. The half mile stretch of sand below was private, hemmed in on either side by huge boulders. Private and vendor-free. He yanked on the emergency brake and looked at her. "Ready for a walk along the beach and then a picnic?"

"It's your turn now," she reminded him, climbing from the Jeep.

He gathered up the picnic bag and they both scrambled down the slick black rocks to a beach with silver sand. Stashing the bag behind a large rock, they took off their shoes and strolled along the edge of the surf, feeling it bubble around their bare feet, teasing and retreating, and teasing again.

"I went into business. Worked in security. Married Kathryn and eked out a living for about two years before I felt like blowing my brains out. She found someone else. We divorced. I quit my job and now you know everything there is to know about Hunter Calgary."

"Mm-hm. So, what's your relationship with Kathryn now?"

"You keep forgetting the rules to your own game."

"All right." She stopped walking and Hunter waited beside her. "As I'm sure you realized last night, Troy hurt me in every way he could. He was in a rage that I had no immediate money, but what really infuriated him was that I didn't care. I used him too, I guess, as my ticket out of that house. When it all fell apart, I lost my courage and let dear old Dad take over again."

"You were pregnant," he reminded her. "And he was physically abusing you."

She nodded.

"And you've been on your own ever since, raising a son alone. Give yourself a little credit, Geneva." He purposely used her given name though it sounded stiff and formal on his tongue. But it kept the distance. That little distance he needed.

"My name's Jenny," she said on a whisper. "But you can call me Geneva, if you want . . ."

And with that Hunter Calgary gazed into her serious blue eyes and leaned in for a kiss.

Jenny had no idea what she felt as she sat directly on the sand and munched a cheese sandwich loaded with horseradish and dill pickle. Not exactly gourmet fare, but she'd never tasted anything better, never felt more ravenous. It was afternoon and the sun was beginning to set. She wanted the day to continue. She wanted to stay here with him and not have to face Magda, Phil, and the others. She wanted another kiss.

How long had it been since she kissed a man? It was entirely too depressing to think about. And when he'd said her name, so seriously, so deeply, it had struck some deep chord inside her that had been left untouched too long.

Hunter sighed, stretched out his long legs on the beach, tucked his hands under his head and closed his eyes. He wore jeans and a black shirt, no collar. Jenny was all too aware of how incredibly sexy he was. She took advantage of the opportunity to really look at him—the biceps that swelled under his sleeves, the rugged jaw, the dark brows and hair that waved just the tiniest bit away from sun-darkened skin.

"It's your turn again," she said, tucking the remains of their sandwiches into the bag and withdrawing the taco chips and salsa. She unscrewed the lid of the jar as she crunched a chip. Then she replenished their wine glasses though neither one of them had swallowed more than a few sips.

"I can't think of anything more to tell you," he said, eyes still closed, looking for all the world as if he were about to fall asleep right there.

"Then tell me about your sister."

His eyes opened and he shot her a hard look. "My sister?"

"Michelle, right? You said she drew caricatures. Does she still?"

"No."

It was as if a cold wind had blown in from the sea. Jenny wondered what she'd said but Hunter was silent for a very long moment. "Do you see her much?" she asked tentatively.

"I don't see her at all." He sat up quickly. "I don't want to talk about Michelle right now."

"Okay." Jenny swallowed, feeling chastised. "I don't have a sister or a brother, but I've got a father with serious control issues and a stepmother who plays tennis, collects jewelry, and pretty much stopped mentally developing at age fifteen."

That brought a smile to his face. "But how do you really feel about her?"

They were back on solid ground again. She was relieved. Munching another chip, she wondered if she should bring up the kiss. It had taken her wholly by surprise, and she felt she hadn't quite surrendered to it enough to enjoy herself. But there was no time. One moment he was looking at her, the next he'd grabbed her upper arms, pulled her forward and kissed her. And there'd been a lurking urgency, though she suspected he'd desperately tried to hide it.

Or maybe she was making too much of everything.

Clearing her throat, she said, "I feel like I'm asking all the questions. It's almost as if you know me already."

He didn't respond to that at all, just leaned over and scooped a chip in the salsa jar.

"So, what do you plan to do when this trip is over?"

He exhaled heavily, cradled his head with his hands again. "Sleep for a year."

Jenny gazed at him, slowly connecting. "That sounds like burnout."

"It is."

"Is that why you quit your job?"

"Uh-huh."

"So, my offer to hire you as a bodyguard won't be accepted?" she asked lightly.

His jaw tightened almost imperceptibly before it relaxed. "Were you serious about that? Do you really want a bodyguard against your ex?"

"Rawley would never understand, and I wouldn't be able to explain. I just don't feel safe right now." She struggled to go on, but her fear was nebulous, based only on her old memories of an abusive man. "I wish I knew what Troy wanted."

"I thought you said it was money."

"Yes. Money's the bottom line. But then there's Rawley . . ." She shivered and rubbed her arms briskly.

"You said he doesn't know about Rawley."

"Not yet, anyway." She grimaced. "But Troy's not stupid, and if he decides to invade my life—and it looks like he already has—then he's bound to run across Rawley."

"What do you think he would do if he found out he had a son?" Hunter asked, choosing his words carefully.

"I have no idea," she answered truthfully. "But it would be awful. Truly awful."

Silence fell between them. Finally, wearily, Hunter responded, "I think a bodyguard might be a good idea, but I don't think it could be me. I don't feel—right about it. What you need to do is learn what's on your ex's mind. He's contacted your father once already. Let him do it again."

"But what should I do if he comes knocking on my door?" she asked, unreasonably hurt by his refusal. "Welcome him with open arms?"

"Call your father. Call the cops. Don't let him pass the threshold."

His swift response was cold and direct. It got to her in a way that she couldn't explain. "You know, you're not helping!"

"I don't like what you've told me about him. I don't trust him."

"But you won't be my bodyguard?" she asked in a small voice.

"I can't."

"Why not?"

He paused for so long she began to doubt that he would ever answer her. Finally he drew a breath and said in a husky voice that got to her way down deep, "Because I feel the wrong way about you, and it wouldn't be wise."

Jenny didn't pretend to misunderstand. "That sounds like an excellent reason to me to take on the job."

"No. You do need a bodyguard, though. Talk to your father. I bet he'd arrange one in an instant."

Was that bitterness in his voice? She was getting so many messages, none of them clear. Maybe it was time to get some answers. "So, what do you want from me?"

"I—" He stopped himself, biting off the rest of what he was about to say. He shook his head and she saw his jaw work, as if he couldn't quite form the words. At last he said, "We're on borrowed time here in Mexico. It's hot and intense, and it won't last past the end of the week."

"But what do you want?"

"I don't even want to say."

"A fling?"

He almost smiled. "You're not the kind of woman to have a fling with,"

"How do you know?" Jenny lifted her chin, not liking the labels he'd already put on her at all. "I can be hot."

That broke him up. His white teeth gleamed in a huge smile and the chuckle deep in his throat sent a thrilling little frisson up her spine.

"You think I'm lying," she suggested.

"No, I don't think you're lying." He sat up and lifted his palms, as if warding off her attack. "I believe you can be . . . hot."

"It's that girl-next-door thing, isn't it? Everyone wants to be my big brother, or my father, or my surrogate something-or-other. No one ever wants to find out about the rest of me."

"Have you given many men the chance?"

Hunter had her there and he knew it. How could he know her so well when she felt he was such an enigma? He doled out just enough information to make her feel she was getting somewhere, but truthfully she knew so little. "Oodles of men," she stated blithely. "Oodles to canoodle with."

"Uh-huh."

She smiled, clasping her arms around her knees and giving in to the moment. "Okay, I lie like a rug."

"What do you want?" he asked with a sudden intensity that caught Jenny unaware.

"I want—something." She licked dry lips. "Maybe . . ."

"Maybe?"

"Another kiss?"

His gaze dropped to her mouth and hovered there long enough to heat Jenny's blood. She was mesmerized by the hard sensuality of his lips.

His eyes were dark and mysterious, on fire with sexual desire. Jenny felt herself lean forward, unconsciously hurrying the invitation. She heard his slight intake of breath and felt the heat of his skin.

At the last moment Hunter caught hold of himself, pulling back sharply. "I don't know what I'm doing, Geneva, and I have a pretty good idea you don't either. Let's get out of here before we both do something we'll regret."

The night sky was filled with stars, but the air was oppressive and smelled of exhaust. Troy could feel himself sweating, which really pissed him off. He hated Houston.

Hated the humidity and the beastly sun and the hostile ground. He'd grown up in southern California, another place he hated. His parents had eked out a living and then placed him in private schools they couldn't afford. He could remember his torn clothes, holes that were mended and mended. The snickers of the girls with the slim tan legs and the frosted, glossy smiles. He'd wanted to attack them. Shove them into the dirt and kick their skinny little asses. Instead he'd smiled and practiced his charm and he'd paid them back over and over again, yet they always seemed to rear up and spit in his eye in the end.

Hadn't that been what Val had done? Sixteen years old and already wise beyond her years. He'd been fifteen. Young and horny and already in and out of enough beds to know what he wanted. Val. He wanted Val. He could still remember the way she smelled and tasted even after all these years. She'd been insatiable. It had been fan-fucking-tastic. But Val had had a roving eye and she soon found a member of the football team she thought might do it better. He could still recall the way she'd laughed when she'd told him about her new stud. Troy had listened in silence, all the while wanting to shove his fist through her teeth to stop the bitch from laughing.

Two nights later he'd waited for her to come home. He'd watched as her football hero dropped her off, one hand halfway up her skirt. She playfully slapped it away as she flounced off in his varsity jacket. Troy grabbed her as soon as the asshole's car roared around the corner, taillights winking out.

"Hey!" she'd said, but Troy simply grabbed her, ground his teeth against hers and tossed her to the ground. She hadn't been scared. She'd been pissed And she'd fought him in silence for a while before finally getting into the mood. Then she'd been hungry for him, talking dirty, egging him on. Then *he'd* been pissed. So, he pulled up her skirt, ripped off her panties and gave her what she'd been asking for, begging for, and he made sure it hurt. She started crying but he didn't stop. He wanted her to pay. Pay hard. And she kept on crying and begging him to stop. When he felt himself about to climax, he pulled out and sprayed semen on her boyfriend's varsity jacket.

She didn't laugh at him ever again.

When he first saw Jenny Holloway he thought she was Val. Same luscious hair, same smile. It had taken Jenny and her uncanny resemblance to his first love for Troy to finally kick Val out of his system.

And Jenny came with money. Truckloads of the stuff. But she was damned annoying. Wouldn't get along with her father. Wouldn't play the game. Didn't know the first thing about sex and didn't want to learn. He'd hit her out of sheer frustration and when he'd seen the wounded shock in her eyes, the disbelief as she brought her fingers up to explore her bloody lip, he'd thought, "Fuck you, Val!" It had felt that good.

But then that bastard Allen had come to the aid of his crying princess. Troy wasn't willing to give up the marriage, especially when he learned that Allen didn't have all the facts. Jenny, bless her cowardly little heart, hadn't told Daddy about her injuries. Still, the fucker had guessed as much. There was just too much in his beady, triumphant eyes to ignore. He knew he had Troy by the short and curlies, and he sure knew how to twist a man's balls. God, how he hated the bastard.

But he did offer a lot of money. A *lot* of money for Troy to get lost. Holy shit. Troy had come out on top after all.

Until that whining bitch Michelle Calgary had turned up pregnant. She'd wanted to marry him, and throughout their relationship Troy had been a model boyfriend. She'd been damn cute. And he'd got her to do some really raunchy stuff, even though she pleaded with him to stop. He could remember one night when she tried to crawl away from him and he just let her have it over and over again, pumping and jerking, with her howling an accompaniment. Just thinking about it still gave him a hard-on. That's when he'd had to hit her, just to get her to stop that godawful noise. She'd begged him to stop, screaming that she was pregnant. In his shocked fury, he'd hit her again.

He'd felt bad about it later, of course. She was so sore she could hardly move for days. When she miscarried she got real quiet. He knew she was thinking about telling that brother of hers. He'd really had to lay the charm on thick, but he wasn't sure she was buying it anymore. She kept going up to the roof to *think.* Troy knew about women thinking. Anytime it had happened, he'd been shown the door. So, he had to stop her and he had. He hadn't meant to. Not that way. Not from the roof.

Involuntarily, Troy shuddered. It started at his feet and swept over him like a tidal wave. God, he hated thinking about that. It made him furious! He'd really loved her. Almost as much as he'd loved Jenny. But women were untrustworthy. They got themselves pregnant just to hang onto a man. Look at Jenny. She had a kid now. Lucky he'd skated out of that one before she tried what Michelle had tried.

He'd run through the rest of his money in such record time it amazed him. But it was just bad luck. Bad investments. At one time he'd been up twenty thousand dollars on the blackjack table! Then it had slipped away and he'd had to pay out another thirty thousand to cover his losses later on. He'd felt like pure shit. Life was so unfair.

Down to his last two hundred dollars, he'd had to give up his beachfront rental and start pounding the pavement looking for a new woman. They were everywhere, but none of them had the bank account he was looking for. Married whores sometimes doled out little chunks of money to him to be their stud. He took it and fucked them like it was a damn marathon. They loved it. But they had husbands. Worse luck, Michelle's thick-skulled brother was an L.A.P.D. detective. He'd wanted revenge after Michelle's accident, and Troy had had to cry foul to get anyone to listen to him and have the maniac restrained. Thinking about Hunter Calgary turned his bowels to ice water. Troy swore a blue streak in his head, snapping himself back to the merciless self-control that had served him so well over the years.

That, at least, was a closed chapter. Calgary had gotten himself fired from the force. Obsession could do that to a person. Troy had hightailed it out of Los Angeles to lay low in Tucson for a while. But when he learned that Calgary had left the state to work in Nevada, Troy returned to L.A. His luck changed when he met Frederica on his second night in a Sunset Strip bar. She was Latina, all heat and fire with a Beverly Hills mansion and an alimony check to make a man kneel down and weep. Her problem was she was manic-depressive. Bipolar. On or off. And when she went off she would lose interest in everything, right down to bathing and eating. Troy didn't live with her, the cagey bitch hadn't let him in that far. So when Frederica went down, he was left dangling, deep in debt and Patricia's pitiful bank account hadn't helped pull him to safe ground.

And that's when he thought about Jenny. Fifteen years had gone by in the wink of an eye. He didn't know where she was, but he sure as hell knew where her daddy lived. He'd waited outside the man's mansion, and waited and waited, until one day the great Allen Holloway finally drove over to that restaurant to look up his daughter. It had been a shock for Troy to realize Jenny was working. As a bookkeeper, in a miserable little restaurant, no less, with some dirty Italian bastard who slobbered all over her, undoubtedly looking for a way into her pants. He'd almost laughed, the guy was so desperate. *It's cold down there,* Troy had wanted to tell him. What women liked was the rough-stuff, but Jenny had frozen up all the more anytime he'd tried that

But then he'd seen Jenny for himself and he'd actually stopped his drink on its way to his lips. She'd been little more than a skinny teenager when they'd parted. Now she was a full-fledged woman, and he hadn't missed her luscious breasts and hips and thighs. Instantly, his plans had changed. He'd originally thought to put the bite on old man Holloway for more money, but seeing how ripe Jenny was, he'd switched tactics, come up with that "making amends" crap. Put right what was wrong. She'd been the ultimate ice princess when he'd known her, but she'd managed to get herself knocked up somehow. Maybe she'd learned a thing or two. Maybe he could teach her another thing or two.

But he had to get into her life. Now. While she was still off gallivanting around. Maybe with some guy. The idea both tantalized and infuriated Troy. *He* was the guy.

That damn dog was stretched across the threshold again, harmless looking enough but Troy knew better. Animals were tricky. He'd never got on with them.

As if hearing his thoughts, the beast lifted its tawny head. A long, low growl issued from its throat. Troy's hands curled into fists. He wouldn't mind strangling it. There was no trusting animals. But he wasn't fool enough to get in a fight with a dog that size.

Still . . . tonight was the night. He could hear a clock ticking in his head. Jenny would be back soon. Very soon. That soccer camp was over Sunday. She'd be back for her kid.

The dog scrambled to its four legs, letting out a nasty snarl. "Relax, Fido," Troy said, knowing it was useless. Instinct sure was a bitch, no pun intended. Dogs sensed his rotten hidden self as if it had an odor they could smell.

More low growling. He should have bought some rat poison and laced a pound of hamburger, but a dead dog would make his breaking and entering seem like something other than random chance and he didn't want that. The screwdriver in his back pocket would help jimmy the lock. His foot banging the door open would finish the job.

And he didn't want anything except information. Unless there was some cash just lying around, but judging by the evidence of Jenny's rather meager existence, he doubted it. Vaguely he wondered how he could have it all again, but he didn't worry too much. Win her over, something like that. Allen Holloway was a heart attack waiting to happen. And he knew the man well enough to know that he'd lost interest in that anorexic wife of his years ago. Sweet little Jenny was all he really cared about. Funny how things turned out.

Why didn't the mangy mutt go home, for God's sake? Troy glared down at the dog. It wouldn't move.

He wanted to lift his own head to the heavens and howl out his frustration. Instead, he concentrated on what he had to do, letting his pulse slow, his brain clear to a single thought. Jenny. Geneva Fucking Holloway.

His.

In control, he stared down at the bristling animal. "Hey, Fido," he said with a snarl as menacing as the animal's own. The beast blinked at him, its lips black and pulled back over sharp teeth. "Come over here . . ."

CHAPTER SEVEN

Deep-sea fishing had not been her idea. Spending hours on a pitching craft with lines strung off the back, hoping to sink a deadly hook into the mouth of some unsuspecting mega-fish left Jenny cold, cold, cold. But sitting around at the villa, or strolling through downtown Puerto Vallarta past the Hotel Rosa held even less appeal. She hadn't seen Hunter since Tuesday and now it was Friday, and she'd thought she might go crazy.

How could a couple of chance encounters with a mysterious man, who had rebuffed her, consume her so? She had a life to live that did not include him. A life, moreover, that was going to be jump-started as soon as she left here, packed up her belongings, and drove out of Houston to Santa Fe.

The pitch and roll of the craft sent a green wave of nausea crashing through her stomach. Cuddling up to the inside wall of the boat, she was almost happy to note that Magda and Alicia were in even worse shape than she was.

"Ohhhh . . ." Magda moaned. "Why didn't I stay home with Phil?"

"Why did I listen to Tom?" Alicia muttered.

"And Phil was feeling better!" Magda continued. "I could be drinking margaritas with him right now!"

"Don't make me sick." Alicia shuddered.

"How much longer?" Jenny asked.

"How can they do it?" Magda lifted her head to glance through the open door to Tom, Matt, Jackie, Lisa, and Sam and Carrie Brickman. They were laughing and drinking Coronas. Sunlight sparkled off the water.

"The women are young," Alicia groaned. "Way . . . too . . . young . . ." She suddenly lurched off her bench and headed for the teensy bathroom.

"Carrie's not that young, she's just . . . better than we are," Magda declared, the back of her hand covering her eyes.

Though she was not as sick as her two friends, Jenny chastised herself for this excursion. She'd chosen it as an escape from her own tormenting thoughts. Talk about choosing the wrong way out . . .

And it hadn't worked. Hunter had constantly been in her thoughts. And all her soul-searching had come down to one inescapable truth: she *wanted* an affair. She deserved an affair. She'd spent way too much time being responsible and serious. It didn't matter that she hadn't had any interest in having fun for intervening years, she sure as hell had an interest now.

And why not? Why the hell not? she argued furiously with herself. Some women slept with scores of men. Why, you couldn't watch television these days without feeling you'd missed out if you hadn't achieved a body count that was too embarrassing to admit to. All she'd had was one man. One. Her ex-husband. Even then she'd known instinctively that Troy's rough methods of seduction were not the way it was supposed to be. There was tenderness in the world, and she sensed a night with Hunter would be filled with those kind of moments.

"Oh, God," Magda moaned again. Then, as if in prayer, "Hurry up, Alicia. Hurry up, hurry up, hurry up . . ."

That, finally, got Jenny's mind off Hunter Calgary and on the more perilous adventure at hand.

At the villa they all looked as if they'd survived some sort of natural disaster. Well, most of them, anyway. Matt and Tom were in fine form, chortling and crowing about the monster tuna they'd managed to haul on board. But Jenny wasn't certain she would be able to look at a can of Bumblebee ever again. Lisa and Jackie were nursing sunburns, and Carrie and Sam were trying to figure out how to ship their catch back to Dallas. She, Magda, and Alicia had a green tinge beneath their skin that washed out all color.

Magda shuddered at the strips of beef soaked in cilantro and lemon, the lavish salad, and the ubiquitous rice and beans. Alicia draped herself over the rail of the patio as if she were some kind of human banner. Jenny actually felt a little hungry. As soon as they'd docked, she'd felt right again, but Magda and Alicia weren't as quick to bounce back.

The only one who had any interest in going into town after dinner was Phil, who'd been housebound for far too long. He begged and begged but was ignored by everyone but Matt—and even he was focused on what Jackie and Lisa were doing—which was creaming their skin with restorative oils. Taking pity on crestfallen Phil, Jenny said, "I'll go into town with you."

He brightened. "You are an angel!" He grabbed up his beret and Jenny held up a hand.

"No Euro-Phil tonight," she said, her lips twitching. "Just good company and Mexican coffee."

"All right," he agreed, dropping the hat. "Coffee with tequila and a whole lot more. Where should we start?" He moved to the phone to call a cab.

The Hotel Rosa . . .

"Anywhere you'd like," was her answer.

There was no further reason for secrecy, as far as Hunter was concerned. Jenny Holloway was safely ensconced with her friends at the villa and any concern for her safety from Troy was going to be in Houston. Still, he walked to a pay phone down the street rather than call from his room. It was his habit to take small precautions. He'd once—only once—underestimated a trigger-happy loser with a bad attitude. The man had followed him back to his apartment and taken a potshot at him. The bullet went wide, and Hunter dropped to the ground, drawing his own gun and holding the man in his sights. "Drop it or I'll kill you," he'd said, and the idiot had flung the gun away as if it were a poisonous snake, then run like the devil was on his heels. He was arrested the next day, claiming the incident never happened. With a bullet in Hunter's apartment door and the recovered gun covered with the perp's fingerprints, it was a slam dunk.

But Hunter never forgot how close he'd been to being killed. He'd underestimated the man. Period. Though he'd been shot at before, and had pots, pans, knives, chairs, whatever, thrown at him, he'd never been caught unaware before or since.

He dialed Holloway's home and got a feminine voice. Natalie. The wife and stepmother. "Is Mr. Holloway in?" he asked.

"May I say who's calling?"

A moment of fast thought. "His partner in the Mexico deal," he said.

She hesitated. "I'm not sure—"

"He's going to want to talk to me," Hunter added in a friendly but firm tone.

That seemed to do it. He heard the clatter of the phone being set down, then staccato footsteps receding. Soon, other footsteps approached. "Yes?" Holloway demanded tensely.

"Nothing new," Hunter said. "She's with her friends. They're protecting her whether they know it or not."

He released a pent-up breath. "He called me," he said shortly. "I was going to call you, but you told me not to. And now you're calling me."

"What did he want?" Hunter asked, ignoring Holloway's fuming.

"Just a friendly chat," he muttered grimly. "A snifter of brandy. A cigarette inside my home. And conversation."

Hunter couldn't imagine Holloway permitting Troy to light up inside his palace. It wasn't in the man's nature. But then he was playing a chess game of sorts with his former son-in-law, one where the rules changed from minute to minute. "What did he say?"

"Same as before. Wants to make amends." Holloway expelled a breath in disgust. "He's just so cool and collected, and the way he smiles makes me feel like I'm the butt of some joke."

Hunter listened silently. He didn't like the sound of Troy Russell enjoying some inner joke. "How long did he stay?"

"Not long." There was a weighty pause. "I don't like it."

Neither do I, Hunter thought. He felt tense and anxious. "I'm coming back to check on Rawley."

"What? No! Russell doesn't know about Rawley. Rawley's fine."

"You're certain?"

"He just talked about investments and wealth," Allen assured him. "As if the bastard had two pennies to rub together!"

"He's counting on Jenny."

"You keep her there as long as possible," Holloway ordered.

"That's not in the cards. She's done at the end of the week and she's going back to her son. There's no changing that."

"Well, find a way!"

"No." The man's controlling nature ticked Hunter off to no end. "How was it left with Russell?"

"He said he'd be in contact. He wants money. He's worming his way back in. I'm afraid Jenny will fall for it."

"She won't let Russell within a hundred miles of her, if she can help it."

"How do you know? Have you spoken with her?" Before Hunter could respond, he ranted on, "You approached her? I thought I made myself clear—she can't know I've hired you!"

"She doesn't."

"Why are you talking to her? I don't think that's a good idea."

The part that wasn't a good idea was his still working for Holloway, Hunter thought. "She's not going to see Russell unless he forces the meeting."

"He will force the meeting. He can't do without money. And he's a charming s.o.b. when he wants to be. Cold as a cobra's heart, but determined. She fell for him once, she could do it again."

Hunter wanted to argue. The reason Jenny had fallen for the creep the first time was because she was so lonely, so desperate to be away from her father and his new wife. But it wouldn't do any good . . . Holloway only heard what he wanted to hear. "She's leaving Sunday. So will I."

"Make sure she's safe."

"I will. Did you notice what type of car Russell was driving?"

"Light metallic tan sedan. Ford Escort, I think. I wouldn't count on him hanging on to it for long. He'll get something else."

On this Hunter and Holloway agreed. Although Hunter felt a gnawing urgency to get back to Houston and check on Jenny's son, he set that aside for the moment. If Russell was contacting Holloway, still making nicey-nice, then maybe he hadn't connected himself to the boy.

But what a bargaining chip when he did. Hunter knew it. And Holloway knew it. "She's been checking on Rawley through her friends," Hunter assured him. "He's at a soccer camp with their son."

"Troy doesn't know about him. Doesn't even know he exists."

"That's what I keep hearing. Are you sure he hasn't figured it out?" Hunter asked.

"He would have mentioned the boy, believe me. He was subtly turning screws every way he knew how." Holloway's tone darkened even further. "He can never know."

"If he's followed your daughter at any time, he could have seen her with Rawley."

"Then obviously he didn't."

"Don't underestimate him," Hunter said now, echoing his own philosophy. And suddenly the hairs on the back of his neck rose. He glanced around, but he was alone. He couldn't ignore that sense of impending doom or his keen intuition. Not again.

"I never underestimate anyone," Allen Holloway remarked in his blithe, autocratic way.

Hunter bit back a harsh laugh.

Jenny clasped the necklace Rawley had given her around her neck, gently touching the pink imitation pearls and examining their reflection in her bedroom mirror. She wanted to be home to make sure Rawley was all right. She was tired of sun and fun. If it weren't for meeting Hunter, she would have counted this trip as more a hindrance than a vacation.

It was time to get to Santa Fe.

She wore a pair of khaki shorts and a sleeveless pink blouse. The necklace had been an inspired afterthought. Slipping on her sandals, she headed downstairs to meet Phil, who was waiting by the pool. The rest of the crowd seemed to have dispersed to their respective bedrooms. It had been that kind of day.

The call came in just as Jenny and Phil were heading to the cab. Phil made a sound of annoyance and had to hurry downstairs to get the call while Jenny waited at the front door. When he called to her, she hurried to answer it, her nerves jumping. "Hello?" she asked anxiously. The only people who knew how to get hold of her were the Fergusons. This couldn't be good news.

"Hey, Jenny," Janice's voice came over the line. "Hi . . . sorry to bother you." She sounded remote, distracted and deeply disturbed about something.

Jenny's heart flipped over and she began to sweat. "What's happened? Is it Rawley? Oh, God, is he all right?"

"Oh, yes, yes. Rawley's fine. Still at soccer camp. Rick went over and checked on both boys today," Janice assured her. "Don't worry about him. It's—your apartment."

"My apartment?"

"Someone broke in."

Her heart raced uncontrollably. "Broke in!" she repeated, stunned.

"I can't tell if anything's been taken. It wasn't disturbed too much. Maybe it was kids," she said with a note of hope. "Benny might have bitten them."

163

"What? Benny? Is he all right?"

"Yeah. He's fine, I think."

"Janice, you're scaring me!"

"No, it's okay. I don't know what happened, exactly There was a scrap of dark cloth on the ground and some tufts of Benny's fur. You know how he likes to guard your door. And Benny's been kind of moving slow the last couple of days. The vet examined him and his ribs are tender. I think the intruder hit or kicked him."

"Oh, no." Jenny swallowed hard. "You're sure Rawley's all right?"

"Fine. Perfect. Except for a slight black eye where he took a soccer ball to the face. I reported the break-in to the police and called your apartment manager."

"Diego."

"Uh-huh. He had someone replace the door this morning. I've got the new set of keys. Diego just wants you to check in with him. And the police suggested you call them after you've looked to see what's missing."

Panic filled her. It had to be Troy. He'd broken into her apartment. She knew it as if she'd seen it with her own eyes. She could hear her own ragged breathing and tried to calm herself. She had to go home. Now. Immediately. "It's okay, Janice," she said automatically, wanting to reassure her friend that she'd done everything she could.

"I wasn't supposed to tell you. Rick wanted me to wait until you got home, since there's nothing you can do about it now."

"You think it was a random break-in?"

"Well, yeah. What else could it be?"

"I'm catching the next flight out."

"Jenny, please don't do that. Please! I shouldn't have called you. Oh, I knew it. I just thought you might need to know."

"Absolutely! I'm so glad you warned me."

"Please don't come back yet. You've only got a couple of days left. Enjoy yourself."

"Enjoy myself!" she said on a half-hysterical laugh.

"Everything's locked up tight. Oh, Rick told me not to tell you! He'll just kill me if you come back too soon. Please, Jenny. Everything's fine. Stay till Sunday. We're talking another day, really. That's all. Please."

Jenny closed her eyes. Every nerve ending tingled. She needed to leave. But Janice was desperate for her to stay. What real difference would it make? She tried to quell her nervousness and think rationally, but all she could see was Troy's smirking face swimming in front of her vision.

"Please, Jenny," Janice went on. A wail sounded in the background at her end of the line. Becky and Tommy were at it again. "Please!"

"I've got to think," she said automatically.

"Don't worry. Everything's under control. Oh, here's Rick now . . ." She sounded distracted. "It's Jenny," she called loudly. Then she whispered, "He wants to talk to you. Please don't tell him I told you about the break-in."

"But—"

"Please!"

The wailing got louder and she heard the clattering of the receiver. A moment later it was picked up and Rick asked, "Jenny? How's it going south of the border?"

He sounded so relaxed that she gritted her teeth. What should she do? Her hand was wet on the receiver. "Pretty well," she answered a bit stiffly.

"So, what time's that flight on Sunday? I'm picking up the boys and then coming to the airport to meet you."

"Um . . . no, I think I'll pick Rawley up, if you don't mind. I'm in Houston by early afternoon."

"Well, okay. Three Winds Camp is a two-hour drive."

"I know. But—uh—I want to pick up Rawley. How's the camp going?"

"They're having a great time. They're already making plans to see each other this summer. And their soccer playing has really improved." He started talking about boys' respective skill levels and Jenny listened silently while her brain whirled ahead.

"Rick, I've got to go," she finally cut in. "I'm just heading out the door."

"Oh, yeah? Don't drink too many margaritas, okay? And quit having fun. I'm jealous." He chuckled. "Maybe we'll see you at the camp when we get the boys. *Adios, amiga.*"

"*Adios*," she responded.

"What's wrong?" Phil asked at the same moment Matt came out of his bedroom. They had both overheard the last few words of her conversation.

Matt said, "The cab's waiting outside."

"Someone broke into my apartment," Jenny revealed.

"Aw, hell," both men said in unison.

"Robbery?" Matt asked.

"It doesn't look like anything's taken, but the only one who would know is me." She chewed her lip. "Maybe I should go back."

"No." Phil grabbed her arm and squired her upstairs and outside to the cab. "It can wait till you get home Sunday.

This is our night."

"Maybe I should come along," Matt started, but Phil adamantly shook his head.

"Go be with your girlfriends. Jenny and I need to get out."

With that he shooed Jenny into the Jeep and they were on their way to the center of Puerto Vallarta. Phil, apparently determined to keep Jenny's mind off the break-in, talked nonstop about the state of the Mexican economy, the fabulous weather and his own return from the "dark side of gastro hell."

He was only partially successful. She still felt Troy's presence as if he were in the car with them. But as they turned onto the main street that faced the beach, she darted a quick look toward the Hotel Rosa. She wanted to see Hunter one last time, no matter what; and she was bound and determined to either find him or leave a message. She didn't want to leave things the way they were. He might have rejected her, but she hadn't imagined the feelings between them. She wanted the comfort of his presence right now, even if it had to be a fleeting pleasure.

Finding no parking place, Phil circled around the block. As they turned down a side street Jenny spotted a man at the public phone. "I think that's Hunter," she said, embarrassed at her unconcealed excitement.

Phil pulled the Jeep over to the curb. Hunter glanced at them, obviously surprised. He hung up quickly and came around the booth to meet them. "Hey, there," he said, gazing softly down at her. "What brings you two back to the city?"

"Phil was feeling kind of cooped up and no one else

really wanted to party outside the villa, so I offered to be his entertainment." She swallowed. She wanted to tell him about her apartment break-in, but it wasn't his problem.

"Looking at those stucco bedroom walls was about to bring on another bout of puking," Phil agreed. "Don't let her fool ya. Had to drag her out of there. She only came 'cause she felt so sorry for me."

"So, where are you two going?" Hunter asked casually.

"I think we'll head to your hotel and get a meal," Phil answered. "Jenny hardly ate a bite tonight, and I'm just glad to be able to eat anything and feel good about it!"

"Care to join us?" Jenny asked, just as casually. She glanced at the phone booth but didn't ask why he was eschewing the phone in his room. Maybe he was just being thrifty. Hotel rates were outrageous.

Hunter hesitated only the briefest of moments. Someone less attuned would have missed it entirely. But Jenny fielded the slight and tried not to let it bother her. She knew why he was doing this. He'd bluntly told her he didn't want to get involved with anyone.

That didn't mean it didn't hurt, though.

They walked toward the Hotel Rosa and into the dining room. A mariachi band was playing in the corner as they were seated, making it difficult to talk, which was fine with Jenny. She couldn't think of a damn thing to say.

"The special tonight is fresh tuna, seared and lightly crusted with a mango-orange salsa," the waiter told them.

Jenny grimaced. "I saw one of those up close and personal today."

"Huge, aren't they?" Phil commented.

"Did you catch anything?" Hunter asked her.

She half-smiled. "A case of seasickness." Hunter flashed her a smile. It warmed her heart, though she tried not to let it. Don't think about him, she warned herself, staring at her menu as if it held all of life's mysteries.

She'd come to Puerto Vallarta for the food, but her stomach still wasn't in the mood. "Soda water," she ordered.

"Black coffee," Hunter added and Phil looked at them as if they'd lost their minds. "I've already eaten," Hunter responded, "but the food here's great."

"Bring on the tuna," Phil told the waiter.

When the fish arrived he smacked his lips, digging in with gusto. Jenny sipped her soda and watched Hunter out of the corner of her eyes. He'd pulled a cigarette from a fresh pack he'd brought with him, tapping it on the table and twisting it through his fingers.

"Quit a long time ago," he said to her unspoken question. "Sometimes the mood strikes, though."

"For no particular reason?"

"It's generally for a reason," he said with a sideways look.

"God, this is good," Phil mumbled around a mouthful. A bit of mango and orange salsa touched the corners of his mouth and he licked it off with relish. "Jenny, my dear, if you serve something like this, they'll be breaking down your door!"

"I'll tell Gloria," Jenny said. Her mind traveled ahead to her plans for the Santa Fe restaurant and all the things she had yet to do to facilitate this move. And then she thought about Rawley. And then she remembered the break-in.

She sighed, feeling Hunter's eyes on her.

"Something wrong?" he asked.

Hesitating only briefly, she decided to tell him everything. "I had some disturbing news before I left the villa."

"What?"

"Someone broke into my apartment."

Hunter's gaze intensified and he dropped the unlit cigarette onto the table, forgotten. "When?"

"A couple of days ago, I guess." Jenny related what Janice had told her. "Do you remember me telling you about Benny? The neighbor's dog? Well, he sleeps outside my door and now he's got some tender ribs. Whoever broke in probably kicked him or something."

"Is the dog okay?" Hunter asked, his voice stony.

"I think so."

"This some random break-in?" Phil asked around a final bite. With a satisfied smile, he pushed his plate aside and settled into his chair.

"It may have been," she said slowly.

"But you don't think so." Hunter was watching her in a way that made her choose her words carefully.

"I'm just afraid—it might have been Troy."

"Troy!" Phil repeated.

"He's back in Houston right now, and I don't really know what he wants yet. He's been in contact with my father." She hesitated, darting a look toward Hunter. "My ex is not a nice man."

"Was anything taken?" Hunter asked.

"I'm not sure yet. I'll know when I get back."

"Russell is bad news," Phil said for Hunter's benefit. To Jenny, who stared at him in surprise for offering up information on her ex-husband, he said, "I don't know that much about your marriage, only what Magda said about whatever you've told her. But I know there's a lot more to that story than you're telling. If that bastard's trying to get back into your life, watch out. You may need a full-time bodyguard, my dear."

Jenny gazed at him. She didn't know how to look at Hunter.

"I'll do my best when we get to Santa Fe," Phil added, "but I'm talking professional here."

"Magda and Phil live in Santa Fe," Jenny explained for Hunter's benefit.

"We talked Jenny into joining us. She's opening a restaurant. Did she tell you?" Hunter nodded. "Riccardo's has fabulous food, but Jenny's talents are wasted there unless Alberto decided to make her a partner."

"I was ready to leave Houston," Jenny said. "Past ready."

"What phase is the restaurant in?" Phil asked.

"Close to done. We've renovated an existing building and thank God for Gloria, my chef, because she's been playing assistant general contractor. She's about driven the workmen crazy, but that's Gloria. She wants what she wants."

"Where are you from again?" Phil asked Hunter.

"Los Angeles."

"You should check out Santa Fe," he suggested.

Hunter didn't respond.

Feeling the conversation starting to die, Jenny put in, "When I drove up to Santa Fe to visit Magda and Phil, that was it: love at first sight."

She felt Hunter's eyes on her and had difficulty meeting his look. His rejection had hurt, no matter how well-meant

171

it was. She didn't share his worries about being her bodyguard and maybe her lover. She would have welcomed both.

"So, L.A.'s your home?" Phil asked Hunter.

"I was working in L.A., but . . ." He left the thought unfinished for several beats, then added, "I'm just trying to figure out what to do next."

"You were in security, weren't you? Well, there's your answer, Jenny. This man should be your bodyguard!"

Phil was so delighted with his own cleverness that Jenny hardly knew what to say. She sensed Hunter stiffen in his chair. "Actually, we've already discussed it," she said quietly. "I offered him a job yesterday as my bodyguard, but he couldn't do it."

"Okay, okay." Phil pushed back his chair. "You two work it out. Whatever the case, Jenny, batten down the hatches and throw the deadbolts. And we'll all meet up in Santa Fe and Troy Russell will be a forgotten piece of your past."

"I hope so."

Hunter felt like an uninvited guest. They were talking around him and he supposed he damned well deserved it. But he could hardly hire on as Jenny's bodyguard when he already had the job.

Still . . . "Maybe I could come to Houston," he said grimly. But he was an idiot. He didn't just want to protect her, he wanted to *be with* her.

Jenny's blue eyes lit up. "Does that mean you will?"

Hunter knew he was playing with fire. He couldn't have it both ways. He and Jenny stared at each other a long, long moment. Picking up the vibes, Phil murmured, "I think this is my cue to leave. You know what, you two? You ought to go with your instincts. Always the best choice. Everything else is just bullshit, y'know? Don't let it dictate to you."

He pushed back his chair and added, "I take it you'll bring the lovely Geneva home."

Hunter nodded.

Phil waved good-bye and left whistling. Just before he disappeared, he caught Jenny's eye and nodded several times like an old sage whose dullest pupil had finally made a bright decision.

"I don't want to force you into anything," Jenny said. "Phil's just trying to look out for me."

"You have good friends." He gazed at her steadily.

"The thing is—is—" She took a deep breath. "Troy is capable of real cruelty, and, if you don't have anything else pending, it would be great if you could—take on the job."

Her words hit like stones. He thought of his lovely, too forgiving sister and could scarcely meet Jenny's pleading eyes. "I can't be your bodyguard and your—date." He regarded her expressive face and had to force himself to continue. "So, you choose."

She swallowed. "That was a pretty harsh rejection the other night. I haven't fully recovered."

"I've been trying to do the right thing all week."

"I wouldn't mind a—fling." She smiled faintly. "But I think I need a bodyguard."

His gaze drifted down the front of her shirt, to the pink blouse that clung to the soft curves of her breasts. "All right."

"All right, what?"

"I want to keep you safe."

"Why can't you be my bodyguard and my date?" she

asked.

He shook his head and stared off into space, lost in grim thoughts. Protecting someone was easy. Protecting someone you cared about was torture. *But it's already too late*, his rational mind argued. *You already care.*

Jenny gazed down at her fingers, surprised to see them clutching the edge of the table. Her heartbeat slowed. Thumped. Hurt. "Can't you answer me?"

"I can't do both because it'll get messy."

She swallowed, darting him a shy look. "I can handle messy. Things have been too clean for a long time." Absurdly, she felt tears sting behind her eyes and she laughed to cover up the emotion. "My mistakes were all a long time ago. And they were big ones." She drew a breath, "But now I think I can take a few chances. And maybe everything won't go wrong this time . . ."

Hunter hated this moment. Hated letting himself listen to her. He gazed into her eyes, lost in the intense emotion in their blue depths. He cursed himself for allowing this to happen—for practically setting it up.

He thought of Allen Holloway. Thought of how the man would react to the idea that his employee was romancing his daughter. No! That his employee was being *asked* by his daughter to engage in a full-fledged affair. The man would be apoplectic.

"You're smiling. I'm almost afraid to ask why," Jenny said.

"I'm a sick man," he said with a silent laugh.

"Is that a yes?" she asked cautiously.

"Come on. Let's get out of here," he said, fighting down another wave of unhealthy amusement. Paying the bill in ash, he ignored Jenny's protests to help. Cupping her lbow, he piloted her out of the restaurant and they walked nto the street in front of the hotel. Just as they reached the orner, the sky suddenly opened up and rain fell in blinding heets, so fast and so hard that Jenny gasped in surprise and pened her palms skyward, as if asking how this could ave happened.

The elemental rain. The sudden cooling of the humid air. The sudden wet skin and soaked clothes. Hunter moved on mpulse and simply pulled her into his arms and hugged er. She came willingly, wrapping her arms around his eck as if they'd choreographed the movement together.

His lips sought hers. Her mouth was soft and warm and urved into a smile.

"Stop smiling," he ordered, his own lips still twisting vryly.

"No."

He kissed her again and felt her hand reach around his eck, holding his face down to hers. His tongue slipped nto her mouth and the heat inside sent thoughts splintering nside his brain. To hell with it. He wanted to make love to Geneva Holloway Russell and he wanted to do it right now.

Jenny's head was swimming, and she was fast losing the ittle self-control she still possessed. This wasn't going to vork. She wasn't the type to have a quickie affair. A one-night stand. A meaningless episode of sexual gratification vhich would leave her feeling wretched the next day. Hunter was right. He should be her bodyguard, not her over. She *needed* a bodyguard. She didn't need a lover.

But why then, did her arms wrap more tightly around im at the thought of letting him go? Why was she pressing her rain-soaked body against his as if she would die without the feel of him close to her?

"I don't know what I'm doing," she said breathlessly, against his lips.

"I don't either." A shudder went through his tall frame. "Come on," he muttered. "Let's get somewhere before I do."

Jenny went willingly, bewildered by her sudden arousal. Her response was so uncharacteristic of her—yet it felt so right. They scurried through the cloudburst to the Hotel Rosa, standing, dripping beneath the archway into the reception area. For a moment they stared at each other. A quivering smile touched Jenny's lips, only to die when there was no answering response from Hunter. His face was tight and intense, almost stern. For a moment she worried he was preparing to say no again, but then he groaned and dragged her to him. Her soft curves melted into his hard, muscular body until he reluctantly released her and they headed hand in hand to the elevator.

Inside his room, she swallowed hard, counting her heartbeats. Her eyes glanced toward the bed. She imagined herself on its smooth cover, naked, with Hunter's body atop hers as she caressed his warm skin and the powerful arms that would hold her close. . . .

He caught her look and held it. "What do you want?"

She opened her mouth. Her mind went blank.

He came to her swiftly, running one hand into her hair, tangling his fingers in the silky tresses, turning her mouth up to his. She went limp. "Everything," she whispered. "I want everything."

No more words were spoken. His hands found the buttons down the front of her blouse. Her own worked on the ones on his shirt. Swiftly shed, their clothes dropped in soft folds around their feet. Once naked, Jenny couldn't help folding her arms over her chest, embarrassed, but Hunter swept her hands aside, replacing them with his own body, his mouth hot on her neck and nape. She quivered. Her legs weren't bone. They were liquid and wouldn't support her. He held her to him and she felt his hardness pressing against her abdomen.

It had been so long since she'd kissed a man. Touched a man. Wanted a man. She found herself desperate to explore every inch of him but was paralyzed by her own fears. He helped her, moving her hand to his shaft as his tongue slipped between her lips.

Jenny moaned.

His mouth pressed lower, as he nuzzled the tops of her breasts, licking and finally fastening on one nipple. His arm held her up or she would have melted to the floor. She was weak with erotic pleasure and when he finally lifted his head to kiss her again, she tumbled against him.

Hunter swept her into his arms and placed her on the bed, then he sank down beside her. She clasped the cover in tight fists when his head sank lower, seeking her most feminine spot, and she cried out when he pleasured her in a way that sent waves of pure desire throughout her body.

It was all she could do to keep from clawing him in her anxiety to feel him inside her. She pulled him to her. When he thrust against her, she pulled him closer.

Hurry, hurry, hurry, she thought mindlessly.

"Geneva," he murmured, as if from a long way away, his hardness penetrating deep.

She cried out. Her body responded with each movement, opening like a desert to a rain after a long, long drought. Her fingers dug into his hips, dragging him deeper. Hunter groaned, struggling to master the overwhelming sensation, but Jenny wasn't having any of it. She wrapped her legs around him and he thrust hard.

"I can't wait."

"Don't," she gasped.

"I want to . . ."

"I want you. I want—" An explosion of pleasure coursed through her and she cried out. Orgasmic waves pulsed through her. She clung to him, riding the sensation, hanging on for dear life. With a groan he climaxed only seconds later and she felt the pulsation of his release. It satisfied her in a way she hadn't believed possible.

Her eyes were shut. She felt afraid to open them, afraid to let go, but Hunter finally stirred. He stayed inside her, however, simply lifting his head and staring into her eyes, his own blue ones dark with emotion and sexual satisfaction.

"I guess that decides whether I'm going to be your bodyguard or not," he said in a lazy, sensual voice.

She felt him harden inside her.

And then he started making love to her all over again.

❋ CHAPTER EIGHT ❋

T here's something I have to tell you."

Jenny opened her eyes in the semi-darkness of Hunter's room. Light filtered through the slatted blinds and she could just see the sheet that covered their tangled limbs. "Oh, no, here it comes, the big confession!"

she teased, burrowing closer to Hunter's side, reveling in the feel of his warm skin against hers, the strength in his muscles, the smooth flesh. She'd never cuddled with Troy. Never.

His fingers trailed along her arm. "I wasn't in security. I was with the L.A.P.D."

Jenny blinked in surprise. "Really?" To his nod, she asked, "Why didn't you tell me before?"

"Because I was put on leave for unprofessional conduct."

"You?" she asked in disbelief.

"I knew that a murder had been committed, but I could never prove it. So, I 'harassed' the man. At least that's what he alleged in his lawsuit."

Jenny didn't respond. Suddenly she realized how little she truly knew about Hunter.

"Then I went to work for a smaller police department, for six years. That job was in Santa Fe."

Jenny could scarcely believe her ears. She drew her arm away from him. "You lived in Santa Fe?"

"I still do."

"What are you saying?" she asked in a small voice.

"I don't like talking about myself. I didn't want to talk about what happened in L.A. And you were moving to Santa Fe, and I couldn't tell you I lived there."

"Why?"

Hunter struggled to explain, but there was no explanation. He could sense how tense she was. If he went into his connection with Troy and her father—and Michelle's death—he was sure he would lose her. "It just seemed too coincidental. I was afraid you would think there was more to it."

Was there more to it? She felt chilled to the bone. "I wish

you had told me this before."

"Before . . . this . . . ?" He ran a caressing finger along the side of her face.

She swallowed. "Yes."

"That's why I'm telling you now."

"I don't like secrets." When he made no response, she felt alarmed all over again. "Hunter . . . ?"

"I think you need a bodyguard. I think your ex-husband is dangerous, and I want to be there to protect you."

She laughed without mirth. "So, now you can do both?"

"I'll have to," he said seriously. "I'm in too deep."

When he drew her into the circle of his arms and began slowly kissing her neck, she didn't protest. The heat he stirred inside her couldn't be ignored and she felt it lick through her like liquid fire. Questions hammered at her brain. Squeezing her eyes tightly shut, she held them at bay. She wanted tonight and she was damned if she would let reality spoil it for her now.

With a supreme effort of will Jenny pushed her doubts aside and gave herself up to the pleasure of the moment.

The bar was country western in theme and music and everyone wore shit-kicker boots and blue denim. Even the women, though their tightly wrapped asses invited a man to give them a slap and a tickle. It was all Troy could do to keep his hands to himself. As a means of distraction, he'd snatched the drumsticks by the snare drum of the so-called band, now on a break, and was rapidly tapping them against the bar as he waited for his beer.

Beer. A cheap drink for cheaper surroundings. He shouldn't be here at all. He had plans, but Jesus H. Christ he was in shock.

Jenny's kid was no bastard. Jenny's kid was his son.

His son!

The beer arrived. Troy tossed some money in the bartender's direction, then grabbed the sticks and rapped harder and louder. "Hey!" came a furious yell, and the drummer with the thick beard and even thicker waist appeared wearing a plaid flannel shirt and dumb expression. Morons. They were all morons. The man yanked the drumsticks from Troy's hands. Troy froze. He wanted to kick the guy in the nuts, but he knew all hell would fall down upon him. He was the outsider here, in pressed chinos and a white shirt, sleeves rolled up to the elbows.

"Hey, little girl," the drummer whispered in his ear. "You're in the wrong place. Your kind of *boy* ain't here."

They thought he was gay? Troy nearly laughed out loud. He made eye contact with a cute little blond in tight, tight jeans and a low-cut bright red blouse, her breasts hanging out. She regarded him anxiously, obviously worried this hayseed would do him bodily harm. "Sorry," Troy said. "Just had a little nervous energy and wanted to work it off."

"Get out of here. Now!"

Troy flushed. He slid off the barstool, hesitating just a moment. The rest of the members of the band had returned and they were all scowling at him.

He walked outside into a coolish March night. Houston. He spat on the ground. He wanted to do some real damage to the fucking assholes.

The door opened behind him and he glanced around quickly. It was the blond. "Whew!" she said. "I thought they was gonna rip you limb from limb."

"Me, too. And it was such a shame. I had to leave a full beer."

She grinned, relieved at his attitude. "I'm kinda fed up with this place. You wanna go somewhere else?"

"Where did you have in mind?"

"We could start at Duffy's and then just see . . ."

He wanted his hands on her. On those ripe breasts and those even riper butt cheeks. He wanted inside her. He wanted to give it to her as hard as he could. He could practically hear her panting and crying already.

She looked a little bit like Jenny.

"Lead the way," he said, smiling.

Jenny woke up with a start, heart pumping, a sheen of sweat covering her body. Hunter lay beside her, sound asleep.

It was nearly dawn. She lay in silence for several moments, willing her heartbeat to return to normal. For a moment she couldn't recall why she felt so anxious, then Hunter's revelations hit her again, full force.

Why had he lied?

She couldn't fall back asleep to save her soul. She thought about her apartment being burglarized Was it Troy? Would he break in as a means to terrorize her? Probably. He delighted in pointless cruelty.

Her next thought was of Rawley. She had to make sure he was all right.

What am I doing here?

Sliding out of the bed as quietly as possible, Jenny groped around for her clothes, feeling a bit like a sneak thief. Her blouse and shorts were still damp from the rain

Shivering inside and out, she pulled on her underclothes, stepped into her shorts and buttoned up the shirt with shaking fingers.

Glancing toward Hunter made her start. He was leaning up on one elbow, watching her.

"I have to go," she said hurriedly.

"I'll take you."

"I can catch a cab."

"I'll take you," he stated again, more firmly, and climbed out of the bed and reached for his own still-wet clothes.

The sky was light gray by the time they reached the villa. As soon as Hunter pulled to the curb, Jenny jumped out. Hunter swung himself from the Jeep and crossed in front of the hood to meet her. She could see how his damp shirt clung to his skin and guessed he was as cold as she was.

"I've got to go inside," she said.

"Can you get inside?" he asked, and belatedly she remembered how Matt had been unable to rouse anyone when he'd come home in the wee hours of the morning. She'd told Hunter the story last night as a funny anecdote about Magda, Phil and the others. Now she saw it as a serious obstacle.

Feeling helpless, she pushed the bell. She could hear its chime inside, but she also knew the bedrooms, each equipped with its own air-conditioning unit, were fairly soundproof.

Turning to Hunter, she wished she could explain her feelings. Then again, she wasn't certain what they were. She wanted to throw herself into his arms and let him take care of everything; at the same time she was afraid of further involvement with someone she scarcely knew. She cringed when she remembered her brave words yesterday . . . how she was ready to make another mistake . . .

He seemed to be struggling with the same issue. "After last night, I thought it was time to get to the truth."

"*After* last night?" She shivered in the cool air. "What about before?"

"There are other things to say," he got out, though it was clearly difficult for him.

"Hunter, I can't hear them right now. I'm sorry. I'm overwhelmed. Do you understand?"

He glanced toward the upstairs balcony. "What are you going to do?"

"I don't know!" she declared, almost hysterical. *Get away from you!*

"I can bring you back later—"

"No! I can't."

Suddenly desperate, Jenny wondered if she was going to have to climb to the balcony herself and beat on the stained-glass panels. Then the front door suddenly swung open and a bleary-eyed Matt stood there, wearing only a pair of black silk boxers.

"Well, hey," he said, running a hand through his tousled hair.

Jenny didn't wait for more. With a terse, "I'll call you," thrown over her shoulder that she didn't mean, she brushed past Matt and hurried up the stairway to her room.

Seven hours later she sat curled in her airplane seat, still as chilled as she'd been that morning. The flight to Houston had been uneventful—and painful. Jenny had never felt more miserable in her life and there was no one to blame but herself. She'd run out on him. One night of mind-shattering lovemaking, and she'd scurried away. She'd been nothing but eager the night before; nothing but a coward this morning. The shower she'd taken hadn't warmed her up much. She'd gotten in, gotten out, then packed her things as swiftly as possible. She hadn't wanted to answer anyone's questions. She'd just wanted to go home.

The questions came anyway. Everyone wanted to know about Hunter. She'd dodged them all with the truthful statement that she had to get back and make sure everything was all right in her apartment and with Rawley, not necessarily in that order. Magda and Phil were all over her, asking questions about Hunter that Jenny simply refused to answer. She couldn't answer them. She didn't know the answers, for crying out loud! All she knew was that she'd indulged in that one-night stand she'd been dreaming about and it had felt damn good.

But her flimsy trust in Hunter had been shattered. She didn't know him. He was a fantasy. That's all. She should have listened to him in the first place and just let him be her bodyguard. But could she even trust him that far? She could just imagine her father's reaction if he learned she'd picked up a complete stranger in Puerto Vallarta, asked him to protect her, then spent one incredible night making love with him.

Apparently her mistakes with Troy had taught her nothing.

And now Troy knew he was Rawley's father.

She shivered again, pulling her sweater more closely around her shoulders. This thought had been knocking around the corners of her brain. Well, if he didn't actually know, he probably suspected. She didn't believe for a minute that he was unaware of Rawley's existence. If Troy was really trying to get back into her life, for whatever reason, then he would have heard of Rawley by now and come to some conclusions.

She'd been denying this thought because it scared her so much. But it was time to face facts. Hunter might be fantasy; unfortunately, Troy was reality. And he had probably come back for Rawley. Her dalliance with Hunter was over before it really began—it had to be. Fooling around with a sexy, mysterious man was pure irresponsibility when it came to choosing between that and the safety of her only child.

You don't even know how to get hold of him.

She shook her head, banishing the thought. She'd booked the first available flight and damned the upgrade charge. She had to go home. She wouldn't let her mind dwell on Hunter—or what he would think of her when he realized she'd bolted not only from his bed but from Puerto Vallarta and his life as well. . . .

The protests of Magda, Phil, Matt, and a few of the others had fallen on deaf ears. A part of her had half-feared, half-hoped that Hunter might come back after her like some white knight, but he hadn't. What romantic claptrap! He was probably glad she'd been so quick to walk away. No man wanted a one-night stand to stick around too long.

Jenny stared out the square airplane window to the limitless blue sky beyond. The drone of the engines made her feel dull and tired. She was glad she'd left before she'd gotten involved with him further, or so she told herself.

She tried to read a magazine, worked on a crossword puzzle, failed in her concentration on both and resumed staring out the window as they came in for a landing. When she got in the terminal she was going to call Janice straightaway. Rawley was getting home tomorrow, but she didn't want to wait. She wanted to pick him up tonight, or at least go see him for herself.

They bumped onto the runway and taxied to the gate moments later. Jenny waited to get into the aisle, feeling impatient, but by the time she'd deplaned and arrived at baggage claim, weariness seemed to drag her bones down. Beneath that she could feel a tenderness inside, the physical memory of a night of lovemaking that still had the power to momentarily stop her breath.

Again, a strange feeling overtook her, that sense of being watched. Shivering, she whipped around. A few people looked back curiously, while others waited for their bags. She started to turn back, feeling foolish, when a familiar profile caught her eye. *Troy!*

Her eyes widened and then the man turned and smiled at an approaching little girl. Not Troy. Not Troy at all.

The man swept the little girl into his arms, then reached out to embrace the young mother. They all smiled.

Jenny turned away. Troy never smiled. Not unless you counted the cold grin of someone who'd bested an opponent. She'd seen that smile in her nightmares over the years.

Reaching out, she grabbed her rollaway off the baggage carousel, set it on its wheels and clicked up the handle.

"Excuse me." Jenny flinched. She glanced at the stern-looking man who'd spoken. "Don't look so scared," he told her as he squeezed past her. "I just wanted to get my bag before it goes around again."

"Oh. Sorry." She grabbed the handle and quickly wheeled it outside into the oppressive Houston air. Muggy. She'd lived here almost all her life but now she couldn't wait to get to Santa Fe's crisp desert atmosphere.

What was wrong with her? She was jumping at shadows.

She took a cab home, watching the familiar landmarks pass by as she neared her apartment: the stop sign with the smiley face in its center; the little strip mall that boasted Michelangelo's Antiques and Magoo's Sunglasses; the pothole in the center of the road just outside the entryway to the complex.

As soon as the cabbie pulled up, she felt her heart constrict. Searching her feelings, she acknowledged her fear of facing what the intruder had done. And her fears for Rawley—and herself.

"Thanks," she said, tipping well as she paid the fare. Pulling her bag to the wrought iron gate of the courtyard, she headed up the outdoor staircase, lugging it to the upstairs landing.

A shiny new doorknob gleamed against a freshly painted blue door. Of course the manager had replaced the door, but it simply hadn't occurred to her until this moment She went in search of him and the new key. Whoever it was could just come back and steal her clothes. She'd be damned if she'd haul that bag down the stairs again.

Luckily, Diego, the manager, was home and had the key ready. He shook his head and murmured how terrible it was for her to be burglarized, a sentiment Jenny fully agreed with. "You want me to check it out with you?" he asked. "I was with the police, you know. Nothing was harmed while I was there."

"I'm fine. Thanks. I appreciate it, and I'm sorry for all the trouble."

"No problem." He waved her away. "You need anything, you come over here."

"Thanks, Diego."

Back at the door, she inserted the key and smoothly turned the lock. The tumblers clicked over and she pushed the door inward, holding her breath as she flipped on the lights.

Jenny tentatively stepped inside and locked the door behind her, feeling instantly lonely. Without her son around, the place seemed desolate . . . and much too quiet. She wheeled her bag down the hall and shot a look toward Rawley's room. The door was closed and she pushed it open.

She smiled. Same utter mess. Feeling better, she examined every square inch of the apartment and ended up in her bedroom. She shucked off her clothes and stepped into her second shower of the day and let the water run over her. She didn't want to think about anything. Not Rawley, not Troy, not Hunter.

Fifteen minutes later she poured herself a cup of freshly brewed coffee and sorted through the mail that Janice had left on the counter. She glanced toward the phone where a triple-fold picture frame held pictures of Rawley when he was a baby, an elementary school kid in soccer gear, and his freshman photo where he stared at the camera with the harsh intensity of a criminal getting a mug shot.

A frisson slid down her back and she glanced around as

if someone had come into the room without her knowing it. She quickly picked up the receiver to phone Janice, who answered on the first ring.

"I'm going to the soccer camp today," Jenny said without preamble. "I've got to pick up Rawley."

"You're back?" Janice asked, alarmed.

"I'm worried. I can't help it."

"Well, don't run over there. Phone first . . . Oh, Jenny, I'm sorry I called you."

"No, don't worry about it," she assured her friend. "Really. I was so ready to come home anyway. I'm glad you called."

"Oh, I know I'm going to be in trouble," she murmured. "They gave us that number for the camp. Let me see . . ."

"I've probably got it here."

"No, it's a different one. More direct. Hang on." Jenny waited while Janice dropped the receiver and went in search of the number. It seemed to take forever. Finally she came on the line with the information. "They're done tomorrow. They're fine," Janice added.

"I know. Thanks." Jenny rang off. Instantly she phoned the camp, then suffered through several people who knew absolutely nothing before she finally got someone in charge. They tried to get her off the phone by promising to have Rawley call her, but Jenny stubbornly refused and eventually someone went in search of him.

"Mom?" Rawley's voice sounded cautious. "What's wrong?"

"Nothing. Now," she said with relief. She had so many things to say and couldn't think of one of them. "I just got back early and I wanted to talk to you."

"Well, okay, but I'm missing the game," he said.

"Go back to it. I'll see you tomorrow."

"Yeah . . . okay," he murmured vaguely, lost in his own interests.

She hung up, so spent she had to sit down. Sinking onto the couch, she held her head in her hands. Her heart beat as if she'd just run a marathon. Parenthood. It made you so vulnerable and children were so unaware!

The phone rang and she jumped to answer it. "Hello?" she said, hearing the lilt in her voice at the thought that it might be Hunter. How silly! She knew better.

There was no response. She listened. The line sounded open, but there wasn't even the sound of anyone's breathing. *Troy.* His name formed on her lips but died, unspoken. She had an eerie feeling about the call. Something like she'd felt at the airport. Slowly replacing the receiver, she stared at it until her eyes felt dry and teary.

She wished Hunter would call.

She knew he wouldn't.

The plane screeched onto the tarmac, bumped hard and blasted forward as if they were launching into space. Not the smoothest of landings, Hunter thought. The woman next to him clutched her throat and made choked sounds of fear, but he simply gripped the arms of his seat and tried not to mind too much that Jenny had walked out on him.

If it weren't so damned infuriating it might be funny. If it weren't so inconvenient, he might sneak away, tail between his legs and forget all about it. Normally he didn't care so much. *Normally,* he stayed away from females who were no good for him.

But there was nothing normal about Hunter's ongoing interaction with Jenny Holloway. Now, he had to chase her down and take the snub as if he were a lovesick kid, unable to leave her alone. And why? Because he'd told Allen Holloway he would protect her!

He slammed the armrest with his fist, which caused another chirp of fear from his companion. "Bad flight," he muttered, but she just looked at him through huge eyes. She was the worst kind of white-knuckled flyer and his dark thoughts and grim attitude hadn't helped the situation. He wondered if she would blink if he ran his hand in front of her face a couple of times. She looked catatonic. Except for the mews of terror slipping from her lips, she seemed frozen in place.

He was glad to finally get out of the plane, and he practically shoved his way through the meandering throngs outside. Humidity enveloped him. He breathed deeply anyway, feeling suffocated and irritable, as if every nerve ending were aflame. Hard to believe that, in the very recent past, he'd suffered from depression and boredom so intense that he'd sometimes wondered if life were truly worth living. Hah! Those days were gone. For a moment he felt a pang of nostalgia. Numbness was better than rawness.

"Oh, hell," he muttered. No, it wasn't. But this was torture and he wondered why in God's name it mattered so much.

He'd broken a cardinal rule: he'd gotten involved with someone outside his social class, someone rich.

And now he had to go find her, come up with some lame excuse about why he was in town, and then protect her from that homicidal ex-husband of hers.

Hunter squeezed his fingers into his palms. Sobering thoughts. He wondered if he should find Jenny first, or go check on her son Rawley. Jenny was pure trouble. Rawley would be a piece of cake by comparison.

"Damn it all to hell," he muttered, heading for his Jeep.

Puerto Vallarta was only hours away, but it was already a long, long time ago.

Sex made a man hungry, Troy thought with satisfaction as he cut into his prime rib. Red juice pooled from its rare center. Red. Like Blondie's blouse.

Her name was Dana and she invited him to her teensy little house in one of Houston's less fashionable neighborhoods. Good old Dana had been around the block a few times, and she wasn't surprised by anything a man might want to do to a woman. The nastier the better. Hell, she thrived on it!

It had been a rollicking good time for a lot of hours, but by the time Saturday night rolled around Troy was pretty sick of her. Her place was a sty: dirty dishes in the sink, wrinkled sheets that smelled of sex.

Suddenly he'd wanted to get away from her. She stank of cheap perfume. He couldn't understand what he'd seen in her in the first place. He was mildly surprised to realize she didn't look like Jenny at all. She was bleached and squat and spewed filthy words in his ear during sex. He felt physically revolted when she drew a thick line of red lipstick on her mouth, then squatted down to suck on him. Watching those red lips as if from a long, long distance away, he suddenly grabbed her by the hair and yanked her away from him, throwing her across the bed. She looked at him in surprise, those red lips a big "O." He'd slapped her hard enough to raise a welt on her face.

After that he'd taken her one final time, pushing her ugly red-smeared face into the covers and climbing on behind her. She thrashed and cried for air. Troy held her face down and she bucked beneath him. *Then* the sex had been good. Yes, indeedy. And when he'd left she'd been sitting up and coughing, head hanging, sobbing a little.

He'd almost gone back for one more bout. God, he loved being in control. But she was just too dirty.

"Coffee?" the waitress asked, breaking into his thoughts.

Troy chewed on a piece of beef, sucking the juice from it. "No, thanks." He watched her walk away. Women were everywhere. They just wanted a man to reach out and grab them.

But Troy wasn't interested. Not tonight. He wanted something better and that something was Jenny. He hadn't realized how much he lusted for her until he saw her again. That lovely, luscious body wrapped around a cold, virginal core. And she came with money! More money than stupid bipolar Frederica, drab Patricia, slutty Val, and that dopey, doe-eyed Michelle Calgary combined.

And she'd had his son.

"Rawley," he said aloud, softly. Maybe he should have whispered the boy's name when he'd called her this afternoon. Hearing her voice had sent a shiver down his spine and a jolt of desire through his veins. Even her frigidity was a turn-on. He'd almost gone straight over there but common sense had prevailed.

Charm was the order of the day. Jenny's charming exusband had come back to make amends, and that's what he was going to get, by God.

When the waitress slipped by, he caught her by the hand, surprising her. "I've changed my mind about the coffee." She threw him a bright smile and Troy chuckled to himself. From a pocket of his jacket he pulled out the game schedule for the Three Winds Soccer Camp he'd found in Rawley's drawer. Saturday night. Final playoffs for the Three Winds World Cup.

He dropped a tip on the table and winked at his waitress, who was taking another table's order. Then he walked out without paying the bill.

Benny's scratching at the door wakened Jenny. She'd fallen asleep on the couch, testimony to her lack of sleep the night before. Exhausted, she opened the door, squawking a bit as the mutt wriggled by her and made for Rawley's bedroom.

"He's not there," she said. "He's still at soccer camp."

Benny came back and laid his head on Jenny's lap. Touched, she scratched his ears, then gently probed his side for the injured ribs. The dog whimpered a bit and shifted away, but his eyes were trusting as they gazed into Jenny's.

"Who was it?" she asked him. "Troy?"

He woofed at her. Lightly. And it sounded so much like an answer that Jenny drew in a quick breath and glanced around the room.

What was Troy's plan? Did he want Rawley? He didn't want her, she knew that. Although that should have made her feel better, she knew she wouldn't rest until Troy showed himself and made his demands clear. For demands there would be. Troy always wanted something.

It struck her how much she knew about him and how clearly she understood his character. Why couldn't she have been so aware when she was young? Why had she felt the need to fight her father and make such awful choices?

But you have Rawley.

"Yes," she answered herself, hugging Benny's silky head close. "Rawley."

The two boys collapsed at the side of the field, sweltering in the heat, heaving with rasped breaths, furious beyond reason. One was blond, one was dark-haired and glowed with the promise of movie star good looks.

"Damn that Berger!" the first one shouted, glaring at the hapless goalie who'd been unable to block the shot.

Berger hung his head. The second boy also gave him a dirty look. He didn't care as much as Brandon did, but he knew better than to go against the tide. There were a lot of players in front of the goalie who could have fought off the opposing team, he and Brandon being two of them. But the goalie always got blamed.

"Now we're out of the finals," Brandon fumed.

Rawley lay spread-eagled on the grass. He just wasn't going to get worked up about the loss like his fiery buddy Brandon Ferguson was. It was over. The camp was nearly over and he was leaving.

He stared up at the glaring lights illuminating the soccer field, momentarily blinded by their brilliance. Above them a few faint stars appeared in the dark blue sky. He clenched his hands. He felt restless, anxious and scared. Scared to leave. He wanted this moment to last forever. He wanted boyhood to never end. He wanted to cry, but he knew that might be the bitter end of his continuing friendship with Brandon.

He wondered sometimes if he cared . . .

"Berger's an asshole," Brandon muttered.

Rawley didn't answer. He thought of Brandon's father, Rick, and let his mind wander down its favorite path. Dreaming, he pretended Rick was his father. Rick would be coming with his mother tomorrow to pick him up. They wouldn't have to be married now. That would be okay. Rick could stay with Janice. She was okay, too. But they would come together as *his* parents and he would have both of them. It was a heartwarming fantasy that put a slight smile on his lips.

"Who's that?" Brandon asked.

"Who?" Rawley didn't even look.

"That man. He's waving at us."

"Maybe he's waving at Berger. Probably ready to scream at him, too," Rawley said with wry humor.

"Uh-uh . . ."

Rawley lifted his head and watched the man approach. He walked with a confident stride, almost a swagger. Sitting up, Rawley waited, examining the newcomer with all the suspicion of any fifteen-year-old faced with an unknown authority figure.

The newcomer stopped directly in front of him, his body silhouetted by the glaring lights.

"Rawley Russell?"

"Yeah?" he responded with just a hint of rebellion. Something skittered down his spine. A premonition. He didn't speak up and tell him his last name was Holloway.

The man reached out and clasped his hand, offering him a smile. "Just wanted to make sure you were all right."

Rawley stared at him while Brandon frowned at the both of them. A long silence ensued while the three of them sized each other up. It was Brandon who broke the moment and demanded, "Who the fuck are you?"

❈ CHAPTER NINE ❈

In the end she decided to go to Riccardo's. Her apartment seemed to have survived the violation of the break-in. She realized some petty cash she'd kept in a kitchen desk drawer was missing, but that was about it. It almost made her feel better, like the burglary was committed by a penny-ante thief. Still, thoughts of Troy couldn't be completely dismissed and she kept thinking about the sound of her son's voice, running it through her mind over and over again as an assurance that everything was all right.

Twice she picked up the phone to call her father. She was desperate to know if Troy had contacted him again. Twice she replaced the receiver, unwilling to open that particular can of worms. No. She would wait. Rawley would be home tomorrow and they would be out of here in a matter of days. She called Gloria and only half-listened to the headstrong chef's list of complaints. After she ended the call she pulled out some boxes, intending to start packing. But she simply couldn't focus, so she decided to go to the restaurant and say good-bye to her friends.

Riccardo's was just as she'd left it: bustling, fragrant with spices and cooking, packed with customers, and under

Alberto's iron-fisted control. He was lambasting one of the junior chefs when she walked in and he stopped in mid-yell.

"*Bella!*" he cried, embracing her warmly.

"Hello, there, Alberto. I see nothing's changed since I left."

"Nothing's changed? Nothing's changed?" He clucked his tongue and stood back to look at her. "You've got a nice color to your cheeks."

"I'm tan," she admitted. "From hours of lazing around in the sun and drinking margaritas."

He tsk-tsked, waving his finger at her. "Naughty girl." But she could tell he was pleased that she'd relaxed. "And what about a fella? Did you meet a nice one, eh?"

That stopped her. Sensing that the other chefs and the waiters had slowed their work to listen, she said, "Everyone's nice in Puerto Vallarta."

"Oh, sure, sure."

"Seriously, Alberto, how's the new bookkeeper?"

He flapped his hands at her. "He comes. He leaves. He complains. I let him go."

"Alberto!"

His brown eyes grew pleading. "Please, will you fix things?"

"I can't. You've got to get someone. I'm leaving as soon as I can!"

"You won't stay?"

"No!" she declared with a smile. "You know I've got my restaurant in Santa Fe. It's practically up and running. And you know you can't leave a restaurant in someone else's hands. Gloria only wants to cook and she's tearing her hair out over all the decisions." She brought him up to date on her conversation with her chef. "So, I'm leaving by the end of the week," she added with sudden determination. "I'm not waiting a minute more."

"Okay." He couldn't have looked more chagrined. "I have called the agency and they are sending someone else. Today." He pursed his lips. "Probably looks like a horse with the brains of a fish."

"Some people think fish are smart. Fishermen who can't catch them."

He sniffed. "All right, go. Go!" He hugged her again.

She relented. "I'll look over last week's entries and see how you're doing. But this is my last night."

His face brightened as if someone had turned on a light. "*Grazie*. Thank you."

Jenny just shook her head. Carolyn breezed into the kitchen and cried with delight upon seeing Jenny. "How was Puerto Vallarta?" she asked.

The thought of Hunter's hard-muscled arms holding her close nearly left her speechless. "Don't ask," she said, infuriated to feel a blush burn her face.

"That good, huh?"

Jenny snorted, tried to lie, then gave up. "Yep."

Carolyn clapped her hands together and grinned like a devil. "Well, it's about time!"

In her tiny bookkeeping room, Jenny tried to hold back a tremulous smile. It wasn't smart to cherish the memories of her brief time with Hunter. Not smart at all. But she couldn't help herself.

Maybe he'll find you.

She told herself silently to get over it, and worked diligently, depressed by how screwed the books had gotten in the space of a single week. Whoever Alberto had hired had not been up to the job. She hoped the next person was more capable.

Finally, carrying the books with her, she headed for the door. Homework, she mouthed to Carolyn as she turned toward the back door.

"Did that guy ever contact you in Puerto Vallarta? Or was he the one you met?" Carolyn teased with a growing smile.

"What guy?"

"Dark hair, blue eyes. He asked about you and I wasn't sure how much to tell. But I did mention you were on vacation there with friends." She hesitated. "Did I do wrong?"

"No. No . . . he didn't contact me." Carolyn could have been describing Hunter, but then she could have described a lot of men, including her ex-husband. She warned herself not to make too much of this. "Did he say he would?"

"He was looking for you," she said. "I told him you were moving."

"Did you tell him where?"

"Jenny, you're scaring me!"

"No, I'm just wondering." Her heart was beating rather fast. "Just in case he looks me up. I take it he didn't leave a name."

"Umm, yeah. His name was . . . Bill . . . something." Carolyn shook her head, glancing toward the main dining room. "It'll come to me. I've got to get some orders."

"Do it." Jenny waved her away, then pulled on the handle of the back door. She took one step, nearly ran into a solid wall of man, then cried out in surprise. Hunter Calgary stood directly in front of her.

"My God!" she whispered, shaken.

"Hi," he greeted her.

"Hi." She looked back, but Carolyn had disappeared into the main room.

"For someone who hired a bodyguard, you sure took off without giving a lot of notice."

Jenny wanted to throw herself into his arms. She hadn't known how much she cared about him until this moment. She was thrilled to see him. Absolutely thrilled! "You still want the job?" she asked in a small voice.

"I still want the job."

She tried to ignore the way Hunter looked. The soft leather of the black bomber jacket he wore; the long, jeans-clad legs; the boots; the denim shirt, open at the throat. He radiated a powerful sexuality she remembered only too well.

"How did you know where to find me?"

"An educated guess." He shrugged. "You said you worked for Riccardo's."

"I'm—so glad you came."

It was her way of apologizing. She wanted to say so much more, but she didn't quite know how. His forgiveness came in a slow smile that started her heart beating in a slow rhythm.

"What made you decide on the back door?" she asked as he walked with her to her car. But then, beside a black Jeep which was much like the one he'd rented in Mexico, there was only one other car—her blue Volvo.

He shrugged. "Seemed like the regulars came through this way. Thought if I came in this way I'd catch you."

"You were right," she said lightly.

They stood awkwardly in the parking lot. She watched the play of the street light on the planes of his face, aware in the growing darkness how seductively sinister he appeared. His handsomeness was evident, but his raw masculinity and sternness overshadowed it. She wondered why she'd never noticed before, and why it didn't bother her more.

"Could we go somewhere?" he suggested.

Should she take him to her place? Should she invite him inside? She wouldn't be picking up Rawley until tomorrow.

"I don't live too far from here . . ."

"I'll follow you."

Jenny told herself she should pay attention to her misgivings as she led the way to her apartment, but all she could think about were flashing images of toned muscles, smooth flesh, hard fingers, urgent lips. She was a basket case in the worst way. She was glad he'd come after her. If he hadn't, she would have gone crazy with remorse.

She watched him remote lock the Jeep, listened to its *chirp-chirp*, then pretended to be concentrating on something else as he moved toward her. She was nervous as a teenager facing her first kiss. She'd been thirteen when that occurred, her lips pressed against Danny Durant's braces until she'd thought they would leave indelible impressions. Nothing much to tell after that. No rampant adolescent desires and fumbling touches. She'd practically run from the scene of the crime, glad she didn't have to do that again anytime soon. But what stayed with her, what she remembered most was her nervousness, nearly the worst she'd ever experienced. Well, it was back.

"It's not too far from here," she told him as she climbed into her car. He nodded, and she turned over the engine, carefully pulling into the street and making sure his headlights stayed right behind her. He parked on the street, met her near the courtyard and they walked inside together.

God. She had to rack her brain to think of anything to say to him. She glanced upward, to her door. "Benny's here," she said with relief.

Hunter followed her gaze. "The dog."

"Yeah."

Jenny hurried ahead to the door. Benny gave Hunter a searching look, growled softly, warningly, then sauntered after Jenny to the interior of the apartment. Hunter followed him inside and Benny stationed himself next to Jenny.

"You've already got a protector," Hunter observed. "A pretty good one, by the looks of it."

"Something happened to him." She massaged Benny's ears until the dog broke into a panting smile. "It makes me furious when I think about it."

Hunter gazed at the dog. "Was anything disturbed?"

"Not that I can tell."

"Mind if I look around?"

She was embarrassed by the way she'd acted this morning. She nodded an invitation. "Be my guest. This is pretty much what it looked like before I left for Mexico."

Hunter prowled down the hallway. Benny couldn't take it. He scurried after him, staying a few feet back, but watching Hunter's every move. The dog wasn't exactly threatening, but he wasn't relaxed. Jenny briskly rubbed her bare arms with her opposite hands, hugging herself a bit. Maybe her nervousness was catching. Or maybe Benny was just being cautious after his encounter with the burglar.

She heard Hunter enter her bedroom, but the thought of him inside her room was more than she could bear. She sprang into action, hurrying to the kitchen to do something—anything. She thought about making a pot of coffee, gave that idea up in favor of something stronger and pulled out a jug of chilled white wine from the refrigerator.

She was just unscrewing the metal cap when he returned. "Not exactly vintage stuff," she said. "But it's what I drink when I'm not south of the border."

He smiled faintly. "I thought you were an heiress."

She snorted and poured them each a glass. "If my father saw me drinking jug wine, he'd have a coronary."

"That's why you drink it."

"I drink it because I like it, and because it's all I could afford for years. I'll keep liking it, because I never want to forget who I really am."

He gazed at her silently.

"*Jenny* Holloway," she said firmly. "Not Geneva Holloway Russell."

He accepted the glass she poured him, sipping it casually, his gaze never leaving her face. "You're both," he pronounced. "And I like the wine, too."

That was enough to send Jenny's nerves into overdrive once again. She sipped and sipped and fought a strange, urgent desire to scream. She wanted him to grab her and press her up against the counter and make love to her in the kitchen. She wanted to feel his possession. She wanted to *live*.

"So, what did you learn in your search?" she asked after a long, tense moment.

"You're tidy. Your son isn't."

Jenny giggled. "That's an understatement!"

"This him?" Hunter inclined his head toward the photo on Jenny's kitchen desk. Jenny nodded. "He looks like you."

"He looks like his father. The eyes are mine, though. And his sense of humor."

"He still at that soccer camp?"

"Until tomorrow."

Benny snuffled against Jenny's hand and she swept her palm over his silken head. Hunter leaned against the kitchen archway, surveying them both. The clock ticked loudly. Feeling breathless, Jenny finally blurted out, "I had to leave. I just couldn't stay any longer."

He gazed at her for a moment. "I didn't like waking to the sounds of you leaving."

Jenny set down her glass. Her hands were trembling. She crossed her arms to hide them. "I know."

"It's all right."

She couldn't read him. Was he saying he didn't want to be involved with her—or that he did? And what did she want anyway?

"I took a chance that the bodyguard job was still open."

"It is. Yes." She nodded jerkily.

Watching her, he added, "You can let me know if there's anything else you want."

"I'm sorry I panicked. It was more over Rawley than you. I got here and I called him and talked to him and I felt better. I probably could have done that from Puerto Val-

arta, but . . ." She shrugged. "I kind of thought I was get-
ing in over my head."

"I thought you left because of what I told you."

"Not totally. I mean, that was part of it. Oh, I don't know
. ." She gazed at him helplessly. "I really am glad you're
ere."

The moment stretched between them. Jenny didn't
other hiding her feelings any longer. She wanted him and
er longing showed in her eyes. She was hungry for his
rms and his touch.

Hunter couldn't miss the message. Deliberately, he set
own his own glass and crossed the space between them.
ust as deliberately he lifted her chin with his finger, and
with sensual deliberation his lips descended to hers, stop-
ing a whisper away. "Let's just see where this goes," he
uggested and it was all Jenny could do to keep from
noaning with desire before his mouth finally possessed
ers.

Her knees weakened. She felt the counter's edge press
nto her hips, felt his hardened manhood against her softer
lesh, felt a wave of pure desire sing through her veins, so
hat her hands were both clutching him and tearing at his
:lothes at the same time.

"I want you," she admitted. "I'm sorry I left."

"Shhh . . ."

He sighed against her neck, a soft, almost erotic sound
hat sent a whoosh of air from her lungs. His hands slid
own her back, cradling her close. He was waiting for her
o make the decision, she realized, and it was a heady sensation. Her hands slid along his belt to the buckle and
slowly undid the clasp. He shifted to accommodate her

exploration, but only after his mouth had found hers again, his tongue moving tenderly inside.

Benny whined and Jenny tried to shoo him away. She wanted Hunter and she wanted him *now*. Stroking the length of his shaft, she marveled at the wanton thoughts that beset her. A tiny voice she didn't believe was hers begged him. "Please," she whispered. "Please . . . now . . ."

"God," he muttered, his hands urgently slipping under her blouse, fumbling with her bra, finally pulling it away from her breasts. His thumb rubbed her nipple, hard. She clung to him with one hand, caressing him with the other.

That was it. Hunter clasped her close, lowered her to the floor, his weight fitting against her, his own body thrusting. Benny had moved to safer ground, pacing near the kitchen archway door, concerned but a bit flummoxed. "Get out," Hunter almost snarled, to which Jenny giggled. The dog slipped down the hall to Rawley's room.

The kitchen floor uncomfortably hard beneath her hips and shoulder blades. Hunter, realizing that, lifted himself on his forearms, which only intensified the pressure of his hips against hers.

"Maybe we should—" he began, but Jenny shut him up with a hot kiss and tugged his jeans partway down.

He broke the kiss with a gasp and shucked the rest of his clothes. Then he bent his head to her bare breasts, suckling one nipple, then the other. Jenny squirmed beneath him. His fingers hooked into her pants and dragged them over her hips. He slipped one finger inside her, and thrust gently, erotically, making her slick with desire. Losing herself in the sensation, she closed her eyes and grabbed his hand, helping him arouse her beyond all reason. She arched, wanting more, all of him, and Hunter thrust himself deep inside her, again and again, until she cried out. They climaxed together, shaken by the intensity of the feeling.

No, don't move," Jenny whispered, as she pulled herself away from Hunter's embrace, pleased by his murmured protests. "I'm just getting a glass of water."

She left him lying in her bed, looking back once to savor the sight of him, gloriously naked on her rumpled sheets. Padding to the kitchen, she poured herself a glass of water and gulped it down—man, sex made her thirsty!—when she heard the dog scratching at the front door.

"Go home," she said through the panels to Benny. She grinned in the semi-darkness. They'd gotten him outside after their initial lovemaking.

Benny whined a little and Jenny shook her head and returned to the bedroom. She sank onto the mattress, then was engulfed in a full leg and arm embrace. Pressing her face to his hair-dusted chest, she fought back another smile. She was grinning like an idiot, too happy for words. She fell asleep thinking, *This is the most perfect moment of my life.*

Later, she would remember that thought and question her own sanity.

She was up at dawn, whistling softly and planning breakfast. It was so incredibly domestic that she smiled at herself. Hunter was in the shower and she listened to the running water as if it were the music of a symphony.

The ringing phone jarred her. Snatching up the receiver, she said, "Hello," without her usual trepidation. In truth, she didn't even think about who might be on the other end of the line. All she could hear was Hunter. He took her sole attention.

"Geneva?"

It was Allen. Her dear old dad. She sighed. "Hello."

"You're back." He was surprised. "I intended to leave a message on your phone. I didn't mean to wake you."

"I was awake."

"You're picking up Rawley from that soccer camp today?"

He was remarkably informed on her life, but then she'd told him her schedule and her father never forgot anything. "Yes."

"I'd like you to bring him over to the house. I just want to assure myself that you and he are all right."

"I can't today. I'm—busy. No, you'll have to—" Her attention returned with a bang. "Has Troy called again?"

He hesitated before saying flatly, "No."

Jenny glanced at the clock. "Why don't we make a date later this week? I'm going to be packing and I need to get some things done." She didn't want to see her father, period.

"Geneva, I want you and Rawley to stay with Natalie and me for a while. It's safe here. Postpone that trip to Santa Fe until we know what Troy wants."

"What?" She half laughed. "I'm moving! I'm not staying with you and Natalie. If you want to see Rawley, I'll set it up. But I'm staying at the apartment until then and I'll be safe."

"How do you know?"

"Because I have someone to protect me now."

She supposed she shouldn't have said it, but as soon as the words were out she was glad. Let him think of it what he would.

"Who?"

"A bodyguard."

"You hired one?"

"I met him in Mexico. He's worked in law enforcement, and he's come back with me to Houston."

"You brought him back with you?" Her father's voice had grown quieter and quieter.

She could just imagine what he was thinking! "Don't panic. Trust me on this one, please. I can make some choices."

"What's his name?"

Jenny pulled the receiver from her ear and made a face at it, annoyed by her father's nosiness. "Hunter Calgary," she stated firmly, as if it would make any difference to Allen.

Silence followed this remark. "You've hired this man as your bodyguard," he repeated, as if he couldn't believe her words.

"He's . . . yes . . . I have."

"He's what?"

"Never mind. I'm happy with the situation, and you don't have to worry about me anymore."

"Are you *dating* this man, Geneva?"

She gripped the receiver harder, closed her eyes and counted to five before Allen exploded with, "I can't believe this. You met a stranger in Mexico and you brought him home. Your gullibility shocks me! Didn't you learn anything from your experience with Troy?"

"Good-bye, Allen," she said.

"I want you and Rawley to stop by, without this guy."

"Don't push me."

"Today, Geneva!"

"Not today. Not—"

"Tomorrow, then."

She drew a breath. "Call me. We'll have lunch."

"Don't be flip. Troy is still out there, wanting something."

Jenny gritted her teeth. "Wednesday night. Dinner. At one of your restaurants."

"They're your restaurants too, but no, I want you to come to the house. Natalie will take care of dinner."

By calling a caterer, Jenny thought, but she knew better than to say it. What difference did it make now?

"Six o'clock Wednesday. And don't bring your new bodyguard."

He practically snarled the last word, and Jenny simmered with all the rebellion of her youth.

She hung up the phone just as the shower ceased. She couldn't wait to get to Santa Fe.

Hunter stepped into the hallway, a towel slung over his lean hips, traces of water still shining in his chest hair. "What?" he asked, reading the expression on her face.

"I'm going to need a bodyguard all the way to Santa Fe," she said.

"I planned on it."

"That's right, you live there." She shook her head in bemusement. How strange the fates were. They were going to be living in the same town!" Maybe we should talk money. I mean, I don't know what you charge . . . but . . ."

He flinched. "We'll talk about it later."

"Hunter . . ."

"Jenny, I don't want to talk about money right now."

"Okay."

"I just want to think about something else," he explained with a sigh.

"Breakfast?" she asked.

"Not yet."

"What, then?"

He stared at her for a long moment. Jenny's gaze moved to his bare chest and she wondered if she were losing her mind. All she could think about was one thing.

He lifted one brow. A slow smile crossed Jenny's lips.

"Again?" he asked in rich amusement.

Reaching for the edge of his towel, she gently began to pull.

I'm heading out to pick up Rawley," Jenny said into the receiver. "Tell Rick thanks. Maybe I'll see him there." She listened a moment to Janice's distracted answers. The twins were stealing her attention once more. "No, really. I appreciate it all. And if you can steal away for a few minutes to say goodbye and have a glass of wine together, just let me know. 'Bye."

Glancing at the hearty breakfast on the stove top, she hurriedly scooped the flour tortilla from its pan, filled it with eggs, chorizo sausage, mild chili peppers, wrapped it up and dribbled salsa across its top. Hunter, who'd been nursing a cup of coffee, watched her deft movements with a smile. "And she cooks, too . . ."

"Don't let this fool you. I've got about three dishes in my repertoire. I understand the financial side of the restaurant business. But I do know how to boil water."

"And she's modest."

She smiled up at him, blowing her bangs out of her face. Quickly she put the other breakfast burrito together and served them at the tiny two-person table against the wall. Hunter sat down across from her, wondering when he'd last shared a home-cooked breakfast with a woman.

"Everything's got that southwestern flavor," she said.

"Fine by me."

"You're easy to please."

He gave her a long look. "Sometimes." Jenny grinned at him and he marveled that he'd found a way back to her. Still, there were tricky issues ahead. He wasn't sure how to handle them.

"I'm picking up Rawley around four. Gotta get this work done and drop it by the restaurant first."

"I've got some things to take care of, too," Hunter said by way of an answer.

"Why don't we meet later? Come in for lunch. I'll make sure Alberto gives us a free going-away meal."

Hunter nodded distractedly, wishing he didn't have to tell her the truth. But there was no way around it.

Feeling her eyes on him, he sent her a smile. "Lunch it is," he said.

"I talked to my father," she admitted, cutting into her burrito with the edge of her fork. "I told him I had a bodyguard."

Hunter froze.

"He was glad."

"Was he . . ."

"But he guessed that we were involved." She made a

face. "I had to practically hang up on him. He wants to see Rawley and me before we leave, but I just dread it. Would you go with us? Wednesday night? He specifically asked for us to come alone, but don't let that scare you. I don't listen to him. I can't! He makes me crazy." She gave a mock shudder.

Hunter swallowed a piece of the burrito with an effort and nodded.

"May I ask you a question?"

He wondered if this was what facing a firing squad was like. "Shoot."

"You don't talk about your family. Your parents, your sister . . ."

"They're—dead."

Jenny's eyes widened. "All of them?"

He knew she was really asking about Michelle. He deliberated a moment, then decided she'd opened the door herself. "Michelle's death was classified as a suicide, but it was something else."

"Hunter . . ." Jenny breathed.

"She was pushed off a roof by a desperate boyfriend. She was pregnant. I followed him and, yes, harassed him. He filed a suit and that's how I lost my job with the L.A.P.D."

"Oh, Hunter."

"It's ugly, but it's the truth." He shot her a wary look. "Sorry. I know you didn't want any more truths."

"I didn't mean that. I just couldn't—process very well yesterday."

"How are you doing now?"

"Better." She studied him sympathetically. "I'm sorry about Michelle and your parents."

"They died before Michelle, one of complications from pneumonia, one of cirrhosis of the liver, both from leading hard lives."

She gazed at him with such empathy that it got to him. He didn't want to talk about any of this. Thinking of Michelle just brought back his churning anger and loathing for Troy Russell.

"Jenny, I—"

She cut him off by jumping from her chair and hugging him close, kissing him tenderly. Suddenly he felt like he couldn't breathe. It hit him like a sledgehammer.

Dragging a breath into his lungs, he said in an unsteady voice. "I'll meet you at Riccardo's."

He left as quickly as he could. The wall keeping his emotions in check was on the verge of collapse.

No, he's coming to meet me here," she told Carolyn.

"The guy from Puerto Vallarta."

"Yes. And Alberto's in a dither, trying to figure out what special thing he can concoct for the 'lovebirds.' "

Carolyn giggled. "Oooh, I love it. After all this time, you find this fantastic man. And he wasn't even the one who was looking for you. Oh, I remembered his name. Mike Conrad. Really handsome."

Jenny shrugged her shoulders. "I don't know the name."

"Well, you've got a guy now, so it doesn't matter. You'll be wanting table seven, I'm sure."

Table seven was in a protected alcove and was reserved for intimate couples. It was said that a waiter had once caught a romantic duo in the throes of ecstasy. The lovers had apparently simply lost their heads over Alberto's fabulous dishes and expensive wines and just felt like making love on the spot. Jenny doubted the validity of the tale, but she could appreciate the sentiment, especially after her blissful nights with Hunter.

"I've never sat at table seven," she said and Carolyn gave her a swift hug.

She thought over Hunter's revelations as she waited for him, sipping sparkling water, as she still had a fifteen-year-old son to pick up. She recognized how hard it was for Hunter to tell her anything about his family, especially Michelle. What a terrible story. She hadn't known how to ask any more questions and besides, it hadn't been the time. Hunter was obviously the strong and silent type, so she considered it a monumental step in building their relationship that he'd managed so much.

She couldn't believe how unfair she'd been to him to run away from him in Puerto Vallarta. It was a wonder he trusted her at all now.

When he walked in, Carolyn was right behind him, her face filled with an expression Jenny couldn't read. Hunter strode to the table and Jenny's heart fluttered. He *was* handsome.

"I thought I was over handsome men," Jenny told him teasingly. "I thought Troy had cured me of that forever, but I was wrong."

Hunter half-smiled.

She wondered if she were falling in love with him. She certainly felt giddy enough right now.

Carolyn hovered by the table. "Jenny, could I see you a moment?"

"Now?"

"There are a few things Alberto hasn't quite figured out. Maybe if you talked to him."

"Maybe I could check into it after lunch."

"I think it would be better now," Carolyn insisted.

Jenny shrugged, momentarily baffled by her friend's strange behavior. "Well, okay . . ."

Carolyn practically pulled her out of the chair and marched her to the kitchen. "He's the guy," she whispered fiercely. "The guy at table fourteen that night. The one that was watching you."

"What guy?"

"The one you're with!"

"Wait a minute." Jenny held up her hands. "You said that the man who asked about me came in here while I was in Puerto Vallarta and that his name was—"

"—Mike Conrad. No. That was a different guy. *This one.*" She pointed in the direction of the dining room. "The one you're with—he's the one who was watching you!"

Jenny gazed at her in confusion.

"Jenny, you say you met him in Puerto Vallarta?" At her slow nod, Carolyn rushed on, "Then he knew who you were. My God, it looks as if he followed you there! He must have been looking for you."

"No, Carolyn!"

"I don't know what he wants, Jenny, but be careful. Please believe me." Her tone was increasingly urgent. "That gorgeous guy out there was watching you like a hawk long before you left for Puerto Vallarta. Jenny, listen to me. *He's the guy!*"

CHAPTER TEN

J enny drew a breath and glanced around. Her hands felt like ice.

"He's never mentioned it? Not once?" Carolyn asked. Jenny shook her head and Carolyn went on, "Then something's screwy. He knew who you were."

"Then . . . then . . . he saw Rawley, too, that night." Fear bubbled inside her.

"He was looking at *you*. Jenny, I think he's been following you!"

That resonated deep inside her. She'd been worried about Troy, but now there was trouble from another angle. Who was Hunter Calgary? What did she really know about him? She couldn't think!

"What are you going to do?" Carolyn whispered, glancing nervously around.

"I don't know."

"Don't go back there!" she urged. "Just go out the back door."

"No." Carolyn's anxiety was infecting her, but Jenny hung onto her control. "He's been nothing but wonderful to me. I'm going to go back there and ask him about it. Just ask him."

Carolyn moaned. "Oh, Jenny . . ."

"Go fulfill your orders," Jenny urged, her sense of responsibility taking over yet again. "I'll handle this."

And with that she headed back to the intimate little table, hesitating as she approached the man she loved and knew so little about.

. . .

She hit him with it hard. One flat question. Hunter had to admire her.

"Have you been following me?" she demanded, tense as strung wire.

He could have lied. He could have said a thousand things. But he could tell her friend had given her the information already. Kicking himself for not remembering he might have been spotted at the restaurant earlier he simply answered, "Yes."

She collapsed as if she'd been held up by invisible strings, sinking into the cushion of her chair, the color rushing from her face. She hadn't expected such a bold reply, apparently.

"I saw you at the restaurant," he continued. "I heard you were going to Puerto Vallarta."

"And you followed me there?"

"More or less. I was there ahead of you."

It wasn't enough of an explanation and though he'd wanted to come clean, he'd wanted to do it in some other, better way. He loathed having to bring up his association with Allen Holloway. He loathed having to tell her that Troy Russell had murdered his sister and that he was afraid for Jenny. He didn't know how to explain his own feelings.

"Why?"

He hesitated.

"No, don't think up some lie," she said tightly. "I don't want to hear some story of how you experienced love at first sight and just followed your heart. I want to know the truth."

"You won't like it."

"I don't like it now. I don't see how much worse it can get."

He cleared his throat. "Your father hired me to protect you."

"*Bella!*" Alberto chimed, holding plates of pasta above his head as he squeezed between the tables and delivered their dishes with a flourish. "For you, my love, only the most special. And you, lucky man. You be good to my daughter. She is an angel."

Jenny felt tears well in her eyes. She could barely see.

"Look! She cries tears of happiness." Alberto leaned down and kissed her on both cheeks, hugging her hard. Then he wagged a finger in front of Hunter's stony face. "You hurt her, you deal with me and my brothers!" Chucking, he moved away, singing a soft Italian ballad on his way back to the kitchen.

Silence followed.

"I have to go," Jenny choked out.

"Don't. Please." He reached out a hand to stay her but she snatched her arm back.

"No . . . don't . . . don't do that. My father hired you? And I hired you?"

"I wanted to protect you."

"Protect me? Oh, you . . . bastard!"

"From Troy Russell. I know him."

That stopped her cold. She gazed at him through tear-wet eyes, but there was no compassion in their blue depths. Hunter's chest constricted, but he could tell she would shrink away if he attempted to touch her again.

"Go away," she whispered.

"I'm not leaving you."

"Well, I'm leaving you!" She stood up sharply. When Hunter made to get up she cut him off with a sharp wave of her hand.

"I want you safe, Jenny. That's all."

"It's Geneva," she managed, then she turned on her heel and stumbled outside.

The drive to Allen Holloway's River Oaks home took a while—long enough for Hunter to run through the scenario with Jenny around in his head about a hundred times. Self-flagellation was good now and again. Kept things in perspective.

He buzzed at the gate and heard Natalie answer tentatively. He explained that he wanted to see Allen and heard only silence for a long moment. Then the gates themselves opened slowly, as if reluctant to swing to the full extent of their arc. He drove to the front of the house, admiring the impressive stone fountain made out of a series of rock slabs. Water cascaded from one level to the next to a deep blue pool at the base.

Out of habit, he remote-locked the Jeep, then wondered why he thought anyone would be able to break inside while parked in the midst of this fortress.

Natalie herself answered the door, giving him a long once-over before she allowed him inside. "My husband's on his way home. He said to let you in," she said in a tone that suggested that this was a task above and beyond the call of wifely duty.

Hunter simply nodded and her pomposity melted a bit. She showed him the way into a high-ceilinged den with mahogany crown molding, a massive stone fireplace, and a group of chairs around a square table of bleached pine. The upholstery was a dark blue and gold design in a decidedly Native American pattern; the chairs were sturdy Ponderosa pine. Whoever Allen Holloway's designers were, they'd followed a distinctly southwestern style. Holloway's preference? Probably. Natalie looked more like the brocade and chandelier type.

"Could I get you something to drink?" she asked, the words sounding stilted on her tongue.

It was Sunday. Hunter had a feeling that it was the maid's day off. "Coffee?" he asked.

"Cream or sugar?"

"Black."

She disappeared in a hurry. Hunter sprawled on the couch, surprised at how comfortable it was. A glance around the room showed other evidence of southwestern influence: small Hopi figurines; a copper Zia sun mounted above a pine sideboard that matched the central furniture; a glass case of pounded silver and turquoise pieces that resembled jewelry but were apparently just meant for display.

Natalie's hands shook a bit as she brought him coffee. She was unattractively thin. Hunter silently compared her to Jenny and wondered how Allen Holloway's marriage was holding up.

Jenny. He had to fight for control. It went against his instincts to let her pick up her son alone, yet accompanying her would have complicated things. He would have been in the way.

Natalie sat across from him, holding a cup of coffee in her anxious fingers. She stirred the dark brown liquid continuously. No cream and he couldn't imagine her dumping a spoonful of sugar into anything she planned to consume. The stirring was for stirring's sake alone.

"What are you doing for my husband?" she asked, surprising him with her bluntness. She set the cup down on the table, the spoon rattling ominously, then she clasped her hands together in a death grip. Her control was downright scary.

"I'm working as a bodyguard to his daughter."

"I saw him, you know. Troy Russell. He pretended not to know me and it took me a while to place his face. He's heavier than he was, but it looks all right. He's still too handsome to trust." She smiled, but it was almost a grimace. The skin was stretched too tightly across her face. "So are you, for that matter."

Hunter shifted uncomfortably. He didn't like being compared to Russell at any level, though he knew they had the same coloring. Michelle had commented on it once. Only once. Because Hunter had snapped at her so ferociously she wouldn't dare to make any kind of comparison again.

"He thrives on intimidation, doesn't he?" Natalie said. "The way he looked at me—that's why I thought about it later. Like he knew something I didn't. Which I guess is the truth." She shivered delicately. "What does he want?"

"Money."

"It's extortion." Twin spots of color reddened her pale cheeks.

"And Jenny."

Natalie sat like a stone. Hunter had just about decided she wasn't going to answer when she said, "He has eyes that undress a woman and it isn't pleasant."

Hunter's jaw tightened grimly. He hadn't seen Troy Russell in years but he knew just what Natalie was talking about. He didn't know what he'd do if he witnessed Russell checking out Jenny like that.

"My husband says I'm a terrible judge of character," she said, crossing her slim legs. "But I can tell you that Troy Russell is not the same as he was. He's far worse now."

"Worse?"

She looked away. "I didn't know him well. I didn't pay much attention to him. He was young and he was Jenny's husband. I didn't have to think about him," she said, turning her gaze back to Hunter. "But the other day . . ."

"Go on," he said, feeling the need to prompt her as she trailed off, lost in serious thought.

"Do you care about Jenny? Allen says you're involved."

Hunter didn't want to reveal the truth to Natalie Holloway. But he couldn't deny he was deeply attracted to Jenny. His feelings for her were real. He couldn't shake the memory of the tears in her blue eyes and hurt turning her voice to an angry whisper.

Natalie was waiting. Her honesty demanded that he be honest in return. "Yes."

"Then you'd better stay close to her. It was just a fleeting impression, but I got the feeling Troy Russell is—" She struggled to come up with the right response, shaking her head and agitatedly fluttering her hands. "He's dangerous."

A feeling of déjà vu came over him. He'd been here before.

Natalie cocked her head a moment before Hunter heard the approaching engine. The nearly soundproof walls blocked most of the noise, but Natalie was attuned to the

house and recognized even the subtlest change. He wa
revising his opinion of her moment by moment. She wa
smarter than he'd guessed, and more intuitive. And deeply
obsessive. Add about thirty pounds, she could even b
called attractive.

Allen arrived with a slam of doors. He stormed into the
den like an angry bull. The man was a classic Type A, o
the verge of a heart attack. No question about it. Jenny wa
going to inherit those millions sooner than her fathe
wanted unless he got himself under control.

*And then Russell will have everything he wants in on
package—and a son to boot . . .*

"Natalie . . ." Allen's tone was curt. She'd risen to he
feet at his arrival and now she stood almost defiantly. N
love there, either, apparently. Not anymore. "I would lik
to be alone with Mr. Calgary. Bring me a bottle of brandy
from the bar cupboard."

She glanced toward a serving cart where at least two bot
tles of brandy glowed in the slanting afternoon light, bu
she left without a word. Allen prowled toward the fire an
back again while he waited for her. He didn't speak a wor
but Hunter could read a dangerous fury in his movements
Natalie returned with a silver tray, a bottle of expensive
brandy and two glasses. Hunter shook his head, but Aller
appropriated the tray and splashed hefty doses for both o
them, offering Hunter a glass without asking whether he
wanted it.

What the hell, Hunter thought, relaxing a bit for the firs
time since his encounter with Jenny. He drank the stuff an
knew he'd been treated to something remarkably good.

"You're sleeping with my daughter?" Allen bit out a

soon as Natalie closed the doors behind her.

Hunter felt a lick of anger, followed by amusement. "Did you expect her to remain celibate forever?"

"I asked you to protect her!" he shot back furiously. "She's not getting involved with an unemployed ex-cop!"

"I believe I'm employed," Hunter responded quietly. "At least I was until now." Drawing an envelope from an inside pocket of his leather jacket, he tossed it on the table. It slid toward Allen and teetered on the edge. "I won't take your money."

"You're a worse fool than I thought. She sure as hell doesn't have any money and she won't take any!" Holloway said triumphantly.

Hunter walked straight up to the man and stared him in the eyes. Holloway was a couple of inches shorter and Hunter overshadowed him, but the older man stood his ground, glaring back at him. "If you think this is about money, Holloway, be careful who you're calling a fool." With that he turned to leave, his thoughts already spinning ahead to Jenny and Rawley and Troy Russell.

"Wait!"

Hunter kept right on going. Natalie hovered in the shadows at the back of the entry. Hunter nodded a good-bye, but his exit was spoiled by Holloway hurrying after him to the car.

"What are you doing? Where are you going?" he demanded.

"I'm going to figure out how to get Russell," Hunter replied. "Be glad there's no link between us, because it's going to get ugly." He swung himself into the Jeep and rolled down the window.

"What are you going to do to him?"

"Don't know yet."

Hunter started the engine and Holloway put a hand on his open window, staying him. He struggled for a moment and Hunter waited. Finally, he said, "Keep them safe." Hunter understood the terse comment immediately: it was a testament to the man's love for his daughter and grandson.

"That must have really hurt," Hunter said as he put the Jeep in gear and Holloway stepped back.

Holloway's acknowledgment was a tight twisting of his lips.

Jenny was shattered. Who the hell did Hunter Calgary think he was, lying to her like that?

He worked for her father!

She'd been fool enough to believe him, too. But the man had been bought and paid for by who else but dear old dad. Why was she surprised? This was just another walk on the same treadmill.

She thumped her hand hard against the steering wheel. She hated him. Absolutely hated him. It was a new emotion. She'd been frightened of Troy and desperate to have him out of her life, but she hadn't hated him. She'd been too intent on survival. There had been no fury inside her. All she'd felt was a need to be free at all cost.

Now she felt fury. Deep-down fury. All she wanted was to claw at Hunter's eyes and kick his shins and belt him hard right in the gut! He'd used her. No, no. Correction. She'd *let* him use her. She'd wanted fun and sex and love and he'd seemed too perfect for words.

Oh, hell. She wanted to die.

And she hated herself, too. She'd been a world-class fool. Fifteen years of staying away from men and then she nosedived into a relationship that was a great, big, fat lie.

"Oh," she said aloud. "Oh . . ."

She drove on, feeling exhausted. To be honest—painfully honest—she'd looked forward to telling Rawley about Hunter. She'd already painted him in as this perfect stepdad. Oh, yeah. She could admit it. She'd been inventing all kinds of happy little scenarios inside her head, mostly unformed, just feel-good fantasies that kept a smile on her face and a spring in her step. Thoughts that made life just a little bit shinier and more wonderful and beautiful.

"You idiot!" she yelled, wanting to scream at the top of her lungs.

She missed the turn-off for the camp, had to double back, railing under her breath all the way. By the time she arrived at Three Winds and stepped from the car, she brushed back her hair and had to remind herself why she'd come. The trip had taken two hours, she realized with surprise. It felt as if it had passed in a heartbeat.

"I'm here to pick up Rawley Holloway," she said to the man behind the rustic front desk. He was dressed in soccer shorts and a shirt with a name tag that read "Tim" clipped to it. He held a soccer ball beneath one arm. The distant shouts and sounds of a ferocious game still in progress drifted in through the window.

"Rawley Holloway . . ." the man repeated, glancing down the list. "Hm. Looks like he's already been picked up."

"What?" Jenny craned her neck to look at the list. "I told

Janice that I would pick him up. When was Rick here? Rick Ferguson," she explained a bit testily when the man frowned.

"This just says his dad picked him up. Let me check with Bruce. He was your son's leader."

"His dad?" she repeated. Maybe they got it wrong. Maybe they meant her dad. Or maybe they'd thought Rick was his dad. Or maybe he was thinking of some other boy.

She followed Tim outside where he signaled to one of the counselors. The counselor jogged over, but before Jenny could say anything, Tim asked the newcomer, "Where's Bruce?"

"Uh, I dunno." The newcomer's name tag read Paul.

Jenny couldn't stand it any longer. "Paul, I'm looking for my son, Rawley Holloway. Tim said Bruce was his leader."

Paul scratched his head and looked around. "Yeah, he's—"

"There must be some mistake," she cut him off, "because the name roster at the front desk says Rawley was picked up by his father."

"Oh, yeah." He nodded. "I remember the guy."

"You do? Was it Rick Ferguson?"

"Uh . . . Brandon's father? No, this was Rawley's dad."

Jenny felt panic rise in her like a tide. "Rawley doesn't have a dad. No one should have picked him up who said he was his dad!"

The two counselors looked worried. Paul offered, "He had his passport. And he showed us I.D."

"Whose passport?"

"Rawley's." Paul shrugged and looked anxiously to Tim for confirmation.

Jenny asked faintly, "Whose I.D.?"

"I don't remember," Paul murmured. "Bruce wasn't around. But Rawley said he was his dad. He wanted to go with him."

"Paul . . ." Tim said warningly.

"Hey, the kid's fifteen. He wanted to go with his dad. He *called* him Dad!"

Jenny held up a hand. Struggling, she asked, "Was his— father's—name Troy Russell?"

Paul's expression cleared. "That's it! Troy! That's the guy. I told you it was his father," he declared triumphantly to Tim.

Tim gazed at Jenny, truly worried. On steady legs Jenny walked to the edge of the soccer field and promptly vomited her breakfast.

If she'd thought the drive down had been fast, the drive home seemed to take an eternity. She couldn't think. Words circled her brain. Phrases. Nothing made much sense.

Rawley was with Troy.

She heard herself sobbing uncontrollably. She should have never let him go to that soccer camp. She should have made him go with her to Puerto Vallarta. She shouldn't have gone to Puerto Vallarta.

"Oh, God . . . oh, please, God . . . please . . ."

She parked on the street outside the Fergusons and ran to their front door, pounding on it like a maniac.

Becky opened it up and said, "Yes?"

"Becky!" Janice yelled from around the corner. "Don't open that door until I'm there!" She came striding into the room, spied Jenny and relaxed. "Don't do that," she scolded her little girl. "You don't know who could be there."

"It's Jenny," Becky said, hurt.

"I know, honey, but it might not have been," she answered in exasperation. Spying Jenny's face, she asked, "What's wrong?"

"Did Rick pick up Brandon? Is he back yet?"

"Yeah, they got in about ten minutes ago. Why?"

"He didn't . . . Did he pick up Rawley, too?" Her voice cracked.

Janice's mouth opened in shock. "No, oh, Jenny!" She grabbed her by the arm and dragged her into the over-crowded living room. Jenny stumbled over a toy truck, and she felt tears fill her eyes anew.

"Oh, Jenn, no. It's okay. I'm sure it's just a mistake. Wait here." Scooping toys and books off the couch, she sat Jenny down. "Rick! Brandon!" She scurried toward the back of the house.

Jenny clasped her hands and stared down at them. She was still in that position, head bowed, praying, when Rick and Brandon came into the room.

"Jenny?" Rick asked, concerned. "Rawley wasn't at the camp when you got there?"

She lifted her head and swallowed. "No."

"Well, where could he be?" he asked. "Could anyone else have picked him up?"

"They told me his father picked him up."

"His father?" Rick repeated blankly. "Who did they mean?"

"Troy," Jenny answered in a suffocated voice.

"*What?*" Rick's jaw dropped. "No. How? That doesn't

make any sense!" He turned to Brandon who was gazing fixedly down at his shoes. "Brandon?"

"Huh." He didn't lift his eyes.

"Do you know anything about this?"

"What?"

"Brandon!" Rick lost patience.

"Brandon, please," Jenny said, lifting a palm in supplication. Brandon darted her a quick look. His stricken face confirmed her worst fears. "Was it—his father?"

"He said he was. Rawley wanted to go with him real bad. I didn't like him!" He shot a frightened glance at his own father. "I really didn't. I told him not to go with him, but Rawley was like in a trance!"

"Whoa . . ." Rick held up his hands. "Start at the beginning."

"Was he tall, dark and handsome?" Jenny asked bitterly.

Brandon nodded and started to cry.

"I've gotta go," Jenny said, clutching her purse. "I've gotta go home and see if there's a message."

"Brandon, why didn't you say something?" Rick demanded, to which his son started sobbing in earnest.

"No, don't," Jenny said, walking to the door in her own trance. "It's not his fault. It's Troy's."

She left her car on the street and walked to her apartment on legs made of lead. She wanted to collapse. At the bottom of her steps she pressed her hand to her lips and clung to the rail for support. But Rawley was Troy's son. He wouldn't hurt him. He was his *son!*

A deep canine growl sounded from above. Jenny forced herself to the upper landing where Benny stood outside her door, facing it, the ruff on his neck raised, his lips pulled into a snarl.

"Benny," she whispered, alarmed, but the dog didn'
move. The door suddenly flung open from the inside anc
Rawley peered out.

"Mom?"

She nearly collapsed in relief. "Rawley!" Tears fell dowr
her cheeks and she gathered her son into her arms, ignoring
his immediately stiffening body in the need to crush him tc
her.

"Hello, Jenny."

The cold voice made her heart stop. Looking over
Rawley's shoulder, her startled gaze landed on Troy Russell standing inside her doorway, big as life. Even his smile
was chilling. She felt a stab of real fear, her only reassurance the continual, low growl emanating from Benny's
throat as the dog intently watched Troy's every move.

❄ CHAPTER ELEVEN ❄

After fifteen years he looked remarkably the same
She walked past him, concentrating on holding
herself together. Rawley was safe and that was al.
that mattered.

"He picked me up at camp," Rawley said as he started tc
close the door.

"Put the dog outside," Troy ordered.

Jenny stated flatly, "Benny can stay," as Rawley reachec
for the dog's collar to obey his father.

Troy's lips tightened. She recognized the signs of his
half-hidden anger. Fifteen years hadn't erased all her memories. Benny snarled and Rawley nudged the dog with his

sneaker. "Hey!"

"You broke into my apartment," Jenny said, keeping her gaze on Troy. "You stole Rawley's passport and you went to his soccer camp."

Troy leaned one hip against the sofa table. His blue eyes were as icy and as calculating as Jenny remembered. He'd put on some weight, but it didn't detract from his overall good looks. In fact, he looked better than she remembered—a fact she fervently wished weren't true. It seemed unfair that someone so vicious could be so attractive. Unfair—and deadly.

"No, I walked into your apartment," he said with an unconcerned shrug. "The front door was wide open. Guess someone broke in while you were gone. I was worried about you. I walked in and called for you and this dog attacked me!" He glared down at Benny who watched him unblinkingly. The dog seemed to recognize an enemy.

"Mom!" Rawley interjected.

"I don't believe you." Jenny swallowed. "You took his passport."

Troy's eyes narrowed. "It was lying beside his pictures. You didn't bother telling me I had a son."

"Mom!"

"He's not your son."

Troy just smiled wider.

"I *know* he's my dad!" Rawley yelled. "I've got his picture!" He started digging into his backpack.

"He's not your son in any way that counts," Jenny responded in a barely audible voice. With as much strength as she could muster she walked past him into the living room and plunked down on the couch. Every muscle felt rigid.

"Mom, Mom . . ." Troy's old picture in hand, Rawley rushed over to perch on the chair opposite her, holding out the photo. Jenny glanced at the faded photograph but refused to accept it. She hurt all over.

Rawley threw a look at his father, then dangled his hands between his knees, the picture hanging loosely from his fingers. Troy's characteristic smirk showed plainly in the photograph even though its edges were ragged with age. Rawley added anxiously, "He came to the camp a few days ago but I knew who he was. I recognized him!"

She met Troy's gaze again. He looked so self-satisfied she wanted to scream. "His name wasn't on the list."

"So what?" Rawley demanded. "He's my dad and he had my passport. That's what counts!"

"I got you that passport to go to Puerto Vallarta."

"I didn't go!" Rawley yelled as if she were completely deaf. "I went to the soccer camp with Brandon! And then Dad showed up and I thought you sent him, and I was so glad!"

Troy's gaze slid down her body, possessively. Jenny shuddered. Memories of his hands on her made her feel dirty and slightly sick.

"But you never told him about me," Rawley pointed out in an injured tone. "You never told him." He pressed his lips together, looking as if he might cry. "Why didn't you?"

Jenny gazed helplessly at Rawley, then slid Troy an angry glance. He lifted one ironic brow. She'd been wrong, she thought. She did hate him. "Because I didn't trust him."

"But I'm his son." Rawley's eyes were huge with betrayal.

"I know." She took a shallow breath. "I'm sorry."

She would have reached for his hand but, anticipating her need to touch him, Rawley recoiled. Jenny's throat closed. If she lost him over this she would never forgive herself.

"We've been making up for lost time," Troy said conversationally. "Played a little soccer, got to know each other a bit."

"Rick never saw you at the camp." She heard how shrewish she sounded and wished she could relax. But not with Troy in the room. That would be like turning her back on a rattlesnake. She could almost feel his intimate gaze crawling over her skin, and shuddered.

"Rick? That Brandon's father?"

Rawley nodded.

Troy laughed without humor. "They got pissed off at him at the camp for telling them how to play the game. He doesn't know how to play the game—at all."

"He knows some soccer," Rawley defended, misunderstanding entirely.

Jenny knew Troy was lying about the break-in. She knew a lot of things Rawley didn't. But now wasn't the time to get into a shouting match that she knew from experience she would lose—and that could turn into something so much worse.

"I thought you were here to make amends," she stated flatly.

"Amends?" Troy's gaze was cold. "Look who's talking."

"What do you mean?" Rawley asked.

Jenny gazed at her son. "Rawley, I need a few moments alone with Troy."

"What for?"

"Please."

He set his jaw and scowled, reminding Jenny so much of Troy at that moment that she thought her heart might break. He was nothing like Troy. *Nothing!*

Without another word he stomped off to his room, slamming the door. For once he didn't play the music full blast. He was listening.

"Jenny, Jenny," Troy said in a silky voice. "You never told me."

"And I never would have," she admitted.

Her defiance clearly surprised him. "Guess it's just lucky I found out, isn't it?" He came around the couch and sat down close enough to brush his thigh against hers. She shrank away involuntarily and he chuckled softly. "Haven't loosened up any over the years, I see."

He had the audacity to brush a curl away from her cheek. Jenny slapped his hand away. They glared at each other and to her horror she saw awakening sexual desire in his eyes. "You little bitch," he whispered.

"Touch me again and I'll have you arrested."

He grinned cockily.

"Have you been following me?" she blurted out, suddenly aware that she'd forgotten how wily Troy could be.

"I coulda come by here anytime I wanted."

"You're Mike Conrad," she breathed.

He chuckled and pretended to shoot her right between the eyes with his thumb and forefinger. "Bang."

Jenny couldn't believe she was having this conversation. "You broke in here. I'll prove it. What do you want, Troy? Money? Did you waste all that money my father gave you? Don't touch me again," she added in a fierce whisper when his hand drew too close to her thigh.

"Come on, Jenny. Open up." He took a lingering look over her legs. She had to resist the urge to clamp her knees together.

"Get out, Troy."

"You can't keep me from my son. Why, I could take this to court. How will it look to have the rich ex-wife keep her son's father in the dark for so long?"

"I'll bring up the past. I'll tell them you hit me."

Jenny could hear him inhale swiftly. The hairs on her arms lifted. He moved fast. One moment he was beside her, the next he had her pinned down, his mouth crushing hers, his tongue all over her lips and in the mouth she opened to scream.

"He'll hear," Troy whispered fiercely, loving his power, gloating under it. "I'll blame you. You, who kept him from his father!"

"Get—off—me!" she demanded in growing hysteria.

"Who do you think he'll choose? Hmmm? *Who?*"

He grabbed her full in the crotch, but then was off her an instant later. His chest heaved from excitement and his pants bulged. He watched her, waiting for whatever choice she made.

Jenny's own chest was heaving—but with terror. All she could think about was escape. *Rawley and me. To Santa Fe.*

"You do it to yourself, Jenny. I'm just giving you what you want." His voice was softer than a whisper.

He hadn't been this aggressive in the past. His cold control had developed into something else—something far more dangerous. He'd always been a bully, but it was overtly sexual now. She knew what he was thinking and her mouth grew dry as desert air.

Her show of bravado was over. She'd lost this round "How much money—will it take?"

"Oh, no . . ." He wagged a finger in front of her nose "I'm yours, honey. You, me and Rawley."

"I'll kill you myself before I let you destroy my son."

His answer was a widening of that awful smile.

Hunter didn't like the way he was feeling. He drove aim lessly for a while, checking his watch, wondering whe Jenny might be back from Three Winds. Probably alread home. With her son. Could he just drop in and see her unir vited, the way she thought of him now?

She hates you. She said so.

He didn't believe it for a moment. But he'd betrayed he and she wasn't likely to forgive him in the foreseeabl future. If he were smart, he'd let some time go by and se what happened a few months from now. Give her time t settle in Santa Fe.

"Damn it," he muttered. Why had he let himself g involved? How had it happened? But just thinking abo her . . . her soft skin and sweet sighs . . . her humor . . . tl sexy way she had of pushing her curls away from her fac

And there was Russell, too. The reason he'd taken th job in the first place. He couldn't leave Jenny alone no even if she threw him out bodily.

He drove to the apartment and parked, walking slow through the courtyard and up the stairs to her door. I knocked lightly. There was no answer. He knocked agai a bit louder. Faintly he heard footsteps come to the do and then he realized he was being examined through the peephole by an unseen eye.

The door opened wide. It was Jenny. A wild-eyed Jenny whose face was white enough to give him real concern. "I'm sorry," he said, not knowing what else to say in the face of her devastation. "I'm sorry. I just want to protect you."

"Too late!" she said, a bubble of hysteria rising in her throat.

"Jenny . . . ?" He stepped inside without being invited, shouldering past her, glancing around, all senses on alert. If he'd had a gun on him he would have drawn it. It was automatic. A cop's reaction.

"He's not here. He left. For now."

"Russell?" Hunter asked, swinging around to look at her.

She nodded. "And my son . . ." With that she broke down, hands on her face, sobbing for all she was worth.

"Jenny." He pulled her into his arms. She resisted for half a moment, then collapsed against him. "What do you mean?"

"He took Rawley." Feeling Hunter tense, she choked out, "No, no . . . Rawley wanted to go. They're just—at the movies." Her last words were a gasp.

Hunter eased her to the couch. Full-blown hysteria was only seconds away. He knew the symptoms—he'd seen them in Michelle after her fights with Troy. "What did he do?" he asked quietly. Michelle would never fully confess, but Hunter knew it was bad.

He wanted to kill Russell.

Jenny wouldn't answer. Maybe she couldn't.

"Did he hurt you?"

"I don't have a mark on me," she said bitterly.

He turned her around by her shoulders. "Jenny, listen to me. I won't let him hurt you again. Do you understand?"

"I can't think. He's"—she quivered beneath his palms—"worse than before."

Hunter's jaw tightened. "He's a sadist."

She sagged against him. "Yes . . ."

He held her close, listening to her shallow breathing. What would Russell do now that he knew the truth about Rawley? Hunter didn't believe the man possessed a conscience. All he wanted was whatever intrigued him at the moment. And money. And sexual power over women.

"He won't hurt his son," Hunter said.

"You said you know him," she answered, her voice muffled against his jacket. "Do you really believe that?"

"I know I won't let him."

"How do you know him?"

He hesitated, certain this wasn't the time to go into the tragedy of Michelle's death. Hearing that he believed Troy had killed her wouldn't do Jenny any good—especially while Rawley was with the man. "I knew him in Los Angeles."

"Did my father contact you?"

"Yes. Through his lawyers."

"I don't understand," she murmured, pulling away and drawing a hand across her forehead. Her cheeks were flushed; her eyes feverish. "I've got to leave for Santa Fe as soon as possible. Tonight. I've got to get away from him."

"I'll go with you."

"I can't—" She twisted her hands together. "I can't ask you."

"I've got to go back sometime. We'll go together."

"I . . ."

The phone rang and they both jumped. Jenny looked toward it as if it were a loaded gun aimed at her, but then she murmured, "Rawley," and picked up the receiver. Hunter followed after her.

"We're back!" Magda's voice came singing over the line. "Jenny, my dear, hurry up and get here. Santa Fe's bee-yoo-tiful. And your restaurant! My God, girl! We drove by it on our way to the house and it's practically ready to go right now." She stopped and listened to the silence. "Are you there?"

"Yes."

"You okay?" she asked with real concern.

Jenny swallowed. She was never going to be okay again. "I'm looking forward to Santa Fe."

"Have you heard from Hunter since you've been back?"

"Yes."

"You don't sound too happy."

"Oh, Magda, I can't talk now. I'll be in Santa Fe by the end of the week."

"Okay," she said, her exuberance doused by Jenny's terse replies. "Hang in there. Phil and I love you lots."

"Love you, too," she said, hanging up quickly, feeling like she was about to break into pieces. She glanced at Hunter, whose strength and silent understanding were what she needed more than anything. She wanted to fold herself into his arms, but she didn't trust herself. And she didn't completely trust him either. Instead she drew a deep breath and said in a steadier voice, "I'm going to start packing." Then she brushed past him on the way to

243

her bedroom closet.

Troy sat through the dumbest film he'd seen in a long time. Some kung-fu thing that was supposed to be smart and funny but he couldn't stand the female lead. Every time she kick-boxed some 300-pound male into submission it was all he could do not to laugh aloud. What she needed was somebody to give it to her but good. She did have fine tits though, held up nice and high with a stretchy top. He just wanted to slap her face hard.

Pulling a pack of gum from his pocket, he folded a strip into his mouth. The kid shot him a quick look and Troy silently asked if he wanted a stick. The boy shook his head. Troy surreptitiously examined Rawley's profile. Looked a lot like Jenny in some ways, but definitely a Russell. Yessirree. He laughed softly to himself, remembering the expression on Jenny's face! Oh, what a bitch! Hiding the kid all these years. It made him want to crow with delight. He had her now. And the old man, too.

The irony was enough to make him roll on the ground in fits of laughter.

"Do you like it?" the kid asked him, so anxious to please that Troy almost ruffled the boy's hair with a sort of affection.

"I like the action."

"Yeah. Me too!" He went back to his absorption in the exciting movie.

Charm. That's all it took. Even with a fifteen-year-old kid. How hard would it be to turn Rawley against Jenny? Not hard at all, by the look of things. And what would she do to win back his favor? Anything, he guessed.

For a few moments he allowed himself the pleasure of picturing her groveling on the ground in front of him, crying and begging. He crumpled up his fist, then released it, smiling. He could have her any way he wanted her. Any way.

Hands and knees. Up against a wall. Across a table. She acted so damn tough but he had her now.

When the movie ended Troy reluctantly ended his pleasant thoughts. He wanted the money, too. And he wanted it soon. He was rapidly running out of cash and he was pretty sure the credit card Patricia had given him was at its limit. The second-rate hotel he was staying at would be wanting him to hand over the card again soon if he kept staying on.

"What do you want to do now?" the kid asked as they left the theater.

"Maybe I should take you back to your mother."

The swift, dark rebellion that crossed his face tickled Troy through and through. "I never want to go back."

"Oh, come on, now. It's getting late. Don't you have school tomorrow, or something?"

"I'm not going back to school here. We're moving." As soon as he'd said it he asked urgently, "Where do you live?"

"I'm kind of moving around right now. And you're going to Santa Fe." It had been a nasty jolt to realize Jenny's ultimate New Mexico destination was Santa Fe. Santa Fe was where that broken-down cop Hunter Calgary had settled after Troy got him fired, and Troy had zero interest in tangling with him again. As far as Troy was concerned, Calgary was a bloodthirsty lunatic, and Santa Fe was too small

a town to hold both of them. He sure as hell hoped Calga
had moved on.

"I don't want to go," Rawley declared. "I never did
want to stay right here with my friend Brandon."

"Now, wait a minute, wait a minute . . ."

"Mom's got a restaurant there," he said, a hint of pri
entering his voice despite his professed desire to stay aw
from Jenny. "It's opening up. Supposed to be really go
food."

He kicked at a stone as they walked toward Troy's rent
car. Seeing the Ford pissed Troy off. He needed a Lexus
a Porsche or a Jaguar. God, how he'd wanted to kill Fre
erica when she'd taken the keys to her spare Merced
back. And all because she was a bipolar freak.

"When are you leaving?" Troy asked.

"I dunno. Sometime this week."

Troy's anger congealed to a cold fury that consumed hi
from the inside out. The cagey old bastard Allen Hollow;
had neglected to mention Jenny's plans. Lucky for him th
motor mouth waitress at Riccardo's had clued him i
luckier still that he'd connected with Rawley because tl
boy was a fountain of information.

"But I'm not going," Rawley said again, full of bravad
"I'll stay with the Fergusons if I have to."

"Now, hold on. I happen to live pretty close to Santa Fe

"You do?"

"You know where Taos is?" Rawley shook his head ar
Troy congratulated himself on familiarizing himself wi
all Frederica's properties. Sure, the place would be locke
up tight, but there was always a way inside. "Got a plac
there. Not much. Just a little stucco ranch house about ;

hour's drive north of Santa Fe."

The boy's eyes shone. "Really?"

"Yep."

"What do you do?"

Troy felt the first twinge of resentment toward the nosy little bastard. "Investments. Stock futures. Stuff like that."

"Oh."

They got into the car and Troy headed back to Jenny's. "I've got some things to do, so I'm going to drop you off and get going."

"You don't want to see my mom again," he said sagely.

"No, your mom's a great lady. Just gotta make an appointment."

Charm.

Rawley seemed to want to say more, but Troy was vastly relieved that he kept his trap shut. When Rawley closed the door, then turned back and asked, "You going to be here tomorrow?" in that casual way kids thought hid anything but their stupidity. Troy had to fight to keep his genial smile in place.

"Probably. See ya, kid."

As soon as he put the car in gear and turned the corner, Troy let out a pent-up breath. He wasn't sure he liked the kid. Too much of a pretty boy. Maybe he'd be better when he got older.

But he sure as hell gave Troy the leverage he needed.

Rawley watched his father's car drive away, the taillights winking red in the evening shadows. He was conflicted with emotions. Mostly he was truly pissed at his mother. She'd pretended his dad was some kind of loser deadbeat.

It was all a fake. He could've been with his dad all this time if she had told the truth.

And she was always on *him* to tell the truth! He marched up the stairs and heard a woof from below. Glancing down, he found Benny loping toward him. "Hey, dummy," he said affectionately. "Why don't you like my dad?"

Benny jumped all over him and Rawley grabbed the dog by the ears in a mock wrestling match. Benny pretended to bite and growl until Rawley glared at him and waggled his finger in the dog's panting face. "Bad dog. My dad's a good guy." Benny's aversion to Troy had been kind of embarrassing.

At that moment the door opened and a strange man stood in the light. The man froze upon encountering Rawley and Benny. Benny growled at the man, then he snuffled at his shoes and looked up like an old friend. The man scratched the dog's ears as if he'd done it for years.

Who the hell was this?

"Who're you?" Rawley demanded.

"Hunter Calgary."

"Mom?" He dodged past the man, alarmed. His mother was nowhere to be seen.

"She's packing. In the bedroom."

Rawley whirled around, filled with resentment. He gazed at the guy, measuring the width of the man's shoulders and the strength of his chest. Not a wuss. Something else. Something he didn't want to think about. "Mom!" he called louder.

"Rawley!"

He heard her muffled cry of relief and that bugged him. She'd been fit to be tied when he left with his dad.

She came out of the room and rushed toward him, hugging him hard once. He didn't generally mind much. She was his mom. But tonight he practically pushed her away and he looked away from the hurt on her face. Guilt gnawed at him, but he turned his attention on the stranger.

"Rawley, I'd like you to meet Hunter Calgary."

"Hi," he said carefully.

"Hello, Rawley."

He wore jeans and a tan shirt and looked like he worked out a lot. Rawley was liking him less and less. Especially now.

"Hunter's a friend of mine," Jenny said into the silence that followed.

Friend? Rawley wanted to scream. *You don't have guy friends!*

"He's helping us move to Santa Fe."

Rawley's head whipped up. "I'm not going."

"Well, of course you're going."

"I'm not. I'm staying here with Brandon."

Jenny started to say something, caught herself, tightened her lips, then pinned him with a certain look that always made him squirm. He tried hard not to move. There were critical issues at stake here. He didn't want that guy to even talk, and he shot him a look that said so. The guy raised his eyebrows quizzically. Rawley couldn't tell if he was amused or not.

"I'm sure this is about Troy," Jenny said. "Trust me. If he can find you in Houston, he'll find you in Santa Fe."

Something weird was going on. She sounded completely defeated. "I like him," Rawley said instinctively.

She nodded. "He can be very charming."

"What's that supposed to mean?"

"He wasn't nice to me, Rawley. If you want to know more, ask. But you're not going to like what I have to say."

"Yeah? Well, he says really nice things about you!" he yelled.

"It's not what he says, it's what he does."

"What does he do? What does he do, huh?" Rawley demanded. Seeing his mom was about to tell him, he cut in, "Don't say it. Don't talk to me. It's all going to be lies anyway. That's what you do. Lie! You lied to me! I'm not going to Santa Fe!"

With that he stomped to his room and shut his door hard behind him. Not a slam. He was just letting them both know that they couldn't push him around.

He pressed his ear to the panels. Footsteps approached and he stepped back hurriedly, grabbed a basketball and began tossing it from hand to hand, as if he didn't have a care in the world. He heard his mother's soft knock. "Yeah?"

Jenny poked her head around the door, her hair swinging away from her cheek. She was pretty, his mom. He was proud of how pretty she was. The other guys kinda got tongue-tied around her sometimes. "I'm tired, Rawley. I'm going to bed."

"What about him?" he asked swiftly, alarmed.

"Hunter's leaving. We'll see him again on Friday. We're going to caravan to Santa Fe. Good night."

He was going to Santa Fe? Rawley flung the basketball down and clamped his teeth together. He didn't swear much. Not like Brandon. His mother would throw a complete fit if she heard him using bad language. But he tried out some choice words in his head to describe Hunter Cal-gary. He whispered them aloud, then glanced nervously at the closed door.

He knew what that guy had to be thinking when he looked at his mom. It really burned him. Why wouldn't she look at his dad? That's what she needed to do. Then he could have his parents back together again.

That's what he wanted.

That's all he wanted.

Hunter let himself out onto the porch and turned around to look at Jenny. Her face was partially shadowed, but he could still see how drawn it was. He wanted to assure her that everything was going to be all right, but he couldn't. He knew Troy Russell, knew how dangerous the man really was. So did Jenny.

At the door Jenny didn't know what to say. Hunter shifted his weight, reluctant to leave. After an uneasy moment, he said, "You shouldn't be alone here."

"I know." She turned slightly to glance at her son's closed bedroom door. "I can't have you here."

"I'm concerned about your safety."

"You don't have to go with us," she said, ignoring him. "We can make the drive to Santa Fe by ourselves."

"I'm going. I'll be here bright and early Friday morning." He cleared his throat. "Still, you need someone here now."

"No, it's okay. Just a few more days. Like you said, he won't hurt Rawley."

"I'm going to be around. Watching."

She nodded. It was a relief to know that if she really needed help it would be nearby. "I hope he doesn't come by again." Hunter gave her a look that said she was being incredibly naive.

"He's going to go straight to your father," Hunter predicted.

"I should call him, I suppose. Warn him."

"I think he'll be calling you," Hunter said, his mouth lifting faintly at the corner.

She lifted her brows.

"He and I had a—meeting—this afternoon."

"He knows about us?"

"I am no longer in his employ."

Jenny mustered a smile. Hunter longed to lean forward and kiss her, but sensing his need, her smile faded. She might never forgive him, he realized. She liked him enough to keep him around, and she knew she needed him right now, but what they'd shared might never happen again. Life was like that.

"Good night, Hunter," she said, closing the door.

He waited until the lights had been turned off before he left to the cold comfort of a night watching from his Jeep.

❈ CHAPTER TWELVE ❈

Built around a central plaza that stood at the end of the Santa Fe Trail, the city of Santa Fe looked like heaven to Jenny. Her pioneer spirit had been born out of an almost lifelong need to escape her roots. She drove around the plaza with its territorial and pueblo-style buildings, art galleries, restaurants, and the Palace of the Governor's Museum. She drove down Canyon Road, once an Indian footpath, now lined with art galleries and restaurants, then headed east to one of the more upscale residential areas.

The condo she'd rented wasn't much fancier than the apartment she'd just left, but it cost more. Still, she'd been lucky. Most of the condominiums in her complex were owner-occupied, but her particular unit's owner hadn't used it much and had finally decided to rent it out. Jenny had been at the right place at the right time. She could have drawn on her inheritance to move into something pricier, but she wanted to plow some of it into the restaurant and keep some in reserve while she waited to see if her venture made a profit.

The grounds were fenced, but she'd been given the entry remote control. As the wrought iron gate swung inward, she felt a sense of intoxicating relief. Safety. A new home. A new life.

Rawley sprawled in the passenger seat, pretending not to look. He'd been an unbelievable pill the whole trip. When he spoke, it was just to remind her how wonderful Troy was, how awful she was for keeping the truth from him, and how unhappy he was to leave the Fergusons.

His attitude certainly put a damper on the whole trip. Jenny, however, had a surprise for him when they arrived, something she'd worked out with the Fergusons and Hunter, and she hoped it might improve his outlook immensely. She glanced in the rearview mirror. Hunter's Jeep was nowhere to be seen. Not that she'd expected it. He'd left about eight hours after her, as it turned out, following her out of town and then doubling back. Still, he was in her thoughts, and though she tried to pretend she didn't care, the truth was she really did.

She hadn't seen a lot of him but just knowing he was around had helped ease her tension. Troy had stopped by twice, both times when Jenny was on an errand. Maybe he'd seen her leave. Maybe he'd seen Hunter's Jeep and figured out she was being guarded. Whatever the case, Troy had checked in with Rawley, cementing his role as "daddy" and drawing Rawley further away from her. Troy now knew where she was going; Rawley wanted him to know everything. She prayed to God he would let them leave Houston without a last-minute showdown.

Out of Rawley's presence, Troy's hidden agenda had appeared: he'd finally demanded money from Jenny's dad. Allen was practically apoplectic. Though Jenny told him not to pay, Allen refused to listen and handed over a substantial amount of cash. Allen made the mistake of telling Rawley that his father was an extortionist, and Rawley had simply disengaged from the grandfather he hadn't much liked anyway. Jenny was both exasperated and infuriated with her father, but Allen once again was unrepentant. It was his way. He would never change.

Allen also had a lot to say about Hunter. "He's a burned-out ex-cop. I'm sorry I hired him. He's just another opportunist looking for a rich woman to take care of him."

"Now that's just plain untrue," Jenny responded. She might have her problems with Hunter, but he was no gold digger.

"You let yourself get involved with him, and he's got your bank account on his mind."

"He's protecting me from Troy. That's all," she answered flatly.

"Don't lie to me. There's a hell of a lot more going on

between you two! He said so himself."

"He was mistaken," she said firmly.

"I hired him to protect you and now we need someone to protect you from him!" He shook his head in frustration. "I'll make sure you're safe in Santa Fe."

"Don't bother. Hunter will be with me," she told him.

"As a bodyguard. If you're so worried about the precious Holloway money, stop throwing it at Troy. As long as you feed him, he'll keep coming to your back door. And that's all I have to say about that."

Her stubborn refusal to discuss Hunter further infuriated Allen, but Jenny tuned out his ranting and raving. She'd given him a stiff hug goodbye and he'd shaken hands with a very cool Rawley. She was glad when their Wednesday night dinner was over and she and Rawley could escape his pretentious River Oaks home. She looked for Hunter's Jeep on the way back but didn't see it. Later that night she peeked through her bedroom curtains and was relieved to see his vehicle parked on the street nearby.

She'd had a final, tearful goodbye with everyone at Riccardo's. Alberto looked totally crestfallen, unable to keep his "daughter" around any longer. He sent her off with a final paycheck plus a bonus that took her breath away. She immediately started making more plans for Geneva's.

Saying goodbye to the Fergusons had been the worst of it. Brandon had just looked shocked and the twins, sensing the attention was away from them, had taken the opportunity to fight. Janice had ignored them, hugging Jenny and urging her to "keep safe" in the wake of Troy's return from nowhere.

That evening Janice had stopped by for a glass of wine

and a last good-bye. She'd also made Jenny an offer she couldn't refuse—the surprise for Rawley—and the two friends had toasted their lasting friendship and promised to stay in touch.

Pulling into the driveway of her adobe-colored condo, she actually grinned from pure happiness. She was free of Troy, at least temporarily, and she was free of her father.

Rawley opened one eye and asked in a bored tone, "This it?"

"Yep."

She wasn't going to indulge his childish behavior. Jumping from the car, she hauled out one of the first boxes. Most of their belongings were coming by truck in the middle of next week, but she'd brought along her most precious possessions on this trip: pictures, mementos, and personal papers. Which reminded her . . .

"Next time Troy calls, tell him to return your passport."

"I know, I know. You've told me enough times."

Jenny fought back a pointed remark as she pulled out her keys and opened the front door. Rawley wanted to fight about Troy and she was in no position to defend herself. Best to let the kid act like a jerk and hope he eventually realized it would get him nowhere.

The place smelled dusty from disuse. Jenny crossed to the sliding glass door, cracked it open, then pulled the drapes. Late afternoon sunlight slanted into the room. She glanced around with satisfaction. In its imperfect way, it was perfect.

It took the rest of the afternoon to unload the Volvo and arrange her belongings. They had no furniture so they sat on the raised hearth of the gas fireplace or sprawled out cross the floor. Jenny had remembered to bring the phone nd she plugged it in and called Gloria at the restaurant.

"It's good you've arrived. They're painting again," Гloria declared with a sniff when she realized it was Jenny. Come over and look."

Gloria wasn't much for conversation.

"I'm going to Geneva's," Jenny told Rawley, slinging the trap of her purse over her arm. "Want to come?"

"Nah."

He looked so forlorn that she hesitated. School had lready resumed after spring break, but they had the whole veekend ahead. Jenny wondered what Hunter would be loing with his time—besides guarding her. She banished he thought as soon as it crossed her mind. She couldn't hink about him in that way. Too complicated. Maybe later, ut not now.

Geneva's was located just off Canyon Road on a side treet. The location had been an art gallery, then a tea shop, hen the owner had taken over adjacent space and added reakfast and lunch. After a messy divorce, the business vas sold and the space sat empty for nearly a year while he opposing parties haggled over the lease. When it was inally free of encumbrances Jenny was able to sign a new ease and begin her own modifications and renovations.

She hadn't been to the site for nearly two months and the hanges stopped her cold. It *was* nearly ready. In fact, as he watched the painters add another coat of dark mustard ellow paint to the thick plaster walls, she caught a whiff f delicious odors mixing with the aroma of paint.

In the kitchen Gloria stood over a small, thin man who vas browning chipotle in a pan. Santa Fe natives were

wont to say, "The chile is king and queen," and Glor
believed it with all her heart. All her dishes were season
with one chile or another, from rocket fuel-hot, to delica
and mild. She made chipotle sauce from browned, almc
burned, jalapeños. The heat of the jalapeños dissipated
the process, but the flavor was like heaven on the tongu
At least that was Gloria's interpretation. But there was r
denying it was fabulous and just the odor—even vyir
with the paint fumes—made Jenny's mouth water.

"I must be hungry," she said to her chef.

Gloria, arms crossed beneath her impressive bosor
glared down at the man, her brown eyes snapping fur
ously, her mouth a taut line. Her hair was wrapped into
tight bun and scraped away from her face. She could I
anywhere from thirty to fifty years of age; it was impo
sible to tell. She was a formidable presence in any kitche
If Jenny had to choose between being the object of h
wrath or Alberto's, she would choose Alberto every time

"We are behind," she practically spat. Jenny wasn't su
whether she meant in the construction, or in the preparatic
of their dishes. When Gloria's back was turned, the ma
gave Jenny a wavery smile. "He speaks Spanish only
Gloria cut in when Jenny was about to say somethin
"He's not too bad a cook, though."

This was high praise indeed. "Maybe you could tell hi
that," Jenny suggested.

"He knows what I think." She jerked her head in th
direction of the seating area of the restaurant where tl
painting was being completed. "I've been yelling at ther
They are slower than snails."

"You've done a great job," Jenny told her. Gloria ha

verseen the renovation work by herself while Jenny wrapped things up in Houston. For her efforts, Jenny had suggested Gloria might want to buy a percentage of ownership. Her father would have choked on the idea, but Jenny knew how important the chef would be to Geneva's success. Gloria was thinking it over.

"I didn't think it would be this far along," Jenny went on. It looks like we could open—maybe—next week?"

"This week!" Gloria declared.

"All right." Jenny grinned. "This week."

"The chairs and tables are ready for delivery."

Jenny nodded. She'd ordered natural pine tables and chairs for the seating area, and for a reception, a restored Spanish writing desk from a tiny antique furniture store further up Canyon Road. Pierced tin lights on dimmer switches hung from the ceiling, and arched entryways were stenciled in motifs resembling the sage and piñon trees that dotted New Mexico's landscape. The final step would be to fill in the traced greenery, making the archways into painted trellises opening room to room.

A row of glass panels along the top of the dining room's northern wall let in bright light inside the room during the day. Without the buildings of the city, the view would be straight toward the Sangre de Cristos mountain range.

Jenny couldn't wait to get started. But first . . .

"I've got some unpacking to do. I've set up my telephone. It's the number I gave you earlier. The one I set up last time I was here." Gloria grunted in acknowledgment. I'll check in tomorrow. When will you be ready for customers?"

"Got people coming to work on Wednesday. Could be

ready to go then."

"We'll do a dry run," Jenny said. "A dress rehearsal witl the waiters. I'd like to get some advance publicity. We'v been running some ads, but I want to set the date the door open. How about Friday?"

Gloria nodded. "I'll get some working this weekend. A coupla dishes need to be learned and I don't have eyes in the back of my head!" She glared at the worried-lookin man.

Jenny let herself out the door. She didn't think Glori gave herself enough credit. She half-believed the woma did have eyes in the back of her head.

At the condo, she realized she hadn't brought any lamps The place was pitch dark. Switching on the lights in th kitchen helped some. "Rawley?" she called, feeling tha fluttery alarm start inside her again.

"Yeah," came the bored answer from down the hall.

The hall light worked, thank God, so she didn't have t trail her fingers along the wall to learn where the door was Peering in his room, she saw that Rawley had moved th phone next to his ear. He was lying on a sleeping bag hands beneath his head, staring, apparently, at the ceiling.

"We've got the little TV from your room," she pointe out. "You could set it up."

"Nah."

"Did you want to call someone?"

"No." His tone was slightly belligerent. "Why?"

"Because you moved the phone from the kitchen. I coul get some calls, too, you know," she pointed out. If Hunte happened to phone, she didn't want to put up with the dark accusatory looks and obnoxious attitude Rawley woul ffect. "Magda or Gloria or anyone. Even the Fergusons."

"Why didn't you get a cell phone?" he demanded.

That stopped her. "Do I need one?"

"Dad got one."

"Oh." Jenny's temper flared. She'd just about had it with his attitude. "Well, if your dad got one, I guess your grandfather's the one who really owns one."

"What's that supposed to mean?" His tone stiffened with warning.

She was instantly sorry for letting her temper get the better of her. "It means you don't know anything about Troy."

"Yeah? Whose fault is that?"

"I'm more than willing to talk about him now."

"You *hate* him," Rawley reminded her hotly. "What are you gonna say? Just tons of bad stuff! When he comes here, I'm gonna be with him."

"When he comes here?" she repeated.

"He lives about an hour away," Rawley told her triumphantly. "In some artsy little town that everybody goes to."

"Taos?" she asked faintly.

"That's it!" Rawley was pleased that she knew it. It did exist, then. He hadn't been completely certain his father was telling him the truth. Not that he would lie, Rawley thought quickly, but his dad was just being careful where his mom was concerned.

Jenny gazed at him with real concern. She could feel the dull, hard pounding of her heart. Just thinking about how Troy had smashed his lips on her and grabbed at her was enough to make her feel ill. She'd thought—prayed—that

Allen's "gift" might keep him at a distance from them for a while. "Rawley, do you know what your dad does for a living?"

"Yeah," he answered, instantly on edge.

"What?"

"Investments," he stated flatly.

"He's living off money your grandfather gave him. I doubt he has any investments. That's why he's back in our lives."

"You just hate him!" Rawley practically screamed at her. "That's your problem!"

"Rawley . . ."

"Just leave me alone," he muttered, flinging himself on his side and staring at the wall. "Shut the door," he added when she didn't immediately move.

All the joy of the day was gone. Jenny let herself into her own room and flipped open her sleeping bag, dropping face down into the pillow. She felt so incredibly tired. Curling up in a ball, she struggled to put her worries out of her head but sleep was a long time coming.

It was dawn when Hunter pulled into Santa Fe. It had taken him a lot longer than he'd planned to get out of Houston. He'd had a bad feeling all day; and only after he'd followed Jenny out of town for several hours had he been halfway convinced she would be all right. He would have kept on going himself, but there was a request he'd needed to fulfill. Something Jenny had asked him to do. The *only* thing she'd said of consequence in the strange silence that had developed between them.

Hunter drove straight to his ranch house, a dusty struc-

ure down a road flanked by sagebrush and one lone ponderosa pine. The pine had been brought in a few hundred
years back, but the sagebrush was native. Couldn't kill the
stuff if you tried. There was something good about fighting
for existence. Better than being handed everything on a
silver platter.

Home sweet home.

With a sigh he climbed from the Jeep. Two hours of sleep
and then he'd be on Ortega's doorstep. Having returned
Holloway's money, he needed a job.

You'll be back . . . sooner than you know . . .

"Damn," he said softly. Ortega had been right.

There was no food in the condo. As soon as Jenny was
through with her morning shower, she slipped into a pair of
jeans and a long-sleeved shirt and a down vest. Santa Fe
was seven thousand feet above sea level and the air was
brisk and cold even though it was technically springtime.

Rawley's door was still tightly closed. She walked past it
and was pulling the keys from her purse when the phone
rang. Quickly she stepped to Rawley's door, hearing his
voice offer a soft, "Hello?"

"Rawley?" she called through the panels.

"I got it," he threw back.

Jenny backed away, seriously uneasy. Maybe it was
Brandon. Maybe some other friend to whom Rawley had
given out his number.

Maybe it's Troy.

A frisson ran down her back and she shuddered involuntarily. Troy had a cell phone. Maybe the reason he'd shown
up so conveniently every time she was gone was that he'd

called Rawley to find out if she were home, then gotten to the apartment as soon as her car was around the corner And since Hunter had confessed to following her these las few days—not Rawley—he wouldn't have been aroun were Troy to simply drop in.

Or maybe Rawley called Troy himself. The thought made her heart ache.

"Is it your dad? If it is, I want to talk to him," she called again.

"I gotta go," she heard Rawley say.

"Rawley?"

"I'm off the phone."

"Was it Troy?"

Silence.

"For Pete's sake," she declared, twisting open the knob and glaring down at her son. "You can be mad at me all you want, but act like a human being. And know this: Troy's a master at game-playing, and he's sucked you in because you don't know the first thing about him. Be careful." She swallowed back her fear. "I love you. And I won't intentionally hurt you."

He opened his mouth to argue and she shook her head fiercely, cutting him off. "I know I didn't tell you where he was. I wasn't sure myself. I didn't want to know. He used to hit me, Rawley. Do you understand that?"

"Mom . . ." He struggled upward, shocked.

"Don't trust him. Don't let him hurt you. I can't—see him. Do you understand?" she asked shakily, on the verge of tears.

"Maybe . . . maybe he didn't mean to," Rawley struggled, unable to hear anything bad about the father who'd suddenly reentered into his life. "Are you sure?" he asked in a pleading voice.

She gazed at him. He couldn't grasp it. He wouldn't. She didn't know what to say. She was no psychologist and she was dealing with tricky issues. Drawing a breath, she said in an uneven voice, "I'm going to the store. I'll be back in a little while."

"Mom . . ."

"I'm too tired to talk about it anymore," she said, and she headed out to the Volvo.

Rawley's defection hurt. Really, really hurt. There was no way Jenny could be that big and brave about it. He was fifteen. A kid. And he wanted a dad more than anything else, something she hadn't really known but maybe could have guessed. But he seemed determined to ignore the truth—even the truth about what Troy had done to her! She hadn't thought she could be more upset about everything, but she'd learned the hard way that there were many, many levels of emotional pain. Children could wound you without a thought.

And wasn't it enough just to have Troy back in her life? Wasn't that enough penance for keeping the truth from him?

She finished grocery shopping and got back to the condo, where she looked inside the bags and almost wondered if she'd picked up someone else's purchases by mistake. She had no recollection of buying the items inside.

"Mom?" Rawley stood at the end of the hall. He wore a baseball cap which shadowed his face. "I called him back. I told him what you said."

"You called Troy?" Jenny leaned her arms on the counter, needing the support.

"He said it was a mistake. He said he told you he was sorry. That you guys were arguing and then he pushed you or you pushed him, or something . . ." He shoved his hands in his pockets and tucked his shoulders in tight. "Is that about right? I mean, is that the way you remember it?"

He glanced up at her, so anxious and afraid that Jenny scarcely knew how to respond.

"He said he's still sorry," Rawley added. "He wants things to be right between you again."

"Sometimes you can't go back," Jenny tried, skirting the issue. Rawley was too hopeful and idealistic to listen to the truth about his father. And she knew only too well how Troy could manipulate people and point the blame in all directions. "There are just too many problems between us."

"Well, maybe, not yet . . ."

"Rawley, not ever," she said softly.

He opened his mouth to say something else when the doorbell rang, a loud buzzing that startled them both. Jenny hurried to look through the peephole, then felt a rush of relief and excitement to see Hunter on the porch. She threw open the door and might actually have flung herself into his arms if Benny hadn't wriggled through and started barking wildly.

"Benny!" Rawley's jaw slackened. He knelt down and grabbed the dog's silky head, to which Benny began sloppily licking him and panting and furiously wagging his tail. "What is he doing here?"

"Surprise!" Jenny shrugged, smiling, watching her son hug the dog and feeling like her heart might break in two

"It was Janice's suggestion and Brandon agreed. He thought you could use a friend."

Rawley wouldn't lift his head. His cheek lay against Benny's collar. Benny kept trying to squirm around and lick his face.

Hunter gazed at the boy and the dog. Benny had whined and thumped his tail and fretted during the ride, but bringing him to Santa Fe had been Jenny's one request. Now, seeing them together, Hunter was glad to have played some part in their reunion.

"Thank you," Jenny said sincerely.

"I might have to get myself a dog," Hunter responded.

Coming to himself, Rawley cleared his throat. He couldn't look Hunter in the eye. "Thanks for bringing him," he managed.

"My pleasure."

Rawley tipped his chin, eyeing Hunter warily. He clearly wanted to ask what Hunter's role was in Jenny's life, but it had been a pretty emotional morning already and he let the moment pass.

Jenny wanted to tell Hunter all about her trouble with her son. She wanted to confide in him, trust him, have him as a close friend. But all she could think about when she saw his lean hips and long legs and wide shoulders was making love to him again, and so she said a trifle breathlessly, "Breakfast? I got groceries this morning."

Rawley looked up, his eyes registering dismay. Hunter gazed at Jenny, his thoughts traveling the same paths hers were. He shook his head. "I'm going to talk to my old boss. Think I need to get a job."

"The Santa Fe police?"

"Maybe."

Rawley gave him a hard, long look. "You're a cop?"

"Was. Expect I will be again," Hunter drawled. "Ortega predicted as much."

"Ortega?" Jenny asked.

"Sergeant Ortega. I thought I'd drop Benny by on my way."

Rawley's interest was piqued in spite of himself. "You're going there now? To the police station?"

Hunter eyed him thoughtfully. "Would you like to come with me?"

Rawley took a step back. He was so easy to read that it melted Jenny's heart. And she wanted to kiss Hunter for picking up the vibes and going with the moment. "Go," she told Rawley. "When you get back, we'll have lunch. It's too late for breakfast anyway."

"What about Benny?"

"He can stay here with me," Jenny said, looking in one of her grocery bags. "I did manage to pick up dog food, I see. The brain is a mysterious organ."

Rawley gave his mom a quizzical look, threw a glance at Benny, hesitated for just a moment, then barreled through the door. Hunter winked at Jenny, then followed after her son.

The heat from that look and the memories it invoked caused Jenny to lean against the counter and blow her bangs out of her face with a weak, "Whew!"

She wished she'd known what real passion was when she was younger. If she'd known what she was looking for, she might not have made the mistake of marrying Troy Russell.

"What a mistake," she said aloud, as she returned to the task at hand.

Thirty thousand dollars had once seemed like a lot of money. Now it was chickenfeed. Holloway had actually managed to give it to him in hundreds. It had been a nice, fat envelope and Troy had gone right out and bought himself a car. They'd hassled him about financing, so he'd just plunked down twenty thousand and settled for a used green Explorer, which kinda stuck in his craw. He'd seen himself driving a white Lexus with gold trim. The Explorer was fine, but there was a ding in the right fender and the black paint didn't quite match over one wheel well. Still, it was better than his piece-of-crap rental.

Next, he'd ordered up a cell phone. God, he hated those salesmen! All dumb as horsemeat, although he'd let them talk him into a program that included free long distance. Might as well keep Jenny within free calling range.

Now, he chuckled as he cruised along the freeway that crossed Texas. Good old 10. He knew it well. You could take 10 all the way across the land. It started in Santa Monica and just kept right on going. He'd have to head northward in New Mexico to reach Santa Fe, but he loved the drive.

"Hey, baby," he said, stroking the dashboard and chuckling some more. He felt kinda horny. It had been a while since Dana and he really wanted to feel some female flesh. He'd flirted around with a gal in a bar last night. Not some dumb shit-kicker place like that country western bar. No, this place had been upscale Houston all the way. A sudden cold snap had brought the women out in furs and the men in suits. Sure, some of the losers wore those western shirts with the slit pockets all embroidered with little arrows on the edges. Bunch of yahoos who thought they were cowboys.

But everyone in there smelled of money and success. He'd cozied up to a lady in a cool white gown, her mink slung carelessly over her shoulders. No Texas accent for her. She was pure East coast and about as frigid as a Nor'easter. He'd watched the diamonds at her neck wink in the light from a series of votive candles. All he could think about was sticking his dick between her dark lips—some ugly new kind of lipstick that looked almost purple. But what a turn-on. She'd smelled like sex, too.

But she hadn't been alone. Just as soon as Troy turned on the charm, up came her husband. Football player size. Looking down at Troy from beneath the brim of the biggest, ugliest cowboy hat he'd ever seen.

"Y'want somethin', friend?" he inquired in a nasty drawl and a smile that said he could read Troy's dirty mind. He was sweating like a hog.

Troy shrugged. "You're a lucky man, sir."

The guy's grin widened. "Yes, I am," he said, sliding an arm around the ice princess. She didn't look any too happy about it. Married him for his money, Troy guessed. Well, he could hardly fault her. The guy looked as if he had truckloads of it. Still, he'd probably smeared his sweat all over her fancy dress.

They moved away from Troy, but Mr. Football Player left his jacket on the stool. Troy casually hooked it, took it into the bathroom, then checked the pockets for money. He was disappointed to find nothing but a couple of match-

ooks and business cards. He threw the coat onto the
rinal. He would have left it there but a memory of Val
ntruded, and he recalled the letterman's jacket she'd worn
ver her shoulders. He could picture this burly monster
ovingly dropping his coat over the ice princess's smooth,
vhite shoulders. With cold precision Troy proceeded to
nasturbate for all he was worth, letting his semen spew
nto the cashmere coat.

He left moments later and laughed all the way back to his
hotel. No fleabag joint for him anymore. Nothing but the
est now, thanks to Allen Holloway, the soul of generosity.

Settling into the seat, Troy tried to put his horniness on
hold. He really needed more than his own right hand to
ake care of the problem, but it was best he left Houston as
oon as possible. He had a few thousand left and nothing
out time to kill.

"Oh, Jenny," he sang softly. "Get ready, 'cause here I
ome!"

❈ CHAPTER THIRTEEN ❈

Hunter tried out the chair at his desk. It squeaked
protestingly as he leaned into its hard back. He was
mildly irritated to realize someone had swapped
his chair for one of their own. The substation wasn't
huge—and it wasn't far away from the main offices of the
Santa Fe Police Department. There were only a handful of
employees here. Hunter couldn't rightly complain, however, since he hadn't completely committed to the job yet.
He'd fully intended to, when he and Rawley stopped by the
station two days earlier, but thinking about Troy Russell

had made him want to stay a free agent, at least until the situation was resolved one way or another.

Ortega, aware that Hunter was sitting at his old desk came to stand in the doorway. The man had a way of bristling even when he was standing still. "So?" he demanded.

"What are these files doing here?" Hunter pointed to the pile dumped in the center of his desk. "Have you been saving them for me?"

"Of course I have! You think I trust anyone else to do your job?"

Hunter drew an exasperated breath. He experienced a sense of stepping into quicksand. Hadn't he escaped this job because of burnout?

"It's raining," Ortega added darkly. "I expect we'll see your smelly friend again."

Hunter almost smiled. Obie Loggerfield was sure to find his way to the station and camp out on the steps.

"What are you grinning about?" Ortega demanded. "You can damn well drive him into the next county. Just keep him away from me."

Hunter's smile turned into an out-and-out grin. Ortega snorted with disgust. Picking up the top file, Hunter examined the case. A rather suspicious death. The wife claimed she'd thought her husband was an intruder and she'd shot him six times, killing him with the second bullet.

"Thought you might talk to Annie Oakley," Ortega said inclining his head toward the file Hunter held.

"What's that file over there?" Hunter jerked his head toward the empty desk at the other side of the room.

"You want it?" Ortega demanded.

Hunter gave Ortega a long look. He knew how irascible he man was. He also knew he generally had a good reason o be. He wanted Hunter on these cases even if he wasn't vet officially a full-time employee. He wanted to whet Hunter's appetite and get a fresh take on the crime at the ,ame time.

Ortega grabbed the extra file and tossed it on Hunter's lesk, smiling evilly to himself. Hunter knew he'd led with lis chin even before he read the account of the UFO that lad landed outside of Santa Fe and whose alien occupants lad taken over the brain of the person reporting the crime. Apparently there was a question of whether the said person vas responsible for igniting the gas tank of his neighbor's pick-up-camper combo, and inadvertently injuring the nan's milk cow, which was standing nearby, in the process. A psychiatrist's report was underway.

"Sounds like the police work's done on that one," Hunter observed.

"That's why it's on the other desk. It's a civil case. The D.A. isn't interested in it. Let the insurance companies haggle it out." He chortled to himself, obviously enjoying unning Hunter around in circles.

Ignoring Ortega, Hunter read the particulars on the rigger-happy wife. Her small ranch lay east of town, near he banks of the Santa Fe River, a nearly dry waterbed that vas an extension of the Rio Grande. Santa Fe's water was drying up at an alarming rate as people moved to the city n droves. A headache for the city leaders that wasn't going o go away.

Picking up the file, he headed for the door. Ortega scowled at him from his office.

"If that stinking bum shows up here, I'm calling you!"

"He actually has a permanent place. In the foothills of the Sangre de Cristos."

"Fine. You can take him there!"

In his Jeep, Hunter swung out of town and down Canyon Road. He'd chosen this case because he could stop by Geneva's on the way. He parked about a block away. It was late afternoon and the lunch crowd was still dawdling a Hunter entered the restaurant. Geneva's had been open a week and its clientele was growing fast. He'd heard people on the street talk about it, and it made him feel proud by association.

True, he wasn't strictly in Jenny's life anymore. She was busy with work and wasn't interested in having him disrupt her frenetic life. Still, he'd taken to stopping in the restaurant in the afternoons and he hadn't missed the lightening of her expression when she saw him. She generally managed to say a few words while he drank a cup of coffee at the bar.

And sometimes Rawley, who bussed tables after school managed a terse hello. This was the extent of their communication, but it was an improvement from the overt hostility he'd first experienced. Ever since Hunter had taken Rawley with him to the station, and Ortega had demanded "Who's the skinny kid?", shooting Rawley a suspicious look as if he were sure the teenager were a juvenile delinquent, Hunter had somehow shot up in Rawley's estimation. Apparently the kid loved the whole law enforcement idea. And though he wasn't keen on Hunter himself, he was willing to put up with him in order to hang around the police station. Ortega hadn't warmed up to Rawley, but

Ortega never warmed up to anyone. And Rawley seemed to embrace the challenge.

It was about all Hunter could hope for at the moment. And though he didn't know where he stood with Jenny, he knew she was relieved and happy that Rawley had some kind of direction—and that direction did not include Troy Russell.

Walking into the restaurant, Hunter spied Rawley clearing off a table. The kid did resemble Russell. Hunter hadn't seen Troy since that time after Michelle's death, but he remembered everything. It was surprising, really, that Russell had managed to sneak into Jenny's apartment and see Rawley without either Jenny or him noticing. Jenny believed Rawley had called his father when she was gone. Hunter suspected that was true as well, and it was troubling to think Rawley was so completely entranced by his father.

God knew what was on Russell's mind. Hunter suspected it was nothing good.

"Hey," Rawley said, glancing up as he carried a tray of glassware from one of the tables to the kitchen bar.

"I'm heading out on a call."

"Can I go with you?" he asked swiftly.

Hunter shook his head apologetically. "The woman I'm interviewing plugged her husband with six bullets as he came into the house through a window. She said it was a mistake, though."

Rawley's eyes widened with interest. "She kill him?"

Hunter nodded. "Yeah, but the D.A.'s stalling. Not enough evidence to get her on a murder charge. Ortega wants me to interview her and see what I think. As a favor to the department," he added with an ironic smile.

"Sounds dangerous."

"Hard to tell until I see her."

Jenny came out of the backroom, leafing through a sheaf of papers. She looked up and smiled in a way that made Hunter's chest feel tight. Rawley's brows came together and his momentary connection with Hunter ended as he grabbed another tray and headed to another table.

"All's well," she told him.

"Good."

"Want a cup of coffee?"

"No, thanks."

They were like two strangers who didn't quite know how to be friends. To hell with that, Hunter thought. He didn't have to examine his feelings too closely to know that he wanted a hell of a lot more than friendship.

"I've had to reassess a few things," he told her.

"What do you mean?"

"You're the hardest-working heiress I've ever met."

"That's a rare compliment coming from you," she said, lifting one brow.

He liked her this way. Happy and relaxed and involved in her restaurant. He hated thinking Troy Russell was out there waiting to spoil it.

Hunter could last a long time in this pleasant limbo. Still, he hoped things would change all the same. Waving goodbye, he headed back outside.

"Wait!"

He turned around slowly. She held the papers close to her breast. "I'm leaving early tonight for the first time since we opened. I was wondering—would you be interested in stopping by? Tonight?"

He gazed at her anxious face. "I guess that depends on what for," he drawled.

"Dinner? Magda and Phil are coming over."

Disappointment swept through him, but he hid his feelings. "You work in a restaurant all day and you still make dinner for guests?"

"Are you kidding? I bring food home. And Magda's making drinks."

"I'll try," he said, and he saw disappointment on her face. "I've got a few things to do," he added. "Work related."

"Oh, okay. Whatever."

"All I'm saying is I might be late."

"We'll wait," she said brightly.

Arms loaded with sacks of food, Jenny could barely get the key in the lock, then nearly toppled one sack as she twisted the handle. She hurried inside and dropped her bags on the counter with a sigh of relief and Rawley followed with a couple more. Too much food, but then Gloria had practically had a fit when she learned Jenny was planning to take home only a few of her dishes. She had prepared them herself and demanded that Jenny and her friends sample everything.

"She's a nutcase," Rawley observed on the ride home from the restaurant.

"She's a genius."

"Same thing."

Now, as Jenny pulled out white takeout containers filled with enough mouth-watering food to feed a small army, she had to admit Rawley was right. "We'll make Magda and Phil take some of this with them."

"We'll be eating it till next week!" Rawley said, unwrap
ping a box and looking longingly at a steaming pile o
tamales wrapped in corn husks.

"Don't think about it."

"We're never going to eat it all. I might as well start."

"Uh-uh. I invited Hunter to join us, too. He's going to b
late, and I realize he won't be able to eat that much of it
either," she added lightly, "but at least he'll help make
dent."

Rawley pulled out another takeout container and stacke
it on two others. He didn't reply.

"I've got to figure out how to keep all this warm," Jenn
rattled on. "They should be here in fifteen minutes, five
Magda's driving." When Rawley emptied the sack an
walked out of the room, Jenny said loudly, "You like goin
with him to the police station."

"I like Sergeant Ortega," Rawley corrected shortly.

"All right," she conceded. "What don't you like abou
Hunter, besides the fact that he's a friend of mine?"

Rawley disappeared into his room, again withou
answering. Jenny gathered up the empty sacks and tried no
to mind too much. It wasn't as if she was doing anythin
with Hunter these days. And where did Rawley get off
anyway?

When the phone rang, she grabbed for it before Rawle
could pick up the extension. Too late. She heard hin
answer, "Hello?" in that eager tone he'd adopted sinc
Troy had reentered their lives.

"Rawley?" Allen Holloway asked.

"Oh. Mom's on the phone." He clicked off.

"Jenny?"

"Hi," she said.

"I was at your restaurant."

"Geneva's?" she asked blankly.

"I came to see you," he said, growing impatient. "I flew to Albuquerque and picked up a rental car. There are some things I want to talk over with you."

Unprecedented. Her father had rarely come across town to her apartment in Houston, and now he'd flown to Albuquerque and driven the sixty miles to Santa Fe? She drew a breath. The vision of having him here with Magda, Phil, and then Hunter wasn't a pretty one. Her father could alienate the most stalwart friend in thirty minutes or less.

"I'm busy tonight," she told him.

"What? You're not at work."

"I'm having guests for dinner."

He sounded taken aback. A moment later, he asked in disbelief, "Are you still involved with Calgary?"

"No. I'm not." She was firm. And mad.

"Then who's coming to dinner?"

"Magda and Phil Montgomery."

"What about Calgary?"

"What do you mean?" Jenny asked cautiously.

"Have you seen him? Is he protecting you?"

"It sounded like you were upset a moment ago when you thought I was involved with him."

"He's a burnout, Jenny. A good officer, I understand, and a decent bodyguard, but he's got a screw loose over his sister's death."

"His sister died a violent death?"

"Yes!" Allen declared vehemently. "And we know who to blame, don't we?"

"Well, for Pete's sake. You're not blaming Hunter, are you?" She was more exasperated than angry.

Allen made a frustrated sound. "No, I'm blaming Troy Russell," he said through his teeth. "In that Calgary and I totally agree. Evidence, or no evidence, he pushed her off the roof. Look, I know he's been obsessed about it. That's why I wanted him to protect you. I figured he was the best man for the job, and we both wanted the same thing. I didn't count on you falling for him," he added in disgust. "I don't want Troy near you and Rawley, but I don't want you jumping into another marriage in the future, either! All right. I'm at your gate. Buzz me through."

Jenny hung up like an automaton, depressing the button that activated the gate. She sat down on a chair in the living room and sat in the dark. Stars were thick in the sky outside and a silvery moon cast elongated blocks of light across the carpet.

Troy had killed Hunter's sister?

She was still sitting in silence when Allen knocked on the door. Rawley, curious, came from his room to see who had arrived. He gave Jenny a strange look as he opened the door for his grandfather.

"You sure need to learn some manners on the phone," Allen scolded him. "Remember who's funding your account," he added with an attempt at humor that fell utterly flat.

"Mom?" Rawley asked.

Allen frowned at her as she rose to her feet.

Troy had killed Michelle Calgary? How come Hunter had never told her?

"Mom?" Rawley repeated tensely.

She managed a watery smile, wondering how in God's name she was going to get through the rest of the evening.

The tale Hunter heard left him feeling sure Ortega had sent him out on this mission just so he could snicker. The woman in question, Bambi de la Croix—her professional name, although she didn't really want to admit that stripping was her profession—was as tired and worn as the flannel shirt he wore to do work around the ranch. She swore "on a stack of Bibles it was God's honest truth" that she had not known it was her husband who'd been sneaking in the window. When asked why she shot him so many times, she said he just kept on coming, so she kept on shooting.

"He should've come through the front door," she said, dabbing at her eyes with a handkerchief. "He knew I had that pistol and that I was scared."

"But you'd locked the front door," Hunter reminded her.

"Well, he was supposed to have his key," she declared in consternation, as if she'd nagged him about this detail forever. "And I was scared about that guy from the club that kept following me. You know what it's like to have someone stalking you, detective? No. Of course you don't. Well, it's real, real scary, let me tell you. And he was a real sicko. I don't give out favors, if you know what I mean, but he kept trying to touch me."

Bambi's face was a study in anger. Hunter thought about stalkers and obsession.

"I didn't dial 911 because I don't have a phone," she added, anticipating the question. "I told the police this already and my lawyer. I'm not changing my story 'cause it's the truth."

Troy Russell couldn't be accused of stalking—yet. And the money Allen Holloway had turned over wasn't blackmail. The burglary hadn't been traced to him, although neither he nor Jenny believed for a minute that he'd happened to show up at the time of the break-in for a visit and had been worried for Jenny's safety. *Maybe I could book him on robbery,* Hunter mused. Troy had taken Rawley's passport.

"It was an accident, detective," Bambi said, bringing Hunter back to the present. "I loved my husband. Everybody knows that."

Hunter nodded. There were reports by the neighbors of amorous foreplay in the front yard a time or two.

"I miss him," she added. "It's not the same, is it? When the person you love is gone. You got anyone special, detective?"

Jenny was special. But she wasn't his. "Has the man who was bothering you tried to reach you again?"

She shook her head. "Guess he figured out I'm a little too handy with a gun. I still keep one loaded, you know. Just in case." Her lips quivered a bit and she reached for a pack of cigarettes, holding it out for Hunter. He shook his head and she lit up. "But now my Bobby's gone," she said sorrowfully, exhaling a stream of blue smoke and looking as miserable as she purported to feel. "What's left?"

Hunter left feeling unsettled. Either she was telling the truth or she was a hell of an actress. Having met her, he was leaning toward the former.

His thoughts turned to Troy Russell—a man on the way to being a stalker as well.

What are you thinking, Russell? What do you want? I'm going to bring you down if it's the last thing I do. Stay away from Jenny, you bastard.

As he pulled into town the rain worsened, turning into an out-and-out downpour. He made the mistake of calling in from a pay phone, just as if he really worked for the police department. Asking for Ortega compounded his mistake. Before he could say one word about Bambi, Ortega practically broke his eardrum when he shouted, "Get this stinking drunk outta here. There are no dry cells in my jail!"

Obie, apparently, had arrived in Santa Fe.

He could have told Ortega it was not his job. He could have said a lot of things. Instead, he decided Obie probably needed a lift, and a water-repellent tarp, and a decent meal. "Gotta make a stop first," he said, realizing he was going to miss Jenny's dinner after all.

Hurrying through the rain, he took the steps to Jenny's front porch two at a time. He rang the bell and waited, hunched into his leather jacket. It was Rawley who answered the door. "Hi," Hunter said.

Rawley's face was a study in conflicting emotions. He held open the door without a word. Benny woofed lightly at Hunter and wagged his tail, and Hunter gave the dog a hard pat on the side which delighted the mutt.

Then he saw Jenny, looking very serious and standing in the center of the living room. Her hands were tucked into the opposite arms of a long-sleeved pink sweater. She glanced to one side and Hunter saw a man's sharply creased trouser leg.

He pushed into the condo so fast he nearly tripped

Benny. Whatever expression showed on his face took Allen Holloway aback. The older man seemed to shrink himself into his chair.

"Sorry," Hunter snapped. He'd thought it was Troy. An adrenaline rush ran through his veins and made his heart race.

"I don't appreciate you seeing my daughter," Holloway grumbled, smoothing his pants leg in an effort to regain his composure. He gave Rawley a meaningful look. "Son, I've got to talk to Mr. Calgary man-to-man. You understand."

"Allen," Jenny lay a hand against her cheek. Her skin was unnaturally pale.

"So, I should go to my room, right?" Rawley tossed out insolently.

"Are you all right?" Hunter asked Jenny, worried.

She swallowed in lieu of an answer, and Allen declared, "She's not your concern any longer!"

"Would you like—a drink?" she managed.

"I can't stay," Hunter said, wondering what Allen had said to her. Clearly something had gone on before he arrived. "I've got to go to the station and run an errand."

"Back with the police?" Allen asked.

"Not completely." He gave Jenny a lingering glance. Her gaze seemed unfocused, as if she were looking at something far away.

"What kind of errand?" Rawley asked, giving his grandfather a resentful look that Allen didn't quite see.

"Relocation project." Rawley was gazing down at his toes, refusing to move. After a moment Hunter invited, "Want to help me?"

"Can I?" Rawley glanced at his mom.

Jenny momentarily surfaced. She pressed her lips together, then said, "Sure," in an unnatural voice.

"You're certain you're all right?" Hunter asked with real concern. What the hell was going on?

"So, you don't want the brandy?" she countered.

He shook his head slowly. Something had transpired between Allen and Jenny, something that involved Troy, he was sure of it. He wanted to demand that they tell him what was up, but Rawley was waiting expectantly by his side.

"We'll be back in a couple of hours," Hunter said tautly. "Sorry about dinner."

Jenny nodded.

"Take the dog," Allen suggested in a tone that made it an order.

Benny hadn't exactly been waiting for Allen's permission. He wriggled between Rawley and Hunter at the door and splashed out into the dark, wet night.

The nightclub was off Cerrillos Road on the southwest side of Santa Fe. It wasn't the fanciest spot, but at least it wasn't a topless, jiggle-it-all, wave your near-naked ass in a guy's face kind of place. Troy had never liked those miserable dives. He wanted something a little more upscale, but he didn't want to go to any of those trendy places around the plaza. Too crowded. Too tight.

He'd checked into La Fonda for the night, which was all southwestern tile and adobe right on the edge of the plaza and boasted being "the end of the Santa Fe trail." The hotel was renown and it had a price tag to match, but he liked being there. La Fonda was famous. Celebrities stayed here.

Troy had expected to find plenty of action but tonight' crowd had been too touristy, the bars filled with familie and couples in khaki slacks and sweaters. What he wanted was a woman wrapped in a tight dress. He didn't even care if she had two cents to rub together because Jenny wa waiting.

He left La Fonda and headed to another area of town.

The club on Cerrillos Road was called Marty's. Marty was a woman, apparently, for the logo was a set of female eyes with long, long lashes done in blue neon. Troy slic onto a stool at the bar. His night with Dana was a lifetime ago and he was hungry for sex. In fact, it was all he could think about tonight, which came as a bit of a surprise. Hi sex drive was healthy, and women were as available as dirt so why was he so edgy? His anxiety and eagerness were new and mildly disturbing. What he really wanted to do was just *bite* the soft, white curve of a woman's neck.

Maybe he shouldn't wait for Jenny. Maybe he should drive over to her place and just take her. Rawley had given him all the directions he would ever need, although the blasted area was surrounded by a perimeter fence and gate That pissed him off. Was she afraid of him?

He'd show her. He'd show her and that fat cat father o hers.

And that other guy. The one Rawley had admitted was sniffing around. Troy had wanted to wring the answers from the kid's scrawny neck. Rawley, after mentioning some guy, had maddeningly refused to give any furthe information. He was protecting the son-of-a-bitch and i pissed Troy off no end. Nobody was going to mess with Jenny. Jenny was his and always had been.

"Give me a scotch on the rocks," Troy said.

The bartender poured him a drink and slid the glass across the bar. There were no women around except for a few shanks with no tits. He'd misjudged the place. No action here.

He drank the scotch and tossed some money down. For a moment he'd wondered if he could skip on the bill but the bartender had a fish eye on him. As he was walking out the door something worth looking at finally came in. She was with her girl friend but she was pert and bouncy with white teeth and a "Hello, there!" on her lips when she saw him.

Charm. That's all it took, charm.

"Ladies, may I buy you a drink?"

They both grinned at him. Two was too many, unfortunately. He was going to have to divide and conquer.

Obie lay in a huddle outside the station front door. A battered hat leaked rain onto a soggy poncho, its bright Navajo design obscured by a layer of filth and grime. One look at Obie and Rawley went dead quiet.

"Why aren't you inside?" Hunter asked.

"The sergeant threw me out," Obie complained. He squinted a look at Rawley, then grinned. About every other tooth was a black gap. Rawley gazed on in fascination. "You kin call me Obie," he said, producing an equally grimy hand from beneath the poncho.

Rawley shook it without hesitation.

"I'm going to have to take you home, Obie," Hunter said. "Thought we might make a stop first for some new supplies."

He cocked his head, birdlike. "Could sleep inside," he

suggested. "Save you some trouble."

"Don't think His Majesty would go for that."

Obie chuckled. "What kind of supplies?"

"The dry kind."

"Well, that suits me just fine, then." He struggled to his feet and Hunter offered him a hand. The rain had liquefied the layers of body oils and plain old dirt into a noxious goo Hunter could scarcely contain a cough as he helped Obie up.

Rawley scrambled into the back of the Jeep to graciously allow Obie the front passenger seat. Benny, who'd been left inside, started whining. Hunter gazed at him for a moment and wondered if it could be possible that Benny, a dog who would roll in anything, was affected by Obie's rank smell.

"Gotta talk to the boss for a moment," he said. "Do you mind waiting?" This was for Rawley's benefit since he was the one forced into confinement with Obie.

"Nope." But he rolled down his window just the same.

Hunter's mind was still crowded with thoughts of Jenny as he let himself into the station. The way she'd acted, as if her brain was stalled and she was going through the motions.

Ortega was waiting for him, pacing his office as if Hunter were already an errant employee instead of someone thinking about taking the job. "Did you see him?" he demanded, jerking his head in the direction of the front door.

"He's in the Jeep. I'm taking him back to his home."

"Home." He snorted, but he didn't add anything further on the subject of Obie. Instead he launched into questions about Bambi. What did Hunter think of her? Did he catch her in a lie? Was she properly remorseful or full of smugness at getting away with murder?

Hunter had no good answers for him, and his saying so just fueled Ortega's frustration. "Tell me something I want to hear!" Ortega demanded.

Ignoring him, Hunter asked, "Whatever happened to the guy who was stalking her?"

"Who?" he asked automatically, then grimaced and dismissed the charge with a wave of his hand. "You fell for that crap?"

"She said she was scared of the guy."

"Lady with six bullets to drill into her old man? C'mon!" Ortega gazed at him almost pityingly, as if Hunter were the biggest patsy on earth. "She's a stripper who does the bump and grind after hours, if you know what I mean. Any stalker of hers was a paying customer."

"Maybe. All the more reason to stalk her. He had a taste, and now he wants more."

"You want my opinion? She bumped off her old man so she could bump and grind without interference."

"She said she thought he was breaking in and that she killed him by accident."

"And you believe her?"

Hunter shrugged. "There's no evidence against her. You knew that already, so why'd you send me there?"

"Because I *want* some evidence! Something concrete!" he snapped, exasperated. "I thought you might be up to the task."

It was a back-handed compliment in a way. No one else had been able to get Ortega what he wanted. He'd hoped

Hunter would. "So, you want me to manufacture evidence?"

That pissed Ortega off, as it was meant to. "Get the hell out of here," he growled.

"How would you protect someone against a stalker?"

He snorted. "Stick to them like glue and hope the perp gets locked up for some other crime before it's too late."

Not exactly a ringing endorsement for the efficacy of one-on-one protection. "You think stalkers ever get cured?"

"No," was Ortega's blunt answer, and though Hunter knew better than to listen to everything his opinionated boss said, he silently agreed on this one. The sergeant gave him a hard look. "Something bothering you?"

Hunter didn't know whether to bring up Jenny or not. "A lady being pushed by her ex-husband."

"Pushed?"

"Meaning he's on the scene, pushing, after a fifteen-year absence."

"Christ, Calgary. This is about that Holloway woman. I knew better than to send you that FedEx package!" He shook his finger in front of Hunter's nose. "I know your history. Better leave that bastard Troy whatever-his-name-is alone."

"That bastard killed my sister."

Ortega folded his arms. "No evidence is really a bitch isn't it?"

"Anything else?" Hunter asked, his own temper rising.

"Just get your smelly rodent friend outta here." He waved in the direction of the front door. "Hell, the way it's raining, he'll probably be back by dawn."

"I'm getting Obie settled for a while."

"Don't count on it," was the sergeant's glum prediction.

Hunter walked out stiffly. He knew Ortega only criticized him for his own good, but it got under his skin just the same. He had to switch off his bad attitude as he swung into the Jeep, however; the stench allowed for nothing but full attention. Drawing in a shallow breath, Hunter threw the Jeep into gear, stopping on the way out of town at a store that specialized in outdoor equipment. He managed to squeak inside just before it closed for the night. Loading up on gear, he hauled it out to the car and tossed it in the back. All the way to Obie's living quarters, the happy recipient couldn't stop thanking him for the sleeping bag and Coleman lantern and waterproof tarps.

"You are a prince among men," Obie declared as Hunter and Rawley helped him get situated.

An hour and a half later, with Obie settled in, a new tarp covering his leaky tent, the soft glow of the lantern escaping from a myriad of holes, like fingers pointing every which way into the dark night, Hunter, Rawley, and Benny started back, windshield wipers slapping out a rhythm.

"Why do you take care of him?" Rawley asked curiously.

"Sometimes people need a little extra care."

"Sergeant Ortega doesn't like him."

"Sergeant Ortega doesn't like anybody," Hunter pointed out.

Rawley nodded, looking older for a moment than his fifteen years. "Are you trying to take care of my mom?"

Now there was a loaded question. Not sure if Rawley's amiable mood would last past the truth, Hunter said, "I like your mom. I don't say that about many people."

"Kinda like Ortega?" He flashed a smile.

"God, I hope not."

Rawley laughed, heard himself, immediately quieted. Hunter could read his mind. A relationship with Hunter meant betraying his father. There was no gray area for the kid and he was struggling to juggle everything and still keep to his own code of honor.

They pulled up to the gate and Rawley punched the keypad numbers to slide back the gate. Hunter drove through and stopped in front of Jenny's condo. There were two cars now instead of one. The Montgomerys had arrived. And Allen Holloway hadn't left.

Hunter, Rawley, and Benny entered with a wet whoosh of rain. Benny jogged over to Magda before Rawley could grab his collar and Benny dropped a dirty, wet paw on her lap.

"Ohmigod!" she declared, more surprised than angry.

"Get that dog out of here!" Allen yelled. His skin turned an ugly red.

"I'm sorry, Magda!" Jenny jumped to her feet. "Come in the kitchen and let me help you. Bad dog, Benny," Jenny scolded, but she couldn't put any real threat in her voice, and the mutt just panted at her and waved his tail.

Hunter was relieved to see she was acting more normally.

Magda gazed down on the smudge. "It's okay," she said, as she followed Jenny into the kitchen. She winked at Hunter as she passed.

Phil shook Hunter's hand as Rawley hauled Benny away from the guests. "We're going outside for a while," Rawley muttered to no one in particular, then he and Benny returned to the rain. Jenny gazed after them, frowning.

"So, I hear you're a citizen of Santa Fe," Phil said. "Small world, huh?"

"Small world." Jenny, or Allen, had undoubtedly filled them in with all the details. He glanced around, amazed by the amount of food displayed on the table. Dinner was long over but there were platters everywhere piled with colorful, spicy southwestern cuisine. If he'd been hungry at all, he would have been in heaven. As it was, he was lost in a swirl of thoughts, all of them centering around Jenny.

The fierce scowl Holloway sent Hunter's way couldn't have been good for the old man's blood pressure. "What is your role these days, Calgary?" he demanded.

"Allen," Jenny warned wearily.

Magda seized the moment to break the tension. "Well, thank God!" she said to Hunter as she held out her arms for a hug. Hunter complied and Magda rolled her eyes in Allen's direction. "It's about time you got here. The party is simply nothing without you!"

Phil sat back down on the couch, also holding a brandy. He plunked on a beret and tilted it over one ear. Though he tried for a jaunty appearance, his expression was slightly strained. "Magda made some margaritas earlier but I'm having a brandy." He lifted his glass in silent invitation.

"Oh, sorry. Are you ready for one now?" Jenny said again, brushing hair away from her face. Her distraction was totally worrying.

"Thanks," Hunter accepted and she walked into the kitchen where an expensive bottle—supplied by Allen, no doubt—sat amongst the plates of food.

"What a kick to have you in Santa Fe," Magda said. "You

should have told us!"

"I should have said a lot of things," he agreed, his gaze still on Jenny.

She said quietly as she handed him his drink, "My father's worried about Troy." She was careful not to let their fingers touch during the exchange. Clearly she was just making conversation in front of her friends. "Would you like something to eat?"

"No, thanks. I don't have much of an appetite."

"You, too?" she declared. The automaton disappeared. He could hear suppressed hysteria in her voice.

What the hell was going on?

"Darling, we were waiting for you," Magda said meaningfully to Hunter. "We didn't want to leave until you got here."

Phil hurriedly climbed to his feet at Magda's cue. Suddenly aware of the beret, he slid it from his head, then stared down at it as if he couldn't understand where it had come from. He added under his breath, "It's good you're here."

Allen sipped his brandy and simply waited.

Hunter realized he was tense, as if he was anticipating some kind of fight. Forcing himself to relax, he said, "We had to take a friend of mine home."

"You weren't working on a case?" Phil asked with sudden eagerness. He seemed relieved by the change of subject.

"Not really." He wasn't about to talk about Bambi de la Croix, and he sure as hell didn't want to talk about stalkers and murder and feeling afraid. But they were waiting for some explanation, so he said instead, "I had to talk to my old sergeant about a few things."

"That sounds ominous."

Now, as Hunter looked around at the expectant faces, realizing they were hoping he would take their minds off whatever had transpired in the room before his appearance, he said simply, "We have a vagrant who appears whenever it rains and camps out on the police station steps. That's about the extent of tonight's crime wave. Rawley and I took him home."

"I wish Rawley would come back," Jenny said suddenly.

"He's got that dog with him," Allen said. "He'll be fine."

"I just don't like to think that he'll go outside the gates."

"I'll find him," Hunter said, heading straight for the door. Stepping onto the porch, he'd just closed the door behind him when he saw the boy and the dog walking beneath the corner street lamp. Rain slanted downward, nearly veiling them. They were both soaking wet.

Hunter eased himself back onto the porch, out of sight, aware that he could ruin the shaky trust Rawley had placed in him by one false move. Reopening the door he nearly walked into Phil and Magda.

Magda grabbed his arm and dragged him back outside. "Her father's scared the bejeezus out of her," she whispered in a rush. "He said Troy killed your sister! Is that true, Hunter?"

"Were you really working for Allen?" Phil asked, sounding disillusioned.

"He was trying to keep Jenny safe!" Magda shot her husband a harsh glare, before turning urgently back to Hunter. "We understand and we're with you all the way. Just do it, okay? Take care of her. Jenny always said Troy was a bastard, but I'm chilled. I mean it."

"So, Allen came to you and asked you to protect her?" Phil pressed.

Before Hunter could respond, Magda cut him off again. "We love her, that's all. And I'm glad I fell into your lap that time in Puerto Vallarta so that you two could get past all the nonsense and meet each other."

"Here comes Rawley," Phil observed.

Hunter glanced around. Head bent against the rain, Rawley was moving their way, Benny faithfully at his side.

Magda squeezed his hand hard. "I'm glad you're a cop, or ex-cop, or whatever. She needs someone in her life who's looking out for her best interests. And it isn't that father of hers. Allen Holloway manipulates everybody without even trying."

"I'm sure Hunter's got the whole picture, Magda."

"He thinks money is all you need. Jenny doesn't want any part of it, though."

"Magda . . ."

"Hey, Rawley!" Magda greeted the boy. She would have scooped him into her arms but Rawley, sensing maternal hugging about to attack him, stayed ten feet out of reach, one hand on Benny's collar. "Oh, don't worry about him, honey. I can clean my clothes. There's still plenty of food," she added, holding up a huge sack. "I didn't make a dent in it."

Rawley didn't respond. Magda gave Hunter another hug, then she and Phil bent their heads against the rain and scurried to their Mercedes. Rawley stared after them, then up at Hunter who opened the door and silently invited him inside. Rawley hesitated, then swept past, a drenched

Benny slipping through before Hunter could grab him again. Allen yelled, "Get the dog out of here!" and Jenny followed with, "Clean up his muddy pawprints, please, Rawley. And take off your shoes."

For once Rawley complied without complaint, dragging Benny to the bathroom for some paw washing and fur toweling.

Jenny sat down quietly on the couch, as remote as the horizon.

Now Hunter knew she was thinking about Michelle's death. Now he knew what had kept her so distant and distracted.

But would she be able to forgive him for keeping the truth from her yet again?

❈ CHAPTER FOURTEEN ❈

She sat deathly quiet in the darkened living room. Allen had finally left after banishing Rawley to his room, railing to Hunter about everything from Troy Russell to preying on his daughter in her distraught state to keeping the truth about his sister's death from her. It was Allen who explained that Michelle had been pushed from the rooftop. Allen, who told about Hunter tracking down Troy. Allen, who warned his daughter to start looking out for herself and stop being so trusting.

He finally left only when he realized Jenny had stopped listening. She was lost in her own world, and neither Allen nor Hunter could penetrate her shell. Now, Hunter stood by the window and wished he could offer some help. He wished to high heaven that Allen had kept the information about Michelle to himself. Hunter hadn't intentionally kept the aspects of his sister's death from her, but he'd wanted to tell Jenny in his own way, in his own time. He knew she was frightened.

"I wasn't sure how to tell you," he admitted now, shoving his hands in his pockets and staring into the black sky. The rain had momentarily ceased, but the sky still looked threatening. He was glad for the unusual weather. He hoped there would be enough to lift the trickling Santa Fe River into at least a gurgle.

She threaded her fingers together. "You're sure he killed her?"

She wanted him to say no. She wanted him to give her some hope.

"I can't prove it, but yes."

"Troy's a bully and he scared me the other day." Her throat worked. "But he couldn't murder someone. Not intentionally!"

She looked away, outside the window. The moonlight colored her profile a soft blue. She was grasping at straws, and she knew it.

"What did he do to you?"

Jenny asked distractedly, "What?"

"When he came by the other day. He did something to you. What?"

"Oh . . ." She rubbed her throat with her hand. "He . . . kissed me." She shuddered delicately with revulsion. "He pressed his mouth on mine so hard it hurt, and then he—touched me—grabbed me—in the—" Heaving a harsh sigh, she said through pressed lips "—in the crotch."

Hunter's blood ran hot through his veins. He felt blinded

with rage. Despite everything he knew about Troy Russell, he'd still believed the man wouldn't attack Jenny.

"It was quick," she said. "He didn't want to be caught by Rawley. He just wanted me to know that he could overpower me, I think."

Hunter couldn't answer. Anything he said might be construed as a vindictive attack on Russell, and he knew that Jenny didn't need his own intense emotions fueling her fear.

"It couldn't have been an accident," she said. Though she stated it as fact, she was hoping he would negate it.

"My sister wouldn't throw herself off a building in despair. She wasn't that desperate, as far as I knew, although she didn't tell me everything. I know he hit her, though. She had the bruises, but she lied about it. I couldn't understand it." He bit out the words. "I still can't."

"I can." Jenny's lips quivered.

Hunter froze, stunned.

"She was ashamed." She gazed at him across the darkened room. "Ashamed that she'd made such a terrible choice. Ashamed to have everyone else be right about him but her."

"I would have done anything to help her. She was pregnant, Jenny."

She flinched. "So was I."

"But you let your father help you."

"He bought Troy off!" she answered bitterly. "Your sister probably felt you would kill him."

This was so patently true that Hunter stopped cold. He'd wanted to squeeze the life out of the man single-handedly. Only Troy's clever sidestepping and accusations of harassment had kept Hunter from attempting just that.

Jenny's lashes fluttered closed. "I just don't want to believe it, even though I know it's true."

He crossed the room and clasped her hands. They were icy. Rubbing them with the pads of his thumbs, he said, "I'm not leaving you alone."

"I'm afraid for Rawley."

He nodded.

With that she seemed to collapse in on herself. He twisted around and sat on the couch beside her, drawing her trembling body to him, half-sitting, half-lying, with Jenny draped over his right thigh.

He wanted to tell her he loved her. The words seemed to whisper into the air, but they were unspoken. "I'm not leaving you," he said instead. "Ever."

Her hands slid across his chest, and he tucked her close.

They fell asleep, exhausted, tangled like lovers.

Rawley awoke to total darkness. Benny lifted his head beside him, alerted to his movements. Absently patting the dog's head, he thought of Hunter Calgary, and got angry all over again.

He thunked his pillow with his fist and crushed it into a ball, then lay back again with his head propped up, staring at the ceiling. A moment later he reached around the bed and grabbed his soccer ball; then, lying back down, he tossed it lightly upward, catching it almost silently.

He almost liked the guy. Almost. He'd brought Benny from Houston, and he let Rawley tag around with him at the police station from time to time. He even put up with all the guff Sergeant Ortega threw at him, which was kinda funny, since it really infuriated Ortega, you could just tell. But Ortega liked him, too.

And then there was that thing with Obie Loggerfield. Phew! What a garbage dump the old guy was, but really cool, too. Rawley liked that His Majesty bit. The guy had a dignity that was real. And Hunter treated Obie with respect, not condescension.

Rawley nearly missed catching the ball. He held it in his hands, listening. He didn't want to wake his mom. She was working really hard and happier than she'd been in a while. Sure, she was out of her mind about his dad, but women were kinda crazy sometimes. Brandon had assured him that you just had to just ignore the really weird things they did.

But he couldn't deny that his mom *liked* having Hunter Calgary around. He cringed at the thought of them dating. The idea gave him a sick feeling in the pit of his stomach. And he knew the guy was trying to move in on his mother. Maybe he hadn't quite succeeded yet, but he didn't seem to be leaving anytime soon. And Christ! He lived in Santa Fe!

Rawley was certain there was some kind of conspiracy there. He wished he could call his dad right now. Was it too late? Probably. Parents freaked if you called them after nine P.M. And what about his mom? Rawley tossed the ball one more time, catching it deftly. He couldn't get a reading on her.

Sometimes she seemed thrilled to have Hunter around; other times she looked worried sick. Like tonight. Something had happened and the only consolation was that Hunter seemed as baffled by everyone's attitude as Rawley did. But he'd hoped Hunter might sort of go away. He still did. He had a dad now, and it bugged him to think that someone else might try to take over. Really bugged him.

Rawley gently dropped the ball on the floor beside Benny. He lay on his side and gazed at the golden-haired mutt. But Benny was resting. He breathed deeply, emitting little doggy sighs that made Rawley grin.

Had Hunter left? Or was he still here?

The grin slid off his face in a flash. Alarmed, Rawley slid out of bed. He dragged a pair of jeans over his boxers, unwilling to have anyone see him half-dressed. Tiptoeing to the front room he stopped short. Blood rushed to his head. They were lying down on the couch together!

His chest constricted. He couldn't breathe. It was a total relief to realize they were fully clothed. They even had their shoes on, he noted quickly, fading back into the shadows of the hallway.

Rawley sneaked back into his own room but didn't undress. He didn't even lie down again. He stood in the center of the room, thoughts racing. He should have told his dad more about that guy. He should have warned him!

Picking up the receiver, he dialed his father's cell phone number from memory. He didn't care if he got yelled at for calling so late. It rang four times before the voice-mail message came on.

"Hi, Dad," he said in a strained voice, glancing toward the door. "Mom's been seeing this guy. You know the one I told you about? He's here and I don't want him here. You need to get here right away. I—" He heard his voice crack and get higher. "Where are you? You said you were coming. Dad! Please! You've got to get here *fast!*"

Troy sat silently in his green Explorer and watched the

gray light of dawn brighten the eastern sky. His mood was black as he sat outside the wrought iron fortress where Jenny had holed up. He could scale the fence somewhere, if he so desired, but he couldn't get the car through without permission from within. He slammed his palm against the steering wheel, then slammed it three more times, grinding his teeth to contain the scream that wanted to erupt from the depths of his anger.

He knew he was being irrational. But he was powerless to do anything other than move forward. He waited for her to come out. He could follow her if she were with Rawley, or if the kid was left inside, he would phone him.

Troy glanced at his cell phone. He'd turned it off for economy's sake. Power down to compensate for the piddling amount of money Holloway had given him. He'd tried to use Patricia's credit card one too many times and had learned that access had been denied.

Access denied.

He threw a bitter glance at the wrought iron fence with its arrow-tipped spikes. They were always trying to keep him out, but it wouldn't work. He was going to eat them alive.

Last night had not gone well. Troy grimaced and growled low in his throat. He'd known two women would be trouble, but his embarrassment was profound.

They'd been more than eager. Heather and Jessica. Friends. He'd bought them a couple of drinks and then had pretended it was time for him to leave. They'd begged him to stay and though he'd merely sipped his own drink, they'd belted back a few of those flavored martinis that were so popular these days until they were totally tanked and inhibitions were gone.

He'd tried to figure out how to divide them. He'd liked Heather better than Jessica. Liked her rounded tits and ass, whereas Jessica was leaner and more athletic and she laughed like a hyena. They'd talked him into coming to their place, a little house on the north side of town down a gravel lane that turned out to be quite attractive. Heather drove their car and Troy followed. He could feel that crazy beat in his head, that need to drum his fingers and jiggle his leg. He wanted to ride Heather like the bitch she was.

But Jessica was there and she was more aggressive. She kept laughing and telling jokes and grabbing him by the arm like they were old buddies. He wanted to slap her silly. He'd tightened up and that's when it had all gone to hell.

They poured more drinks. Vodka with a spray of soda and tiny ice cubes. Troy held his glass but never took a swallow. It seemed like his vision was filmed in red, somehow, and all he could see was Heather's bouncing butt cheeks. He finally reached over and squeezed. She slapped his hand away, but playfully, and then Jessica went in for the kill. Coming up behind him, she clamped that big ugly mouth on the back of his neck, sucking and moaning while her fingers traveled downward and played with him through his pants. He lay limp. And even when Heather approached from the front and slid her tongue between his lips, Troy couldn't get aroused. He felt used. Trapped. Claustrophobic and subservient.

They did their utmost, but Troy yanked away from them. He grabbed Jessica by the throat at one point, until her eyes bugged out in surprise. *Then* he wanted her, but he wanted her down on her knees. When he tried to push her down she resisted and yelled; and then Heather started yelling and yelling and Troy felt like his head was going to explode.

They were laughing when he left! *Laughing!*

Humiliation burned so bright he felt like he was on fire. And it hadn't burned out yet.

Running a hand through his hair, he knew he looked like hell. This wasn't the Troy Russell of old. He'd lost something. He wasn't sure what, but he'd lost it just the same.

He sat for another hour, wondering if he should call Patricia and try to mend some fences. He could go back to L.A. and make nice and she would take him back. She wasn't all that attractive, though—and she wasn't that wealthy. If he really wanted to play the whipped puppy he could go back to Frederica. If she were on an upswing she would take him in, no holds barred.

But he couldn't imagine being their stud. Either one of them. For the first time in his life Troy didn't trust his cock. Last night had shattered his confidence. Women were such ball-busters. They thrived on humiliating men. They laughed and pointed.

You had to teach them respect. You had to beat the fear of God into them.

He'd always known it, but it suddenly sounded like an epiphany. He had to make them cower and cry and gaze at him in fear.

He got an achingly stiff hard-on just thinking about it.

Jenny awoke to a sense of heat and confinement. Her arm was numb and she realized it was crammed beneath her and she was pressed into the couch, her legs entangled with another body. Hunter's.

She jolted to wakefulness and her sharp movement made him stir. While she assimilated the situation, he said lazily, "I took your shoes off."

She gazed down at her stockinged feet, wiggling her toes. "Thanks."

"How are you feeling this morning?"

"Cramped." With that he turned on his side, facing her. The moment lengthened. "I have to brush my teeth," she whispered through tight lips.

He grinned, and his smile was just too devastating. It shattered her strength. In one sinuous move, she freed herself from his embrace and headed into the bathroom, groaning at the sight of her wild hair and rumpled sweater. Brushing her hair and teeth, she scurried into her room and changed her wrinkled pink sweater and creased trousers for a black sweater and slacks to match.

She returned to the living room to find him gone. She looked into the kitchen where Hunter was fiddling with her coffee maker. The sight was so domestic she felt slightly breathless.

I want this, she thought fiercely.

"Here, let me do that," she said and proceeded to make coffee as he settled onto one of the stools she'd brought from Houston and leaned his elbows on the kitchen bar.

His silence unnerved her and she threw him a look. "What?" she demanded.

"You okay?"

"You mean after my near breakdown last night?" She watched the coffee begin to run rapidly into the glass carafe. "I've been living in a little fantasy world ever since

I got to Santa Fe. I pushed all my problems aside and thought they wouldn't follow me here, but then my father showed up and told me . . ." She lifted a hand helplessly, then dropped it to her side. "I think Troy would do anything," she admitted, meeting his gaze directly.

"I do, too."

"You've met him," she said, as if the thought were new. Maybe it was. She hadn't been thinking all that clearly last night.

Hunter nodded.

"I wish you had told me."

"I was supposed to watch you, not meet you. I didn't plan to tell you anything."

"But later," Jenny insisted. "After we—were together. You should have told me."

"And if I had?"

She blinked. "I would have thrown you out of my life and screamed at you for working for my father." She gazed at him in a way that constricted his heart. "What can I do? I want a restraining order against Troy. I can't bear that he sees Rawley! And he won't quit. I really do know that, even if I've been trying to repress it. He'll follow us and follow us as long as my father keeps paying him."

It wasn't just the money. Hunter knew it, and maybe Jenny knew it, but he didn't say it aloud. Troy was toying with Rawley to torture Jenny. And both Jenny and Rawley stood to get hurt.

She poured them each a cup of coffee. He couldn't bear thinking how Troy intended to hurt Jenny.

"Ortega wants me back, but I'm not going yet."

"I'll pay you to stay with me," she said quickly.

"I'm staying with you anyway. What about Rawley? How's he going to feel about this?"

"He won't understand," she admitted tiredly, "but I can't say that I care right now."

"Russell will show his hand eventually. I want to be there when it happens. So, I'm sticking to you like a leech, like a lover."

Her eyes left his, looking anywhere but directly at him. With a small swallow, she admitted, "I hope so."

Hunter relaxed the muscles in his back. He hadn't even realized how tight they'd been until now. "Come on. I'll take you to my ranch. I, too, need to brush my teeth, and unless you plan on plying me with more fabulous southwestern food, I also could use some breakfast. This time I cook."

She smiled at him, delighted by his suggestion. "I don't have to be at the restaurant until later."

"Gloria could run that place blindfolded, with her hands tied behind her back, and in a wheelchair, even if she were Geneva's only employee."

Jenny laughed. "She's fierce."

Hunter basked in the sound of her happiness. "I'm scared of her."

"Uh-huh." She lifted her cup to her lips, her eyes crinkling at the corners with mirth.

"I'm serious. That's really why I stayed with you last night. The dreams, you see." He gave a mock shudder. "I need protection."

"Let's go to your ranch," she said, and there was a wealth of meaning in her words that Hunter didn't miss. He slid a look over his shoulder, in the direction of the hall and further down, Rawley's bedroom.

Jenny took the initiative, heading to Rawley's door and rapping lightly with her knuckles. When he didn't respond, she turned the knob. "Rawley?"

"What?" was the surly response.

"I'm going out with Hunter for a while. Do you want to come?"

"Where are you going?" he demanded.

"For a drive. Then to see his ranch."

Silence. "I wouldn't want to intrude."

"You wouldn't be," she assured him, ignoring his martyred tone.

"I'll just stay here. I've got homework for tomorrow."

"All right," Jenny said, closing the door softly. Through the panels Rawley yelled, "How long will you be gone?"

"A couple of hours."

When he didn't respond Jenny came back into the kitchen and raised her eyebrows.

"Let's vamoose," Hunter said, grabbing his rain-spattered leather jacket. He glanced outside. The rain had let up and the air felt drier already. Soon Santa Fe would return to its usual crisp, cold dry desert.

Jenny tossed on a wind breaker and they headed outside. She'd put on some light cologne and she smelled like heaven.

"I'm glad he wanted to stay," she admitted.

"Not as much as I am."

They ran to the Jeep, holding hands, dodging the shrinking puddles and laughing.

The black Jeep came through the gates and turned toward

town. Troy was so absorbed in his own problems he paid it scant attention until he caught a glimpse of Jenny's profile. Adrenaline shot through him.

Who was she with?

He was instantly infuriated. Rawley had told him there was a man sniffing around her, and though Troy had minded, he hadn't considered him serious competition. Jenny was the ice princess. She didn't take lovers.

Suddenly Troy wasn't so certain. Anger flooded him in red-hot waves. Goddamn the bitch! She was doing it on purpose to taunt him.

He swore violently, coldly under his breath, twisting the ignition, only to let it die a moment later. If Jenny was out with her lover, Rawley was in. Switching on his cell phone, he realized there was a message. Growling in frustration, he punched in his code and listened to Rawley's young voice telling him that his mother was involved with this guy.

Troy shivered. There was no time to waste. He phoned Rawley back and the kid answered on the first ring.

"Hello?"

"Hi, there, Rawley," he said, forcing a lightness to his voice even while inside his head he was screaming. He shook his head, trying to clear it. His control was slipping

"Dad!" He sounded relieved. "You got my message?"

"Just did. I was thinking about coming over and checking this guy out for myself."

"You can't! They just left together."

Troy squeezed his fist closed and held it as tight as he could. "Really."

"I don't know about him. I just wish he'd go away

Why'd he have to show up now?"

"Hey, I'm in the neighborhood. What's that code for the gate? I'll just come on in and we can do something together."

"Great!" Rawley rattled off the numbers and Troy burned them into his memory.

"See you in a few," he signed off. He was half tempted to chase after Jenny but he hadn't lost it completely. Oh, no. Troy could play a waiting game if he had to.

He unfisted his hand and stared at the fingers. He wanted to strangle someone. Someone with blue eyes and a false smile. Someone frigid and beautiful. Someone wealthy . . . who would be wealthier as soon as her old man popped off.

That thought cooled his killing fever a little.

Hunter's ranch lay nestled in a small valley, tucked against the rolling hills outside of Santa Fe. Jenny stepped out of the Jeep and Hunter held open a gate made from coyote fencing. They walked along a pebble-lined path to the front door, which he unlocked. Holding open the door, he allowed her entry.

The place was small and fairly bare, little more than a cabin. The furniture was knotty pine and a stack of wood lay on the slate hearth of a river-rock fireplace that rose to the ceiling. Two doors jutted off one end, and she could see the curved bar that led to the kitchen. It was tidy and spare and cozy enough to elicit a pleased, "oh . . ." from her lips.

He shrugged, somewhat embarrassed. "I haven't done much to it, besides repair the outside fence. No livestock. I bought it with the furniture from a gal who was getting married and moving to Phoenix."

"It's really nice," she said, meaning it.

"I could make a fire," he suggested.

"I could make breakfast, if you have some supplies."

"I said I'd do that," he argued.

"Oh, come on. Let me have a task."

Hunter lifted a brow. "Good luck. There's bread in the freezer. Cereal. No milk. Frozen bacon. Anything perishable perished while I was gone."

"More coffee?"

"Instant."

"Fine by me."

"Forget it," he said, changing his mind. "I'll take you to breakfast."

"In a while," she said, enjoying the moment.

While Hunter attended to the fire, Jenny rummaged around in the kitchen. It was fun and slightly dangerous to peek into his life. Clearly he hadn't made much of one for himself in Santa Fe. The place felt untouched, in a way. As if it were waiting for someone to take it over.

She boiled water in a pan and poured it over instant coffee crystals. Handing Hunter a cup, she inhaled the aroma.

"Not the best if you're used to lattes and espressos," he observed, taking a mouthful.

"I can deal," she said.

She sat down on the couch as the fire got going. "I'm going to take a quick shower," he told her, and was gone before she could answer. She heard the water start up and had to close her mind to the vision of him naked . . . and wet.

Fifteen minutes later he returned wearing clean jeans and

a loose gray sweater, his hair still glistening with water. His feet were bare. Pouring himself another cup of coffee, he asked if she needed a refill. Jenny shook her head.

He stood in front of the fire. Jenny crossed her legs. She wanted him to kiss and caress her, make love to her. She could scarcely think of anything else.

Hunter studied her, taking his sweet time about it. She wore jeans and a black sweater that stretched lusciously over her breasts. Her sleeves were rolled up and he could see the delicate band of her gold watch. She looked like money even in casual clothes. He reminded himself silently of all the reasons he should not get involved with a wealthy woman.

None of them seemed to matter.

"What are you thinking about?" she ventured.

He shrugged. "Uh, what we should do about Troy."

"That's not what you were thinking about." He lifted his brows, waiting. She swallowed, then said softly, "You're thinking about what I'm thinking about."

"Which is?"

She climbed to her feet and came to stand beside him, her back to the fire. "Well, we're alone at last."

"Ahhh . . ." He slid her a look. "That's not what I'm thinking about."

"It's not?"

He shook his head. "I'm way past you. My mind's already traveled in that direction. . . ." He indicated his bedroom door. Sliding one hand around her back, he dragged her close, his breath ruffling her hair.

A delicious shiver slid down Jenny's spine. "My father won't like this."

He kissed her neck tenderly until she sighed with pleasure.

"My son won't like this, either." Lightly she nipped his earlobe with her teeth and pulled ever so slightly.

"Yeah, but I like it," he pointed out, pulling her to him and kissing her boldly on the mouth, his hands digging into her hair.

Jenny's knees went weak. "So do I," she said, drawing in a shaky breath, and that was the end of their conversation.

❖ CHAPTER FIFTEEN ❖

They rode back to Jenny's condo in satisfied silence. Lovemaking had made them incredibly hungry; and when Hunter's stomach growled, Jenny dragged him off to Tía Sophia's, a favorite Santa Fe breakfast spot for locals and tourists alike. They had to wait in a minuscule foyer before being seated but Hunter held her close the whole time and Jenny simply let herself forget all her problems while in the comfort of his arms. They ordered blue corn tortilla dishes, breakfast burritos, and *mucho caliente* enchiladas to share, and they both drank plenty of water to douse the flames.

"I hope Rawley made himself something to eat," she observed as they turned in to the gate. "There were enough leftovers to feed an army, but he prefers traditional breakfast food."

"Hmm . . . I'm pretty sure I've lost a layer of taste buds.'

"You didn't have to order extra hot," she pointed out.

"I'm a man. I wanted to impress you."

"You already did that," she said with a sideways glance

then was mortified to feel a blush crossing her face.

"You said you could be hot. You were right."

"Funny."

They walked up the stairs together. Jenny would have liked to hold hands, silly as that might look, but she knew Rawley could be peeking out the window and her son needed lots of time to adjust to Hunter. They were making progress, but she didn't want to ruin things by pushing too hard.

"Rawley?" she called as she stepped inside the condo. A glance at the spotless kitchen said her son hadn't fixed himself breakfast. If he had, the place would have looked like a tornado had hit.

Glancing at the sink, she expected to see the two coffee cups that she and Hunter had left but one of the cups was shattered into a dozen pieces, as if someone had dashed it into the sink with real force. It gave her a bad feeling.

Benny whined and scratched at the door from inside Rawley's room. Jenny quickly released him and let him outside. "Rawley?" she called again.

No answer.

She glanced toward the carport across the way where her Volvo still sat. "For a moment I was afraid he'd taken the car! He's fifteen and he wants to get his learner's permit, but I wanted to wait till we were settled."

"Where would he go?" Hunter asked, and something in his tone alarmed Jenny anew.

"Well, he could be in the neighborhood."

"Without Benny?"

She hesitated. "Maybe he's left a note . . ."

She searched his room, the living room and kitchen but

found nothing. Frightened, she struggled to understand what had happened. He was probably fine. Just hanging around somewhere nearby. He didn't have any close friends yet that she could call, and unless there was a number on the caller ID . . .

"There's a private call that came in not long after we left," Jenny said, staring down at it. She swallowed hard. "He told me Troy has a cell phone."

Hunter couldn't offer false hope because he'd been thinking the same thing.

Jenny dashed to her room, heart pounding. Against her jewelry box was propped a white envelope. She tore it open, scanned the contents, and let out a cry of anguish. Hunter hurried to her side and took the note from her shaking hands.

Mom,
   Sorry I had to leave without calling you. I'm just on a trip with Dad. I'll call when I get a chance. Don't worry. I didn't want to go back to that school where I don't know anyone. I'm okay. I promise I'll be back soon.
                                        Love,
                                        Rawley

"He's kidnapped my son," she whispered. "Troy's kidnapped my son."

"Shh . . ." Hunter said, drawing her close. His own heart pounded heavily, his own worry for Rawley taking over.

"While I was making love to you . . . he stole my son."

"Don't panic. Rawley went willingly. We'll get him back."

"We need to call the police. We need to stop him right now! Call your sergeant friend," she demanded urgently, pulling away from him to gaze pleadingly into his eyes. "Call him and tell him what happened."

"Who knows how long they've been gone? They're probably outside the Santa Fe department's jurisdiction by now. We can call the state police, but . . ."

"But?"

"They're not going to get too excited just yet. Troy is Rawley's father. Rawley said he'd call you."

"What's that got to do with it? He has no right!"

"I'm telling you how the law will look at it."

"Don't you care? Don't you care *at all?*"

Hunter gazed at her. Her accusation hurt even though he understood it was out of fear. "I'll find Rawley." He dropped his arms from around her, his mind already swirling ahead.

"What do you mean? Where will you look? What will you do?" Now that Hunter had said he was leaving, Jenny's anxiety intensified.

"Troy was last living in the L.A. area. He knows people there."

"But . . . but that's California! Rawley said his father was moving to Taos. He might be there."

"I'll check it out."

He sounded so uninterested in her theory that Jenny clutched desperately at his sleeve. "What's wrong?"

"Jenny." He disengaged her tense fingers and dropped his hands lightly on her shoulders. She trembled beneath his grip. "Do you have Troy's cell phone number?"

"No . . . no . . ." She shook her head. "Unless Rawley

wrote it down. He had the number." She tore away from him and ran into Rawley's bedroom, frantic with fear. Her eyes darted every which way. Yanking out drawer after drawer, she rummaged through his belongings. She took a step back, one hand pressed to her lips. "He's taken some clothes. A lot of them!"

Hunter's expression grew grimmer, if that were possible. He rifled through the clutter in Rawley's desk drawer. Candy wrappers, paper clips, a stapler, and blank note pads—the usual. No doodlings or numbers of any kind.

"There's no phone number, is there?" she said hopelessly.

"He'll call." Hunter was positive.

"They're on a trip," Jenny said, rereading the note with renewed hope. "Just a trip. They could be back tonight."

He didn't know how to tell her she was wrong. He knew Troy had taken the boy a lot farther than a day trip would allow. He knew it like he knew when bad things were about to happen.

"I'll get him back," he said in a tone so intense it caught Jenny's fragmented attention.

"How? What do you mean?" As he turned to the door she demanded, "Where are you going?"

"L.A. Like I said, it's where he's been these last fifteen years. I know all the names of Troy's friends and his ex girlfriends."

"But you've been in Santa Fe for six years. You said so yourself!"

"Like Troy, I still know people in L.A. And I have friends on the force who think I was justified in following Russell and making his life a living hell. Friends who've kept their eyes on Russell's habits."

"You're scaring me," she said in a small voice.

"I'm glad I didn't take my old job back," he said soberly.

She knew what he meant. She understood that if he were an officer of the law he would have to abide by certain rules. And when it came to Troy Russell, Hunter didn't want to abide by any rules.

She swallowed hard, holding back tears. "Do you think your friends can find him?"

"I'll find him."

"Are you sure?"

His answer was a faint, twisted smile that said this show-down with her ex-husband had been a long time coming. "Keep Benny close," he said, and then he was gone.

Rawley sat in the seat, his baseball cap pulled down over his eyes, his arm wrapped around the soccer ball in his lap. He chewed gum. Big Red. His father's favorite and now it was Rawley's too.

His dad was in a great mood. The best. Rawley had begged Troy to take him along, and he'd had to plead like hell to get his dad to listen. But it had all worked out great. Now, they were on their way to who knew where. The thrill of excitement burned bright. He did feel a little bad about his mom, though. She would worry, he thought guiltily. A lot.

But he didn't give a damn, really. Not really. She was hanging out with that Hunter Calgary and having him around wasn't what Rawley wanted at all.

"Are we going to your place in Touts?"

Troy smiled. "Taos," he said with a snort which Rawley

couldn't quite understand. "Nah . . . I had somewhere further in mind."

"But we'll be back by tonight, or so . . ."

There was silence for the next couple of miles. Rawley felt his first prickle of unease as the car sped down the road, sagebrush and scraggly trees no more than a gray-green blur. He reckoned they were heading west. He was pretty good at directions.

With an effort he tamped down his feelings. He'd been so glad to see his dad when he'd showed up this morning. A feeling of pride had actually stolen over him. When his dad walked into a room, he just took over.

Benny's snarling had spoiled the effect and Rawley had been forced to drag the dog by the collar into his bedroom. When he'd returned it was to find Troy staring down at the two coffee cups in the sink. "So, your mom had a friend spend the night, huh?" he'd asked casually.

"Nothing happened between them," Rawley assured him as quickly as he could. "He just stayed here."

"Where?"

"On the couch," Rawley answered with difficulty.

"You sure?"

Rawley's heart slammed against his chest. He didn't like thinking in those terms, and his expression must have shown it because Troy said, "Think they might have snuck around? You know what I mean."

"No!"

"What's this guy like?" He picked up a coffee cup from the sink.

"He's just a guy. I don't know!"

"But you don't want him around, do you?"

"Hell, no," Rawley said loudly, testing his father's reaction to having him swear.

His dad grinned. "I don't want him around either. You know, I've always regretted how things turned out between Jenny and me. I made a lot of mistakes, but we were good together."

"Then, you gotta help me get this guy out of here. He's a policeman, sort of."

"What do you mean 'sort of'?" Troy asked sharply.

"He used to be. And they want him back at the department. His sergeant always yells at him, but he really wants him—"

"His *sergeant?* Here in Santa Fe?"

"Uh-huh, he's—"

"What's his fucking name?" Troy demanded, throwing the cup in the sink and shattering it.

Rawley just stared. "Hunter Calgary."

His father's reaction was nothing short of explosive. He clasped his hands into fists and backed away from the sink as if the coffee cups were somehow dangerous. Rawley glanced around in fear, wondering what had happened.

"Do you—know him?" Rawley asked in a thin voice that scarcely sounded like his own.

Troy turned around, his back to Rawley. His hands closed and opened, closed and opened. "He stayed the night with your mother?"

"I said he was on the couch."

"But what's their relationship?" he demanded impatiently.

"I think . . ."

"You think *what?*" Troy whipped around, clearly in the

grip of some serious emotion.

"I think she likes him," he admitted, afraid, knowing i was exactly what his father didn't want to hear.

"Is she with him now? That's *the guy?*"

Rawley nodded, miserably, feeling like the situation wa somehow his fault.

Troy's eyes closed. He relaxed his hands and drew sev eral deep breaths. It was like yoga, or something . . . som kind of relaxation technique that Rawley had heard of.

"Hunter Calgary." Troy opened his eyes and regarde Rawley with new control. "Do you know who that ma is?" Rawley shook his head vehemently. "He's on a cam paign to ruin me. If he's seeing your mother, it's because h wants to get to me."

"Why?"

"Because he's a lunatic. You know why he's not policeman anymore? Because he followed me like a do and threatened my life."

Rawley tried to put this picture of Hunter together wit what he knew about him and failed. Still, his father wa clearly affected by the man. This was no act.

"How did Jenny meet him?"

"I don't know."

"At the restaurant?"

"I—don't know."

"Has this been going on a while? Why didn't you tell m about it sooner?"

"It started when I was at soccer camp! Maybe—mayb they met in Puerto Vallarta?"

"Impossible." Troy paced to the window, pulled back th curtain, looked out. "Does the old man know?"

"Grandpa Holloway? Yes. He's here. He stopped by last night."

"He met Calgary face to face?"

"I went to my room," Rawley said apologetically. "I didn't pay much attention, but yeah. They were here together. I think they knew each other already."

That really got him. Rawley was sorry he'd brought the whole thing up and now wished to high heaven he'd never called his father. But was he right? Was Hunter after his mom because he wanted to get back at Troy?

"Why does he hate you so much?"

"Because he blames me for the death of his sister."

"What?" Rawley asked faintly.

"I was involved briefly with his sister and he couldn't stand it." Troy regarded him for a long moment. "Are you old enough to handle the truth?"

"Sure. What do you mean? Of course I am." Rawley was slightly offended.

"It's dirty."

Rawley inwardly recoiled. He knew dirty. He'd seen his share of dirty pictures and films, and he knew what it meant to fight dirty. But there was a whole swirl of adult meaning in his father's tone. In truth, he wasn't sure he *was* old enough to handle the whatever his dad was about to say. "What's dirty?" he asked reluctantly.

"I think there was something going on between Calgary and his sister. The kind of thing nobody likes to talk about, you understand? He was jealous of me. He didn't like me going where no man—other than big bro—had gone before."

His meaning slammed into Rawley's brain. "I don't

believe it!"

"I told you you wouldn't like it."

"That's just—*sick!*"

"They're both sick. And that's why she committed suicide by throwing herself off a building."

"No . . . no . . ." Rawley raised his hands, warding off the words as if they'd been physically thrown at him.

"Why don't you ask him, if you don't believe me?" Troy stalked toward him, a black rage building.

Rawley was taken aback. "I can't do that!" he choked out, afraid that he was suddenly about to cry. Sometimes he didn't understand himself at all. "I just want to get the hell out of here!" he practically screamed.

Benny whined and scratched at the door. Troy glanced down the hall, then back at Rawley. "You could never do that to your mother," he said slowly.

"Why not? She's with a guy who does it with his sister!"

Troy shook his head, never taking his eyes from Rawley's face. Rawley could feel himself start to crumple under that intense scrutiny and he wanted to run and hide. "But that would really scare her," Troy pointed out meaningfully.

"I don't care!"

"And I would look like the bad guy. She would think I took you away when you didn't want to go."

Rawley realized his father was seriously considering the options. "Take me with you. I don't care where! I just want to get out of here."

"I'm not sure . . ."

"I'll write her a note. I'll tell her not to worry . . . that I'll call her. Please!" Hoping he could convince him, Rawley begged again, "I won't be any trouble. I promise."

"Is your grandfather still in town?" Troy asked, a total non sequitur that made Rawley afraid he was trying to change the subject.

"I think so. We could go to your place in . . . in . . ."

"Taos," he replied absently. "Where's he staying?"

"My grandfather? La Fonda."

Troy blinked several times.

Rawley got the impression of a computer making zillions of connections.

"All right," Troy said slowly, reluctantly.

"You mean we can go away?" Rawley was afraid he'd misunderstood. "Like, right now?"

"I have to stop by my hotel and check out," Troy said, sounding faraway, as if he were talking to himself. Rawley had to fight to keep from jumping up and down and waving his hand in front of his face.

"Okay. Let me write Mom a note and grab a few things. Just wait . . . okay?"

"Don't let the dog out," was his father's response and Rawley had hurried to get everything together before he changed his mind, as parents were wont to do. When he returned he had his bag in one hand, his letterman's jacket in the other. Seeing his father's gaze at the jacket, Rawley said quickly, proudly, "I got called up to the varsity play-offs, got a few minutes of playing time, so they gave me a varsity letter."

Troy had seemed transfixed for a few moments before shaking off whatever was affecting him. He'd told Rawley to get in the car and they were on their way.

They'd made a stop at La Fonda—his father's hotel, too,

as it turned out—then they were on their way. Rawley had rattled on about nothing for the first hour or so, but then he'd just kind of slowed down and started to worry. It didn't help that it now sounded like they might be gone longer than he'd originally planned. Not that he didn't want to leave, but he felt kind of bad for his mom, too. And Benny.

He didn't know how to feel about Hunter Calgary.

"So, how far are we going?" he asked again, since his dad didn't seem to be planning on answering him.

Troy was smiling to himself, driving with one hand, his eyes hidden behind sunglasses. "Didn't you just say something about how you wanted to learn to drive?"

Rawley perked up. There was nothing he wanted more. "Well, yeah!"

"When we get going a little farther, I'll turn over the wheel."

"But I don't have my learner's permit."

His father glanced over at him, smiling slightly. "Who's going to know?"

The phone rang within minutes after Hunter's departure. Jenny snatched it up and couldn't prevent herself from asking desperately, "Rawley?"

"Geneva?" her father responded, sounding as desperate as she did.

She sank onto the couch. Benny moved in close beside her, on alert, attuned to her anxious mood. "Oh, hi," she said, then added unnecessarily, "I thought you were Rawley."

"Is Rawley all right?"

Alarm shot right to her heart. "Why?"

"Because I had a meeting with Russell. He called me here at La Fonda!" He sounded offended by Troy's choice of venue. Allen did not like being accosted on what he considered his own turf. "He wanted to meet in my room. I told him I'd give him fifteen minutes in the lobby. When I went to . . ."

"You saw Troy this morning?" Jenny cut him off.

"Yes. That's what I'm trying to say!" Allen declared huffily. "And I'll tell you what—he's showing his true colors. Now he's demanding five hundred thousand dollars! Can you imagine?"

Ransom! It was turning out just as she'd suspected. "You mean—you mean—for Raw—"

"He said he wanted to go into business with me. Invest in some California real estate he wanted to develop. He said a lot of things."

Jenny's head swam. "Was Rawley with him?"

"What? No. He was negotiating, Jenny. *Negotiating*." He snorted. "He doesn't even bother with that 'make amends' line anymore. It was just a matter of time. I turned him down flat."

She couldn't breathe. In a suffocated voice, she asked, "What did he do?"

"The bastard smiled and said, 'We'll see about that.' That's what he did. Then he left." Finally Allen heard what she'd said through his anger and disgust. "Where's Rawley?" he demanded suddenly.

"With Troy."

"When? Are you sure? What do you mean?"

Jenny told him what little she knew about Rawley's

leaving with Troy, ending with the note.

"He hasn't called yet?" Allen asked, not waiting for an answer, knowing she would have told him if he had. "So, he went of his own free will. Damn it all, Jenny. Where were you when Rawley left?"

"I was with Hunter." The silence was damning. Jenny flinched in spite of herself. She said, as an afterthought, "Hunter's gone to find Rawley."

"Where?"

"I don't know. Maybe Los Angeles . . ."

"I hope he kills him," Allen said distinctly.

Jenny was shocked by her father's words. Shocked because she knew he meant them. "I just want Rawley back safe and sound."

"I should have paid him the money."

"Troy would have just kept asking for more."

"He thinks he's got the bargaining chip to end all bargaining chips." Allen coughed several times. "The sly bastard," he added, a hint of reluctant admiration in his voice. "He does." He coughed again, harder.

"Are you all right?" Jenny asked.

"Fine." He cleared his throat. "Call me when Rawley calls you."

She heard his deep concern. "I will."

She just hoped that phone call would be soon.

Troy could scarcely contain his glee. Talk about the rabbit falling into the snare, his eager son had begged to go with him. Begged! And he'd stalled the kid, pretending that it was an imposition.

Christ. He should have demanded more from that old

bastard. Five hundred thousand was chicken feed. And now he possessed the golden goose . . .

Oh, Jenny, Jenny. Soon you'll be begging, too. On your knees. Just like that squealing bitch Michelle.

"What are you smiling at?" Rawley asked, his own lips curving as if he could somehow divine Troy's thoughts.

If he only knew.

"As soon as we cross the border, I'll turn over the wheel," Troy said expansively. He didn't give a damn about the Explorer. He was going to have a Porsche, better than Frederica's piece of rundown shit. He'd drive it right up to her door and lay on the horn. She'd be sorry she threw him out. Bipolar sicko. Maybe he'd slip it to her for old time's sake. When the mood struck, she was red-hot and ready for anything. No crying and whining from Frederica. No, no. She gave as good as she got.

He really ought to see her again, he decided. Give it another try. A dress rehearsal before opening night with Jenny. He'd wasted way too much time with Patricia. Frederica was the one.

Eat that, Heather and Jessica! he thought with a jolt of remembered fury. When Frederica came on to him, everything was functional below the belt. Yessirree. She could really get him going. It wasn't his fault Heather and Jessica couldn't get him hot. It was theirs!

Of course, with Frederica, there were those downturns. Those times when she was a lifeless mannequin. He'd managed some sex with her then, but it was like trying to wake the dead.

"Across the border?" Rawley repeated, frowning.

"Yeah. When we hit Arizona."

"We're going to Arizona?"

What was this? "Getting cold feet?" he asked. The kid was starting to squirm and that annoyed him.

"No . . . I just . . ." He shrugged and fiddled with the zipper on his letterman's jacket. "I just wanted to know where we're going."

Troy's gaze fell on the bright blue "M" blazoned across Rawley's jacket that stood for whatever high school the boy had attended. He thought of Val for a moment. Val.

The Explorer drifted to the side. He yanked it back on the road and said flatly, "We're just driving, son."

Thoughts of Val reminded him of Jenny and that, in turn, reminded him of Calgary. Troy flexed his fingers around the wheel. Thinking about the man made him sweat, which also pissed him off. Calgary was dangerous. Troy instinctively knew the man would kill him if he could. And what was he doing with Jenny?

Jenny was *his*, now and forever. Given enough time, Troy would come up with the perfect plan to have her and the money, too.

❈ CHAPTER SIXTEEN ❈

He could have driven, but Hunter wanted to get to L.A. as fast as possible. Catching the first available flight out of Albuquerque, he was in Los Angeles by early evening. He rented a Jeep, one exactly like his own. Grimly, he put the car in gear and headed into a mess of commuter traffic.

He hadn't been back in a while, although the memories were still raw, crowding his brain. But this time he was on a mission to straighten out the events that had led to his exile from the City of Angels, and he didn't care how he did it.

He had two buddies, both still detectives on the force, one in vice, one in burglary and theft. He also had a pretty good friend in homicide, but Hunter's insistence that Michelle's death was murder hadn't set well with the boys in that department. They'd thought differently. For his efforts Hunter had earned a penalty and a warning to leave Troy Russell alone. He'd ended up quitting rather than living under that dictum.

Carlos Rodriguez worked vice and lived in South Central. By a realtor's standards, it wasn't the best neighborhood in town; it certainly had its share of crime. But Carlos lived within a large Hispanic section where most of his neighbors were trusted close friends. Hunter knew many of them, so he wasn't worried when he passed several sinister-looking groups of young men who glared at him as he drove by. He pulled in front of Carlos's modest home, strode up the sidewalk which was lined with bright flower boxes and rang the bell.

"Hunter!" Tina Rodriguez declared in delight. Carlos's wife had always been fond of him and she threw open the screen door and hugged him close. She was five feet two in socks and built tough. "What are you doing here?"

"Looking for Carlos. He on the job?"

"You know he is. Busting the hookers and junkies." She sniffed. "You still in Santa Fe?"

"More or less. Could you give him my number?" He scribbled down a phone number from an airport hotel which he'd never forgotten. "I'm checking in there later. I also want to see Mammoth."

"Getting the old gang together again." She smiled. "Don't you be like those boys on the street out there, eh?" She jerked her head in the direction of the street toughs gathered outside. "No trouble."

Hunter smiled. "No trouble."

Her expression clouded. "Is this about that man who killed your sister?"

Hunter regarded her with affection. Carlos and Mammoth and their wives had never questioned whether he was right or not. They believed him. "I'm afraid it is."

She gave a quick sign of the cross. "That is for you."

"Thank you."

He left feeling somehow better, lighter, ready to face the fire. He was going to get Russell this time.

Next, he checked into the hotel—a euphemism since it was barely more than a two-story motor court built in the thirties—and settled in to wait. He'd brought along the information Ortega had sent to him in Puerto Vallarta, even though it had more to do with the Holloways than Russell himself. Still, it gave him a picture of Russell, and even with the passing of years, he knew he'd immediately recognize the man.

Two hours later Carlos phoned. "Hey, man!" he declared. "What you doin' back in the city, huh? Thought you was run out of town on a rail."

"Just couldn't stay away. I've got people to see."

"Uh-huh." Carlos's tone grew sober. "I know where some of 'em live."

"Figured you did."

"Russell's friends keep crossin' my path, again and

again. There's an apartment in El Segundo. Really funky place, y'know? Ratty lives there. Betcha that's where Russell shows up."

Ratty was Hunter's own nickname for one J.P. Graef. The man looked like a rat, with a pointy nose, big ears, and a narrow face. And every place he'd ever lived looked like a rat's nest: dirt and papers and clutter and a stench that pervaded everything.

Carlos rattled off the address. "You want me to go with you, man?"

"Not while you're gainfully employed."

"That doesn't sound good."

"Russell has someone with him. His son." Hunter gave Carlos a quick recap of Rawley's relationship to Russell. "I'm working with the boy's mother and grandfather."

Carlos whistled softly. "You better take either me or Mammoth with you."

"I'll let you know if I need backup. For now, I'm on my own."

"You always were," Carlos said softly. "Don't forget about us."

"Never."

Friendship. Something he'd let slide. Something he'd nearly forgotten about while he'd been holed up in Santa Fe, trying to heal. Ever since he'd connected with Jenny Holloway he'd discovered himself again. It was amazing to realize how much he'd nearly thrown away forever, and how important it was to keep one's perspective.

Ratty's apartment was easy to pick out amongst the fifty or more units in the dilapidated complex. A stack of old newspapers, boxes, and bottles lined the area outside his front door. His fellow slum dwellers apparently felt he should keep his filth to himself for as Hunter pulled into the parking lot and examined the area from his Jeep, Ratty's neighbor to the right came out of his door and kicked the pile viciously with his foot before stalking to his car.

A riot light atop the building next door lit up the place like a prison yard. It seemed like someone wanted to keep a sharp eye on the tenants of the—Hunter strained to read the faded, unlit sign—the Roseland Court. Still, the over-hang of the deteriorating roof offered deep shadows near the doorways and any number of nefarious doings could be managed by an enterprising criminal.

Ratty had been an acquaintance of Troy's, not because they were alike in any way, but because Ratty worshiped the ground the urbane Troy Russell walked on. He was happy to grovel, happy to be used. Troy didn't even pay him. Apparently allowing him to remain just outside his inner circle was enough for Ratty.

It was Ratty whom Hunter had shaken down to find out where Troy was on the night of Michelle's death; Ratty who had squealed about Troy's involvement with another woman, several other women; Ratty who clung to Hunter's leg and begged him not to tell Troy who had led the police to him. Hunter had kept the promise.

And in the end it hadn't mattered. Hunter had found Troy in the arms of some bimbo and had jerked the naked man out of bed, strangling him to within an inch of his life while the woman clutched the covers to her breasts and screamed at him to stop. All Troy knew was that Hunter had crossed the line, and the fact that he'd been caught in bed with another woman attested to the fact hat he hadn't been with Michelle.

Hunter tried to get the rap to stick. He pointed out that here were gloves in Troy's car and that he could have worn hem while he was with Michelle, effectively leaving no prints while he pushed her off the roof. But *could have* wasn't good enough. He told them how Michelle had confided in him, had said she felt Troy would rather see her dead than be the father of her child. *Insubstantial.*

All anyone cared about was that Hunter had physically attacked Troy Russell, and that Hunter continually harassed and threatened Russell at every opportunity.

End of story.

Until now.

No lights shone in Ratty's windows. Nothing. If they were driving, Russell hadn't had time to get here yet. Throwing the Jeep into gear, Hunter decided to cruise by a couple of more addresses that he'd gathered and saved over the years, some of Troy's innumerable bedmates.

Hunter had a feeling he'd be back.

Rawley's hands were sweating on the steering wheel. He could hardly concentrate. Twice he'd run the right side wheels off the pavement into the dirt. Twice he'd jerked the car back, overcorrected, and slipped into the other lane. Worst of all, he knew he was disappointing his dad. He didn't know the first thing about driving, and for the second time that day he felt near tears. Now it was night and he wasn't sure how to say he wanted to quit and just go home.

"Why are you slowing down?" Troy demanded.

"I'm kinda tired."

"We're still fifty miles outside of Phoenix. Go ahead."

Rawley swallowed. "I really don't want to."

His dad gave a disparaging groan, but Rawley pulle[d] over to the side of the road anyway. His arms felt lik[e] weights. His dad hadn't seemed to mind his erratic drivin[g] which was totally weird. He just kind of chuckled deep i[n] his throat. Like it was a thrill a minute even though Rawle[y] had felt close to passing out.

Troy took over the wheel and they drove in silence to th[e] outskirts of Phoenix. Rawley thought they would sto[p] there, but they drove straight on through. "Where are w[e] going?" he asked.

"Stop asking." Troy was curt. "We're going to go as f[ar] as we can go."

Rawley stared through the windshield, watching hea[d] lights passing them in the opposite lane. That lane heade[d] east, toward Santa Fe, toward his mom. Reaching deep i[n] his pocket he fingered the pink beaded necklace he'd take[n] from her jewelry box. He hadn't known why he'd done i[t] It was his birthday gift to her. But in the heat of the mome[nt] he'd just grabbed it and taken off.

Now he was glad.

"I should call my mom," he pointed out.

"Not yet."

"She'll have the cops on us."

Troy threw him a harsh look. Rawley shrank back at th[e] venom in that dark gaze. "Well, let her. They'll have a he[ll] of a time finding us, won't they?"

Intimidation normally didn't work on Rawley. H[e] resented authority like every normal fifteen-year-old. H[e] was just quieter about it than his friend Brandon. But h[e] was stuck in a car with a virtual stranger, he realized now, and he wasn't sure what to do.

"Wouldn't it be better to just call her?"

Troy swore pungently. "She'll send her boyfriend after us. Is that what you want? The guy who screws his own sister? You want him, huh? You want the guy that slips it to her when she's sleeping, then covers her mouth with his hand so mom and dad won't hear?"

All lies, Rawley had a feeling. The more Troy embellished, the clearer that was. He could feel his stomach tighten with fear. He understood at last. But it was too late.

Escape was all he could think about.

Jenny had gone to the restaurant. She needed something to do. She wandered around the kitchen and thought about Rawley. She could visualize him bussing tables and seating customers.

Troy, don't hurt him.

Her jaw set. She was experiencing a little of that cold control her ex had once possessed. If he possessed it still, she hadn't seen any signs of it. Troy wasn't the same. He was looser, wilder, more dangerous. Capable of anything.

After an hour of watching the clock, she headed home. She'd been keeping a vigil by the phone and that hadn't worked. She'd hoped Rawley might call if she were gone, yet been afraid to leave. Finally, she'd bolted from the condo just to save her sanity. Now, she drove over the speed limit to get home and check the messages.

None.

One glance at the answering machine and Jenny collapsed. Head in hands, she wept tears of fear and fury. Ten minutes later she was on her feet, pacing. She had to *do* something. Why had she let Hunter leave? She should have gone with him. Except if Rawley called . . .

Magda. She would have Magda stay here while she went to find her son. That was the answer. With no plan fully formed, she headed to the phone. Hand on the receiver, she almost cried with relief when the phone miraculously rang.

I have to go to the bathroom," Rawley said.

"You're going to have to hold it."

"I can't," he answered simply.

Heaving a sigh of disgust, Troy pulled into a service station. To Rawley's consternation, his father followed him inside. Hell of all hell, Rawley couldn't pee. His father watched him like a hawk. But his nerves had tightened up and no amount of silent pleading could get his body to work. "I guess I was wrong," Rawley mumbled, shoving past Troy on the way to the car.

It happened so fast he was still reeling with shock. One moment he was stepping out the bathroom door, the next he was slammed up against the wall. Before he could move, his head was slammed hard again against the tile wall. His ears rang.

"Don't fuck with me," his father told him.

Rawley lowered his lashes. Every instinct told him to go for it, just hit him and take him down. But Troy had a good twenty pounds on him and an unpredictable temper.

"You wanna call Mommy? Fine. Get in the car and I'll give you the cell phone. But after you say hello, turn it over to me."

"Are you kidnapping me?" Rawley asked him bluntly.

"Hey, kid, you begged to come with me. Begged!"

"Guess I made a mistake."

They stared each other down. In the end Troy started laughing. He clapped Rawley on the shoulder and guided him back to the Explorer. "All right. I was mad. I didn't want to stop. Here." Troy handed him the cell phone as he shut the passenger door. Rawley would have jumped right back out with the phone in hand, but Troy didn't immediately move away.

What time was it? Three o'clock in the morning. Rawley placed the call and the line rang and rang. Finally, the answering machine picked up. "Hey, Mom?" His voice cracked. Suddenly he couldn't go on. Troy peeled the phone from his limp fingers and said, "Jenny?" then realized he'd gotten the machine. After a moment of thought, he said, "Where the hell are you in the middle of the night? Have you spoken to your dear old dad? He and I have a deal going. When this thing all gets settled, you can join Rawley and me. One big happy family, just like it should've been fifteen years ago. You better not be fucking around with Calgary."

With an effort Troy cut the connection. He really wanted to swear at her, tell her what a whore she was. But the kid was about to break down and this was the moment to go, go, go.

He couldn't wait to get to L.A. He was so horny he could scarcely think straight. He'd wanted to beat the shit out of the kid, but that wasn't going to work.

Patricia, he thought. No. Frederica. Maybe she was on an upswing and they could fuck themselves silly.

"Stop blubbering," he said harshly as Rawley lay like a

limp rag in the passenger seat. Troy made one step toward the hood of the car and he heard Rawley's door open. Surprised, he jumped back and slammed the door against his son's hand and heard his howl of pain. He slammed the door twice more, but the kid had jerked his wounded fingers free after the first time.

Behind the wheel, he reminded him tightly, "I told you not to fuck with me."

Next stop, the City of Angels.

Jenny sat in a chair at the side of the hospital room. If she'd been the least bit tired she would have nodded off. As it was, she stared at her father's sleeping form and the frightening sight of tubes connected to the line of monitors recording his vital signs.

The call had been from a member of the hospital staff. Allen had suffered a heart attack. A small one, by cardiologist's standards, apparently. She could hear Allen yelling in the background, still seeking to control, and she'd been so disappointed that it wasn't Rawley that at first she hadn't understood what had happened.

When she'd finally connected all the dots she called Magda, got her machine, and left a message saying she was going to the hospital to be with her father and could Magda please come over and stay by the phone? She would explain all later.

Magda and Phil had showed up at the hospital instead. Jenny could scarcely convey everything that had happened—including Rawley's sudden trip with Troy, which had probably been the trigger for Allen's heart attack. She tried to give Magda her keys, but because Jenny hadn't adequately explained the situation, neither of the Mont-gomerys understood her urgency about Rawley.

Finally, Magda grabbed her arm. "Are you saying he was kidnapped?"

"It amounts to that."

"Where did they go?" Phil wanted to know.

"I have no idea."

"What's the status on your father?" This, too, from Phil.

Jenny shrugged helplessly. Tests were being run. As an afterthought, she made her way to a pay telephone and called Natalie. Another answering machine or voice mail. Well, it was the middle of the night. She could scarcely blame her for not wanting to answer the phone.

She left a curt message. "Hello, Natalie. It's Jenny. My father's had a heart attack, but is doing okay so far. He's at St. Vincent Hospital. I'll call you in the morning."

Magda and Phil hung outside Allen's room, looking oddly sick themselves under the unforgiving fluorescent lights. "You didn't have to come here," she said again.

"Of course we did!" Magda hugged her hard for about the tenth time.

"But as long as you're up, I really need someone to go to my place and check the messages. Rawley should have called by now."

"When did he leave?" Magda asked, finally under-standing the gravity of the situation.

"This morning. Late morning." She felt close to tears again. "While I was at Hunter's ranch."

"Oh, honey. Don't feel guilty. Please. Rawley wanted to go, right?"

She nodded. "He took a bunch of clothes . . . a lot of

341

them. Maybe he plans to—stay with Troy."

"Oh, that won't work." Magda shook her red curls. "Troy'll get sick of him." Jenny blinked at her. "Well, from what you've said about him, he doesn't exactly have the patience of Job and fifteen-year-olds can test the best of us. I mean, Jenny, Rawley's great. But he's a teenager."

"You think he'll want to come back?" she asked hopefully.

"Of course he will. You're his mother."

"Jenny!"

It was Allen's voice. Jenny scurried back into his room. "Don't yell," she said in a whisper. "Please. Take care of yourself." She glanced at the monitors as if she could make sense of the readouts. The narrow green lines peaked and dipped and waved.

"I'm fine," he declared impatiently. "Have you heard from Rawley?" He started coughing and Jenny touched his shoulder.

"Dad, please," she implored.

He waved a hand at her, unable to speak for a moment. "You need to pay him the money," he finally rasped out.

"Five hundred thousand dollars?"

"How much is your son worth?"

"Priceless, and you know it. And you also know it doesn't work that way. Rawley's got to want to come back."

"Pay Troy the money and he'll drop Rawley like a hot potato."

"Dad—"

"Just do it, Geneva. Call my lawyer. Joseph Wessver. Tell him to set it up. He'll know what to do."

Jenny gazed at her father in concern. He looked terrible. Sick and old. They'd fought about money for so many years. "You bought me out of my marriage. Now, you're going to buy me my son back."

Allen managed a faint smile. "Best investments I've ever made."

Leaning forward, Jenny kissed him lightly on the forehead. She saw the glimmer of tears in his eyes as she turned away.

Hunter woke up with a jolt. He'd cruised by some of Troy's other previous haunts, then had drifted back to Ratty's and fallen asleep. Now, he watched the rust-bucket Chevy nose into a spot. The engine sputtered and quit. The door flew open and Ratty himself climbed out. Stretching, he reached in the back of the car and hauled out what looked like several thousand dollars worth of electronic equipment. Hunter watched him make several trips up to his apartment.

"A little breaking and entering, Ratty, old boy?" Hunter whispered to himself. "A little burglary and theft? That how you're surviving these days?"

He was going to have to call Mammoth when this was all over and get Ratty's ass hauled into jail. But not now. Not yet.

He dozed off again, fitfully.

Dawn was breaking as the green Explorer slipped into the parking lot and found a place next to Ratty's Chevy.

For Rawley, it was a living nightmare. And it was all his own fault. Why hadn't he listened to his mother? *Why?*

This man wasn't his father. There was something wrong with this man. He was nervous as hell. Chewing gum and jiggling his leg. It was like he was high on something. Maybe meth. But Rawley was beginning to suspect Troy's drug of choice was intimidation—and sex. The last part was because of the way he talked.

"You had sex yet?" Troy had asked him as they hurtled through the night toward the west coast.

Rawley had carefully couched his response. In the short time he'd been with Troy he'd learned it was best to offer as little information as possible. "I've been with girls," was his answer. In truth, he'd had a few wild rumblings that had come pretty close to the real thing. But he'd never actually done it. Too many consequences he wasn't ready to deal with. He wasn't one of those guys who carried condoms and he was bound and determined to avoid STDs at all costs.

His answer got Troy's leg jiggling. "Your mom's a cold bitch. Real icy. She needs a good—"

"Shut up about my mom!" Rawley had yelled without thinking.

"You ever thought about her that way?"

Rawley had seen red. He knew his dad was trying to work him over, but that was low. Low and dirty. His father's smile gleamed unpleasantly in the dark car.

"Go ahead, kid," he said, enjoying the malicious game. "See what it gets you. Come on, crybaby."

Troy's hand had slipped down into his jacket pocket. Rawley froze. He sensed without being told that Troy was going for a gun.

"My mom was right about you," Rawley said.

"Your mom needs a lesson in how to be nice to a man. And I'm going to give it to her."

Not if I cut off your balls first, Rawley thought without a qualm of guilt.

Get out of the car," Troy said now, pushing Rawley roughly out into the early dawn chill. Rawley wasn't asleep but he was slouched in the seat, thinking hard. Escape was everything. He had no money. Not a dime. But if he could get to a pay phone he could call his mother collect.

He stepped from the car. Troy was beside him in a flash, waving him up the stairs. Rawley had to step around the junk collected outside the door. "Hey, there, J.P.," Troy called as he pounded on the door. "Open up this pigsty!" A lot more pounding ensued before a weasly looking guy finally slung open the door.

"Troy!" he crowed in delight.

Rawley took a step back, but was grabbed by the collar of his letterman's jacket and thrust inside a dark, smelly room.

Hunter hadn't brought a gun. He didn't own one. He'd carried one when he was on the force but had turned it in when he quit. Though he'd pulled his gun often during the course of duty, he'd almost never fired it.

Now he wished to high heaven that he owned one. Walking in on Troy and Ratty unarmed was just plain foolish.

He debated calling Carlos and Mammoth. They would come if he asked. They would come fully prepared.

But they would play by the rules, something, at this juncture, that Hunter wasn't prepared to do.

He couldn't figure out Rawley. The kid had seemed kind of reluctant to go in. Or was he just sleep-deprived? He and Troy had been on the road a long time. Uncertain how to play this, Hunter hesitated.

There was a pack of cigarettes in the glove box. He pulled it out and played with one, unwilling to actually light up. He must be getting over that addiction as well as his burnout, he decided. He certainly felt alive and sharp this morning.

The morning wore on. About nine o'clock a couple of young kids flew out of unit sixteen and began playing in the strip of dirt to the side of the asphalt. The sun burned hot in a smoggy gray sky.

There had been no sign of life from Ratty's apartment since Rawley and Troy entered. No lights. No sound. No stirring, as far as Hunter could tell.

Thinking it over, he decided it was time for a confrontation, gun or no gun.

He climbed out of the Jeep and up the stairs. The kids playing in the dirt paid no attention to him. In the boxes of junk outside Ratty's door he spotted a length of metal casing about three feet long. Not much. But it could sure inflict some damage if the blow was right.

Hunter weighed the weapon in his hand. He glanced at the door.

He knocked loudly.

Ratty answered, blinking in the light like the rodent he was. Hunter shouldered past him and found Rawley two feet on his left, scrambling out of a sleeping bag on the floor and rushing toward him, his face alight with joy.

Hunter picked it all up in the split second before his gaze found Troy Russell. The man had a gun—and he was pointing it directly at Hunter's heart.

"Move and I'll kill you," he stated flatly.

"Hello, Russell?" Hunter answered calmly.

❊ CHAPTER SEVENTEEN ❊

S tand still," Troy responded. "Drop that. Get your hands up."

Hunter slowly released the piece of metal casing gripped tightly in his fist, eased it gently to the floor and lifted his hands.

"Hey!" Ratty called from behind Hunter's right shoulder.

"J.P., get your car warmed up," Troy yelled at him.

"But I—"

"Get that piece of shit moving!" he snarled through his teeth. Ratty hurtled down the outside stairs, knocking over boxes of his treasured junk in his haste.

"Shut the door," Troy ordered Rawley.

Rawley was breathing hard. "Wait . . . wait a minute . . ."

"Shut—the—fucking—door."

"You're not going to shoot Hunter."

"Just do it!" Troy fairly screamed.

"Go ahead," Hunter said softly. Russell's loss of self-control worried him. He'd had no idea the man had changed so much.

Rawley hesitated. He didn't want to comply. His heart was pounding fast. He instinctively gauged the distance between himself and Troy.

Troy read his mind, and it pissed him off no end. He

would have to shoot the stupid little bastard and teach him a lesson.

In that instant, as Troy moved the barrel in Rawley's direction, Hunter twisted and pushed Rawley away with all his strength. The bullet blasted with a loud bang and the hot, distinctive smell of cordite. Hunter felt the pain as if from a long distance. Rawley sprawled on the ground. A tangle of legs and arms. Fighting back a wave of shock and pain, Hunter gasped, "You okay?"

Troy gazed at the gun in surprise. He watched Calgary stumble forward. How loud was the sound? As loud as he imagined? Jumping forward, he yanked Rawley to his feet. The boy, stunned at first, became a wild animal, attacking and growling. "I'll shoot him! I'll shoot him again!" Troy screamed. "I'll shoot him!"

Rawley froze, his breath coming hard and fast. Troy could scarcely see straight. The kid had kneed him in the groin and it hurt like hell. But the gun was an equalizer. He held it through waves of pain, weaving it between Rawley and Hunter, concentrating on Hunter who was clutching the windowsill with one hand, the other arm hanging loosely.

"You won't win, Russell," Calgary gasped out.

"You're already dead." Troy waved the gun. Rawley crouched low, his attention distracted by Hunter. Troy stuck the hot barrel in the boy's ribs. "Come on," he ordered roughly.

"I'm not leaving him."

"Jesus, you little bastard. Get out before I shoot you, too."

"You won't shoot me. I'm your link to my grandfather's money."

"I don't give a damn who you are!"

"Rawley . . ." Hunter drew a breath. He was wounded in the shoulder, numbed by shock but shaking almost uncontrollably. "Don't argue with him." *Don't argue with a man holding a gun.*

"Hunter . . ."

"I'm okay. Really." He was. He was pretty sure he was, anyway.

Blackness crept over him, obliterating all conscious thought. A minute passed. Maybe hours. Suddenly, he came to, aware that he'd fallen onto the sleeping bag. The sticky black stain was from his own blood.

Blinking he saw the room was empty.

How long had it been? Struggling, he got to a sitting position, fighting off waves of nausea, the nasty after-effects of shock. A glance at the sleeve of his leather jacket wasn't particularly alarming. There were a couple of tears surrounded by blood but nothing to reveal the damage done.

Stupid, stupid, stupid, he berated himself. He hadn't believed Russell would be so psychologically fractured as to try and shoot his own son. He had believed some familial bond, and Troy's own desire to keep the golden goose alive, would keep Rawley safe from his father's violence.

He'd let Russell get away. He'd let him take Rawley, and there was no question Rawley's life was in danger.

With an effort Hunter got to his feet, shaking his head a bit to clear it. He needed medical attention, but going to a hospital emergency room would only complicate things. They would recognize a gunshot wound and then a hornet's nest of questions would be thrown at him. Once the police got involved, Hunter would be completely removed from the investigation.

But there was Carlos . . . and Mammoth.

He staggered down the hall to the bathroom. Ratty, for all his clutter, kept this room relatively clean, Hunter was relieved to see. His reflection stared back at him from the medicine cabinet mirror. Grim, white face, set jaw, blue eyes simmering with fury. His hair was rumpled and standing in stiff licks. He hadn't shaved and the rough stubble on his chin added to his menacing look. Anyone who saw him in this state would run the other way.

"Damn . . ."

With his uninjured left hand he opened the medicine cabinet. Inside was a tidy array of toothpaste, toothbrush, mouthwash, cotton balls, rubbing alcohol, hydrocortisone cream, and a roll of gauze. Gritting his teeth, he slowly removed his jacket. The right sleeve stuck a bit, ripping wounded flesh. Shaking, he yanked the coat off and flung it to the floor. His blue shirt was spattered with blood, and the right sleeve wasn't even blue any longer. Unbuttoning the shirt, he peeled it away, closing his eyes and concentrating on a vision of Jenny's beautiful face.

All the while a clock ticked in his head. How far away was Troy? Where would they go? To one of Troy's ex girl-friends? Doubtful. How would he explain Rawley? Russell didn't have many friends left in L.A. He didn't have many friends, period. Hunter put his mind to the task as he ripped off strips of gauze, dousing them in rubbing alcohol.

You know how he thinks. He's a coward. He wouldn't stick around. He would hightail it from the scene of the crime and go . . . *where?*

Gently, gently, he poured rubbing alcohol onto his wound. A growl erupted from his mouth. The stinging pain made his eyes water. When the first wave was over, he twisted his arm and examined the damage. The bullet had passed through the flesh, but it had obviously spiraled and done some serious damage to his upper arm, twisting through the flesh. Possibly hit the bone, maybe chipped it. Maybe not. Hunter could move his arm some. It hurt like hell, but mostly from the tearing of muscle. The central artery was intact. He could still make a fist if he concentrated hard and ignored the pain.

Just a flesh wound. He smiled without humor. The ugly mass of ravaged tissue still seeped blood at an alarming rate. Closing his eyes, he lifted his arm, keeping the wound above his heart. He used the alcohol-soaked strips of gauze to disinfect the raw tissue, gritting his teeth and hoping he wouldn't faint.

In the end he wrapped the rest of the gauze around the wound. Not too tightly, but snug enough. As soon as the first aid was done he felt better, clearer. Running cold water over his face, he glanced around Ratty's place. Ratty was half his size, but Hunter needed a shirt. His jeans, though spattered with blood, simply looked as if they were in need of a good cleaning. He threw water on the spots just in case, smearing the blood into indeterminate grime.

A shirt was going to be hard to come by. He settled for a black T-shirt folded neatly on top of Ratty's beat-up chest of drawers. It stretched to fit him, but didn't hide the gauze. A further search revealed a long khaki raincoat tucked in the back closet. Hunter struggled into it. It was at least a size too small but bearable if left unbuttoned. At least there was ample room in the sleeves.

Once more he examined himself in the mirror. He smoothed his hair with his hand. He tried on a smile. He was going to have to catch a flight and he didn't want to frighten the airport employees.

He'd pass.

Emptying his belongings from his jacket pockets, he left his clothes where they lay. He wouldn't be wearing them again. On his way out, he thought of the phone. Did Ratty even possess one?

Sure enough, behind a pile of junk in the bedroom was a black telephone with a remote handset which was nowhere to be seen. He finally found it in the kitchen, next to the remains of breakfast. He dialed Carlos first at the L.A.P.D. and didn't leave a message when he learned he wasn't at his desk. Ditto for Mammoth. Instead, he called Ortega who answered in his clipped, impatient way.

"I'm in L.A., but I'm flying back to Albuquerque as soon as I can."

"You sound awful."

"Russell has kidnapped his son, Rawley Holloway. I'd bet they're heading back your way, because Russell's been getting money from Allen Holloway. I'm sure he's using Rawley as leverage. I'm going to call Jenny and warn her. She knows Rawley's with Russell, but the kid went willingly. At first—things have changed. Write this down." He drew a breath and gave Ortega Jenny's phone number and address. "Holloway's in Santa Fe visiting Jenny."

"Holloway's at St. Vincent Hospital," Ortega informed him shortly. "Heart attack. Your friend Jenny called me this morning, looking for you."

Hunter blinked. "Heart attack?"

"Apparently a mild one. What the docs call a warning. Your friend Russell tapped him for five hundred thousand. He didn't pay, then he learned Russell had taken his grandson and *bam*, he's in the hospital."

"Jenny told you this."

"Yeah. Russell left a message on her phone that shook her up. Something about how he and the kid and her should be together again." Hunter absorbed that bizarre idea until Ortega spoke again. "Where the hell are you?"

"L.A. But Russell left a while ago."

"You saw him?" Ortega sounded grim. "You confronted him?"

Hunter did not want to go into what had transpired. He knew Ortega would chew him out to within an inch of his life. He hadn't even wanted to tell him he was following Troy, but Rawley's safety came first.

Looking through the window, he said, "They could be in a beat-up Chevy, early 80's, blue, maybe an Impala, or a green late 90's Explorer with temporary plates."

"What if he's still in L.A.?"

"I've called a couple of friends on the force. They'll get back to me, but I know he's left here. I can feel it. I foiled whatever he planned to do. I'll have my friends tie up the loose ends, maybe check out the ex-girlfriends."

"You coming straight here? You part of this police force again, Calgary?"

Hunter thought about Troy Russell, and his anger congealed into a hard knot. "When I get back."

"Don't you harm one hair of the bastard's head."

"Goodbye, Ortega."

"Listen, Calgary—"

He hung up and called Jenny.

With a fierce determination, Jenny threw her packed bag in the back of the Volvo. She was buying a cell phone, first thing. She hadn't bothered with one before but now she was desperate to be able to call at any point, from nearly anywhere. Troy's call had fired her up. She needed action.

The hospital would be her first stop on her way out of town. She knew her father would ask her where she was going. She had no answer. Hunter was in L.A., and that seemed like a good place to start. She wanted to be with him. She wanted to be part of the chase. She needed to think she was helping.

She jumped when the phone rang. Gingerly, she picked up the receiver, forcing herself not to gasp out Rawley's name.

"So, you sicked your lapdog on me," Troy said conversationally. "Sent him right to me. That's what he is, a lapdog. Sitting on your lap."

"Troy," she said carefully, heart racing. "Could I talk to Rawley?"

"Has Allen changed his mind about the money he owes me?"

She exhaled heavily. Yes, she'd expected him to say something like that. Greed was what drove him—that was perfectly obvious and she'd accepted it from the start. But she'd harbored some small belief that he couldn't help but love his own son. Now, she knew how silly her hope had been.

"My father's in the hospital. He instructed me to call his lawyers."

"The hospital? Tsk, tsk. He looked like the same old fat cat when I saw him."

Her control snapped. "You threatened him, Troy. That's what happened. And he suffered a heart attack and is lucky to be alive." Her voice shook. "Now, put Rawley on the phone!"

"Have you called those lawyers yet?"

"No. And I'm not going to until I talk to my son."

"Well, your son isn't with me right now. Don't worry. He's somewhere safe. But until I hear that money's been transferred into an account with my name on it, you won't be talking to him."

"Have you hurt him?" She couldn't stop herself, couldn't stop the crack in her voice.

"Jenny, honey. Of course not." In a silky voice he added, "I want to see you, babe. Real soon. Without your lapdog. It's my lap now."

"I can't transfer the funds without an account number. What bank and where—"

He cut her off. "Get the lawyer ready. I'll come find you and we'll take care of things."

"I won't do anything unless you put Rawley on the phone."

"The hell you won't!" he growled.

"I'm hanging up, Troy. I don't believe he's with you."

He swore pungently before he clapped a hand over the receiver for a moment. Then Rawley said, "Mom?" in a way that turned her knees to water. She sank onto the couch, hand to her mouth. She would have cried if there were any tears left but she simply sat in numb fear.

"Rawley, oh, God. Rawley. Are you all right? He hasn't hurt you, has he?"

"No."

"Are you in L.A.? You sound like you're in a car."

"Yeah . . ."

"Can you . . ." She gathered her wits with an effort. "Can you give me this phone number? It doesn't show up on caller ID."

"Yeah, uh, have you talked to Hunter?"

The desperation in his voice sent a thrill of fear through her. "No. Why? What happened?"

In a rush, he said, "Seven one three, four four three—"

She heard a brief scuffle. "Rawley! Rawley!"

"I'll call you," Troy said through his teeth. "I'll call you."

"If you hurt him, I swear you'll pay."

"Yeah, mama bear? Put on something sexy for me. None of those jeans and sweaters. I want my girl in satin. No pants." A smile entered his voice. "And no panties."

He hung up. Replacing the receiver in the cradle, she stared at it, thoughts swirling. It rang beneath her hand. "Yes?" she asked tensely.

"Jenny."

Hunter's voice nearly did her in. "Hunter!" she exclaimed in relief, hysterical laughter bubbling up. "Oh, Hunter! I'm so glad to hear from you."

"I'm on my way back. I should be there late this afternoon."

"To Santa Fe?"

"I had a face-off with Russell in L.A."

"A face-off?"

"I can't talk about it now," he interrupted her, and she thought he slurred his words a little. "I'm at the airport. I've called Ortega. He knows Rawley's been kidnapped."

"Troy called just a moment ago. Rawley was with him." There was a moment's hesitation. "Hunter? Did you hear me?"

"Yes." He spoke with an effort.

"Are you all right?" she asked in fear. "Rawley wanted to know if you were all right?"

"What did he say?"

"That's all. But it scared the living daylights out of me. You sound funny, though." She paused. "What kind of face-off did you have?"

"Rawley knows what a bastard his father is."

"What did Troy do?"

"He's—" Hunter sucked in a sharp breath. Dodging this question was difficult. "My flight's being called."

"What did he do?"

"We had a fight. Jenny, listen, Ortega told me your father had a heart attack."

"Yes, but he's doing okay so far. Troy wants five hundred thousand dollars put into an account in his name. I'm calling my father's lawyer and setting—"

"No! Don't turn over the money. Don't even start the process."

"I'm just going to call Joseph Wessver."

"You're not going to solve this with money."

"You don't sound right," she said. "Are you sure you're okay? If Troy will trade Rawley for the money, I don't care what it costs!"

"He won't trade him!"

"Well, I'm not going to risk his life on that chance!" Jenny found herself practically shouting.

"Your father just wants to buy you out of another tough situation, and *it won't work!*"

"Don't tell me what to do," she declared in a quivering voice. "Troy will take the money, believe me," she added more to convince herself than him. "He wants the money. I've got to get it to him."

Hunter swore beneath his breath. "He wants something more. Russell's a psychopath. He's over the edge."

Dry-mouthed, she whispered, "What are you saying?"

"Forget Daddy's fortune. The money isn't going to help now."

"I'm calling the lawyer," she said in sudden decision. "I'll pay whatever I have to."

"You sound like your father."

"Well, I'm his daughter," she shot back.

"You both think money will solve anything."

His bitterness took her aback. She straightened her spine. "That's right. And I'm just like your ex-wife, too. We're rich and we can buy anything! Well, damn you, Hunter Calgary. I'm going to buy my son back!"

She slammed down the receiver. Her thoughts were for her son. Hunter's words had terrified her. ". . . he's a psychopath . . . he's over the edge . . ."

Troy's going to hurt Rawley! The realization was like an arrow striking the center of her heart. She paced the room, frantic with fear, her gaze glued on the phone. If she could buy back her son, she would spend every last dime of her money and her father's money.

She couldn't leave now. She had to stay. She had to

wait for Troy.

Three hours later the phone finally rang again.

Rawley sat in the passenger seat of the dirty silver Dodge van. Troy's friend J.P. had a slew of cars, apparently, ready at a moment's notice. They'd driven half a block and Rawley had been roughly thrown into his current position. J.P. had driven one way and they'd headed another.

He was sick with fear, especially for Hunter. Hunter had saved his life. He knew that. It resonated deep within him. He owed the guy so much. Especially since Rawley had wanted to believe all the bad things his father had said about him.

His father.

The man beside him was very different from the urbane stranger who'd approached him at soccer camp. He'd unraveled somehow. Something weird and ugly had taken over, as if an unseen hand had peeled back the outward layer.

Hunter. Rawley felt like throwing up. What if he was dead? He'd fallen to the floor, fighting consciousness, telling Rawley to go with Troy in order to save his life. But what about *his* life? Was Hunter Calgary even alive?

"Hey." His father elbowed him. "Why are you so quiet?"

Rawley wasn't going to think of this psycho as his father any longer. He was simply someone bad. Someone with a gun in his left jacket pocket that Rawley couldn't reach. Someone who talked about his mother as if she were his personal whore.

"I asked you a question!"

"I'm tired."

"You think I killed him, don't you? I hope to hell I did! That bastard's been fucking your mother. You should be happy he's dead."

Rawley didn't rise to the bait, even though he was ready to fight the sexually twisted man who'd kidnapped him. He was no father. No father at all.

Don't die, Hunter. Please. Don't die.

They were crossing the border into Arizona. He could see the stations on the opposite side of the freeway where cars were stopped and checked to see if fruits and vegetables were being brought into the state. If they were going that way today, he would jump out of the car at that point and scream for help.

But he was on the other side, hurtling into Arizona where he guessed they didn't give a damn about insect infestation because no station was visible and no one was stopping them to ask.

Arizona was only one state away from New Mexico. Troy was taking him back, but not for any purpose meant to benefit Rawley.

For the first time in his life Rawley longed to be in school. Yearned for the homework and exacting teachers and silly classmates. He also wished he'd had sex with that girl that one time. It might have been his only chance.

An hour later they stopped at a filling station. Troy looked like death warmed over. He eased his shoulders back, started to step from the car, slipped a hand in his pocket and silently warned Rawley not to make any sudden moves.

To hell with that. Rawley started counting in his head. One . . . Troy took a step toward the pump. Two . . .

Another step. Three . . . he reached for the handle.

Rawley exploded out of the car and sprinted to the mini-mart, slamming his arm against the door and bursting inside to the amazement of the girl at the counter. She froze, one hand above the cash register.

"Back door!" he said. "Where is it?"

Her eyes traveled toward an area that included the restrooms. Rawley ran, skidded, and grabbed a door handle as Troy, face livid with fury, charged after him. Rawley yanked open the door. A short hallway. Another door.

"Stop, or I'll shoot," Troy said with dead calm behind him.

Rawley didn't wait. He grabbed the handle, twisted and bolted to freedom. Swearing, Troy chose to run after him rather than firing a gun in this public place.

There was nothing on all sides of Rawley. Sagebrush and dirt and dry yellow grass and saguaro cacti standing at attention. The one in front of him was giving the whole world the finger. Far in the distance were rolling hills, also dotted with saguaro. He'd read once that saguaro grew only in Arizona, and only in one part of the state. Maybe it was true, maybe it wasn't. But they were here now and might be all he had to hide behind. He ran and ran, distancing himself easily from the panting, infuriated monster trying to stay on his heels.

"Years of soccer practice, you bastard," Rawley whispered fiercely, and he kept on running.

CHAPTER EIGHTEEN

Hunter landed in Albuquerque, feeling half dead. His car was waiting for him but his fingers were heavy and sluggish with the keys. It was only an hour's drive to Santa Fe but it had grown dark and the night was clouding over, cloaking the stars one by one. Looked like more rain, he thought with an exhausted sigh. It was difficult enough to see already.

He hoped Ortega had Russell in his sights. He drove with that one thought in mind. His arm throbbed dully, sending out blistering jolts of pain whenever he moved too quickly.

He drove straight to Jenny's condo. It took three tries for him to get the right code punched in at the gate. His brain just wasn't working right.

He drove to her place and pulled to a stop. For a moment he rested his head on the steering wheel, woozy with exhaustion and a nameless emotion. Call it fear, he thought.

Staggering up the stairs, he got to the bell and pressed hard, leaning against it with all his weight.

She opened the door. "Hunter!"

He staggered inside.

Jenny looked him over, not knowing exactly what was wrong with him, but it was obvious he was sick. "You've got to see a doctor."

"No. I need to call Ortega. See if he's picked up Russell."

"You're feverish," she said, having felt his forehead. He was sprawled across her couch, wearing a raincoat that was a couple of sizes too small. A black T-shirt strained across his chest, emblazoned with filthy words in Gothic script. Where had he gotten those clothes?

"Hunter."

"Give me the phone," he ordered, but he couldn't rise to a sitting position.

She didn't like being ordered around, but she knew he was half out of his head, his brain tracking Troy Russell even if his body couldn't. For that she loved him, even if he did think she was a rich bitch who poured money away like water.

Benny sat next to Hunter's head and wouldn't budge. Jenny handed Hunter the remote handset.

Ortega answered on the first ring. "Any news on Russell?" Hunter demanded.

"Haven't picked up either of the cars yet."

Hunter scowled. "Bet Ratty provided another one. I'm here with Geneva. I'll call back." The receiver slipped from his fingers. Jenny replaced it gingerly. His left hand shot out and grabbed her by the arm. "Don't leave," he whispered.

"You need to get those clothes off."

"I can't do it," he admitted, grimacing in disgust at his own weakness.

"Stubborn as a mule," she muttered. "Let me . . ."

She helped him struggle out of the coat. The blood-soaked gauze and purpling skin beneath gave her pause. "My God, Hunter. What happened?" she asked shakily.

"Russell took a potshot at me. Hit my arm."

"That's a gunshot wound?"

" 'Fraid so. That's why I can't see a doctor. They'll have to report it."

She gazed at him in disbelief. "Don't be crazy. You need medical attention."

His teeth gritted. "Not yet. If this gets reported, it'll all come out and they won't let me go after him."

"The authorities," she said, a statement rather than a question.

"I just need—some rest. And brandy, if you've got it."

"I'll see if I have some more gauze," she said, slipping from his grasp and heading to the bathroom.

He was asleep when she returned. She had some butterfly bandages and antibiotic ointment, a fresh roll of gauze and some tiny scissors. She had no intention of waking him to redress the wound, but his eyes fluttered open.

"I'm sorry," he said.

"For what?" She began to unwrap the wound, her hands trembling a bit at the sight of the ravaged flesh.

His good hand slid up her arm from her elbow. He gazed at her in a way that melted her heart. "You're nothing like Kathryn," he said softly and she impulsively leaned in to kiss him. A few moments later, breathless, Jenny drew away and turned her attention to the task at hand.

"Where are you going?"

"To get you a stiff drink. You're going to need something more than a kiss to get through this next part."

"I've been through it once already today," he murmured.

She returned with brandy and continued unwrapping the wound. Hunter closed his eyes and kept the glass to his lips, swallowing hard every time Jenny pulled a little too hard and tender flesh ripped apart. By the time she finished she was sweating.

She went to her bathroom and found a bottle of painkillers. Shaking three into her palm, she brought them back to Hunter who swallowed them with the brandy.

"Drugs and alcohol," she said.

"Hey, knock me out. The medical way," he murmured, his eyes closing in utter exhaustion.

It was dawn when the phone rang. Jenny had the handset next to her ear in the bedroom. The phone barely chirped when she answered it.

"Get in your car and drive north," Troy's voice directed. "Stop in Taos. Go to the Taos Inn. You know it?"

Jenny listened hard to hear if Hunter had picked up the phone. She didn't want to wake him. She didn't even want to involve him in his current state. "Yes, I know it," she whispered. The historic Taos Inn was an old adobe building right in the center of the tiny town.

"Check in."

"Are you in Taos?"

"I'll call you at the hotel . . ."

She hung up, frightened, heartsick about Rawley. A terrible feeling was building inside her. The Volvo was already packed. She'd done that yesterday when she'd felt an urgency to chase after Hunter to L.A.

Should she wake him? Should she tell him?

She ran through the shower and slipped into jeans and a sweater, fully conscious that her outfit was exactly what her ex didn't want to see. She carried her sneakers in her fingers and tiptoed out to the living room. Benny softly woofed at her and snuffled her hand.

Hunter woke, tried to sit up, caught in his breath, and

demanded sharply, "Where are you going?"

She didn't like lying, but she knew he wouldn't approve. "I'm getting us breakfast."

"I don't need anything."

"You need lots of things," she said with a smile that felt as false as it was.

"I don't want you to leave."

"You're in no condition to do anything. We'll talk when I get back."

He struggled to get to his feet and Jenny hurried to help him back down to the couch. "I feel okay," he said, his eyes searching her face. "Aren't you worried Russell will call while you're gone?"

"Well, yeah. Of course. Um . . . tell him not to hurt my son."

They stared at each other. Jenny quickly put on her shoes, grabbed her purse and headed for the door. She knew he knew she was up to something. Turning back, she said brightly, "When this is all over, let's go stay at the Taos Inn."

She left before he could get to his feet.

The Taos Inn had a room available at four P.M. Jenny checked her watch. She wondered if she should call Hunter and tell him what she was doing. She could call his sergeant and leave the information. But she could predict what would happen. The Santa Fe police would inform the Taos police and officers would come to her aid and . . . and . . .

She could almost hear the gunfire. She knew Troy would smell a trap. Rawley would get hurt . . . badly hurt. A moan

)f protest left her lips. She couldn't do it.

But if she called Hunter he would come. Put himself in
langer when he wasn't physically up to the task. Troy had
;hot him, the bastard!

She shivered, thinking once more of her son.

Oh, Rawley! Please, please be safe.

Jenny stepped outside the hotel onto the sidewalk and
watched traffic cruise by. The air was crisp, dry and bright
with sunlight. Window-shoppers stopped along the way,
gazing in the shops and galleries.

She crossed the street and tried to do the same, wan-
dering aimlessly, checking and rechecking her watch. She
wore only her white cotton sweater and jeans, not enough
to keep her from shivering. There was a winter nip still in
the March air.

Or was that from nerves? Fear? She didn't want to think
about it.

At four o'clock she checked into her room and called the
hospital. Her father sounded groggy, so she tried to make
her conversation short.

"Have you found Rawley yet?" was all he wanted to
know. She told him she was waiting for a call from Troy.

"Did you call Wessver?"

"Yes," she said. She had called the day before not long
after slamming the phone down on Hunter. "I'm calling
him again as soon as I'm off the phone with you."

"Jenny, promise me you'll take the money."

"I'll take the money," she said automatically though
Hunter's words still stung her conscience. He felt she was
making the same kind of mistake her father always had.
She knew he was right. But her son's life was at stake!

"It'll flush him out." Allen coughed again. "Do it Geneva." She heard someone say something to him and realized Natalie was by his side.

"I'll call Wessver right now," she assured him.

She didn't, though. She hesitated. She thought of how Hunter would handle this situation and she called her own number quickly, before she could change her mind. There was no answer and she hung up after a while, afraid all over again. What if he were unable to get to the phone? What if he were lying there, needing help?

She was deciding what to do when the phone rang. "Jenny . . ." Troy said in his caressing way that made her stomach sink.

"Let me talk to Rawley."

"What about the money?"

"I called Joseph Wessver, my father's lawyer. He's calling me back."

"You disappoint me. You really do. You'll have to check out."

"Check out! Troy, I'm waiting for Wessver's call. I have to stay here."

"I want you to go back to your lovely little condominium. Wait for me there."

"Troy—" she protested.

The line went dead.

She went downstairs but she didn't check out. Instead, she extended her stay for several more days and she left her bags in the room. She didn't know what Troy was up to, but at least she'd let Hunter know where she was.

She walked out to her car in the gravel lot behind the

Taos Inn. She'd inserted the key when she felt him come up behind her. Gasping, she had instant thoughts of kicking and screaming and biting, but she recognized the gun against her ribs for what it was.

"Jenny . . ."

Troy's breath on the back of her neck revolted her. "Where's Rawley?" she whispered.

"Safe. I'll take you to him."

"I'm not getting in a car with you."

"Then I'm going to go kill him right now."

"I'll call the police. They'll pick you up."

"You'll never see him again."

She couldn't bluff her way out of this. She had to play along—for Rawley's sake.

"Get in the car, Jenny."

She thought he meant her car, but he guided her toward a silver van with California plates. She balked, but he just shook his head and smiled.

She climbed in the passenger seat.

Damn his arm, his weakness. Damn Jenny and her lies.

Hunter dragged himself to his Jeep and drove to the station, pinpoints of light dancing in front of his eyes. He stumbled inside.

"Jenny's in Taos. At the Taos Inn. I think Troy Russell told her to go there."

"What the hell happened to you?" Ortega demanded, helping Hunter to the chair next to his desk.

"Did you hear me?" Hunter asked tersely.

"Your lady's at the Taos Inn. I got it."

"No sign of Russell?"

"Not so far. You're not moving your right arm," the sergeant observed, frowning.

"I got in the line of fire."

Ortega swore a blue streak and glared at Hunter. "You're gonna end up at St. Vincent's right beside her old man."

"I'm going to Taos."

"You won't make it in that condition. What the hell are you wearing?"

"Her son's shirt and jacket. Better than what I had before." He moved to the door.

"Here . . ." Ortega grabbed his own leather jacket off a peg and tossed it Hunter's way. "It's raining out there again," he said in disgust. "Feels like it's been raining forever."

Hunter drove straight to Taos, Benny sitting upright in the passenger seat. He made the trip in record time even though the rain was mixed with snow and the roads were growing slushy. He arrived at the Taos Inn and parked next to Jenny's Volvo. Here the snow was sticking and he could see several sets of footprints outside her driver's door. Snow had been brushed from the handle, but was rapidly piling up again.

Stepping inside, from the cold to sudden heat, he felt slightly dizzy. He was running on adrenaline and willpower. Neither was doing much good for his overtaxed body. He walked up to the desk clerk and asked him to ring Jenny's room. "No answer, sir."

"Ring it again."

The clerk lifted his brows, clearly thinking Hunter was on the make. "Still no answer, sir."

Hunter nodded, troubled. He walked back to his Jeep. A

set of deep tracks, from a truck or van, had gouged through snow into mud. By the looks of the snowfall, it had left only a few minutes ahead of him.

What if Russell already had her . . . ?

He went back to the desk clerk. "Do you have a Troy Russell on your guest list?"

"Sir . . ."

"He would have come in yesterday or today. About my height, similar coloring. Probably driving a car with out-of-state plates. California, most likely. He's this woman's ex-husband and he's kidnapped their son. Just tell me if he's on the guest list."

Reluctantly, the clerk scanned the list, then shook his head.

"How many single men have checked in today and yesterday?"

"I'm not allowed to give out that information."

Hunter inwardly berated himself for not asking Ortega for his police identification when he'd had the chance. He was heading to the pay phone to take care of it when he heard, "Excuse me."

A young woman in a long black coat and fur cap gazed at Hunter thoughtfully. "A man checked in this morning, early. He had similar coloring." She pursed her lips. "He was driving a silver van with California plates. He bragged that he owned a place around Taos, but he was locked out or something. He wanted to drive me past it and then go to lunch. I refused the invitation."

"Did he say where it was?" Hunter asked.

She shrugged. "Go out Kit Carson Road."

"I need to check Jenny Holloway's room," Hunter

ordered the clerk. "She might need help."

"I'll check it, sir."

Hunter followed after him, much to his frowning dismay. Once the door was open, he shouldered past the younger man, ignoring his protests. Jenny's bags were there, untouched. Nothing in the room had been disturbed. But that didn't mean nothing had happened.

The drive was short. Jenny wondered if she could jump out and run, but she kept hoping Rawley was at their destination. She knew she'd played right into Troy's hands. He was violent, a sexual predator who liked to hurt and dominate women. He'd grown from a bully to a full-blown psychopath. She didn't doubt that he'd killed Michelle Calgary.

And she didn't doubt that he would kill her and her son if the mood suited him. Hunter had been right. Money was only part of Troy's obsession.

"Put this on," he said, dragging Rawley's jacket from the back of the van. There were no seats in the van except the front two.

"I'm not that cold." She was freezing. The rain was mixed with snow at this elevation, but she balked at anything he might ask of her.

"Put it on."

She did as she was told and the familiar scent of her son wafted up to her nostrils. Swallowing back a new wave of terror, she fought to think of something to do. Maybe if she could connect with Troy on some level, appeal to what little good there was in him . . . "Rawley was called up to the varsity playoffs as a freshman. That's how he earned his letter." Maybe Troy would be proud . . .

"I told you not to wear those jeans."

"I'm not going to wear a satin skirt in this weather."

"Take them off."

She had to reason with him. She knew he would hurt her if he could. Physically and emotionally. She had to out-smart him any way she could.

The snow fell faster, turning into slush, which piled up along the edges. "I'll take them off when we stop."

With that Troy cranked the wheel and they were sud-denly bumping along a side road almost hidden by the snow. After about a half mile, he pulled in front of a ram-bling stucco house made to look like adobe, its *vigas* sticking out, its porch, railings and roof frosted with white.

"Whose place is this?"

"Mine," Troy said.

"Are we getting out of the van?" she asked when he didn't make any move.

He wagged his head from side to side, as if it were a game. "I like it right here, don't you?"

"Not really."

Pulling out a new, oversized pack of Big Red, he folded a cinnamon flavored stick of gum in his mouth. "Kissable," he said. "Want one?"

She shook her head. Her mouth was dry.

"C'mere . . ." He dragged her forward. "You're scared, aren't you?"

"Yes," she answered honestly. "Is Rawley inside?"

"Rawley, Rawley, Rawley . . . the way you talk about him, I wonder if you've gotten in his pants."

Her heart lurched in horror. "He's our son, Troy. He's

your son."

He yanked her mouth to his, nearly choking her with his thrusting tongue. She tasted the cinnamon gum. He had a gun in his jacket pocket. The cell phone must be in the driver's door. Where was a weapon? What could she use?

"Get in the back!" he rasped, suddenly pushing her away, shoving her through the seats and following right behind her. "On your hands and knees."

"Troy . . ." She warded him off with her hands, but there was nothing in his eyes but malignant lust.

"Hands and knees, baby. Come on. Hands and knees. Now take off the jeans real slow . . ."

Hunter got onto the main road, headed south, then east on Kit Carson Road. It wasn't as long as Santa Fe's Canyon Road but it boasted galleries and eateries and a few bed and breakfasts. It soon petered out to a small road lined by skinny pines weighted with fresh snow. He turned off to follow a set of tracks down a drive, finding only a bright red Chevy truck parked in front of a small house. He returned to the main road, berating himself for wasting precious time.

Oh, Jenny, hang in there.

I think I want that piece of gum now," she said in a strangled voice.

"You're stalling."

He was waving the gun at her now, letting her see his power. Her terror must have been written on her face no matter how she tried to hide it because his smile got wider.

"You're getting me hot, Jenny, my love," he whispered,

shaking one knee as he sat across the van from her. "Raging hot."

"Oh, no . . ." she said weakly.

This wasn't the same man she'd married. He was long gone. Fifteen years gone. But she hadn't realized what a monster Troy had become.

He grabbed the pack of gum and threw it at her. She flinched, picked up the pack, then turned around to stare down the barrel of his gun.

"Don't fuck with me," he whispered.

She had to keep him talking, but she was nearly frozen with terror. "If you kill me, you won't get the money," she pointed out reasonably.

"I'm not going to kill you," he said, as if she were extremely dense. "Sounds like dear old dad's about to leave this world, and that means all the money goes to you."

"Why did you kill Michelle Calgary?"

"You've been listening to your lapdog. I didn't kill Michelle. She fell."

"You pushed her. She made you mad, and you can't stand that. She told you she was pregnant and you didn't want her or the baby."

"She was a crybaby. Cried all the time."

"She was going to tell the authorities that you hit her and abused her. She was going to do what I should have done all those years ago."

"You've got a nasty little mouth," he said angrily. "Just like Michelle. She cried and whined to that bastard brother of hers, the one you let into your bed. You did, didn't you, Jenny? You let him have sex with you."

"You killed her," she insisted carefully.

"Jenny . . ." He cupped her chin in one rough hand and shook her head slowly from side to side. "Michelle never listened. It was her fault. She just—wouldn't—listen! You need to listen. Now, get on your hands and knees. Don't make me make you."

She would rather face the gun than comply to his wishes. Deliberately, she pulled out one stick of gum, unwrapping it slowly and sliding it into her mouth. He watched her like Benny watched the bag of kibble whenever she was about to feed him.

She was feeling strangely calm. She needed to know where Rawley was, but she had to have the upper hand. "It's kind of warm," she murmured, trying to shrug out of Rawley's jacket.

"Don't take it off," he bit out.

"Why not?" She kept pulling her arms from the sleeves, watching him. His gaze was on the jacket, his breath coming hot and fast.

"Lay it down," he said jerkily.

She did as she was told. "Come on, Val," he urged. "Come on, Jenny." She didn't move. Suddenly, his eyes glazed over and to her extreme disgust and amazement, he unzipped his pants and stroked himself until he came, squirting semen all over the jacket.

She didn't wait. She kneed him in the crotch for all she was worth. Too preoccupied to anticipate the blow, Troy crumpled up, moaning. She scrambled to her knees, but he lunged at her, hitting her head with the side of the gun which slipped from his fingers. Her hand fisted, connecting with his chest. She felt his teeth sink into her shoulder and she cried out. Her hand scrabbled around, searching for the gun. She found the pack of gum instead.

He tried to pin down her arms. They were both breathing in hard gasps. With all her might, she shoved the pack of gum into his open mouth, momentarily choking him.

He spat out the thing and attempted to bite her again. Jenny kicked and flailed. She realized their fight was arousing him again. She hadn't done enough damage.

They were both panting, silently struggling. He grabbed her arms, but she wrenched one away. The gun was to her right, lying on the carpet. She grabbed for it but it skittered further toward the back of the van. He hit her full across the face and snatched at it himself. Jenny twisted, trying to get one knee up. When he shifted to stop her, she wrenched around, reaching out with all her might, her fingers finally closing on the gun's butt.

A second later she had it pointing at his forehead. "Move and I'll kill you!" she screamed.

He froze.

"Where's Rawley?"

He didn't respond. Just stared at her through cold eyes.

"Where is my son?" she demanded. Was the safety on? Could she pull the trigger? Kill him point blank? "Tell me where he is, you bastard!"

"You can't do it, can you?"

"Where is he?"

"Oh, Jenny." Watching her, Troy pulled slowly back, a smile forming on his lips.

She wanted to shriek with frustration. She couldn't look at him. He would never tell her. She knew that now.

"Come on, honey," he whispered.

"Stop it. Don't touch me. Please, Troy. Tell me he's alive."

"Well, of course he is." He yanked the gun from her nerveless fingers.

Jenny's shoulders sagged and she closed her eyes. She was spent. Weary enough to pass out on the spot. The click of the safety brought her eyelids flying open. The gun was trained on her face.

"Beg me some more, Jenny. I like it."

She said nothing.

"Come on, Jenny. 'Please, Troy, please. Pretty please.' Say it." With his free hand he reached for the button on her jeans. She slapped him away.

"Say it!" he ordered, yanking hard on her zipper.

Her hands clamped over his, stopping him. He pushed the gun into the skin of her cheek.

"You scared? You scared, Jenny . . . huh?" He leaned down on her, pushing her into the carpet. "Come on, baby," he crooned. She could feel him hard against her, pushing rhythmically. "C'mon, c'mon, c'mon. 'Pleeease . . . Troy . . .' " He fumbled with his own buckle. She heard the jingle as he hurriedly pushed down his trousers.

Her hand curled and flexed. She would grab right where it hurt and twist with all her might.

The gun was now pressed to her throat. He started to lick her lips. "You used to like that. Remember?" he whispered. His tongue grew more sloppy, sliding around her mouth and in and out of her lips. He grunted and pushed against her, his hands seeking to dig inside her jeans.

Jenny tensed, ready to strike.

The side door of the van suddenly flew open. One moment Troy was on top of her, the next he was yanked back as if he'd suddenly learned to fly. Jenny scrambled to her knees and pushed herself out of the van after him.

Hunter had Troy by the neck and was squeezing the life out of him.

❈ CHAPTER NINETEEN ❈

H unter . . ." Jenny clambered out of the van. Troy's eyes had rolled back. His pants were down at his knees.

A low, ferocious growl warned her not to move. But it was Benny, transfixed by the sight of the man who had beaten him.

"Hunter," she said again. "Please . . ."

"He killed my sister."

"He knows where my son is."

A moment passed. Slowly, Hunter released the fingers of his left hand from around Troy's neck. He gazed at the man for a long moment, monitoring the labored rise and fall of his chest, willing him to live just a little longer. Troy started to fall, but Hunter clamped one hand on him, pinning him in place. Benny sat below, mouth drawn back in a vicious snarl, low growls issuing steadily from his throat, the hair on the back of his neck as stiff as his four legs.

Troy coughed and touched his throat as he came to. Jenny belatedly thought of the gun, somewhere in the van.

Hunter said, "If you move, Benny will rip you apart and I'll just sit back and watch."

"You strangled me," he whined.

Hunter's cold smile was an echo of Benny's snarl. "Not well enough, apparently."

"Where's Rawley?" Jenny asked.

Troy glanced around. Thoughts of escape were clear in his eyes. He looked down at the clothing ignominiously circling his ankles, but when he reached to pull up his pants, Benny clamped his teeth around his wrist.

"Tell her where her son is," Hunter warned.

"Get the damn dog off me."

Jenny grabbed Benny by his collar. "Come on, boy. Over here." She was shaking all over with relief. She was so glad to see Hunter. So glad.

Troy pulled on his pants, staggering a bit. In a flash he leapt for the open door of the van.

"The gun!" Jenny called as Benny jerked from her grasp and charged after him in a flying leap.

Hunter was only a second behind.

A bullet exploded within the van. All Jenny could see were Hunter's legs hanging out.

"Benny . . . ?" she whispered in horror.

Hunter slowly levered himself out. He shook his head and tears sprang to Jenny's eyes. He reached over and brushed her hair out of her face, a soft smile crossing his lips as he looked at her. "No," he murmured. "Benny's got his jaws around Russell's throat. The bastard shot himself in the foot."

Three hours later, with Troy at St. Vincent Hospital under armed guard, awaiting surgery to his shattered foot, Hunter and Jenny stood in the waiting area. Sergeant Ortega had met them—and he ordered Hunter into the emergency room to have his own injury attended to.

Left with the sergeant, Jenny sat in a chair, clasping and

unclasping her hands.

"We'll find Rawley," he said.

She didn't know what to say. Excusing herself, she went to check on her father who was sitting up and looking marginally better. Natalie sat in a nearby chair, legs crossed, elegant and composed.

"Jenny," Allen said in alarm, staring at her.

"I'm okay." As quickly as she could, she brought them up to date on the latest events. They both watched her gravely the whole time.

When Jenny was finished, he asked, "Did Russell do that?"

"What?"

He gestured to her face.

Her fingers explored the growing puffiness and bruise from where he'd struck her. "Oh."

"I hope he rots in hell," he muttered.

"He didn't tell us where Rawley is. Even Benny couldn't get it out of him."

"They'll find him," he said, repeating Ortega's assurances. Jenny smiled weakly. "How's Calgary?" Allen asked gruffly, as an afterthought.

"Getting looked at."

"Jenny—"

"Don't tell me how to feel about him. I know how I feel. I love him, and nothing you can say can change that."

"He saved your life, so say thank you and let it go at that."

"Allen," Natalie murmured disapprovingly.

"Just stop," Jenny told him.

"Okay, okay." He lifted his hands, warding off any more

criticism, before dropping them weakly to his lap.

"Hunter Calgary is the best thing that ever happened to me. All I've done is go against his advice and wishes, and he thinks I'm a spoiled rich girl whose daddy buys her out of trouble, again and again."

"That's not true. You've been living on your own for years—much as I hate to admit it."

Jenny started to laugh. She couldn't help herself. "Don't try to be reasonable now. Not after all these years. You'll only confuse me."

Natalie arched an amused brow. Maybe she wasn't as bad as Jenny had believed all these years.

"I want you to be with someone you deserve," Allen said bullishly. "Hunter Calgary saved you, and I feel he ought to be rewarded. But that doesn't alter the fact that he's an unemployed ex-cop and a burnout case."

She sighed. Her father wasn't going to change. Picking up her windbreaker and purse, she gave him a meaningful look.

Allen frowned, sensing a trap.

"He's going to be your son-in-law," she said. "If he'll have me."

You didn't lay a hand on him, did you?" Ortega asked Hunter after the probing and antisepsis and stitching and bandaging were done. Ortega had seen the blue and purple bruises on Troy's throat.

"Not a hand," Hunter lied cheerfully.

Ortega grunted. "He'll still scream police brutality. He's the type."

"He was trying to rape her. Had her at gunpoint."

"Nice," he muttered, grimacing.

"Benny deserves a medal. Got anything for canine courage?"

Ortega grunted again.

They left the emergency room together. "You're a lucky bastard," Ortega remarked. "That bullet could have taken off your arm."

Hunter nodded soberly, but he was thinking about how Troy had aimed for his only son. A moment of madness? Probably. But it could have had lethal results.

Jenny met them in the waiting room. Her beautiful face was drawn and white. "How are you?" she asked.

"On painkillers. The real thing."

"He's fine." Ortega's look squelched her rising concern. "I'm gonna wait for Russell to get out of surgery. Why don't you two get some rest?"

Hunter and Jenny left him at the elevators and walked outside. Twilight had come upon them and the snow glowed a soft blue in the fading light.

"I keep thinking he'll just show up. Maybe he got away from Troy."

Hunter nodded. "Let's check the condo phone."

"I'll drive."

There was no message on the answering machine, but there were three hang-ups from telephone numbers with varying area codes. "Maybe it's Rawley!" she said with renewed hope. Benny's ears lifted at her tone and his tail wagged.

"The last call was early this morning," Hunter observed.

"Well, maybe he's just not somewhere he can get to a phone."

A sudden silence divided them. There was a lot more to say and neither of them knew how to begin.

Finally, Jenny cleared her throat. "I know you're still a little woozy after all that, but at least let me say I'm sorry. I shouldn't have left without telling you where I was going. I just didn't want you to get hurt."

Hunter shrugged. "Let me ask you a question." He paused, remembering their game. With a faint smile, he added, "Then you can ask me a question."

Jenny shot him a look. "Okay."

"You put yourself in extreme danger. If something had happened to you, why did you think I wouldn't care?"

She gazed at him, gauging the seriousness of his words. "Do you mean that?"

"You keep forgetting your own rules. Answer the question first, then ask."

Her lips twitched in spite of her overriding worry about Rawley. "I was thinking about your shoulder. I didn't want you to tangle with Troy, because I was afraid he might hurt you. I wouldn't be able to live with myself if anything happened to you because of me."

"You needed protection," he insisted. "That's why your father hired me in the first place. And I would do anything to protect you from Troy. But because you didn't tell me, I damn near got there too late!"

She put a finger to her lips. "Shh. You're forgetting the rules. It's my turn to ask a question." She paused. "And just for the record, I said I was sorry."

"Where's the question?" he said, only slightly mollified.

"I'm not like your ex-wife, Hunter. I know you think I have no concept of money, but I do. But don't expect me to act rationally when my son's gone God knows where." She swept her arm in a wide circle, close to tears again. "But I'm glad you arrived when you did," she added in a small voice. "Thank you."

Hunter reached his left arm toward her and she hurried to curl up next to him, to hear his heartbeat and know she was safe. He inhaled deeply of her delicate scent, loving the closeness. Their game, for the moment, was over.

"Do you think Rawley's alive?" she finally asked. "Please don't lie."

"Yes, I do. I think he's been calling."

"Well, then, where is he?"

Resting his cheek against the silky crown of her hair, Hunter wondered the same thing.

Jenny wouldn't have believed she could sleep, but though her mind raced and raced, her body relaxed. She and Hunter spent another night on the couch, and in the morning they stirred themselves awake.

At nine o'clock the phone rang. "Give me Calgary," Ortega barked into the phone, irascible as always.

Hunter frowned. "Hello."

"This blasted rain's brought your bum friend back and he smells like a garbage dump. Get him outta here. And are you working for this department, or not? If so, get in here."

"I've got to take Jenny to pick up her Volvo in Taos."

"Well, isn't that nice. Russell looks as if he'll walk again, more's the pity. Talk about shooting yourself in the foot!" He laughed harshly.

"I'll stop by and check on Obie." He hesitated. "Nothing on the boy yet?" He saw Jenny stiffen and look his way.

"Not a damn thing."

"What did he say?" Jenny asked as Hunter hung up. He shook his head.

"We'll break Russell. We'll make him talk."

"But every hour that goes by is just—" She broke off, unable to continue.

"Come on. We'll stop by the station and I'll figure out what to do with Obie, then we can get your car."

"Who's Obie?" she asked without any real interest.

"Just a crazy old guy who doesn't like the rain."

The snow had melted into puddles. Rain still fell lightly but the storm was passing. "That'll probably be it till next winter," Hunter observed. "Not a lot of precipitation around here, normally."

Jenny stared out the side window of the Jeep. "I had all these dreams about my restaurant and a new life. The hell with it. Only Rawley matters now."

"We will find him," Hunter said with grim determination.

"He would have come home by now. He wouldn't let me worry."

"Don't think that way."

"I can't help it," she said in a suffocated voice.

Hunter moved his injured arm to touch her fingers. She lifted tear-drenched eyes to his and his gaze moved over the bruise on her cheek. "I love you," he said.

The tears spilled down her cheeks and onto her hands. She loved him, too, but Rawley was still out there somewhere. Alone? Hurt? She had no way of knowing.

Obie Loggerfield stamped his feet outside the door of the

police station. His fingers were frozen. He didn't have his poncho on and that sure as hell didn't help things. Damn, whoever invented rain, anyway.

The sergeant stood inside the doors, hands on his hips, scowling like the mean bastard he was. To Obie's utter shock, he suddenly thrust open one side of the glass double doors and ordered, "Well, get in here."

"Thank you, sir," Obie said respectfully as he crossed the threshold and dripped melting snow and rain onto the floor.

"Keep it right there." He pointed to a square of linoleum. Enough room for one old bum, in Ortega's opinion.

"I wish to see Detective Calgary," Obie said, sweeping his knitted cap from his head.

Ortega gave him a look. "Why do you come all this way, just to have him drive you back?"

Obie stuck out his chest. "I have an important message for him."

"Yeah, right. They're all important." Shaking his head at the puddle forming at Obie's feet, he strode back to his office.

Jenny sat frozen in the Jeep beside Hunter, keeping her mind on routine matters and off Rawley.

"I have to call Gloria," she said dully.

"You know that Gloria can handle the restaurant's operation. The paperwork will wait for your return."

"What's going to happen after I get my car?" she asked. "How many hours do I have to wait until . . . ?"

Hunter interrupted her. "Troy'll talk," he said with grim confidence.

"I don't know . . ." She'd had him at gunpoint and he

hadn't coughed up the information on Rawley's where-abouts. He'd known she was serious and still said nothing.

They pulled up a block from the station. Hunter opened her car door and Jenny stepped onto the wet street, avoiding the dirty snow that lined the curb.

Lights were on in the police station. Hunter held the door for her and she stepped inside. An indescribable odor hit her nose and she glanced over at a begrimed man in ragged clothes who shivered in the entryway, water pooling at his feet, his brown stocking cap held deferentially in his hands.

"So, Ortega let you in," Hunter said. "Where's your coat?"

"Had to give my poncho away."

"Who was the lucky recipient?"

"A friend in need."

Hunter noticed that the door to Ortega's office was open. "Stay here a minute." He motioned for Jenny to follow him.

Obie called, "I need to give you some information, Detective Calgary."

"I'll be right back and we'll drive out to your place." He placed his hand on the small of Jenny's back, guiding her inside. "That's Obie," he said in her ear. "An olfactory delight."

"He's very nice," she said as they walked toward Ortega's office. "He gave his poncho to someone who needed it more."

Hunter smiled. "Hard to imagine who that could be." He stuck his head around the doorjamb and spoke to Ortega. "Your dedication is a thing of beauty."

"Don't get all gooey on me. Get your smelly pal out of

here and buy him a cheap raincoat. He's giving our station a bad odor, so to speak."

"When can I see Russell?"

He shot him a look. "You taking your job back?"

"Depends on when I can see Russell."

Hunter glanced at Jenny who said, "He knows where my son is."

"I'm aware of that, Ms. Holloway. Russell is in big trouble. He shot Hunter in California, and he took a minor across a couple of state lines." He pursed his lips. "There's a second kidnapping charge in New Mexico—" He inclined his head in Jenny's direction. "Not to mention attempted rape and assault. Lieutenant Perkins has detectives waiting to interview him already."

Hunter glared at Ortega, who added tersely, "You're out of this one, Calgary. For a lot of reasons. That bullet wound being one of them."

Jenny gazed from one to the other, her anxiety mounting. "What does that mean?"

"It means I don't get to talk to Russell myself," Hunter bit out.

"The department doesn't want to risk being slapped with a lawsuit," Ortega explained. "They would keep Hunter Calgary and Troy Russell in opposite states, if they could."

"So, when will these detectives talk to him?" Jenny wanted to know.

"Soon."

She had no faith in any of this. Troy wasn't going to give Rawley up. Why should he? He'd believed he could get away with anything where his long lost son was concerned.

Sergeant Ortega wanted to go over a few more aspects of

the case with Hunter, and Jenny could take a hint. She stepped out of the room, signaling that she would wait in the hall. Walking around, healthy and basically unharmed, had a nightmarish quality to it when she had no idea what Rawley's condition was.

She sank onto a wooden bench. Realizing Obie was still waiting patiently in the anteroom, she reminded herself to be polite and got up. Obie seemed to be a caring human being who deserved better than being forced to wait on a twelve-by-twelve square of linoleum.

"Hey, there," she said. "Why don't you come in and sit down?"

"Oh, the sergeant wouldn't like that."

"You're freezing. It's warmer in here. I want you to come in." She held out a hand to him.

Obie hesitated, his eyes darting warily toward Ortega's open door. The rise and fall of authoritative voices seemed to intimidate him.

"Come on," Jenny said, holding her breath a bit.

Obie stepped into the brighter light, blinking a bit. His hair was a rat's nest. She doubted it had been combed in years. Still, he self-consciously pulled lank strands behind his ear and lifted his chin. A beard had been hacked at and hung lopsided from his jaw.

Around his dirt-grimed throat he wore a necklace of pink fake pearls.

Jenny stared. Her hand flew to her own throat. "Wh-where did you get that?" she whispered, her voice failing her for a second.

Obie looked down at himself, alarmed. "What?"

"The necklace."

"Oh!" His face split into a grin. "That's from my friend."

"The one you gave the poncho to?" He nodded vigorously. Jenny swallowed, scarcely able to breathe. "Is this friend a teenage boy?"

Obie lifted his chin. "I never asked his age. Wouldn't be polite."

"Is his name . . . Rawley?"

"You know him!" Obie said in delight.

Jenny swayed. She held her arms out for balance, overwhelmed with relief and about to faint. Obie darted forward and caught her. "Detective Calgary!" he called.

Hunter instinctively leapt from his chair at the tone of Obie's voice. Seeing Jenny in his arms, he rushed forward and gently drew her toward him. "Jenny" he whispered, alarmed at her paleness and the tears filling her eyes. But a smile trembled on her lips. She couldn't speak. She reached a finger toward Obie and touched the incongruous string of pink pearls circling his neck.

Hunter gaped. He remembered it from their days in Puerto Vallarta—Jenny had said it was a birthday gift. "You got that from Rawley Holloway!" he snapped at Obie.

"A gift!" Obie declared. "A gift, sir!"

Jenny was nodding. "And he gave Rawley his poncho."

"What?" Ortega demanded behind them.

But Hunter was already helping Jenny to her feet and hustling Obie out the door.

Obie's tent was surrounded by snow. Hunter screeched to a halt outside, but Jenny was out the door before he'd yanked on the brake.

She ran to the entry flap and flung it aside. Rawley looked up, gasped, then threw his arms around her as soon as she entered and buried his head in her shoulder. Jenny laughed through tears of joy. "I love you. Oh, God. I missed you. I was so scared."

"I tried to call . . ." he choked out. "But you weren't there. I was afraid he was—"

"Shhh. Don't talk," she ordered, stroking his hair, then asked in the next breath, "How did you get here?"

"Where is he?" Rawley asked fearfully.

Hunter stuck his head inside the tent. "Troy's in police custody," he informed him.

Rawley released his grip on Jenny. "Are you all right?" he asked Hunter. "I thought he shot you."

Hunter took a deep breath and said, "I'll tell you all about it. Want to continue this reunion in fresher air?"

Rawley gazed down at the filthy poncho Obie had lent him and said, "Guess I'm kinda used to it." He peeled off the poncho and said solemnly to Obie, "Thank you."

"Keep it," the old man said magnanimously.

They managed to convince Obie that he needed the poncho more than Rawley. During the drive back to the condo Rawley sat in the back seat with Jenny. Holding his mother close, he explained what had happened, recounting his escape from Troy and adding, "I got away about an hour over the border from California into Arizona. I just ran and ran. Eventually I circled back to the road and I got picked up by a trucker. I wasn't even hitchhiking. I know it was dangerous, Mom, but it was better than running into Troy.

"I got another ride outside of Phoenix from a couple of

guys driving a farm truck. Then an old codger who could barely stay on the road. I gotta learn to drive," he added seriously. "Right away. I mean, I had to hold the wheel half the time to keep us on line."

Jenny said, "I'm just so glad you're okay."

"Then we got into New Mexico and I got scared he would find me. I was scared for everybody." Rawley shot a look to the front seat where Hunter stoically drove on. "So, when I recognized the foothills I got out of the car and went to find Obie. He said he'd go get Hunter. I knew you'd said Hunter had called, so I figured he was still alive . . ." He drew a sharp breath and expelled it. "Did he do this?" Rawley asked, looking at the bruise on Jenny's face.

"He didn't get away unscathed," she responded.

Rawley's face darkened. "I'll kill him."

"There are a few of us ahead of you," Hunter drawled. "Might as well wait your turn."

As they reached the outskirts of Santa Fe, Jenny burst out, "Let's go to your ranch, Hunter."

Rawley pricked up his ears. "Ranch?"

"Is that all right?" Hunter wanted to know.

"Where's Benny?"

"We'll pick him up on the way," Jenny said.

An hour later all four of them jumped out of the Jeep and into the fast-vanishing vestiges of snow. Benny barked joyously and ran around the perimeter of the house. Jenny could scarcely release her grip on her son, but Rawley was eager to chase the dog.

"The recuperative power of youth," Hunter said, unlocking the door.

He made a fire while Jenny stood in the center of the

room. "This feels more like home," she said lamely, trying to explain her desire to come here rather than her own condo.

"It's not as fancy."

"I love it. Just the way it is," she said firmly.

"Good."

They locked eyes.

"You told me you loved me," Jenny said haltingly, and I wasn't able to tell you how I felt about you." She swallowed. "Do you still feel the same?"

"That was just a few hours ago."

"I know. But do you still feel the same?" she asked again.

"Yes."

She stopped and smiled. She loved him so much. And she suddenly wanted to tell him before another moment passed.

"And?" he questioned, waiting.

"I love you, too," she said simply and when Hunter opened his arms, she hurried into his strong embrace.

He nuzzled her ear. "If this feels so much like home, do you think you could live here?"

"Yes," she answered promptly, happily. "But can *you* live with someone who's going to inherit—the amount of money I'm going to inherit?"

"Half of New Mexico, half of Texas, and half of Arizona?"

"I think it's only a quarter of Texas," she murmured.

Hunter laughed. "To be honest, no."

"No?"

He spread his palms. "Look around you. I'm not going to change."

"Well, neither am I!"

"So, what would you do with all that money?"

Thinking about it, she said, "Maybe I can talk my father into donating to some philanthropic causes. That's what I would do. Give most of it away." Jenny felt as if she'd suddenly discovered something that was always there. She'd been hiding from who she was. Denying that she was Allen Holloway's daughter. But it wasn't going to work. She was going to have to face the responsibilities that she'd been born into whether she liked it or not.

"Is it my turn for a question?" Hunter asked.

"I have no idea," she said with a grin.

"Would you marry me?"

He took her completely by surprise. She pretended to consider for a moment. "Well, I don't know. I come with a fifteen-year-old son and a dog of indeterminate parentage. Do you think you can handle that?"

"Hm . . ." He rubbed his jaw, then looked down at her, amusement in his eyes.

She hugged him as fiercely as she dared, remembering his injured arm.

"I guess I could take a chance," he said.

"Then the answer is an unqualified yes," she said, tipping up her chin. Hunter's mouth slanted tenderly down on hers.

By the time Rawley and Benny came inside, the fire was licking vigorously around a stack of pine logs, the fire crackling with pitch, and Jenny and Hunter were warming themselves in front of it. They'd jumped out of their embrace like criminals caught in the act at the sound of Rawley's return.

Rawley was oblivious to their mood as he joined them

for some heat.

"Oh, my God. You need a shower," Jenny declared, wrinkling her nose. Rawley smelled like Obie.

"I could use one too," Hunter observed. To Rawley he called, "I'll get you some clean clothes."

Thrilled with happiness, Jenny used the time to investigate Hunter's refrigerator. She was suddenly ravenous, and she didn't care what she ate. In the end she made grilled cheese sandwiches and heated canned chicken soup for one and all.

Rawley arrived first, his hair wet. He looked awfully scrawny in the clothes he'd borrowed from Hunter. His expression was grim. "Something wrong?" Jenny asked, her heart leaping.

"I saw his arm."

"Oh." Jenny nodded. "He's lucky." Thinking how she would feel if something had happened to Hunter, she shook her head. "We're all lucky."

When Rawley didn't respond, she slid a sandwich his way, encouraging him to eat it. Hunter appeared a few moments later, also with damp hair and in clean clothes. She noticed how tired he looked.

"It's not exactly gourmet fare, but it's hot," she said and set his bowl down in front of him at the pine table.

He looked up at her. "It's perfect," he said simply.

"Thank you, Hunter," Rawley said, staring into his bowl of soup.

Jenny gave him a quizzical look. He sounded so solemn.

Hunter had lifted his spoon. Now, he twisted it between his fingers and looked over at Rawley's bowed head. He seemed to know something Jenny didn't because he shrugged and said, "I'm just glad you're okay."

"Am I missing something?" she asked.

Rawley lifted his eyes to hers. "My—father—" He changed his mind and said, "Troy pointed the gun at me. He would have killed me except that Hunter jumped in the way."

Jenny gazed wordlessly at Hunter. Seeing her look, he shook his head. "Don't make more of this than it is."

"More of this!" she repeated. "You saved my son's life. You could have been killed!"

"But I wasn't. We're all here. And I'm sure as hell glad I asked you to marry me before, or I might believe you said yes out of gratitude," he added casually, spooning up his soup.

Rawley snapped out of his funk. "Mom, are you going to marry Hunter?"

"Yes."

He blinked a couple of times, tore off a hunk of his grilled cheese sandwich and threw it to Benny who caught it with one snap of his jaws. Smiling, Rawley stirred his own bowl of soup. "Do I get to be best man?"

Hunter grinned. "Well, I don't know. It's you or Obie."

Rawley shot him a look of real affection.

Two weeks later Jenny had moved most of her personal items over to Hunter's ranch. He'd taken back his job with the Santa Fe Police Department, much to Sergeant Ortega's delight, and Rawley was back in school. Hunter's proclamation that Gloria could handle the restaurant and then some had turned out to be more than true. Jenny felt superfluous, and for once, she was glad.

When Hunter returned that night, he was greeted by Benny—who was wearing a Mexican hat on his head. "What's up, boy?" he asked, baffled. Benny regarded him woefully. "You look like hell."

Inside the ranch house someone had strung chili lights around the fireplace and a brightly colored serape was draped over the couch.

"What is this?" he asked Jenny, noticing the white peasant blouse and brightly colored skirt she wore. "Did Cinco de Mayo come early this year?"

"I'm recreating Puerto Vallarta with whatever I could find," she said. "Rawley's working rather late at the restaurant tonight. Gloria just needs him there, I guess."

"I see . . ." He winked as she handed him a beer and clinked her own bottle against his. "No margaritas?"

"Can't face them after that trip and Magda's blender-bombs the other night. Tequila overload." She gestured to the couch. "Sit down."

He did as he was told and she picked up the remote for the television and VCR. A moment later an old movie flickered on the screen. "*Night of the Iguana,*" she told him.

"And here I thought we were going to make out on the couch," Hunter said lazily, examining the way her blouse slung over one shoulder. His finger tugged gently at the edge of the elastic.

She arched a brow. "What do you think the serape's for?"

Hunter grinned. Her lips just looked too kissable to ignore. He leaned in and breathed into her mouth. "Olé . . ."

Center Point Publishing
600 Brooks Road ● PO Box 1
Thorndike ME 04986-0001 USA

(207) 568-3717

US & Canada:
1 800 929-9108